IN THE MOON OF ASTERION

REBECCA LOCHLANN

Also By Rebecca Lochlann

The Year-god's Daughter

The Thinara King

The Moon Casts a Spell

The Sixth Labyrinth

Falcon Blue

When the Moon Whispers

Swimming in the Rainbow

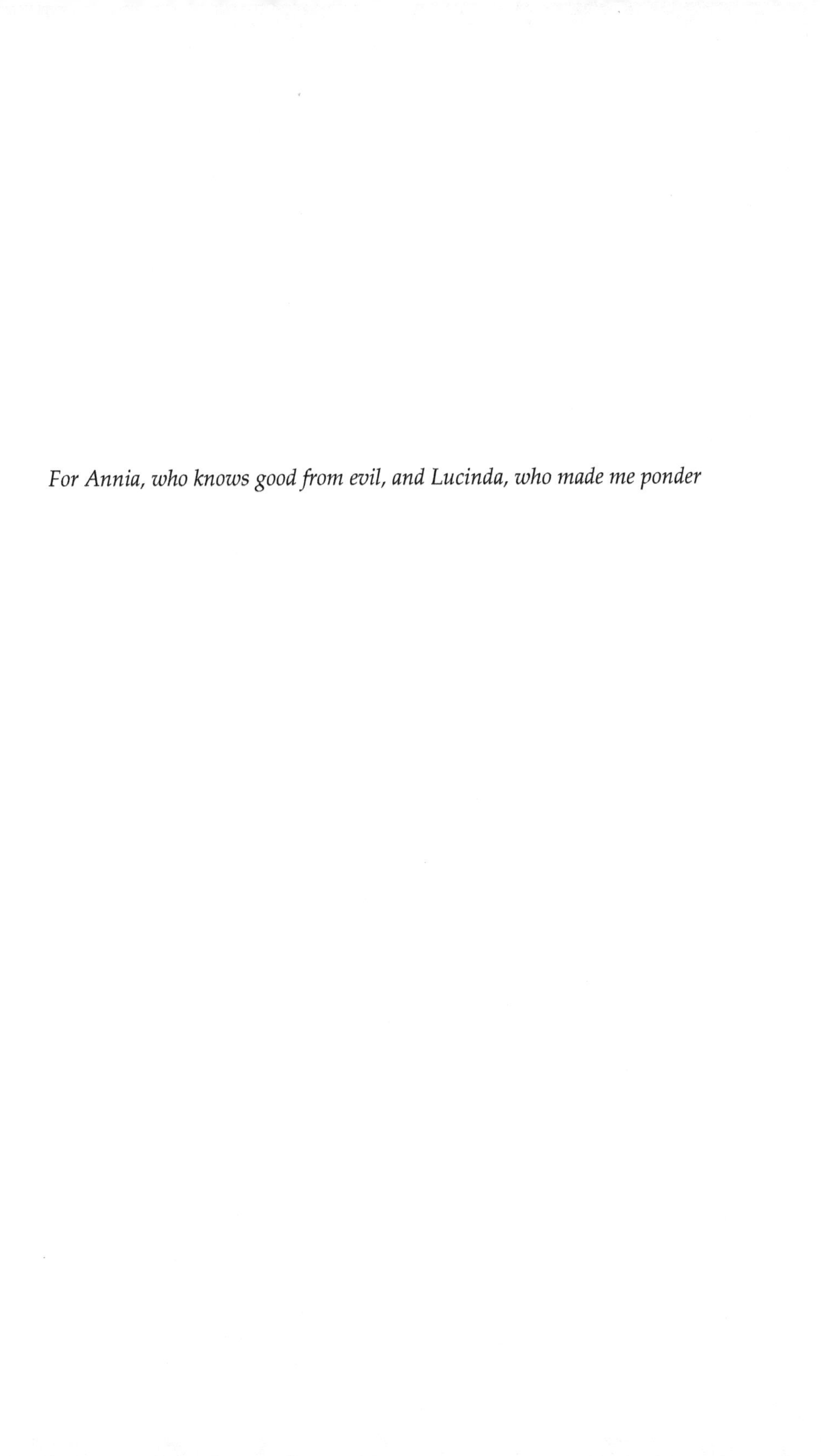

For Annia, who knows good from evil, and Lucinda, who made me ponder

In the Moon of Asterion

Rebecca Lochlann

Erinyes Press

Book Three

The Child of the Erinyes Series

Maiden

"Minotauros," "the bull of Minos," was not a true name. For the inhabitant of the labyrinth the names "Asterios" and "Asterion" have come down to us, both synonymous with *aster*, "star." ... No Greek myth attaches to these names. No luminous aspect of the Minotaur was accepted by the Greeks outside of Knossos, but the Knossos coins bear witness to a star in the labyrinth, to the lunar nature of Ariadne" (105-106).

~~~*Dionysos: Archetypal Image of Indestructible Life*, Carl Kerenyi
Copyright 1976 by Princeton University Press
Used by permission

</div>
~~~

Cretan Calendar

1ST LUNATION MOON OF WHITE LIGHT: KING SACRIFICE

2ND LUNATION MOON OF FIGS AND ACORNS

3RD LUNATION MOON OF FIELD POPPIES

4TH LUNATION MOON OF WINEMAKING

5TH LUNATION MOON OF THE OLIVE HARVEST

6TH LUNATION MOON OF FLYING SWANS

7TH LUNATION MOON OF DRENCHING RAIN

8TH LUNATION MOON OF ASPHODEL AND HONEYSUCKLE (ARIDELA'S BIRTHDAY)

9TH LUNATION MOON OF FLOWERING APPLES

10TH LUNATION MOON OF WATER FERNS

11TH LUNATION MOON OF FERTILE WILLOWS

12TH LUNATION MOON OF LAUREL LEAVES (MENOETIUS AND CHRYSALEON'S BIRTHDAY)

13TH LUNATION MOON OF MEAD-MAKING (THEMISTE'S BIRTHDAY)

PART I

The Beast

Moon of Asphodel and Honeysuckle

FROM THE ORACLE LOGS
Themiste

WE ARE FREE!

The Butcher is dead!

Our queen is restored to her throne!

Kaphtor thunders with these shouts. The people make merry day and night.

Though the worst is over, I remain uneasy. I want to return to a time before these barbarians unleashed their disaster upon us. I will not draw an easy breath until the earth swallows the blood of our newest bull-king, Chrysaleon of Mycenae. On that night, I will drink mead and dance in the light of Iakchos. I fear him. I distrust him. None are safe while he lives. Yet, I confess this secret, as I must, to the Oracle Logs...

I am drawn to him as I have never been drawn to any other man.

EVERY ROW OF BENCHES LOOKING DOWN UPON THE FAMED BULLRING AT Knossos groaned under the weight of multitudes. Those who couldn't fit inside crowded thick as schools of anchovies across the plain. All wanted to be a part of the triple-tiered festival—Queen Aridela's seventeenth birthday, the annual observance of Velchanos's rebirth, and the feting of their mainland liberators.

Kaphtor was free—to survive, to grow, to recover. Harpalycus, cursed prince of mainland Tiryns, the Usurper and Oppressor of their beloved island, had been defeated in a victory of such glory it would never be forgotten. His head now rotted on the tip of a spear outside the palace of Labyrinthos.

In the underground chambers beneath the ring, Aridela and her friends were nearly finished dressing, ready to begin the much-anticipated celebration. One handmaid adjusted Aridela's diadem while another finished rubbing kohl along her eyelashes.

"Color has returned to your face, Aridela," Neoma said, and slipped between the two women to give the queen a spontaneous hug. "You look well and strong, at last!"

"Freedom and victory have granted us both new life."

"Do you remember how we used to fight and try to outdo each other over petty things? It seems lifetimes ago."

Aridela nodded ruefully. "Yes, we are changed. How could we not be?"

"Was it by design, I wonder?" Neoma touched the shallow dent in her forehead, a permanent reminder of the night when stones had fallen like deadly spears from the sky. "I thought this would make things difficult, but the opposite is true. My lovers are so many I cannot choose between them." Her boisterous laugh echoed off the walls of the chamber. "I suppose it could be because they curry favor with the queen's cousin."

"For some men, that could be a hindrance rather than advantage."

They giggled like they were still ten years old.

Selene, also dressed lavishly, appeared in the doorway from the outer corridor. "I have never seen anything to compare with this crowd —not even your mother could draw crowds like these." She lifted her heavy, elaborately braided and bejeweled cream-colored hair so she could fan her neck. This Phrygian warrior, a princess in her own right, had slaughtered many enemies in the battle to free the island, and she had saved Aridela's life more than once. "They grow impatient, and it is stifling down here. Soon they will break the stands beneath their feet. Are you ready?"

As Aridela turned from Neoma, an eager *yes* on the tip of her tongue, a dizzy spell spiraled in the abrupt, unexpected way it had, leaving her ears humming, her eyesight spackled, and her balance in jeopardy. Such attacks were frequent since Harpalycus had stabbed her, and ending the life of the infant in her womb had made matters more precarious. Rhené, Kaphtor's royal healer, blamed the affliction on an excessive loss of blood, and dosed her patient daily with noxious concoctions of half-raw meat and boiled ox bones in an effort to rebuild her strength.

Usually she either fainted or vomited, but this time, hallucinations flooded—dazzling, terrible flashes from the two months Aridela spent as Harpalycus's captive and personal plaything. She grabbed Neoma's shoulder as a litany raced through her mind of his drunken assaults, the filth of the straw mat in her cell, the cruel eunuch's daily beatings, and the leather thongs biting into her wrists.

Chilling echoes replaced the lively chatter. Deep within, as if dredged from her soul, another voice drowned out everything else.

We will make ourselves barren. No more children. No more love. Not until they all lie dead. Then we will begin again.

The chamber walls melted like wet paint, vanishing into a different scene. One amongst a crowd, Aridela huddled on the side of a steep hill, soaked by cold rain. Above, on the summit where her voice would carry, a woman with long dark hair shouted these words. Some members of the crowd wept. Some were angry. Many raised their fists.

If we are barren, Aridela wanted to ask, *how can we begin again?*

Neoma drew Aridela out of the vision and back to the present by clasping her chin and gazing with alarm into her eyes. "What happened? Is it the wound?"

Selene crossed the space and joined them. "Are you strong enough to do this? You're shaking. You're pale."

Aridela composed her senses in the comforting, familiar scents of dust, wood, sweat, and unguents that for centuries had permeated these walls. Her hand rose to the healing puncture above her heart and pressed; beneath her skin, she felt the steady beat of her heart. Harpalycus had done his best to end her life, yet through Athene's divine intercession, she had survived. In the end, it was Harpalycus who failed, who lost everything, who breathed his last in the blood and gore of battle.

The strange, otherworldly vision made no sense, and this was not a day for somber reflection. "Yes!" She gripped her old friend's hand. "I am strong enough. I'm ready to begin life at last, to see Kaphtor begin again." An exhilarating shiver ran up the back of her neck as she pictured her mother. *Be happy, isoke,* Helice would say if she were here.

Iphiboë felt close as well. Her beloved sister, a nervous, shy girl terrified of lying with a man, had willingly sacrificed herself to calm the Lady's anger and bring mercy to their people, and in doing so, had become Kaphtor's most cherished treasure.

Squaring her shoulders, Aridela managed to push away the nauseating whirl in her head.

Cheering and the deafening stamp of feet vibrated the ground as Aridela followed Selene into the ring. Leaves and flowers fashioned from feathers and cloth rained over them. Aridela held Selene's waist, Neoma held Aridela's, another woman held Neoma's, and so on. Together they formed a long, winding, triumphal line. In imitation of the divine serpent, they would weave through the opened sections of the labyrinth, leaving behind a fresh, clean skin, and later, when night fell, smoke from offerings would be sent into the heavens from every mountain sanctuary.

Though the people cheered, Aridela felt a subtle change in mood. Who could miss how sunlight bounced off amber and obsidian where once it was gold and lapis? Real flowers remained scarce, so these poor substitutes of cloth were thrown. Hunters searched for meat yet found little, and sickness stole more lives every day. The harbors were bereft of Kaphtor's famed fleet; now they were crowded with ships belonging to King Idómeneus, King Eurysthenes, and the defeated Harpalycus.

She, too, careened between despondency and elation. After many tears and arguments, she had convinced Rhené to put an end to her pregnancy, just six days after the battle. The healer couldn't manage the task during Harpalycus's occupation because she had no medicines, and she flatly refused to attempt pricking Aridela's womb with a sharpened instrument, declaring the queen would surely die.

Rhené again balked after the battle because of the near-fatal knife wound above Aridela's heart. She relented only because she couldn't argue with the fact that the longer they waited, the more risky any method would become.

After prodding and poking her, Rhené declared it unlikely the child was Chrysaleon's, claiming a lack of hardness she said would be typical in a woman's third month, but she was forced to speculate, as Aridela could not recall whether her monthly course of blood had ever flowed after Harpalycus made her his prisoner. The royal augurers had no better luck divining an answer from the portents and entrails.

Kaphtor's queen choked down foul-tasting brews and endured a suppository of birthwort. After a day and night of ripping cramps, pain that left her helplessly screaming, and profuse bleeding that Rhené and her attendants all but failed to stop, she lapsed into unconsciousness. While she floated ever closer to the land of the dead and the severing of her moera, the unwanted baby was expelled.

Had she stopped the life of Harpalycus's offspring, or Chrysaleon's? The answer always twined away in a bewildering black maze. One was understandable, even necessary, the other a blistering torment. Only the Immortals would ever know the answer.

As she and her sisters danced around the arena, Aridela waved and blew kisses to the audience. The crowd returned her effort with ringing cheers. Her task as queen was to revive their confidence, no matter what personal grief she suffered. She, Themiste, and Chrysaleon, with the intercession of a mollified Lady Athene, would reinvigorate their island, and they could all start over—perhaps with a new baby.

Harpalycus tried to break your spirit, Menoetius had told her one cold winter night. *He failed. You have far more courage than Chrysaleon.* Fresh confidence surged through her veins and her smile brightened as she remembered how his words helped bring back her will to live. She gave a lively toss of her head, sending her hair flying, and the crowd's cheers intensified.

The women circled the perimeter of the bullring seven times while the spectators made a thundering drumbeat with their feet. Continuing through the wynds of Knossos, the dancers shed layers of their skirts and threw bits of colorful cloth.

They crossed the viaduct and glided through the olive groves, accompanied by swarms of boisterous admirers.

At the palace, they entered the processional corridor and danced their way past newly painted frescoes of smiling youths, their arms filled with rich offerings. On they went, circling columns, spinning across terraces, and marching over balconies draped with bright banners.

Their supporters thronged the courtyard as the cavalcade wove down the steps to the underground, where laborers had cleared rubble and hoisted support pillars to create pathways for them.

Deeper and deeper the women danced, singing songs of purification. They stopped only to put out bowls of milk for the holy snakes.

Up and out they climbed, back through the courtyard to the north gate, past the charging bull fresco, which still bore cracks across its middle.

Tomorrow morning, the foreign kings and their armies would depart. They had enjoyed half a month as Kaphtor's venerated guests while waiting for King Eurysthenes to recover from his wounds. Tonight they would be feasted. Though the meal might not compare to Kaphtor's feasts of old, even now skilled cooks were roasting ibex, poaching seafood, baking bread from mainland grain, and arranging bowls of dried fruit.

Yesterday, Chrysaleon had announced his intent to accompany his father back to Mycenae, "To settle old affairs," he told Aridela. He also wanted to see what damage had been wrought throughout the islands.

His decision added to Aridela's emotional struggles. The Zagreus was never supposed to leave Kaphtor. They couldn't conceive his child if he was gone. And they had already lost so much time. Now they would lose more. Worse, he'd failed to disguise his eagerness to be away, to engage in a new adventure apart from her. She could hardly blame him.

At the fall of dusk, King Idómeneus was lifted onto the royal dais in the feasting hall. Placing his thin, cold hands over Aridela's and Chrysaleon's, he gave them his blessing.

"Our lands are now joined," he said, his voice weak and quavering. "May your womb be fruitful. May the isle of Kaphtor return to its former glory."

Aridela smiled and bowed as courtesy demanded, though she knew his words were a blatant lie. She and many others had overheard the vicious encounter between Chrysaleon, Menoetius, and their father. The very night of Kaphtor's triumph, with Harpalycus dead, his army in ruins, his surviving warriors hiding in any cranny they could find, Idómeneus had summoned his two sons and proceeded to give them an uninhibited taste of his displeasure. The king's healers had raced past Aridela in the corridor at Labyrinthos, pausing for no more than the briefest salutation.

They mean to slaughter you like a pig, Idómeneus had raged. *Do your vows to me mean nothing? All this for lust of a woman.* To Menoetius he shouted, *You promised me you would protect your brother.*

At Idómeneus's peremptory gesture, Aridela leaned closer and allowed him to kiss one cheek, then the other. His watery eyes remained bitter, yet she felt no animosity. Only compassion, which she tried for his sake to hide.

The scent of death lingered on his flesh. No matter what his healers proclaimed, Aridela felt certain Idómeneus did not have long to live.

Chrysaleon had told her of Harpalycus's boast that he'd had the king poisoned with hellebore. The poor man's unhealthy color, palsy, and emaciation gave weight to the claim.

The mainland nobles drummed their cups against the tabletops as she and Chrysaleon stood before them, holding hands. She wondered if any were displaying their true feelings.

Gelanor sat next to Aridela at the high table. His rapt gaze leaped from the dancers to the wall hangings to the tables thick with nobles. Being but three months older than she and fascinated with everything having to do with Kaphtor, Chrysaleon's younger brother had quickly become her friend and confidant.

"My mother named him before she died," Chrysaleon said. "He lives up to her vision, laughing so often, over anything at all, we suspect his mind is weak."

Gelanor sneered and sent his brother a crude gesture.

"And you have a sister?" Aridela asked.

"Bateia. She is betrothed to King Eurysthenes' son."

"My lady." Gelanor leaned on one elbow as he regarded her. "There is a story that Goddess Athene buries the moon in your mountains when it vanishes from the heavens. Is this true?"

The words sent Aridela back to the day she leapt the bull. How long ago it all seemed. Chrysaleon had regaled her with Alexiare's tales. She'd told him of her father, and showed him her prized necklace, the charm she'd thought lost forever.

She touched the silver links at her throat and met Chrysaleon's amused gaze. *Back where it belongs, thanks to you.*

That was the day she had asked him to remain, to fight in Kaphtor's Games and find glory, for one year, as sacred king.

"I believe it is true," she told Gelanor. "Every year hunting parties make their searches, but no mortal has a chance of finding the Lady's hiding place."

Chrysaleon's faint, intimate smile told Aridela he recalled that distant day as well. When life was simple. When she was carefree, happy, newly in love, and quite ignorant of what horrors were about to descend.

Now that he was clean and richly attired, Gelanor bore little resemblance to the blood-spattered warrior she had fought beside on the battlefield. His innocence and naivety were evident, but earlier, during the formal speeches, his face had displayed an ominous frown as he stood next to his father's litter.

She was queen of Kaphtor again because of these men. Honor, gratitude, and gifts were being heaped upon them. Yet in six short months she would reward all they had done by overseeing Chrysaleon's ritual murder.

Aridela lowered her gaze and tried to fight off a sudden queasiness she suspected was caused by guilt rather than a supper swimming in rich sauces.

If only her mother were here. Helice would know how to handle this delicate situation. She would find a way to satisfy Idómeneus, Gelanor, Chrysaleon, and the Immortal Goddess.

Duty and obligation lay heavy as a yoke over her shoulders on this night that had been designed for joy.

She didn't want Chrysaleon to die. Yet she dared not confess her selfish desire to anyone. She could do nothing to save him. Instead, she must stand with her head lifted and her grief hidden as his blood seeped into the earth, as he looked his last upon her, as his manhood was carried to the sea.

Blinking back tears, she turned to her consort. "Are you taking your slave with you to Mycenae, my lord, or leaving him here with me?"

"I cannot leave him here," Chrysaleon said. "That old man is far more trouble than he seems, and loves to interfere in matters beyond his station. Who knows what mischief he would cause while I'm gone? Change your mind and come with me. It will be a short stay—a fortnight, no more." He added, low, "We can use that time to begin a child," and kissed her palm.

They had already discussed the impossibility of this. Rather than restating tired arguments, Aridela said, "Would that not make your many citadel women jealous?"

Startled surprise, followed by a hint of uneasiness, flickered across his face. She turned away, giggling.

Aridela's stewards had scoured the palace and town to obtain suitable offerings for King Idómeneus, King Eurysthenes, Prince Gelanor, their officers, and men. Merchants who had squirreled away their wealth to protect it from Harpalycus donated it now in hopes of gaining favor with the queen. Presented with much fanfare were gifts of golden tripods, carved signet rings portraying full-breasted Athene with lions at her side, miniature bulls carved from crystal and onyx, bolts of Egyptian linen, and delicate quartz jars filled with Cretan oils.

Idómeneus in his turn gave Aridela an exquisite painting made especially for her. It depicted Athene herself, brandishing a spear on the summit of a hill, flanked by two lionesses. The High King told her it was a likeness of the stone carving he'd had constructed for the main gate into his citadel.

The night wore on. Idómeneus was carried off to his bed. Many left for other entertainments and the feasting hall grew quiet. Aridela and Chrysaleon made excuses and slipped away to stroll through the neglected palace garden.

Jeweled rays of lavender offered a new dawn's subtle promise. "I will bring it back," she said, struck with fervor at the beauty in the heavens. "I will make Kaphtor as great—no, greater—than it ever was."

Chrysaleon placed her hand on his arm and covered it with his own. They walked on without speaking, their steps making no sound on the dirt footpaths.

As they detoured around the skeleton of a dead bush, they nearly ran into Menoetius. Leaning against a stone pillar, the last remaining piece of an elaborate arch that had once framed the outer entry into the garden, he was staring into the sky. He straightened at their appearance, obviously as startled as they.

Guilt prompted Aridela to step away from Chrysaleon. She fancied Menoetius noticed, and felt her cheeks flush.

After Chrysaleon took her from the cave in the Araden mountains, Menoetius returned to Selene. He hardly spoke to Aridela. In fact, she'd scarcely seen him since the battle. Obedient as always, he bowed to Chrysaleon's wishes and hers, unspoken though they were.

Chrysaleon cuffed Menoetius on the shoulder, oblivious or dismissive of the tense atmosphere between his consort and half brother. "Where have you been hiding? I can never find you these days. Is that milky Amazon girl roping you to her bed?"

In this brief space before sunrise, the sky deepened from lavender to purple, much like a vast royal robe soaked in the precious dye Crete's fishermen extracted from snails. Such a richness of color made it hard to determine any subtleties, yet Aridela acutely sensed Menoetius's desire to escape.

"Leave off, Chrysaleon," he said. "I don't ask what you do with your time."

"Let every foolish wench on Crete invite you to her bed. Why should I care? I alone possess the queen of women."

"Chrysaleon." Aridela's attempt at criticism was interrupted when he plucked her into his arms and swung her in a dizzying circle. So close were they to Menoetius that her heel struck his shin.

Setting her down and holding her fast, Chrysaleon gave her a long, suffocating kiss, effectively halting her sputtered protests. He lifted his head and shouted, his words bouncing off the crumbling walls. "The queen of Crete is mine!"

"You show me little respect, Zagreus," she said, her face burning.

"My property. My chattel. My slave." Lowering his voice, he added, "My wife, my love, for as long as the pyramids stand in Egypt."

"An earthshaking could bring those down tomorrow. What of you? Are you my property and slave?"

He dropped to one knee and pressed her right hand to his forehead before kissing it. "Command me. I am yours."

Tears stung her eyes as she drew him upright. "Who will make me laugh with you gone?"

Chrysaleon squeezed her hands, but she thought she caught the slightest hint of that anticipation she'd noticed when he first told her he meant to go.

Menoetius stepped away. She swung toward him, startled and guilty.

The bow he offered was rigid and formal. "I leave you to your privacy," he said, and stalked toward the palace, swiftly vanishing into murky violet shadows.

Aridela realized what she'd said and how it must have sounded. She was glad the dim light would disguise this persistent guilty blush.

"Not him." Chrysaleon sent a derisive laugh after his brother. "Women find Menoetius alluring because he frightens them, makes them shiver and feel alive. They fantasize about taming the ugly beast of Mycenae. But when his true nature is revealed, they run away as fast as they can."

He wagged a finger at her. "Stop frowning like that or I will think you are one of those simpleminded females."

"I assure you I am not simpleminded."

He laughed. "Until recently I suspected my father preferred the bastard over his true son. I was ravaged by jealousy. He is older than me, you know, by a few breaths."

"Yes. I know." Menoetius had described how the brothers came into the world almost simultaneously, from different mothers—one the queen of Mycenae, the other a slave.

Tilting his head up, Chrysaleon contemplated the sky. "At last I know differently. My father is angry and must shout his curses, yet I saw his pride. He has disavowed Menoetius, though, for allowing me to compete. Menoetius has become a man with no home. It is me Idómeneus values."

Aridela stiffened. "I will not stand for this. Menoetius has twice saved my life. If your father cannot see his worth, his home will be here, with us."

Chrysaleon kissed her again and guided her backward, into the still-deep shadows behind the ruined arch. As he drew her to the ground, he said, "I suspect you are too soft to be queen. Did I say I was disavowing Menoetius? He is still my brother, as far as I'm concerned. And my father will forgive him when he calms down. He always does."

A small, pale lizard, the kind with bumps that looked like armor, skittered across the pillar. She couldn't help smiling as it paused and seemed to peer at them. She'd caught one when she was little and kept it as a pet, toting it around on her shoulder with a tiny leather leash.

It seemed a good omen.

"I overheard King Idómeneus the night of the battle," she said between his kisses. "He was so angry. I feared for you. I thought he might have you both killed."

"If you knew him better, you would understand." Chrysaleon hiked up her tunic as he nuzzled her throat. "His anger is what made it clear. He wishes Menoetius, not me, was facing death at the midsummer moon. That was the plan, you know. Menoetius was supposed to compete in your Games. My father considered him expendable."

His callous statement brought back the confession Menoetius made when they were living in the Araden mountains. *If Chrysaleon had obeyed our father, I could have been your partner in the cave. I could have won the Games and become your consort. Only the gods will ever know what difference it might have made.*

Chrysaleon lifted his face from hers long enough to add, "Be cheered it was me who fought for you and won." He grinned. "My humorless brother would have made your life as grim as the ash-buried isle of Callisti."

2

Moon of Asphodel and Honeysuckle

"WAS IROS WITH CHILD?"

"Yes, my lord." Theanô kept her eyes downcast, her hands folded, her stance meek.

Chrysaleon wasn't fooled. "You had her killed."

She sent him one glance, just enough to refresh his memory. She had beautiful eyes, his lover of old—sultry grey irises emphasized by kohl-darkened brows. Every part of her was seductive and well kept. Jewels accented her long, fair hair, but it only served to remind him of Aridela's, scorched off during the blaze of heat and fire that decimated her island. Theanô's flawless skin was kept pale and pure in milk baths, while Aridela's would bear scars for the rest of her life. Chrysaleon couldn't help admiring the curves that filled out the delicate pleats of Theanô's gown. She, unlike Aridela, had missed no meals. He knew he should be angry, but after the extraordinary months he'd only just survived, he could hardly remember Iros, the child-wife imposed upon him not long before he and Menoetius set sail for Crete. He couldn't recall what she looked like but for her mousy brown hair, though he had no trouble remembering Harpalycus's claim that he, not Chrysaleon, was the father of her unborn child. King Lycomedes had deliberately attempted to foist his son's cursed offspring off as Chrysaleon's. Just the thought of how close it had come to success made Chrysaleon's teeth grind and the tic under his eye throb.

14

It was hard to be angry. But Theanô must learn she had taken too much upon herself.

"How did you know?" he asked, when she made no response.

She shrugged, the movement drawing attention to her breasts. "It was common knowledge among women that Harpalycus initiated his sister soon after she began her monthly bleeding. When King Lycomedes urged the marriage so desperately and wanted it done so quickly, there could be no other reason."

She took a step closer and stopped. Chrysaleon smelled the rose oil she often used, and which reminded him of better days. He knew if he touched her skin, it would be soft and smooth. By the gods, it felt good to be home, good to walk in a place untouched by havoc except for a sprinkling of fine ash, which affected nothing. The blast that threw him off his feet on Crete had also been heard and felt in Mycenae, but the mainland suffered no mountainous waves, no poison fire-clouds, and only minor earthshakings.

"The child could have been mine." He allowed a hint of threat to lace his tone. "Do you think I didn't lie with her before I sailed?"

Ah, there it was—a flash of fury, quickly masked. Jealousy was the true core of her actions, not a desire to protect him.

He fingered the perfectly shaped curl in front of her ear. She smiled. She couldn't know he was picturing Aridela's hair. After that calamitous night, which had gradually come to be known by all Cretans as the "Destruction," after Queen Helice moved her court to Natho, a village on the southern coast, Aridela's handmaids had set out to save their mistress's charred hair. They sheared off the burned ends and drenched it in special revitalizing salves made from olive oil and herb essences. It continued to grow, even when she was Harpalycus's starving captive. Now, as snow finally retreated from the plains and mountain slopes, it was glossy again, and brushed her shoulder blades.

For some reason no mortal could know, his hair had merely singed at the ends. Such tales abounded, of buildings, bronze, and tile disintegrated from heat and fire while a half step away, feathers, lamps, and linen remained unaffected. The Goddess selected what would burn according to her whim. It remained a matter of puzzlement as to why she chose to incinerate her beloved child's hair while leaving the barbarian's intact.

"Chrysaleon." Theanô placed her hand on his cheek. "I have longed for you in the night."

He smiled and she returned it. He saw she was no longer afraid of his anger. Her other hand trailed up his thigh, fingertip by fingertip.

He used her then, as he would a nameless woman caught in battle. He wanted to see if she would allow it. He threw her backward onto his bed and when he was finished, he rose, leaving her to drowsily grasp at him, her coiffed hair tangled and her gown torn.

Chrysaleon looked down at her. The words of Aridela's dead father floated through his mind. *Finally, an age will come when woman will embrace her own degradation.*

"Perhaps I will take you to Crete," he said, "and give you to my wife."

Her eyes flew open. She sat up. "You want me to serve your Cretan whore?"

He seized her by the throat, his fingers pressing hard enough to leave bruises, so she wouldn't forget too quickly. "Apologize for using that word."

She pulled at his hand but couldn't break his grip. "You're a fool," she shrieked. "They'll slaughter you and she will take your killer into her bed. You are nothing there but a goat. You could have married me and ruled your whole life."

His grip tightened, forcing her to wheeze and gasp. He dragged her off the bed and threw her to the floor. "We will see who is slaughtered."

She started to say something but instead pressed her lips together and breathed out, sharply. Rising, she straightened her gown and walked, a bit unsteadily, to the door.

"Keep close to the citadel," he said. "In case I need to have another pregnant girl murdered."

She paused. Half turning, she sent him a narrowed stare redolent with hate. "Long before that day comes, you will be dead." She tucked her loosened hair back into its network of silver and crystals before adding, "And the world will forget you."

THE SUMMONS ARRIVED IN THE MIDDLE OF THE NIGHT, TEN DAYS AFTER Chrysaleon and his father took up residence at Mycenae's citadel.

Chrysaleon rubbed his eyes as he strode toward the king's bedchamber. Alexiare struggled to keep up, his stick tapping hastily against the flagstones.

Throwing open the door, Chrysaleon took in the scene before him. Bateia crouched in a weeping knot on the floor beside the bed. Gelanor stood over her, his hand on her shoulder.

The great King Idómeneus, always ruddy, loud, and robust, was now so emaciated he hardly made a lump under his purple wool blanket. Bereft of hair, his head resembled a skull with eyes. Chrysaleon suppressed a shiver as he grasped the dying man's skeletal hand.

"My lord." Chrysaleon gritted his teeth, unable to keep his nostrils from flaring at the stink.

Sores had eaten away the inside of the High King's mouth. They broke open at the slightest movement of his lips, bringing helpless tears of pain to this fierce warrior once dubbed the "Mad Lion of Mycenae."

"Crete," Idómeneus whispered. It was all he could manage. His voice grated and failed.

It was true, what the healers said. Idómeneus would not survive to morning. As he stared at the fraying threads of his father's moera, Chrysaleon realized the death obligations and associated uproar would force him to remain at least another month. He had promised Aridela he would return in a fortnight. It was a promise he now knew would be broken.

Idómeneus's fingers tightened around Chrysaleon's. He tried again. "You. High King. You. Not Gelanor—" He fell back, his eyes closing. Tears coursed over his frail face and watery blood seeped from the corners of his mouth.

"Allow me, my lord." Alexiare cleared his throat and proceeded at Idómeneus's nod. "Your father has proclaimed you his heir. He wants you to abandon your role as consort on Crete."

Idómeneus raised his head, clutching at Chrysaleon's arm.

"I will tell him, my lord." Alexiare helped the king lie back.

"You must take his armies and overthrow Crete as Harpalycus tried to do. It must be done now, before Queen Aridela rebuilds her country's strength."

Chrysaleon stared at his sire's waxy face and tried to dislodge the constriction in his throat. "I'll do it some other way."

"There is no time," Alexiare said. "Soon the summer sun will beat upon Kaphtor's soil, bringing the rise of Iakchos. You must use any means to halt the great sacrifice." Sending Gelanor an apologetic glance, he added, "Your brother, though highly favored, does not possess the necessary—strength to hold Mycenae's throne."

Ruthlessness. That is the word you avoided, old man.

"It's true," Gelanor acknowledged quietly in answer to Chrysaleon's gaze. "The Kindred think me weak." He lowered his head. "They don't fear me as they do you."

Chrysaleon could only swallow again as he watched his bold plans swirl away, taking Aridela with them.

"Menoetius might succeed, my lord," Alexiare said with a raspy cough, "if you truly wish to abandon your birthright and give your crown to him. If your desire is to follow the path of Crete's previous kings...."

"Watch yourself."

Alexiare inclined his head. "Then your choice is made. The High King's legacy cannot be lost."

Idómeneus touched Alexiare's wrist. Again the slave seemed to read his master's mind. Gently, he slipped the gold seal ring off the king's finger and held it out.

Overthrow Crete, when the people cheered him through every town and village, proclaimed him their greatest hero, gave him the finest of all they had left and showered him with trust? Chrysaleon couldn't rid himself of this obstruction in his throat. In the garden, in the aftermath of love on the day he'd sailed, Aridela confessed her council's initial fears, their distrust of Mycenae. The shame she felt was clear as she apologized for their suspicion.

He *would* end the king-sacrifice. He wanted the glory of it, and refused to die in such an ignoble fashion, nor could he lose Aridela. And he would never give up Mycenae. He would find another way.

Taking the ring, he jammed it onto his middle finger and met his father's gaze. "Be at peace, Father. Know as you travel to the shadowlands that I will triumph over our enemies."

Idómeneus again motioned almost desperately. Alexiare nodded and asked everyone in the room to leave, including Gelanor and Bateia.

When they were alone, Idómeneus beckoned. Chrysaleon bent closer, accepting the imminent, pitiful death he saw in the once-great ruler's eyes.

"The star." Water flooded from Idómeneus's eyes. "Menoetius."

Chrysaleon stared helplessly.

"King Idómeneus refers to the star that flew across the sky when you were born." Alexiare's features remained woodenly expressionless.

"What about it?"

"Have you never heard that this star actually appeared during your brother's birth, my lord, and by the time you came forth, it had passed on?"

"Yes." Chrysaleon's brows lowered at the annoying memory.

"That rumor is true, and some have not forgotten. The king's royal guard, for instance. Menoetius is captain in more than name." The slave's injured voice deteriorated to a harsh whisper. He broke off in a spasm of coughing.

Chrysaleon wasted no more than an instant on Alexiare's struggle to speak. No doubt there were many who believed Menoetius—first-born, acknowledged by the High King, adored by the elite force he commanded, and additionally blessed by a mystical heavenly event—should be next in line for the crown of Mycenae, son of a slave woman notwithstanding.

Idómeneus watched Chrysaleon work this out. "You," he whispered. "My son."

Alexiare covered the king's hand with his own. "You both love Menoetius," he said, "but he is dangerous to you now. Your father regrets acknowledging him, raising him with you as though he were a prince. You must do whatever is necessary to make your claim to the throne unchallengeable, by Menoetius or anyone."

Chrysaleon's breath froze even as odd relief flooded. He bowed his head in affirmation and obedience.

"Proud." Idómeneus's translucent eyelids squeezed closed. His lip drew up and his breath caught before he exhaled in a long, final wheeze.

Chrysaleon kissed his father's forehead as Alexiare opened the door. "Trust me, Father. I won't fail you," he said, his words lost beneath the women's mourning wails.

3

Moon of Flowering Apples

From the Oracle Logs
Themiste

Our future lies before us, open, unhindered, like damp clay ready to be formed into a design of our choosing.

Long ago, through trial and error, priestesses on the lost isle of Callisti discovered something miraculous. If they collected ash from the holy mountain and worked it into their gardens, it increased the fertility of the soil. Too much suffocates, but there is an amount which, if properly applied, acts like a hero's blood. We of Kaphtor do not know the secrets those women had years to perfect, but if we want to survive, we must learn—and quickly, for our crops still languish, half a year after the Destruction.

Our farmers predict nothing will ever grow again on the eastern half of our island, but the central plains and western precincts were not so damaged. Every able-bodied man, woman, and child is eager to work the soil and plant the new seed brought by our mainland saviors.

I record with gratitude that some of our ancient olive trees withstood the cataclysm of earth and sea. Without this small mercy, Kaphtor would quickly fall into decline and eventual oblivion. Many did die, though. Our Egyptian comrades bemoan the loss of the oil they crave. We graft, dig new trenches, hoe, and add dung, as Lady Athene taught us when the world began. In our *valleys and on our mountain slopes, we clear away dead grapevines and prune those that still live.*

In our towns, laborers sweep up ash and haul it away to be covered over in pits. With prizes of pottery, weaving, and crowns of grapevines, we give the work a celebratory air.

We have coaxed a few shipmasters from other countries to Kaphtor. Along with those of ours who survived, they oversee the construction of new vessels. From morning to night, one hears the crack of whips as woodcutters drive oxen from the forests, carrying supplies of lumber to the coasts.

My old chambers in the labyrinth are slowly being unearthed. Every recovered tablet brings relief and joy, but so far, only shreds of the papyrus prophecies have been found. These are forever lost if I fail in my task to rewrite them from memory.

Night brings dreams of Callisti and the malignant rage inside Alcmene, its once-lovely mountain. I know not who named this peak "Wrath of the Moon," but I suspect it was an oracle, acting in obedience to a vision of terrible foreshadowing.

CHRYSALEON HAD BEEN GONE HALF A MONTH, YET AT NIGHT ARIDELA still reached for him in their bed and longed for his company by day.

Not surprisingly, when she contemplated what he might be doing, her thoughts often turned to Iros, his Mycenaean wife.

Harpalycus's devoted slave and lackey, Proitos, had described her as a mere girl, but Harpalycus had declared she was carrying his child when given to Chrysaleon as a prize designed to strengthen ties between Mycenae and Tiryns. Iros must be very near to her lying-in by now. What would Chrysaleon do about the baby? Aridela had no illusions about Harpalycus's offspring being raised as a royal Mycenaean heir. She could only hope Chrysaleon would have enough mercy to let the infant live. What would he tell Iros of his commitment to Kaphtor and Kaphtor's queen? What would her reaction be? Had she wanted to be her brother's lover, or Chrysaleon's wife?

Aridela's mind dredged up question after question about this faceless woman. She obsessed over what was to come, and how it would affect the girl who had not seen her husband in nearly a year. She hoped Iros would not feel hurt or abandoned, but the twist of guilt in her stomach offered a more likely and unpleasant truth. She knew how she would feel if Chrysaleon informed her he loved another woman and was going away, never to return.

She also struggled with weariness. It was almost impossible to concentrate during the endless interludes trapped in stifling chambers, listening to her council drone on about restorations and rebuilding. All she wanted to do was sleep away the days until her consort returned.

Rhené grew increasingly concerned about this lethargy, worried her patient might still be losing blood from some hidden place. She boosted the portions of boiled bone broth and raw meat, insisting Aridela consume them three times a day, and covered the stab wound with smelly pastes of barley and old wine, ground up pine cones, olive oil, and goat's fat. Another requirement was that her charge spend a portion of every morning on the roof terrace, for Rhené was a great believer in fresh air and sunlight.

The healer forbade any council member except Prince Kios from visiting Aridela while she was taking her morning rejuvenation. She was to rest, breathe, and give no thought to duties or political concerns. Kios was the only one of the council who could be trusted to follow Rhené's wishes and bring up nothing stressful.

Aridela generally fell asleep while a musician plucked his phorminx and Kios described cooking with his favorite spices and herbs.

For longer than you can imagine, I will be with you, in you, of you, and nothing can ever part us.

As always, the oath brought a sense of completion to Aridela's mind. She was no longer sure whether Chrysaleon spoke it or Menoetius, but that didn't seem to matter. The two brothers often merged in her dreams, taking on each other's characteristics, making her long for one, then the other.

I will have victory, Aridela, Menoetius whispered against her ear.

Not even death can part us, promised Chrysaleon.

I am the one with true power. I have defeated death, and will live forever. One day, all people, all civilizations, will worship me.

This voice drowned out the voices of love. Harpalycus bent over her, his blue eyes cold as a shark's.

If you do not quicken soon, I will hand you over to my men.

Aridela woke, sweating, shuddering, her heart thudding like it meant to break through her ribs and burst from her chest. She gasped, trying to breathe. It felt as if she were being throttled.

Ashes. The acrid smoldering stench that was the smell of Harpalycus. It surrounded her and filled her mouth.

Her eyes flew open. She shrieked.

A man was bent over her. The smell of Harpalycus was everywhere.

She struck out, flailing, clawing at him. He held her upper arms, forcing them down.

One brow lifted as he grinned. There was that look she would never forget, of lust and cruelty, of pleasure drawn from pain.

Again she shrieked. Her throat went raw from screaming, and caused tears to stream. She fought in earnest, kicking, thrashing.

He won't take me again. I'll die first.

"My lady?" The man's smirk vanished. "My lady, please!"

She blinked as his voice penetrated her terror. This man was not Harpalycus. He was much older. His hair was grey and his eyes darkest brown, not blue. His clothing was humble, the coarse tunic of a slave or manservant. His face was smooth-shaven, in the manner of one of her people.

But she couldn't stop gasping like a fish thrown onto the deck of a ship. She shrank from him, moaning. He released her, fell to his knees, and covered his head with his arms. "I beg your forgiveness, my lady," he cried. "I was collecting your soup bowl and saw your blanket had fallen. I was putting it over you."

She hardly heard his babbling through the roar in her ears.

"Aridela?" Themiste's worried face swam into view. She pressed her hands to Aridela's cheeks. "Are you ill? Shall I get Rhené?"

Still Aridela couldn't speak, couldn't catch her breath. She tried to blink away the tears that made everything so blurry.

More faces appeared, the musician's and the handmaid's. Both were frightened.

"Leave us." Themiste's curt order sent them all scurrying, none with more alacrity than the slave, who rose, bowed, and fled, no doubt to the shrine, where he would pray for his life.

The smell of smoldering ashes dissipated on the morning breeze.

Themiste sat on the edge of Aridela's couch and stroked her hair. "What happened?"

Aridela drank from the bowl the oracle held to her lips before she could manage a croaking, "Harpalycus. He was here."

"Harpalycus!" Themiste continued to smooth her hair and wipe tears from her cheeks with a corner of the blanket. "Well, it was only a dream then. Drink a bit more."

Aridela obediently sipped the barley brew, though it made her want to gag.

"Do you remember now?" Themiste asked. "Harpalycus is dead. You killed him. We can go and look at his rotted head, if you like."

Aridela sat up and peered from side to side, half-expecting to see the chamber where Harpalycus had raped her, his soldiers who had looked on, and Lycus, also forced to watch.

But she lay on a comfortable divan, safe on the roof at Labyrinthos. The sky was blue, with a few puffs of innocent cloud. A robin chirped in the rafters. Themiste's presence was close and soothing. To further quiet her fears, Rhené hurried across the terrace toward them, no doubt alerted by one of those Themiste had sent away.

"What happened?" the healer asked as she drew near.

"She had a bad dream," Themiste said. "She is better now."

Themiste rose so Rhené could examine her charge. She peered into Aridela's eyes and mouth and smelled her breath. Pulling off Aridela's tunic, she felt the queen's heartbeat then cupped her breasts. The healer's eyes narrowed and her head slanted.

Aridela shivered, though the morning was pleasantly warm.

Rhené had always been diligent and painstakingly exact. Her ability to discern the slightest changes in body or mood, no matter how small, was legendary.

She leaned back, her brows lifting. "You are with child," she announced.

Themiste's mouth opened. Her eyes widened then she laughed. "Ah, now it becomes clear."

Aridela wasn't so easily convinced. "How can this be?" Only a month had passed since Rhené had freed her of the last baby. She knew she wasn't wholly recovered. Such unexpected news, on the heels of believing Harpalycus had returned from the shadowlands bent on persecution, made her head reel.

"I am not surprised," Rhené said in her usual blunt, almost caustic way. "I know you disobeyed me and lay with the Zagreus before he left."

Aridela flushed. It was true. The very morning he sailed to Mycenae, in the barren garden. Their lovemaking had been violent and satisfying. Knowing they would be separated for far too many days, she had put Rhené's instructions out of her mind, telling herself that joining with the Zagreus in the garden would instill it, and her, with fertility and new life. Perhaps it had.

"Surely it's too soon to tell." Themiste took Aridela's hand. "You could be wrong, and making her hopeful for nothing."

"I am not wrong," Rhené said. "There are too many signs. She has been throwing up. She is always sleeping. She won't even taste honey now, she who has always wanted honey on everything. Her breasts have changed. And now these nightmares. I recognize the signs her body gives us. That is all."

The bad dream was forgotten as Aridela allowed herself to believe.

She was with child. Chrysaleon's child.

Themiste laughed and hugged her. Even Rhené smiled.

"I must send a messenger to Mycenae." Aridela leaped from the couch, already composing in her head what she would write.

4

Moon of Flowering Apples

CHRYSALEON'S HAND SMOOTHED THE EMPTY SPACE NEXT TO HIM ON THE bed. The slave girl satisfied his lust before he sent her away, but did nothing for the deeper ache that, these days, none but Aridela seemed equipped to ease.

A ship from Crete had arrived, bringing him an unforeseen and stunning message. His queen's womb had quickened.

The announcement immediately sent his mind back to their tryst in the ruined gardens, since that was the only time it could have happened.

If Rhené had witnessed what they'd done, drenched in the iridescent glow of dawn, made more ferocious by the knowledge they would not see each other for many days, she would no doubt have gelded him then and there, as she'd strictly forbidden any relations until the queen fully healed.

Chrysaleon was pleased and proud, and could easily picture Aridela's happiness. But deep inside, a dark, shameful irritation reared, wearing the face of Harpalycus. His detested rival's triumphant, laughing image managed to taint what should have been a joyous revelation.

He thrust this niggling repugnance into a far corner and returned his thoughts to the pleasure of that last morning in the garden, but his frustration only increased. What was she doing while he lingered on at Mycenae? He wanted her now, warm and willing against him. He needed to bury himself inside her and eradicate the sickening knowledge that Harpalycus had taken her too. It annoyed him that she was so far away, that he couldn't board a ship and go to her, or better yet, summon her to him like a High King should.

As he rolled onto his side he felt the thickened scar on his thigh, a permanent memento from the night he had killed Crete's sacred king and won the title for himself. He remembered the suffocating, tear-inducing smoke in the labyrinth, the way the youth tried to escape his fate, the gold apple rolling across the dirt.

Who will slay me?

In his mind, he saw Aridela holding her ivory-topped scepter, standing aloof and regal while the new winner of the Games lifted the double axe to separate his head from his neck.

Renewed fury heated his blood from carnal simmering to a resentful boil. Jumping out of bed, he threw open the doors leading to the terrace. Chilly night breezes caught one of the heavy oak and bronze-inlaid portals, slamming it against the wall with a reverberating thud.

He walked out and set his fists against the balustrade. The moon, waning but still fat, sent milky light over the surrounding mountains. Cool breath from their summits lifted goose flesh on his arms. The Mycenaean plains had not escaped the chill that transformed Crete from a place of sultry heat into one of snow and ice. All the seasons everywhere seemed turned on end since the night of raining fire and ash.

At least the seas were tranquil. His people called this the month of sailing, for the waters between the mainland and Crete traditionally became passable; Cretans called it the Moon of Flowering Apples, though now, for the first time, many feared their fragile apple trees might never bloom again.

To him it meant that in four months, he would fulfill his dreaded destiny under the white light of the star Iakchos.

He returned to his chamber and stirred the hearth fire. No matter how furiously his thoughts circled in their search for a way to achieve his desires, he couldn't unravel the knot that proclaimed the king of Kaphtor must die.

A hesitant knock broke the silence.

"Who is it?" He threw the bronze poker into the corner, where it landed with a sharp metallic rattle and skidded across the flagstones.

Alexiare opened the door. He remained there, looking uncertain.

"You are restless tonight, my lord," he said, his voice still painfully hoarse from translating the dying Idómeneus's wishes. "Is there anything I can do?"

"Go away," Chrysaleon said impatiently, but as his slave turned, he changed his mind. "No, wait. Sit with me, old man."

Alexiare shut the door behind him then crossed the room and closed the doors to the terrace. "May I ask what disturbs your sleep?"

Chrysaleon felt as worn as if he'd run a grueling footrace only to finish last. "I wish Harpalycus still lived. I would skin him, piece by piece, and revel in his screams. I feel him laughing at me from the shadowlands. He murdered my father and somehow, managed to escape my vengeance."

Alexiare nodded. "Ah."

"I cannot believe the king is gone."

"It is a testament to his strength that he forestalled the poison as long as he did."

Chrysaleon paced, repeatedly fisting his hands as he thought of the tortures he would like to inflict on the dead prince of Tiryns.

"Is that all?" Alexiare frowned as he watched Chrysaleon stalk. "I thought you resigned to your father's death. Does something else trouble you? Perhaps I could help." He hobbled to the table, poured mead into a gold cup, and handed it over.

Chrysaleon leveled a speculative stare at his slave as he accepted the drink. "You lived on that god-cursed island, and you've made it clear how much you admire them. Where do your loyalties lie?"

Alexiare bowed stiffly; that and his sharp exhale betrayed his annoyance. "Your father trusted me more than his own council. Have I not always kept your secrets?"

Releasing an explosive sigh, Chrysaleon sank into the carved olive wood chair next to the hearth fire and swallowed the mead in one gulp. "Then tell me, old man. What does a king do, when he makes a vow he cannot keep?"

"What is the nature of this vow?"

"The oldest one—the fate of all Crete's consorts. I knelt before them and swore I would die for the land. The people trust me. If I muster my armies and invade, I will have to kill Aridela. If I don't, neither she nor her people will stop until a dagger finds my heart."

Other than the slight lift of one brow, Alexiare showed no sign of surprise. "My lord, you can either die in the sacrifice, or refuse and declare war against your wife."

Chrysaleon laughed cynically. "This oath hangs over me like a blood curse." He rose and paced again, corner to corner. "The Cretans believe the bull-king joins with Athene and achieves everlasting paradise. His spirit is reborn in the new crops. But I have no wish to enter paradise yet or return as a stalk of barley. Why did I agree to this? Was it lust, as Menoetius and my father claim? The day I watched her leap that bull, I think I would have agreed to anything. I did not consider the future. I never pondered how quickly the months would pass. Harpalycus and the cursed Destruction have stolen much from me...."

Throwing himself into the chair, Chrysaleon raked through his beard and snarled his resentment. "*Fuck.*"

Alexiare picked up another cup, but instead of pouring a drink, he merely transferred it from one hand to the other. "King-sacrifice is a most holy custom, my lord, more ancient than you know. The land's fortune centers around the death and rebirth of the year-god. Until the earthshakings, fires, floods, and frost, Kaphtor was blessed in every circumstance. They believed their abundance sprang from an unfailing performance of the sacrifice. Once, in fact, it was believed necessary to conduct it twice a year, at each solstice." He paused, his shoulders slumping, and sighed. "Man's nature strives for power and leadership, but in these lands, becoming the most powerful man also means certain death. Of course you want to change the tradition, my lord. For you, this is not the way things should be."

Chrysaleon's hands cupped the boar's heads carved into the chair's armrests. His fingertips traced their sharp tusks. "Someone must have given me one of those potions they're so fond of there. What else could explain how swiftly and easily she enslaved me?" Disgust wormed like serpent venom through his veins. "Those slaves at the bullring could have put anything in the wine I drank that day."

"I should have tried harder to prevent you from getting caught up in their ways. You did promise me you wouldn't...but I should have known the challenge would be irresistible."

Chrysaleon glared at him.

"Forgive me, my lord." Alexiare lifted his hands in a placating manner. "Though the rituals and beliefs of our two lands seem similar, they are not. Here, the Lady is subservient to Hippos Poseidon and his young brother, Zeus. Not so on Crete. There she rules supreme. She has no husband, and males give their lives in service to her."

Alexiare's eyes began to water. He coughed in severe, hoarse expulsions. Without asking permission, he poured mead into the cup he held and drank deeply. It helped only a little, but he wiped away what spilled into his beard and rasped on. "You were born to rule by might over a land of warriors and horsemen. Dying in a dark labyrinth, unarmed and helpless, can never be your moera. The men of Kaphtor seek out this fate. They see it as the greatest glory they can ever achieve. But not you, my lord, no. This is not the right end for you."

"It's more than that." Chrysaleon held Alexiare's gaze. "When I sailed to Crete, I had no premonition of my father's death. The citadel was secure. Now all he won depends on me, for Idómeneus was right about Gelanor. If I bow to my fate, the Kindred Kings will lay siege. They'll steal my throne in half a year. Gelanor does not yet understand the lengths men will go to win what they want."

"His is a peaceful nature. Prince Gelanor is more suited to composing songs and breeding horses than making war."

Restless frustration nagged Chrysaleon back to his feet. He picked up the sword he'd used in Crete's labyrinth and frowned at the hilt, with its carved ibex and stylistically curved horns. "Aridela was pregnant when I found her in the Araden mountains."

"She was?"

He nodded. "She ended its life somehow. Women's mysteries." He stabbed the point of the sword into the tabletop. "Harpalycus forced her, and she would not bear what could have been his."

"My lord." Alexiare couldn't hide his shock and dismay. "I am sorry to hear it."

Chrysaleon gritted his teeth and clenched his fists as rage thundered through him. "He did it to ruin her for me. Otherwise, he would have killed her."

"Do not let him succeed." Alexiare kept his voice low.

There was no answer Chrysaleon could make. The old man knew him, knew Harpalycus's attack was one that would spoil any other woman in his master's eyes. But it wasn't so easy to dismiss *her*, the queen of Crete, as if she were any woman.

He hadn't been told very much about what Harpalycus had done, nor had he asked. Though his desire for Aridela remained powerful, it was becoming harder to deny the faint aversion that had begun to chew at the edges of his thoughts when they were together.

He yanked the sword out of the tabletop and pointed it at his slave. "Today a messenger brought me news that her womb has again quickened. This time there is no doubt about the father. I want that child. I want to be surrounded by our children. Then I will have my revenge on Harpalycus."

"Ah." Alexiare grinned and drew in a deep breath, obviously relieved. "Happy tidings and good fortune. See? Your revenge is already complete, my lord. Harpalycus is dead and you are alive, fathering children and ruling as High King over all the Kindred."

The statement, meant to bolster him, had only a brief effect. "My thoughts are like a madman's. They offer no peace. Do I stay here? Demand Aridela join me and give up her throne?"

Alexiare's wheezing escalated, betraying his anxiety. "She will never do that."

"So I must relinquish my father's kingdom to Menoetius and become Crete's sacrifice. Laughed at by the Kindred as a woman's plaything, led to my own docile murder at the rise of Iakchos." He stared at the pelt of the lioness on his wall. The creature had tried to slay his bastard brother, but Chrysaleon killed it instead. His warriors had hung it on their prince's bedchamber wall as trophy and reminder of his victory. He crossed to it, running his fingers over the stiff, dusty coat. "Am I to kill Menoetius?" It sounded strange in his ears, speaking such a thing. A shiver ran through him. He shrank from the idea, yet was oddly attracted to it at the same time. Like a bothersome conscience, Menoetius made him feel edgy, uncomfortable…inferior. "Is that what the king tried to tell me before he died?"

"Your choices are not easy, my lord—but there is one more. You could disavow your union in the interest of Mycenae. Aridela can keep her queenship. Your brother need not die. I don't think she would bring her armies here to force your hand, even if she still had power enough to do so. They can find a new king. Those who have never trusted you might even welcome such an event."

Chrysaleon found himself grinding his teeth again. He breathed in and out, seeking to disperse the irritation inflamed by his slave's suggestion. "If I did that, the Kindred would believe me afraid. Afraid of a woman, hiding behind my throne to escape her." He pressed his knuckles against the flutter of the tic beneath his eye. "And I would lose Crete. If Aridela succeeds in returning strength and power to her island, it would forever needle me, what I let slip away."

He paused. His words left an echo in his mind. More than losing Crete would needle him, if he faced the truth. "Live my life without Aridela?" he said, considering it, then shook his head decisively.

"What you suggest is a death sentence. Every bit as much as the other."

Glimpsing the cynicism on Alexiare's face, he turned away. He'd never managed to fool the old man. Life wasn't a tragic play performed in a marketplace. He could live without Aridela, in luxury, with power, and there would be women in plenty. But he didn't want to. Even if it meant he had to murder Menoetius. Even if it meant others had to die. He wanted what he wanted. Aside from that, there were many who would believe him cursed if he defied his sworn destiny. All eyes would be upon him, waiting for the wrath of the gods to rend him into bloody fragments. Much as he wanted to dismiss such notions, he couldn't. Not after what he had witnessed and endured on Crete.

Furiously raking back his hair, he said, "Everything comes down to the one knot I cannot untangle. I must live and die as my moera decrees, and the queen of Crete must live at my side. The only way I can see to unravel the knot is for Aridela to voluntarily end the sacrifice." Peering into the smoke-blackened rafters, he gave another humorless laugh. "And how, by all the gods, can I make that happen?"

He smashed his fists against the pelt. The unyielding stone beneath sent a brutal shock up his arms and into his shoulders. "Why does she not agonize over this as I do?"

Alexiare shuffled toward him. "All Cretans believe Queen Aridela is a descendant of the Lady. I am certain she does not wish for your death—her love and respect for you are clear. But the sacrifice is part of her as much as the beat of her heart." His voice lowered. "Long years have I lived on the Rock of Mycenae. Before that, it was Kaphtor, and before that, Ephesus. The things I have seen have left me skeptical. I no longer believe sacrificing the bull-king makes the crops grow. Nor do I believe gods and goddesses punish and reward us according to their whims. There is simply life, my lord. Then death. It's easy to see around us. In some lands, men rule over women. They worship powerful gods but have never heard of Poseidon. In others, women are proclaimed as embodiments of a fertile mother-earth, but the names of their goddesses are foreign to us. We are locked in an endless, petty struggle, though surely we must have been designed to complement and support each other."

"You only say that because you were not there. The fire didn't sear your throat. You didn't watch bodies burst open. Never again can I dismiss the gods after living through that night." Even as he spoke,

Chrysaleon remembered the dead hero, Damasen, who described what life would become when the Lady was forgotten. Alexiare's conjecturing returned Damasen's prophecies, word for word.

The female will be considered the substance of corruption, and every manner of evil toward her will be overlooked.

"Of course, my lord." Alexiare bowed his head, but almost immediately smiled. "This is the adventure my mother promised me. I feel it."

"What are you talking about?"

Alexiare's eyes gleamed beneath his stringy brows. "Before she died, she told me if I remained in Mycenae I would have an adventure, and that it would change the course of the world." He retrieved the poker and bent to refresh the sputtering fire. "I want to offer you yet another choice, my lord, one I doubt you have considered. You may not find it to your taste, and I must give it more thought. But I have the glimmerings of an idea."

"If you suggest I slip a dagger between Aridela's ribs while she sleeps, I will throw you over the balcony."

"No, nothing like that."

"Then why would I not like it?"

"Because you are a man who will run to the forefront of battle beating his shield, shouting to draw your enemy. You are not one to work the actions of others through shadows, secrets, and trickery." Tears streamed over Alexiare's cheeks in his struggle to speak. By the end, his voice was nearly inaudible.

Chrysaleon frowned. "I am tired, and you are prattling."

"You always have been impatient. I believe there may be a way to defeat the king-sacrifice. But it will require tact and subtlety. I wonder if you are capable of controlling your nature to achieve your aim. My lord."

Chastised, Chrysaleon could think of no retort and merely stared, astonished at his slave's audacity.

"I want you to live your life, to see your children grow." Alexiare was forced to whisper now. "And I want to help the queen. She must not realize as an old woman that she put you to death for nothing. I can think of no way for you to win but through cunning strategy. Can you deceive her, and every other person on Crete? It's the only way—I am certain of it."

Chrysaleon paused. "Tell me more," he said at last.

THE FUNERAL GAMES LASTED A FORTNIGHT. THE SWEARING OF LOYALTY BY the Kindred took most of another. Kings and their retinues crowded into every spot big enough to hold a pallet or clump of straw.

Chrysaleon faced and fought warriors and princes who hoped to defeat him and seize the High King's throne. The games, contests, and feasting—not to mention the punishing of Harpalycus's father, King Lycomedes of Tiryns, left hardly any time for plotting, missing Aridela, or even thoughts of his own approaching death.

When at last it was finished, winter had slipped into a lush, cool spring. Chrysaleon and his slave journeyed to the holy shrine near Sparta, for Alexiare thought they should begin with whatever prophecies the famed oracle might give, and construct a plan based on her revelations. That way, if the gods existed, perhaps they would be appeased.

Oracles had served here as priestesses to Mother Gaia for countless centuries, but in one of the villages they passed through, they learned that Spartan warriors, in a training sortie, had lately overthrown the shrine. Now priests managed the rites in the names of Poseidon and Zeus, and the oracle lived more as a prisoner than a revered prophetess.

Warm, sunny weather heralded their arrival. Crested hoopoes sang beside a river sparked with gold, and delicate poplar leaves fluttered in ecstatic breezes.

No one cared that he was High King of Mycenae. He and Alexiare had to wait their turn while other votaries underwent the required purifications.

At last two boys approached and led them to a quiet pooling in the river. White-robed maidens, never lifting shy eyes from their task, bathed them, rubbed unguents into their skin, and led them to a rock cleft from which a spring bubbled. Both drank purifying water from bronze ladles hanging on hooks. The girls placed fillets of apple-spray on their heads and pointed to a narrow, well-worn path between the rocks.

The track was steep and slippery, forcing Chrysaleon to hold Alexiare's arm so the old man wouldn't lose his balance. Eventually, they came to a dark slit-like opening leading into the cave.

Strong incense permeated the air inside. A boy in a pristine tunic gestured to yet another opening in the stone beyond.

Once they entered the inner sanctum, they saw the oracle, she who the boy had called Daphoenissa. She sat upon an impressive gypsum throne—one larger even than Aridela's.

Smoke drifted, translucent in the glimmer of cresset lamps. A python's thick body coiled around the throne, its head resting on the woman's bare feet.

Chrysaleon caught the faintest whiff of blood beneath the incense.

Daphoenissa appeared to be asleep. But when Chrysaleon's sandal grazed the edge of a stone, she opened her eyes and stared at him without blinking. Her eyes were cold and colorless, very much like the serpent's. Tilting her head infinitesimally, she drew in a breath as though scenting him.

"Your desire travels to me on the wings of my doves," she said, her voice echoing slightly. "You are the king who would rule beyond his appointed time."

Chrysaleon knelt, furious that he couldn't suppress a flush. Unclenching his jaw, he said, "I am." He refused to believe she had omnipotent power—one of her attendants must have told her he was on the way up. But how did she know his predicament?

She rose. The hem of her long white gown rippled as the disturbed python lifted its head. "What can you offer in return for this gift?"

"I have land, gold, precious oils, ivory, spices. I have ships and warriors. Horses."

"Such things are meaningless to the Immortals."

"What do they want of me?"

"Something that could make death beneath the light of Iakchos seem easy in comparison."

"I will give anything the gods require."

Alexiare pinched his arm and spoke a soft warning, but Chrysaleon shook him off. The woman's contempt was ill concealed. He would rather die in her serpent's suffocating embrace than show hesitation or fear. No wonder the short-tempered Spartans had subjugated her.

She watched him without expression, as though giving him an opportunity to change his mind. Slowly, her head slanted the opposite direction from before, and one of her fine dark brows peaked. Again she breathed in. He felt her slicing through his soul.

"Women use curses to make themselves appear powerful," he said to Alexiare from the corner of his mouth.

Stretching out her arms, Daphoenissa stared above their heads into the cavern's echoing depths. "The king who would overturn his vows must lie with the moon upon the earth. One shall spring from the holy womb who will devastate the most ancient of rituals."

Two handmaids came forward. As they guided her off the dais, Chrysaleon realized she was blind. The three stepped into the shadows behind the throne. Chrysaleon rose, thinking himself dismissed, but Daphoenissa stopped and turned. In a measured voice she said, "Slay the Lady's Earth Bull and rule until the sun and moon shift into perfect alignment."

The air grew still and silent. It felt like her blank, expressionless eyes were boring a hole in his forehead.

"Then you will die, Lion of Mycenae."

5

Moon of Flowering Apples

Aridela weathered a punishing morning in the judgment chamber, one strident with arguments, claims, supplications, and the usual tiresome accusations.

She was in trouble with her council. All but her aunt Oneaea had survived Harpalycus's invasion; most were now angry because Aridela had allowed Chrysaleon to leave Kaphtor. His father's death and the obligations that event placed upon him compelled him to remain at Mycenae longer than he'd expected, and for that, the council blamed her. As though she knew all along this would happen—as though she'd planned it. A few of the members declared they were happy to discard him, and hoped he would never return, but the common people adored their sacred king. Not a day passed without a bombardment of peasants and handmaids asking for news and wanting to know when their Zagreus would again walk upon Kaphtor's soil.

Tired, exasperated, cringing beneath the pounding throb of a headache, Aridela finally dismissed everyone, including her retinue, and went off in search of peace and quiet. She soon found herself wandering the gardens adjacent to the breakfast hall. It was hard not to think of how it used to be—the scent, the color, the swift flash of larks, swallows, doves, and the occasional visit from an eagle or kestrel. It was painful to remember how often she, in the company of her mother and sister, had played here when she was little. This was where she had made love to Chrysaleon before he sailed to Mycenae, and where the baby she now carried was sown.

The first time Harpalycus attacked her was in this garden. He had given her a glimpse of the evil inside him. If only she could have seen what was to come. She would have had him put to death then and there.

Kaphtor's gardens, once famed far and wide, were now little more than bare earth. Dead limbs and ash-smothered foliage had been hauled away, but the laborers were too busy elsewhere to plant anything new.

She made her way to one of the few surviving trees, a maple, standing in isolation near the far wall. As she came closer, she spotted a man squatting on the ground beneath its branches. Turquoise shadows showed her the rim of one ear, a fall of dark hair carelessly tied back, and bent shoulders covered by a quilted tunic, for the mornings were still chilly.

One of the gardeners, no doubt. Disappointed, she chose to walk on and not disturb his work, though she'd hoped to spend whatever brief time she could steal sitting in solitude, listening to breezes play amongst the maple's leaves.

His head lifted. As he perused the canopy above, she recognized that profile. It was Menoetius. Flooded with guilt and uneasy conscience, she took a few steps backward, as unobtrusively as possible, but it was too late. He turned and looked at her, silent for one instant too long before saying, "Aridela."

She floundered for a greeting, but he moved them past the awkward silence by motioning her over. "You must see this."

Reluctantly, she approached and stood beside him, surprised when he reached up and clasped her fingers.

She had made every effort to appear strong, happy, and confident since the day Chrysaleon left for the mainland. As she always seemed to be mired in clusters of priestesses, councilors, friends, hangers-on, or handmaids, there hadn't been much time to indulge in self-pity.

But lodged inside, continually pricking at her thoughts, was the awareness that every morning brought closer the rise of Iakchos; each night that passed with Chrysaleon far away at Mycenae was one less they could be together. Twice during the council meeting, she had caught herself recklessly daydreaming of covert methods to prevent or postpone the king-sacrifice.

Menoetius's casual gesture dissipated her control. She bit her lip, harder than she intended, breaking the skin and tasting blood, but the pain helped her maintain her composure.

He had been courteous, if remote, since their return from the Araden mountains. He never reproached her. Perhaps he was as embarrassed as she about their intimacies, and glad to have been wrong about Chrysaleon's death, pleased to see her reunited with her rightful consort.

"What must I see?" she asked, fortified by these reassuring thoughts.

He gave her one of his very rare smiles and tugged on her hand.

She knelt. Almost hidden by shade and a few tufts of grass, several delicate pinkish-tinged flowers were sprouting. They were wild lilies, common in the old days, but these were the first she had seen since the Destruction. Their petals pointed sharply toward the sky like miniature flames. A few had opened, revealing deep yellow centers.

Elation and relief welled. It was easy to believe the old adage that pregnancy caused unpredictable and sudden changes in mood. She heard herself laughing and said, "Shall we construct a shrine?"

"A temple."

She allowed the weight of the council meeting, Chrysaleon's absence, and her guilt to slide away as she and her accomplice settled on the ground like sentinels, circling and protecting these frail symbols of recovery. Even her headache eased. "Do you think Kaphtor will ever be as it was?" She smoothed the earth gently with the tips of her fingers. "It has been months, yet hardly anything grows."

"Your hair has grown."

She self-consciously touched the side of her head.

His smile and a hiked brow mocked her feminine embarrassment. "The land will recover as well," he said without a hint of doubt.

"Elasa and the eastern regions have been abandoned," she reminded him.

"But the wheat in Messara shows astounding growth."

"Yes. They think the ash contains some invaluable elemental property. I hope it's true."

"What will you do with this garden? I remember how much you loved it."

"I want an arbor fashioned of grapevines." She gazed over the barren paths. "It will take a long time to mature, but when it does, it will be heavy with grapes, covered with leaves, woven through with flowers and herbs. I will make this garden a place of refuge, one that every land will attempt to imitate."

He nodded and looked pleased.

They fell into comfortable silence. Aridela relaxed, no longer fearing he would raise unpleasant subjects. As sunlight pierced the last remaining threads of mist and the chill retreated, she was soon overwhelmed with the need to sleep, another bothersome mark of pregnancy. She leaned against the maple's trunk, her cheek pillowed in the crook of her arm. Closing her eyes, she listened to doves coo, leaves rustle, and branches creak, as she'd longed to do all morning. Menoetius's quiet presence sparked memories of their cave in the western mountains, of waking in the night and seeing him wrapped in his magnificent tiger skin on the other side of the fire pit. If she made any sound, no matter how slight, he always opened his eyes, leaving her to wonder if he ever got any rest. Somehow, though they rarely spoke, his regard enveloped her in a sense of safety and comfort.

Only he would ever know how deeply she had dropped into hopelessness and despair, how she had prayed for death, or how the cave shadows had persecuted her—at least in her imagination. Only Menoetius would ever know how far she had come since.

But for him, she would have returned to Chrysaleon still contaminated by Harpalycus's torture. She would have gone on idealizing death, and might have continued to seek it. She loved Chrysaleon for his heroism and courage, his determination, his ardor, but she knew the sort of wounds seared into her by the Usurper were beyond his ability to grasp or heal. They would have festered. They might have consumed her. It was Menoetius, wounded himself, who understood. It was he who convinced her that no matter what Harpalycus did, he failed to touch her in any way that mattered. Because of Menoetius, she released the shame, the rage, and hatred. She returned to Chrysaleon with her old fierce strength and resolve, very nearly the Aridela he had always known.

When she thought back on how it all unfolded, she saw the blessing in being sent into the mountains with the one person who knew how to mend her. What if they had taken her to Knossos right away? What if she had never experienced the benefit of Menoetius's own unique pathos, which in turn created his perfect empathy? Things might have turned out very differently.

It was ironic. She owed not only her present happiness to this man, but her very life, and the life of the baby growing inside her. She wanted to tell him how grateful she was, but she feared her confession might make him think something had changed, when it couldn't—not as long as Chrysaleon lived. It might spoil the easy, relaxed camaraderie they were enjoying now. It could propel them back into the pain of that last day in the mountain cave.

There was another reason, a memory from that day, which stopped her tongue. He had said something that had gone on haunting her, something she had never confronted him about or revealed to anyone else.

Do you think I have never raped a woman?

She only knew him here, on her island. Could he be so different at Mycenae? The image of Menoetius, brutalizing, outraging a woman as Harpalycus had done to her threw everything she thought she knew about him into doubt.

Yet, as she had told herself many times, he hadn't harmed her. She wasn't sure why she hadn't demanded an explanation immediately— maybe because of the intensity of his anger. Now so much time had passed, she didn't know how to ask, and little by little, the question had expanded in her mind to encompass Chrysaleon as well. She had heard ugly rumors about mainlanders, and all the war-loving tribes who burned the land from Ephesus to Selene's country and beyond. It was said that Mycenaeans in particular employed all manner of atrocities to subjugate and seize power—that they used rape to further crush the spirit of their defeated enemies. It was hard not to believe those tales after Harpalycus.

The possibility of her beloved consort engaging in such horror made her feel sick and acutely disloyal. She reminded herself that when it came to rumors, every mouth added a little to increase their audience's shock, until truth and facts were lost beneath imagination and exaggeration.

Aridela rested her free hand on her stomach and deliberately turned her mind to the coming child. *Lady, bring me a daughter*, she prayed as she created fantasies of wavy golden hair and eyes like Chrysaleon's. Her daydreams brought back Chrysaleon's tenderness, his vows of love, his poetry. *How could I have known before I came here,* he'd said the night of the cataclysm, *that your waist would fit my hands like it was made for them? That your body would mold into mine and mine into yours as though we were fashioned within the same womb?* And there would always be the indelible memory of how he had used his own body to shield her during the Destruction.

Remembering his words of love caused her mind to war again with her heart.

I don't want him to die. I cannot let him die.

Perhaps he would defy his vow and stay in Mycenae. Part of her wanted him to. At least he would be alive, even if she never saw him again, even if his abandonment forced them to be enemies and brought humiliation upon her.

Such thoughts were a betrayal, sacrilege, and selfish. They might draw the rage of Athene. But her heart didn't seem to care about consequences.

She opened her eyes. Menoetius was leaning against the trunk beside her, looking up through the maple's branches. This side of his face was nearly flawless—only one narrow ridge of scar running along his jaw. Seeing it brought memories of the handsome youth he'd once been, and their time together before Chrysaleon.

Impulsively, she said, "I wish I could know your mother. I wish she would come back."

He glanced at her before returning his gaze to the leafy awning. "I am going there—to Ys. When Chrysaleon returns."

"What?"

His gaze remained fixed. He didn't speak.

"No." She cleared her throat and ordered herself to display more queenly control. "I know you have always wanted to find her. But it's so far." Logic suggested it would make things easier if he left. With time and his absence, her guilt might lessen. She might forget the mountains. The cave. That last day.

But even as she had this rational thought, she heard herself say, "Kaphtor needs you." She worked to keep her voice impersonal. "This child I bear will need your wisdom and guidance." She stopped herself from adding, *When its father is gone.*

His jaw clenched. How well she remembered that habit of his from the mountain cave. Caught up in her misery and grief, she had reviled him, called him a coward. He had never returned her abuse but his jaw clamped, over and over again, as he fought for control over his anger.

It was hard not to reach up and press her fingers against that tense spot. Hard not to say, *I will need you.* She forced herself to swallow the words. The confession of love she'd once made followed by her abandonment spoiled any hope of real trust between them. Yet, despite their misunderstandings and discomfort, despite hardly ever seeing him, she always knew he was there, somewhere in the corridors or chambers of Labyrinthos. She relied on knowing he was there, that she could call and he would come. Menoetius was a man who would keep his vows. In a strange way he had proven that when he'd bound her to the log in the cave. It would have been easier to let her run away and be done with her.

Nothing can ever part us, he'd said that day on the precarious cliff, before Chrysaleon found them. Chrysaleon had parted them effortlessly, the instant she heard his voice.

As Menoetius turned towards her, she had a sudden, startling revelation. Her mind soared, higher and higher into the heavens.

Drifts of shadow, speckled with sunlight, cast just the right clarity, imbuing the incredible color of his eyes, like jeweled blue fire.

When very young, she had enjoyed a strange, solitary intimacy with a friend no one but she could see, a lady she called "Mother." She'd forgotten all that long ago, but now those memories returned.

The eyes looking at her from Menoetius's face carried her back to those distant days. They were the eyes of that beloved companion.

She took a steadying breath. His shrewd gaze must not discern the unraveling of her determination. It would always be this way—a struggle to deny the part of her that needed him in a way Chrysaleon would see as a betrayal.

"Forgive me." She pressed her palm against his. "I am selfish. The mystery of Sorcha calls you. You want to go, to discover your own glory apart from Mycenae and Kaphtor. We will miss you. You will always be remembered for the sacrifices you made."

"Sacrifices?" His head jerked. He stiffened and pulled his hand free.

Oh, Menoetius, you are so much more complicated than your brother. It takes only a smile or lovemaking to please him. You wind and tangle like the labyrinth that leads to the holy Earth Bull.

"I want to give you the honor you deserve," she said. "You are my brother, as you are Chrysaleon's."

He blinked, drew in a breath, and returned his gaze to the upper reaches of the tree.

She'd made things worse. His body looked rigid, his shoulders tight.

"I am always tired but I haven't been sleeping well," she said. "Would you stay with me here? It's peaceful, and no one would dare disturb me with such a fierce guardian." She took his hand again, lacing her fingers through his with a conciliatory smile.

He hesitated then seemed to relax. "No one will molest you."

She closed her eyes and again rested her head on her arm. Sleep had been elusive, easily disrupted by the slightest sound, leaving her weary and out-of-sorts.

Mistress, give me strength, she prayed as she had that last day in the cave. *Help me do as you wish.*

The dream began, as it often did, with her bull leap, and Chrysaleon lifting his dagger in salute. That triumph faded and she woke in an unfamiliar place. She saw a circle of faint starlight far above, but everything around her was impenetrable blackness. When she extended her arms she encountered a cold, encircling barrier that felt and smelled like wet wood, and she stood in a puddle of water.

She cupped her hands around her mouth. "Is anyone there?"

A muffled sound filtered through the walls of her prison, a low growl, reminiscent of the lions Helice kept in the halcyon days before fire and ash burned away the golden age of Kaphtor.

Again she searched, more desperately, for any crack or imperfection that might provide a means to escape.

"There is no way out."

Water splashed over her ankles as she swung around. "Iphiboë," she cried. "Is it you?"

Hugging her sister was like grasping a cloud. Iphiboë disintegrated then reformed when Aridela stepped away.

"Iphiboë, where have you been?"

"Cocooned within peace." Even her sister's voice sounded insubstantial, like the softest breeze. "I have returned to tell you what you need to know. It's hard for you, little sister, to do nothing. Did not your inflexible will force the warrior Menoetius to bind you in the cave?"

"What good does doing nothing bring? Should we not strive to create our fates, to fulfill our moera?"

The light around Iphiboë shimmered like the fine netting, covered with crystals and polished disks, that hung over Aridela's bed. "A war began on the night of the Destruction, and it will last longer than you can dream. If you could see the length and breadth of this war, you would lose hope. That is why my Mistress hides the future from you— from all her children. You stand at the center. Yet you must deaden your nature and do nothing. It is for those who have defiled her to construct the bridge back. You are the promise. The purpose. The quest. In striving for you they will, I pray, return to her bosom, and bring the world with them. It is the only way."

Goose bumps washed across Aridela's arms. "I cannot do nothing. If there is to be another war, I will fight."

"Yes. But not for a long, long time, and until then, you will suffer, for you are the betrayer as well as the promise."

"Who have I betrayed? Tell me." Furious, Aridela tried again to grasp her sister, but it was no use.

Iphiboë's gaze held such sorrow it frightened Aridela, made her want to cry out in protest. "You cannot know everything, Aridela. This is our Mother's design. You must relinquish your power if you ever wish to understand the plight of those for whom you battle. It makes me weep to see the misery you will endure, the mistakes you will make. You have already made many. But, my sister, your suffering hones you, as it does your champion."

Iphiboë leaned her head to one side. "Do you hear the growl of the lion?"

"Yes, what is that?"

"The lion is the changing world. Velchanos must defeat it if you are to be freed and the approaching upheaval thwarted. Yet he must also submit to it, allow himself to be consumed. Oh, how I hope he finds the courage to face the beast and fulfill his obligation."

The growl outside expanded into a snarl then a terrifying roar, making the walls of Aridela's prison shudder. She pictured the lion turning its massive head up to the sky as it gave voice. Instinctively she shrank and covered her ears. "What is happening?" she cried, making the sign against evil, but when she turned back to Iphiboë her sister was gone and she was alone. Something flew out of the dark and latched onto her wrist, squeezing, harder and harder, until she thought her bones would snap.

Heart pounding, she opened her eyes and took in the waking scene. The garden was peaceful, silent but for the drone of cicadas and the desolate call of doves. There was no raging lion. No dank, chilly prison. Sunlight rather than starlight bathed the ground. Next to her, though, Menoetius's face was contorted. Sweat poured off him. It was he who squeezed her wrist, his grip unyielding and painful.

An instant later his eyes opened but they were blank, unseeing; with a miserable groan he released her, bringing his forearms up and covering his face as though to ward off a blow.

"Menoetius." Aridela grabbed his arms. "Menoetius!"

His fixed stare gradually cleared and gained awareness. "Aridela?"

"I am here—you are with me. In the garden." She pressed his fists to the warm flesh below her collarbones. His expression was wary and she thought he might need to know she was real.

He glanced around the enclosure and up into the softly swaying branches before sighing and freeing his hands. He rubbed his eyes.

She sat beside him, drawing her knees up to her chest, and waited.

"I had a dream." His face was pale, tired-looking, as though he hadn't been sleeping any better than she. He was only twenty-three, but right now he appeared much older.

"So did I. There was a lion."

He stared at her, frowning, as though trying to decipher a language he had never heard before.

"It roared," she said, delving into her mind for the details and dismayed to realize they were already fading.

He drew in a sharp, shuddering breath. "It's real? Is it here?"

"No, no," she said, understanding. "I was dreaming. We were both asleep. There are no lions here anymore."

His gaze narrowed and she nodded, reassuring him without words. His jaw clenched. Unclenched. He spoke hoarsely. "I told you that the first time I saw you, when you were bleeding in the shrine, I knew I loved you."

She hesitated no more than an instant. "Yes."

"I knew it because you are the lady from my dream. Realizing it was like climbing out of an abyss. It was like seeing green grass after enduring a thousand years of winter."

"The lady…from your dream?"

"For years, every time I have fallen asleep, I see the same thing— you, trapped inside an oak tree. To get to you, I must pass a lion. It never leaves. Never sleeps. It will kill anyone who confronts it." His voice dropped. "I have to fight this lion if I am to free you."

His words sparked a memory. Something about the lion in her dream. *The lion Velchanos must defeat.* Who had said that? Her sister! Iphiboë! Aridela's flesh prickled. She felt the presence of Goddess Athene, and knew these intertwined dreams were sent for a reason.

Menoetius watched her carefully. "Long ago, when you drew the wrath of the bull, I saved your life."

She encased his hand between her palms, fighting a sudden burn of tears.

"I had gone into the shrine at Labyrinthos to offer Athene my devotion—to ask what she wanted of me. This was her answer." He gestured with his free hand toward his face. "She sent the beast that did this. In sleep and waking, there are lions." He dug four shallow trenches in the dirt with his fingertips as he said, "I have never had enough courage to fight the lion in my nightmare, though she promises it will bring an end to all misery, even my own. I am a coward, and she knows it. That is why she punishes me."

At last, Aridela understood. It was this curse causing his bitterness, not the scars. In his waking life a lioness nearly killed him. When he slept, another lion mauled him endlessly. Pity washed over her.

He looked away from her as though he couldn't bear to see her expression, and she knew she must tread very carefully.

"My dream, too, was strange." She rubbed his knuckles as she tried to bring back the details. "It was dark. Iphiboë was with me. A lion was roaring in the distance." She pondered, silent until he blinked and returned his gaze to her. "Menoetius, I remember something. When we were on the mountain, you said Athene caused the lioness to attack you. That it was her punishment for leaving me."

"Yes."

"What would have happened if you hadn't been in the shrine that day? I would have died. You think the mauling was her answer, but I think you are wrong. She sent you there to save me. I was the answer, yes? She only punished you later, when you left me. She put us together that day; she wanted you to stay. But you didn't. You ignored her command and returned to Mycenae. That is why she punished you. If you stay here with me now, isn't that as good as fighting the lion? Do what she wants. I promised I would make you judge or advisor. I want that still. Stay. Stay with me."

He frowned.

The need to convince him intensified. "You swore to me that day on the cliff, that if I fell over the edge, you would jump after me and break my fall. Did you lie?"

"I don't know." He wrenched his hand from hers and immediately seized her wrist, pressing his fingertips over the pulse beating there.

His stare was anguished and accusing. *Did you?* his eyes asked.

There was the Goddess again, her gaze demanding. Aridela's flesh crawled. She felt the pounding of her pulse beneath his fingers. Yes, she, too, had been given a command, and she, too, had ignored it.

Frustrated and filled with doubt, she pulled her hand free and hunched over, pressing her face to her knees.

That last day in the mountain cave returned vividly. It had taken more strength than she knew she possessed to resist him. Had she followed the Goddess's wishes by refusing him, or had she misreck-oned everything?

He said nothing. Finally, she wiped away the tears on her cheeks and broached what lay between them. "I promised to savor every day I have with Chrysaleon. It is a small thing, is it not, to be with no other until Iakchos rises and he meets the winner of the Games, his brother in death…his cabal? To do otherwise would hurt him. He would feel betrayed." She added, both to Menoetius and the Goddess, "It's only three and a half months." Wrapping her arms around her knees, she studied the desolation that had once been a lush, vibrant garden. "These are your customs which direct me, which I try to recognize. They are strange. It is not our way. Our queens have never been ruled by such constraints. If I wished, I could take any man I wanted into my bed and suffer no condemnation. No consort reared on Kaphtor would be offended." Returning her gaze to his, she added, "My mother chose to give her loyalty, her love, and her body to no one but my father when he was bull-king. I follow her lead. I want to dignify her memory, and my father's, as well as Chrysaleon. Do not be angry with me about this, Menoetius."

His gaze faltered and fell. "In my land, a woman's needs, her desires, mean nothing. She must obey if she wants to live. If I had not been mauled, I might feel as my countrymen do."

Aridela waited, watching resistance play across his face and finally evaporate. He drew in a deep breath and released it slowly. "What you offer Chrysaleon is different. You give it freely, without coercion, without fear." He inclined his head, a little reluctantly. "This is not our time. It belongs to Chrysaleon, though I doubt he understands the value of what you give. I ask but one thing. Let us sit here awhile longer, until the sun reaches the western roof of the palace—" He pointed. "You can see it's almost there. I won't touch you. I only want to look at your face. I want to hear of your days, your tasks and plea-sures, the judgments you make, your thoughts. This I ask, the man who has twice saved your life, and it is a much smaller thing."

She thought of the lilies, thrusting so bravely from the soil, wanting to live, to thrive, to offer beauty—as he was doing, with a pure and open heart. That last day on the mountain returned vividly to her mind. Rainbows danced and frothed through her blood, enticing her. Listening to the cadence of his voice, seeing what lay in his eyes, gazing upon his beloved, scarred face, all these heightened a desire for more—a need to play out that last day to the conclusion they had both wanted.

She knew his true intent. He meant to coax her into acknowledging what lay unfinished between them, and perhaps give in to it. What he asked was not small, and she didn't trust herself to keep it so.

Harpalycus had ripped all semblance of choice from her. That could never be changed or forgotten. But Menoetius had returned her strength, had given her back the ability to determine her own course. She could act like a queen. She could put her vow to Chrysaleon above her secret weaknesses, even if they weren't as secret as she believed. "No," she whispered, squeezing handfuls of her tunic in her fists to keep them from stealing out to his.

Breezes played with his hair. It had grown. She imagined watching it run, glossy and sleek, between her fingers, but she kept her hands clenched and met his gaze, forcing her eyes to give no hint of the rainbows darting through her veins.

His face turned to granite. His jaw worked and he rose abruptly. "I won't stay here. Your goddess can kill me. I wish she would."

"What of your oath?"

"All your oaths are to Chrysaleon. You give nothing and ask much in return." He stared down at her, and seemed a stranger—a foreigner.

She opened her mouth, wanting to say *I need you*, but hesitating. Before she could gather the courage, he turned with a growl of disgust and abandoned her, leaving nothing of their time together but a drone of cicadas and cold, yawning regret.

SELENE LOOKED UP AS MENOETIUS STALKED INTO HER CHAMBER, HIS expression black with rage. She set down the knife she was sharpening. "Leave us," she told the handmaid. The woman bowed and slipped out of the room.

"What troubles you?" She asked as she crossed to him and caressed his hands.

He swiveled and threw up his arm, knocking her away. "Don't," he said, grimacing.

She stepped back. "Menoetius. Your face is filled with hatred."

He seized her and bent her backward until she feared for her spine. He kissed her, staring into her eyes, but she felt he didn't even see her.

She drew him onto the bed. The way he ripped her tunic reminded her of warriors fresh from battle, men surprised to be alive.

This rough lust was at odds with his usual tenderness. She pulled him closer, sliding her legs around his hips. "Yes, my love," she said. "I am here."

It was over quickly. He fell upon her, heavy and still, then rolled off and turned away.

She stroked his hair. Unsheared since before he came to Kaphtor from Mycenae, it spilled through her hands like a gleaming fall of water.

"What has happened?" She rose on one elbow, frowning at his inflexible shoulders.

In a halting, hoarse voice, he said, "Chrysaleon."

"What of him?"

He faced her, seized her hands and kissed her palms. "He is my brother. I came here with him, knowing his mind, believing as he did, but now that I know you and Ar—the queen, I cannot stand by and say nothing. I cannot."

This last he spoke with such despair that Selene gathered him into her arms and held him like a child. "Tell me."

"He deceives you."

Selene drew away just enough to look him in the eyes. "How?"

"Chrysaleon vowed he would win Crete for the glory of Mycenae. He means to halt the king-sacrifice. Your people will be his slaves."

"Chrysaleon, a traitor, like Harpalycus?"

Menoetius gripped her arms. "He won't stop until he destroys the Goddess-of-Life-in-Death and makes her subject to his gods."

Selene stared, too shocked to speak.

"I won't stay to watch it happen." Menoetius's eyes narrowed. "I will leave. I mean to make my way to the country that birthed my mother."

"No!"

His jaw clenched. "Come with me."

"I...."

"Come with me, Selene." He pressed her cheek to his throat. "I want you with me."

She pulled back, blinking away the sting of tears. "I am with child."

It was his turn to stare.

She nodded. "The night before you took Aridela into the mountains. Remember? The Moon of the Olive Harvest."

He was quiet then he smiled. "Yes." He reached for her again, turning her so her spine rested against his chest. He put his arms around her, his hands on her abdomen.

"Are you pleased?" she asked.

He kissed her and held her face. "I am pleased," he whispered.

She watched him swallow, watched the faintest hint of moisture gather in his eyes, and was deeply moved. "I wondered if you would ever notice," she said lightly, to preserve his pride.

He laughed. "I thought you were eating more."

"Even if I were not having your child, I would not go," she said. "I cannot leave Aridela. I won't leave her. Especially if what you say is true. She will need me, and you, too."

"She doesn't trust me."

"Of course she does."

"No. I kept secrets from her. Secrets Chrysaleon revealed. Now she thinks he's the truthful one and I, the liar."

"What secrets?"

He looked away. Then he shrugged and faced her. "My father wanted to add Crete to his holdings, make it his possession. That is the only reason we came here, to find a way to overthrow you. I am as guilty as Chrysaleon. My only desire was to make my father proud. Chrysaleon told Aridela. I didn't. That is why she trusts him more than me."

She asked with her eyes what she could not bring herself to ask out loud.

"I have not felt that way for a long while," he said. "Since…that first night in the Cave of Velchanos."

"You are one of us."

He nodded.

She rose from the bed, straightening her tunic. "We must go to Aridela and tell her what you've told me." She picked up the knife she'd been sharpening. "Somehow, I always knew this about Chrysaleon. But I could never make her listen."

"No."

She turned to him, surprised. "No? You cannot mean to think I won't tell Aridela of this."

He came to her, took the knife, and placed it on the table. "I want to see Chrysaleon when he comes back. Perhaps something will have changed, as it did for me. Maybe he will return ready to fulfill his promise."

Selene snorted. "You don't believe that any more than I do. He's High King now. You can't think he'll want to give that up. Not for us, not for anyone."

"Swear to me you'll say nothing. I need time. I must be certain. It is not so easy to betray my brother and my king, to knowingly draw the wrath of the Erinyes. Swear to me."

"Very well. But you must promise me something."

"What?"

"That you will not leave us. This is your home. I am giving birth to your child. Promise me you will stay."

He paused, finally nodding. "I won't leave unless you go with me."

Selene turned away, swiping at tears. "Aridela loves him," she whispered. Fear and hopelessness crept through her limbs like a wasting illness. "Mistress, if this is true, take vengeance upon him alone."

6

Moon of Water Ferns

CHRYSALEON TOSSED HIS HELMET TO ALEXIARE AND STRODE ACROSS THE beach to clasp Aridela's outstretched hands. It meant something that she'd come to the harbor instead of waiting like a queen for him to come to her at the palace.

"At last," she said, her smile as brilliant as the face of the moon.

The shadows that had lingered beneath her eyes after Harpalycus stabbed her were gone. Her skin was lustrous. Perhaps the intensity he thought he glimpsed behind that smile was no more than imagination, from so many days of being overtly judged by too many people. He bent and kissed her, breathing in her musky scent. "My nights have been dismal," he said, and in that instant, he spoke the truth.

Her laughter sparkled. She wound her arms around his neck. "My Zagreus. My beloved. And now, High King of Mycenae."

He frowned.

"Forgive me." She drew back, pressing her hand to his cheek. "I mean no disrespect to your father."

"He died before his time." Clasping her waist, he said, "I see no evidence of a child."

"She is there. Rhené is certain of it."

He nuzzled the perfumed flesh under her ear. "That is what you want? A daughter?"

"I pray for a daughter. She will be everything to me, as I was to my mother. Everything. She will be my heart and heir."

Alexiare cleared his throat behind them. "The litter is ready, my lord."

"Shall we go to our chamber?" Chrysaleon brought her fingers to his mouth.

Her eyes grew dark and her cheeks filled with color in the way he'd remembered and missed.

"Yes."

CHRYSALEON LEANED AGAINST A STONE WALL OUTSIDE THE PALACE. HE pressed his knuckles against the irritating tic beneath his eye and tried to coax some morsel of strength from his limbs. If the wall weren't there to hold him up, he feared he might well sprawl on his face.

Being with her after so long was almost like drowning.

"My lord?" Alexiare's mouth curved in a knowing smile as he held out a leather flask.

"Why are we stopping? It's cold." Chrysaleon took the flask and drank. Honey and spices flavored the mead. A few sips warmed him, numbed him, and made him even sleepier.

"Someone is coming to lead the way. Apparently we cannot hope to find Themiste's chambers on our own."

Chrysaleon took another swig then forced himself to stop. He wanted more, but for the task at hand, he needed to be clear-headed.

"Where does the queen think you have gone?"

"Out to inspect the land. She hardly woke when I told her, and asked no questions."

Alexiare nodded.

The sky lightened to an endless expanse of silver. Alexiare stamped his feet and rubbed his hands together.

"Go over it again, old man," Chrysaleon said. "Repeat the oracle's words."

Though he'd done so numerous times, Alexiare's damaged voice held no hint of impatience. "Sir, the lady prophesied that the king who would break his vow must lie with the moon upon the earth, one whose womb is holy."

The two had gone over and over these words on the voyage to Kaphtor. "You're certain this means Themiste."

"Her womb is consecrated, belonging solely to her Mistress. She possesses as much, if not more, power than the queen. Daphoenissa promised that from this womb one shall be born who will change ancient rituals."

Chrysaleon felt his blood heat, which helped make him more alert. It could be the mead, but more likely it was the idea of bedding Kaphtor's high priestess. He had wanted to taste that flesh ever since his death-dream. The fact that he'd just come from a sleepless night of sex with Aridela made no difference.

His next thought cooled the ardor. "Does it mean something will happen to the child Aridela carries? Why else must I make another with Themiste?"

"It may simply mean the oracle's child will achieve your wishes. Queen Aridela may bear a child to you as well, my lord. I hope so."

"And the last part?"

"I wish we could be more sure of that. 'Slay the Lady's Earth Bull,' Daphoenissa said. "But while you are Kaphtor's consort, you are the Lady's Earth Bull. She seems to be saying you must kill yourself to win more time." He shrugged. "In this, I feel I am failing you—" Alexiare remained quiet awhile then said hesitantly, "Your father told me he was quite certain Menoetius would cause you harm, if nothing was done to prevent it."

Again he fell into silence. Chrysaleon had another sip of mead and let him think. Menoetius. What could his bastard brother have to do with all this? The oracle had said nothing about him, and Chrysaleon had far too willingly put Idómeneus's warning out of his mind. He much preferred overthrowing Crete in some way that wouldn't hurt his position or his wife's affections, if a way could be found.

Finally, giving a heavy sigh, the old man returned from his ruminations. "For the present, we should follow the only course that makes sense—striving to achieve both your desires and your father's." He pulled on his earlobe and squinted at his master. "I think I have the beginnings of an idea."

A robed figure emerged from beneath an archway and paused, looking around.

"What is it?" Chrysaleon said. "Be quick."

"Ask Themiste for another year. Tell her you have been cheated of yours. She will refuse. Then ask for a smaller boon, one she can more easily grant—to pick your own cabal. If she agrees, tell her you choose Menoetius. I'll explain later."

Chrysaleon nodded. The figure had spotted them and was approaching. He straightened, planting his feet firmly. "I will do this if

I can. But Themiste's vows are sacred to her, and she isn't gullible. I don't see how—"

Alexiare clasped Chrysaleon's arm and spoke into his ear. "Minos. That is Themiste's secret title. It is forbidden for you to say or even know. It means 'Moon-Being.' That is how I knew Daphoenissa was speaking of her. I wasn't sure I should tell you—there are heavy curses attached to women's mysteries." With a sideways, sardonic smile, he released Chrysaleon and stepped back. "If any living man can cause the high priestess to stray from her vows, it is you, my lord." He sobered. "Use her secrets to your advantage, but be careful."

Their guide lifted her hood, revealing a young, solemn face. From her height, build, and features, Chrysaleon decided she couldn't be more than twelve.

"Follow me," she said.

They fell in behind her. *Moon-Being*. This proved they were following the right path. His slave's oblique warning notwithstanding, Chrysaleon felt, clear into his bones, that he must make this plan happen, even if he had to rape the woman.

They walked along the palace's west wall. Greedy vendors, harried craftsmen, builders and architects, clerks and messengers, would soon crowd its precincts. Right now it lay empty and silent but for a lone raven that sidled away from them, and a disinterested slave sweeping the flagstones. Presently they came to an inconspicuous portal between two pillars. Their guide opened it and stepped through.

Many of the labyrinthine corridors beneath the palace were still buried in rubble. Those under the eastern precincts might never be restored. But much had been done to improve the west side. Chrysaleon lost track of their direction as they followed the girl through narrow maze-like hallways, lit by intermittent wall sconces. In places, rough wood beams temporarily supported the ceilings. Every now and then the creak and groan of weakened, damaged wood broke the silence. Dust lay thick and heavy. Their steps caused it to billow, which in turn made his nose itch. Nothing looked familiar. He could only hope as they went on that the Goddess wouldn't bring Labyrinthos crashing down on their heads and put an end to his plots against her.

The dim tunnels brought back his fight with Lycus for the kingship. It seemed eons ago, almost as though it had happened to someone else, except for those times when the healed-over thigh wound ached or he noticed the white scar on his forearm.

At last they stopped at a plain wooden door.

Their young guide held up her hand. "Wait here," she said, and slipped inside.

Soon Themiste herself opened the door. Near darkness prevented Chrysaleon from guessing what she might think about this unexpected visit.

"Zagreus."

He knelt.

"Why do you kneel?" she asked. "Are we not old friends?" She held out her hands. He took them, rose, and didn't let go.

"Yes." He looked into her face. "I hope so."

"Come in. I am anxious to hear all about the mainland."

At her glance, Alexiare bowed and backed away. "I will wait here, my lady," he said.

The room Chrysaleon entered was large but austere, and appeared to be under construction. Flickering cressets sent shadows dancing across unadorned walls and piled crates. Chrysaleon surreptitiously examined his surroundings as Themiste gave him a faint smile and the barest inclination of her head, motioning him to wait as she went off with the girl who had brought them.

The only thing of note was a rectangular pit in the center of the room, which he knew Themiste used to give the monthly oracles. He could just make out frescoes painted on its walls, displaying the Goddess in a few of her Cretan guises. He saw Dictynna, who gave favor to fishermen, Britomartis of the wild things, Eleuthia the pregnant mother, and Athene the benevolent gift-giver, holding what looked like an olive branch in one hand and oak leaves in the other. Dominating the other paintings at one end of the pit was her most ancient guise, as White Goddess, lady of the moon. Brightly painted tripods held lit braziers, bathing the pit in a soft glow. On the northern ledge, three wooden staffs rose, the tallest in the center, each topped with the double axe and doves, crafted in what appeared to be solid gold. Amidst all this beautiful artwork lay a jumble of pots, brushes, and sponges, indicating the paintings were new. The room smelled of paint, plaster, clay, and straw.

At the far end of the chamber, Themiste kissed her young attendant on both cheeks. The girl bowed and left through an arched opening.

A black snake slithered across the floor and disappeared into the shadows, reminding him of the serpent in the labyrinth on the night he fought the battle to become Crete's king.

"I am sorry, my lord," Themiste said as she returned. "Your father was a wise and gracious man. These last terrible months have been difficult for us all. I grieve with you. He will always be remembered for his aid in our most desperate time. Who knows where we would be now without it?"

"He was a great king." Suddenly nervous, Chrysaleon wiped his palms on his tunic. Alexiare's words echoed. *Moon-Being. Heavy curses attached to women's mysteries. Use her secrets to achieve your desires, but be careful.*

She worried her lower lip with her teeth. He fancied she was nervous too, and wondered why. Then she smiled. "Tell me of this curse you fear," she said, guiding him by the elbow to an embroidered curtain hanging over another doorway. Pulling it aside, she led him into what must be her private chamber. It was smaller than the other, warmer and well lit, with chairs, a table, and a center hearth. In one corner, almost beyond the circle of light, lay a great bed robed in purple.

Chrysaleon watched smoke from the fire being sucked up somehow through a square hole in the ceiling, leaving virtually none in the chamber to sting their eyes. All of Labyrinthos was crammed with pipes, breezeways, and ingenious methods of increasing the comfort of the inhabitants. The structure truly was an awe-inspiring achievement.

He and Alexiare had planned the lie carefully, going over it again and again until Chrysaleon could recite it without pause. More sure of himself now, he spoke without hesitation. "When the Kindred Kings attended my father's funeral games, one who would steal my place came also. He was my father's son from a liaison with a princess of Gla. He thought himself of better blood than me, since my mother came from Seriphos and was not pure Achaean."

"What blood did she carry?"

"She was part Cretan," Chrysaleon said. "Have I not spoken of her?"

"No, my lord."

"She was a priestess, before my father took her away."

"I see." Her eyes widened so briefly he almost missed it. "Perhaps that is why you so easily adapted to our ways." She sat in one of the chairs at the hearth fire, and he took the other.

"During the troubles you called me Chrysaleon," he said. "What has changed?"

She blinked and concentrated her gaze on the flames. "You have become Kaphtor's hero as well as royal consort to the queen. Now you are High King in your own right, of Mycenae, the mainland's most powerful citadel." Color rose through her face like embers consuming pale wood. "Chrysaleon." Her voice stumbled, and her fingers knotted together on her lap.

He pushed away gnawing fear at his trickery, hoping Alexiare was right in his interpretation of Daphoenissa's prophecies. He didn't like to think what vengeance the Goddess of this land could take upon him, and tried not to remember the night of searing wind and blizzards of ash.

"The boy had a following," he said. "He won several tourneys— archery, the foot-race, and the javelin-throw. I watched him, but I wanted peace, and let his braying arrogance go by me. There has been too much death and war in my life of late."

"Yes." She seemed absorbed in his tale, and nodded.

"He mistook my patience for weakness or fear. One evening at supper in the hall, he stood before the Kindred and challenged me for the throne. I had to fight him. We did so in the citadel precincts with all the kings watching. I killed him, and was cleansed of the death at the shrine of Poseidon."

"Then why…." Her face displayed puzzled concern.

He leaned closer. "I still feel it." He struck his chest with a fist. "Guilt lives in me over his death. He was a boy, the same age as Aridela. As my brother, Gelanor."

"Oh," she said softly.

His lie was working. Her brown eyes, so large and lustrous, were eloquent in their sympathy. "Can you free me of it, Themiste?"

She swallowed. Her knuckles whitened. "We will go to the sanctuary of children. I will cleanse you at the altar myself. Have you not told Aridela of this? Why do you come to me in secret?"

He lowered his head. "The shame…."

"He made a man's challenge." She touched his forearm and left her hand there, warm against his flesh. "He would have killed you and stolen your rightful kingdom. You had no choice. Rulers must defend their own."

Bringing her hand to his lips, he kissed it. "You have the wisdom of an old woman, my lady, for one so young and beautiful."

Her fingers trembled. He looked into her eyes steadily.

"Wine, before we go." She pulled her hand free, rose, and retreated to a cabinet where she collected a matched pair of engraved cups.

He made sure to touch her as she handed him one. She looked at the pitcher, the fire, the shadows. Everywhere but at his face and her bed.

Somehow, the Spartan oracle had known. She had spoken true prophecy. Rape would not be necessary. One thing Chrysaleon knew was how to tell a woman wanted him. He also knew how to play the game of seduction with hesitant virgins.

They sat before the fire, sipping a mixture she professed to enjoy, of wine and honey. He refilled her cup twice while regaling her with stories from the feast of his kingship, anecdotes of the Kindred Kings who came to Mycenae as his guests, of the gifts they brought and the lion and boar hunts. She relaxed. Her smiles grew frequent, even charming as she described the day Rhené told Aridela she'd conceived.

Chrysaleon more somberly related how little damage the mainland suffered. "There," he said, "no ships were lost. The country of my birth remains strong while Crete struggles."

At her frown, he added, "You are in more danger than you know."

Those glorious eyes widened again. He saw fear and anger. "Another invasion," she said quietly.

"I can keep you safe, my lady. I have intimate knowledge of the Kindred."

"You will advise us?"

"I will share all I know. Every one of my Mycenaean warriors will be yours to command."

She smiled her relief and he continued. "I ask but one favor in return. Much of my year as sacred king is gone. Grant me another. You need me to live another year, lady. Only I can control the Kindred until Crete regains strength."

She blinked and returned her gaze to the fire. He cursed himself for being too blunt, too swift in his demands. He didn't possess the gift of spinning smooth lies without planning them out first.

As he tried to construct a way to repair his mistake, she spoke. "You are right," she said, bringing her gaze, rife with compassion, back to his. "You have been cheated by events you could not control. I would give you what you ask." Her brow puckered. "Gladly, I would. But, my lord, I cannot, for the same reason you ask it. Everyone was cheated. There has been too much death and destruction. Our land withers. Aridela uses what riches are left in trade for grain. Can you not imagine the rage our Lady would level upon us if we abandoned the vow? This sacrifice above all others must take place. The people are already talking of how it will complete our supplications for forgiveness. I dare not change or stop it."

He looked down at his wine cup, putting on a convincing frown of disappointment.

Softly, she said, "I am sorry," and again touched his arm.

"Grant me this then," he said. "Let me choose my own cabal."

"I cannot do that either," she said, now guilt-stricken as well as sympathetic. "The Games must be played. How else can the next bull-king be chosen? He must win his place through strength and cunning, as you did."

Defeated, Chrysaleon could only wonder how Alexiare would have handled this, how his slave's ability to weave words might have turned it all to his advantage.

He swallowed some wine. It was far too sweet. Honey belonged in mead, not wine.

A log fell, sparking, causing Themiste's eyes to narrow against the flare of light. Finally, she said, "My lord, I feel churlish refusing you anything, after all you have done for us. It seems to me it's the sacrifice that cannot be ignored. It also strikes me that no one is in any mood for Games. Why do you want to choose your own cabal? And who is it?"

"Menoetius. If I cannot pick the manner or day of my death, at least I would like to choose the one who spills my blood. I want the last face I see to be that of my brother. And I know that of all men, I can trust Aridela to him."

Her eyes sparkled with tears as she nodded. "Did he agree, my lord? We no longer force men to compete. His heart must be willing."

"He knows." As his lies piled higher, Chrysaleon could only hope their weight wouldn't bring his brittle obelisk crashing down. "I spoke to him about it last night. He cares as much as I do about Kaphtor, and has given his allegiance wholly to the queen." He hadn't even seen Menoetius since his return from Mycenae, but she couldn't know that.

What was Alexiare plotting? At this point, Chrysaleon could only follow his slave's instruction and hope the purpose would become clear.

"I may be able to grant this request," Themiste said. "Of course I must speak to the council about it. As long as Menoetius is willing, there might be a way."

"I am grateful." An odd prickling crawled through the back of his neck, almost of anticipation. He didn't dwell on it but moved quickly on to the last part of his planned lie, that which would hopefully make

Themiste feel closer to him in spirit. "My sister Bateia has asked me to release her from her betrothal. She claims a desire to serve the Lady, and wants to dedicate her womb to Athene, as you have done."

"It is the call of her mother's blood," Themiste said.

He left his chair and knelt, almost touching her knees, gazing into her face with all the ardency he could muster. "If you would take her, it would put my mind at ease."

Her breasts rose and fell beneath her tunic as though she struggled to catch her breath. Her eyelashes swept down. Timidly, her fingers grazed his cheek before she clenched her hand into a fist and pressed it onto her lap. The firelight made her hair look redder—reminiscent of his death-dream, and lent a glow to the blue crescent moon upon her forehead.

"I had thought to make Aridela my successor," she said, leaning toward him. "Now, of course, that cannot happen. I must find another. Of course I will take your sister. If she is called to it, Bateia could wear the bull's mask for Kaphtor."

Bateia would be furious; she had wanted to marry Eurysthenes' son since she was a child, but she would comply. He would see to that.

Was he becoming like his father? He remembered how angry it made him when Idómeneus ordered him to marry Iros, and how carelessly the king dismissed his son's protests.

Rising, he bent over Themiste and gave her a formal kiss on each cheek. He felt her quiver and heard her indrawn breath. Her hands clasped his forearms, but she didn't push him away.

A short space of downy-soft skin separated him from her mouth. He covered it swiftly. "The moon guides me…Minos," he whispered.

Another indrawn breath, this one ragged. She stiffened. He feared he'd gone too far. But then her hands slipped up his chest and around his neck. The softest sigh escaped and she murmured, "As it bids me follow."

With a body as slender and nearly as small as Aridela's, it was an effortless task to pick her up and carry her to the bed.

7

Moon of Water Ferns

"Release her," Chrysaleon said.

The soldier holding the eagle removed its leather hood and lifted his arm; the bird spread her wings and soared into the heavens with an eager cry.

Chrysaleon's attention was diverted from the beauty of the raptor's flight to Menoetius, cresting a nearby hill. His bastard brother shaded his eyes as he peered up at the eagle, then he turned and descended, swiftly crossing the field toward Chrysaleon, his singular white and black cloak billowing in the chilly breeze.

Even from a distance Chrysaleon could see how much thinner Menoetius had grown in his absence, yet he looked harder too, as though he'd kept up with or increased his training. That Phrygian bitch probably forced him to spar for the pleasure of bedding her.

The Spartan oracle's advice hummed through Chrysaleon's mind. *Slay the Lady's Earth Bull and rule until the sun and moon shift into perfect alignment.* Alexiare still wasn't certain what Daphoenissa meant when she spoke of killing the Earth Bull, but he'd set his mind on the coil while Chrysaleon was occupied with Themiste. Once his master returned, after they left the labyrinth where, Alexiare cautioned, "anyone could be listening," he shared a rudimentary yet inspired plan.

Chrysaleon was more than pleased, eager to get started. If Alexiare was right, and if everything progressed to their advantage, he would in one act save his own life, rid himself of the threat to his Mycenaean crown, and fulfill an oracle's prophetic instruction.

As he squinted at his approaching brother, a dark, burning need blossomed inside his chest. His hands curled into fists; he had to force himself to relax them.

Months ago, Harpalycus had banished Chrysaleon to the Knossos labyrinth, intending to let him slowly expire. As he lay in that dim prison, starving, thirsty, hovering ever closer to the shadowlands, Chrysaleon had experienced a dream or vision, one where Menoetius transformed into a bull and gored him. It had unfolded with such clarity, menace, and significance Chrysaleon never forgot it. Nor had he forgotten how, in the dream, Aridela accepted what Menoetius did—even wore an expression of satisfaction.

As the bastard approached, he relived the dream and wondered if the god of his fathers, Immortal Poseidon, sent the memory of it in warning.

The tic beneath his eye began to throb.

Everything hinged on Menoetius. If he refused to serve as cabal, all their plots would disintegrate. Chrysaleon would die beneath the light of Iakchos, slaughtered by some Cretan. Menoetius would go on living, free to do whatever he wished. He might manage to steal Mycenae's throne. He could gather power and support here, on Kaphtor. Aridela thought so highly of him, she might assist his ambitions. He could father children, watch them grow, and live a long life.

The possibility made Chrysaleon's teeth grind.

He smiled even as his eyes narrowed and his mind formed the resolve. *You will lose to me, brother. You won't have Mycenae or this island. I will see to that.*

"Well?" Menoetius effectively interrupted Chrysaleon's spinning conjectures and doubts. "I see you survived the swearing in, so you must be High King. How does Mycenae fare, and Gelanor, and the Kindred?"

"Mycenae is in loyal hands, with Gelanor as my custodian. My father's most trusted advisors will assist him."

They gripped right arms, gradually increasing pressure as always, to see who would relent first.

This time Chrysaleon did.

"You look tired." The faint lift of Menoetius's eyebrow was the only indication of his surprise. "Are you sure you wish to hunt? Perhaps your bed and a warm posset are all you can manage today."

Chrysaleon laughed. "I have missed your mothering ways. In Mycenae I had only my own poor resources."

The eagle dived upon some creature. They walked towards her, the serving men following at a discreet distance.

"I regret not being there to celebrate Idómeneus at his funeral games," Menoetius said.

"Safeguarding my queen was more important." Chrysaleon frowned. "Harpalycus has caused much damage. Some of it can never be put right. We did capture the one who fed the poison to Father. He was tortured and put to death."

"The Kindred swore fealty?"

Chrysaleon nodded. "All, including Lycomedes. He denied any knowledge of Harpalycus's schemes and claimed he had disowned him."

"And?"

"I have not forgotten the number of warriors it took to invade and hold Crete's cities. Lycomedes' entire army, as well as conscripts. I let him languish in the catacombs awhile then I killed him myself. His youngest son swore terrified fidelity. He sits on his father's throne at my pleasure, and rules under the guidance of my council. Tiryns is now wholly subject to Mycenae."

"That must be sweet vengeance."

The eagle had snared a rabbit. Chrysaleon sliced a generous portion of thigh for her before handing the carcass to one of the men.

"Let us free ourselves of prying ears." As Chrysaleon turned to dismiss his attendants, he caught the eagle handler, an older, grey-haired Cretan, staring at him. Though the man lowered his face swiftly, it was too late. Chrysaleon saw such bare, malignant hatred it made him forget what he'd been about to say.

He'd never seen this man before. They'd brought him along because he fed and cared for the raptors, and the birds were comfortable with him. No doubt he was just another discontented peasant who wished for something beyond what his moera had dealt.

"Give her to me," he commanded curtly.

The soldier, bobbing his head, stepped closer so Chrysaleon could take the sturdy oak pole supporting the eagle. "My lord," he muttered, keeping his eyes downcast.

Chrysaleon waited, but the man never lifted his gaze from the ground. Maybe he had imagined that seething hatred. He took the staff, running one hand soothingly over the bird's wings. "Be off with you," he said, "All of you."

The men bowed and began trudging towards the palace. Chrysaleon watched them, but the eagle fluttered restlessly, taking his attention. By the time he'd hooded her and moved her from the staff onto his forearm, the men were halfway up the hill.

"Did you see that?" he asked Menoetius.

"What?" Menoetius was staring at Mount Juktas, a brooding frown on his face. He squinted at his brother. "See what?"

"Never mind." Chrysaleon perused the luxurious cloak Menoetius wore, feeling the old sense of covetous jealousy. "You look more a Cretan than these slaves," he said. "You're wearing their womanish linens instead of good Mycenaean leather. And what is this? No beard? Have you turned into one of them?"

"I grew tired of being stared at and called a barbarian," Menoetius said with a shrug. "It means nothing."

They walked on, stopping to inspect the sprouting barley and wheat, and the dusty green olive trees along the lower slopes of Mount Juktas.

"How many of these were lost?" Chrysaleon asked.

"Most. The queen tells me it will take more time than we or our children can live to bring them back."

"But some did survive?"

Menoetius nodded. "The groves to the east of Phaistos and west of the Ida mountains will still produce. The people seem to think you helped bring about this miracle."

Chrysaleon plucked a bunch of tiny budding grapes from a surviving vine and examined them. They looked healthy and blight-free. He was no farmer, but these were some of the brightest, firmest young grapes he had ever seen.

"The queen, of course, they exalt above all." Menoetius cut into the vine's dewy green center. "They say new life sprouts because she was reunited with her throne, but your praises follow close behind. They never thank the Lady these days without including you. The mainland barbarian has become their savior."

"You sound as though you doubt their wisdom." Chrysaleon frowned in mock suspicion. "Or is this more of your tiresome envy?"

Menoetius laughed. "I have everything I could wish for. Reverence is heaped upon me as well as you, and I have a woman of beauty and fire in my bed...as do you."

"Yet something is missing?"

Menoetius shrugged. "Things have become boring. There is no war to plan. No lions to hunt. No overthrow to plot."

Chrysaleon recognized this for the fishing attempt it was, and smiled. "The mainland kings watch me. I can imagine the wagers they have placed on how it will turn out—what I will do to keep myself from being slaughtered like an ox."

"Idómeneus didn't die agreeing to your sacrifice. I know it."

A nearby flock of sheep grazed peacefully. White gulls soared like swift moonbeams through an azure sky. It hardly seemed, on such a pristine morning, that the earthshakings, suffocating ash fall and Harpalycus's brutal occupation had ever happened. Mother Gaia, given time, always found a way to renew herself. "My ship passed the destroyed isle," Chrysaleon said. "There was a burning stink and boiling cauldrons of steaming water. As for the land, all that is left is a sliver." The back of his neck crawled at the memory. "Is it a sign, do you think?"

Menoetius shrugged.

"We beached and explored. There are no birds. No plants or trees. Ash is everywhere. There is no hint of its great cities, or of those who lived there. Remember the mountain? The one that gave the island its name? Callisti. Most beautiful." He faced his brother, watching for any reaction, however minuscule. "With his last breath, Father ordered me to invade Crete. He respected Helice, but that meant nothing at the end. My kingship and my life were more important."

"What did you tell him?"

No more than the briefest narrowing of the eyes. As usual, his brother hid his thoughts with skill. "What could I say? He was dying. I agreed, to give him whatever peace I could."

"But you will disobey?"

Menoetius would not be easily fooled. Chrysaleon had already decided to dance with the truth, so his lies would be more believable. "I promised Aridela I would lay down my life for her. Can I turn on that vow and invade like the Butcher of Crete?" Suddenly hot, he unfastened the clasps at the neck of his cloak and removed it, tossing it on the ground.

His brother's gaze sharpened. "So you will submit to your fate after all? Stand unarmed in your own grave while one of these Cretan shepherds slaughters you?"

"Not a Cretan. You."

A slight hesitation, a tilt of the head. "Me?"

"Themiste gave me leave to pick my own cabal. I picked you." *His heart must be willing.* What if Themiste asked Menoetius why he had agreed? What if Menoetius guessed his true role? It all seemed too shaky and fragile. Chrysaleon wiped sweat from his forehead.

"Why me?" Menoetius stared at him, his jaw working.

"As you say, a Cretan would be more than eager to kill me." Chrysaleon lowered his voice and placed one hand on his brother's shoulder. "I have been working the tangle. Testing the means to avert their customs. So has Alexiare. He and I sought answers at the oracle's lair near Sparta, from a blind seer they call Daphoenissa."

Something, perhaps disappointment, seemed to pass across his brother's face, but it was gone too soon to be sure. "Did you receive one?"

Chrysaleon shrugged as he recalled her vague words. "In a manner of speaking, but I have yet to understand how it will help."

"What did she say?"

"That I must lie with a holy woman—'the moon upon the earth,' she called her. We thought she must mean the priestess, Themiste. I did so this morning."

Menoetius stopped in mid-stride. "Are you saying you bedded the virgin oracle?"

"It was a simple matter, easily accomplished. I suspect from her eagerness she has long wanted me to take her."

Menoetius snorted. For once he made no attempt to hide his thoughts. "She has gone her whole life resisting any such temptations, and you managed it in one day—one morning." He shook his head as mingled disgust and disbelief ran across his face. "I cannot doubt the gods direct your fate. But how does this avert your death?"

"The oracle we consulted said there would be a child—one who will change the sacrifice."

They stopped by a swift stream and Chrysaleon loosed the eagle. He shook the ache from his arm then leaned on the staff as they watched the bird glide joyously into the blue firmament.

"Any child you get on Themiste won't be born until long after you're rotting in the earth," Menoetius pointed out.

"The Spartan oracle may have used her prophecies to trick me as I attempt to trick the Goddess who has been stolen from her. The child may indeed change the sacrifice, after I die."

"No more than you deserve." Menoetius gave him a sideways smile. "Then why lie with Themiste?"

"I vowed to halt the sacrifice." Chrysaleon mused on the image of his future sons and heirs. He wanted to have many, one after another, all growing into warriors and kings. A pity, almost, that the bastard would be dead, and couldn't see it happen—that is, if everything went as it should. "Aridela is pregnant and if I chose correctly, Themiste will be as well. Both infants will be of my line. My blood will rule this land, one way or the other." He searched the sky for the eagle and saw her circling above a stand of dead tamarisks. One of those murderous poison clouds must have descended there, killing every one. "I asked Themiste for an extra year. She refused me. But, if she quickens, perhaps her heart will soften. Or something else might present itself if I follow the Spartan woman's advice. I know I can change things to my benefit, if I can just have more time." He made an abrupt dismissive gesture. "Oracles speak in riddles. I guess at her meaning. She may not have meant Themiste at all. The truth is if we cannot determine a way to change or halt the custom, you may very well be forced to kill me at the midsummer rites." He laughed, but he watched.

A flush crept up Menoetius's face and his hands balled into fists. "You'll have to find another man to help you trick these people. I won't be here. Now that you're back, I am leaving."

Surprise brought Chrysaleon up short. "You cannot do that."

"I thought you would be pleased. You have long distrusted me— since we were children, in fact. I mean to leave this place and never return. I will sail to the mainland and from there make my way west until I reach my mother's country."

"You will leave me to be slaughtered?"

"How can my being your cabal stop that? Someone has to kill you —I don't want to be the one. It was your choice to become bull-king of Crete. Idómeneus and I tried to talk you out of it. Even these people tried. Do you have a plan that makes any sense? More than oracle ramblings and smoke-fed prophecy? If so, tell me what it is. If not, I leave you to your schemes."

Chrysaleon leaped upon his brother and knocked him to the ground, smashing him on the cheekbone and eyebrow with his clenched fist. Menoetius stabbed his knee into Chrysaleon's ribs and threw him off. He rose and backed away, blood dribbling from a gash gouged into his cheek by Chrysaleon's seal ring.

Chrysaleon sat on the ground, breathing hard. *Maybe it's enough. If he never comes back he will no longer be a danger to me. I never have to see him again.* But as soon as those thoughts formed, another one crowded behind. He looked up at Menoetius's defiant face.

The bastard makes plans to leave, while I cannot. Even if I find a way to live, I am still trapped here, while Menoetius is free to go anywhere he wishes. Who is to say he will go to his mother's country? He could recruit his royal guard—they would do anything for him. With their help, he could oust Gelanor and the council. He could seize control of Mycenae, all while I am forced to remain here, helpless to stop him.

"You are still subject to me," he ground out. "You will stay, if not willingly, then as my prisoner." He got to his feet, dusting off his hands.

"Are you certain you have made the right choice?" Menoetius swiped at the blood on his cheek. "I may be more eager to kill you than any Cretan on this island, given the chance."

Chrysaleon almost trembled in the throes of his rage. He wanted to reveal what their father had said on his deathbed. How satisfying it would be to bruise Menoetius with Idómeneus's final words while giving his true and rightful son permission to kill him. *Cunning strategy,* Alexiare had said. *It is the only way.* He had expressed doubt that Chrysaleon could control his impulses long enough to follow a delicate and complex plan.

As they stared at each other, bristling like feral animals, Chrysaleon suddenly saw the truth. His brother had tricked him. From the instant Menoetius joined him on this plain, everything he had said had been a ploy to ferret out his plan. Why else would he give a show of support, then, when he'd received every tidbit he thought he would get, inform Chrysaleon he was abandoning him?

He needed to make Menoetius believe he had a say. The bastard must believe it would, in the end, be up to him, that he would make the choice to either save Chrysaleon or kill him.

Forcing a smile, Chrysaleon said quietly, "It is true. I have not yet conceived a real plan. I named you my cabal hoping it may help when the time comes, that's all. I need you, my brother. You are the only man on Crete I can trust. I ask you to do this for me. You and I will work together. Together we will find a way to overcome the sacrifice that doesn't involve invasion or slaughter. I know you care about these people, as do I. I don't want to harm anyone. When we've succeeded, I swear I will outfit a ship for your use and you may go anywhere you like. It is only a few more months. Surely you can spare me that."

Menoetius's inner struggle played across his face—loyalty fighting anger and distrust, and something else, something not so easy to read. It almost seemed like regret. Chrysaleon waited, hoping his mollifying tone would make Menoetius believe he had triumphed in their clash of words.

"As you wish," Menoetius said finally.

At last, things were clear. Chrysaleon would feel no guilt. He would pull this thorn from his flesh and squash it underfoot. He would be free of that which had goaded him from birth.

He gave Menoetius a friendly cuff on the bicep. "And if I fail to come up with a way to succeed, then you may have the joy of killing me."

Menoetius flushed.

Chrysaleon laughed and went off, whistling to the eagle.

8

Moon of Water Ferns

From the Oracle Logs
Themiste

Lady Mother, can you forgive?

Nephele, who asked to serve me after Laodámeia's death, does not understand. She weeps, frightened of the terrible calamity she believes I have foreseen, but I cannot tell her this secret. I am too ashamed.

No one stays with me now but Io, my serpent. She won't let me touch her. Can she not see how wretched I am? She has no pity, she who also dedicated her untouched womb to Goddess Athene...and has not broken her vow.

I allowed the Zagreus of Kaphtor, our holy bull-king, to lie with me, to spirit away what was claimed at my birth by Goddess Athene. To use it for his own pleasure.

I feel my longing for him even as I write these words.

I understand.

The Lady sees through my lies. Though I may kneel until I am a white-haired crone, this need I cannot quell is my truth. There is no genuine remorse within me. I tremble for him even as I weep before my Goddess in shame.

No wonder she will not appear or send me a sign.

CHRYSALEON FOLLOWED ALEXIARE INTO THE PALACE'S LOWER passageways. "All of Knossos is buzzing about this. The moon waxes, and there is still no sign of her. Could she be dead?"

"No, my lord. The queen would know of an event so tragic, and she would tell you."

"The seer of Sparta said nothing of this uproar." Chrysaleon scowled. "What if Themiste confesses what she has done?"

"The holy oracle's womb is dedicated to the Goddess. If she admits her crime, the queen will be forced to cast her out, or worse. There's much for Themiste, and Kaphtor, to lose. I doubt she will confess."

They fell silent as they traveled deeper into the underground tunnels. "Are you sure this is the way?" Chrysaleon asked at last.

"I marked it well."

Their lamps illuminated only a meager circle around them.

"Why does Crete's revered priestess hide herself down here in this tomb?"

"She used to have chambers on the other side of the palace, but they were destroyed, along with, I hear, many irreplaceable tablets." Alexiare peered around, frowning. After some time he murmured, "Ah yes," and resumed walking. "I believe she prefers the underground. She is accustomed to it, I suppose. And she cherishes her solitude." After they walked several more steps, he added, "Guilt could be causing this withdrawal."

Chrysaleon rubbed his temples. "I'm the one who tricked her. Do you think I suffer no guilt?"

"I knew you would not like the means of escaping your vow. It may not be too late to change the path you've chosen. Ask Themiste's forgiveness. Accept whatever punishment will appease Goddess Athene."

"She may already carry my child."

With a sly glance, Alexiare said, "That is unlikely. It was only once, was it not, my lord?"

Chrysaleon stopped and faced his slave. "Toy with me, old man, but I believe I will take the advice you give in jest. I will tell her we made a mistake. I will pray to the Lady for forgiveness, and ask for Themiste's as well. I will undergo the blood cleansing. I would rather die in their sacrifice than live this lie."

Alexiare's doubts were betrayed by the slightest lift of his brow.

At length they came to the innocuous wooden door leading into

Themiste's chambers. Alexiare stepped into the shadows while Chrysaleon rapped.

"I cannot see you, Nephele," a weary voice said. "Leave me in peace."

"It is Chrysaleon," he said.

After a long silence, the door opened a little. "Go away." Her voice was muffled.

"You have to speak to me, Themiste."

With a protesting squeak, the door opened farther. Chrysaleon's lamp illuminated her pale, tired face, tangled hair, and shapeless robe.

He crowded into the room, closed the door behind him, and set his lamp on the floor.

"Themiste." He seized her hands, which trembled almost violently within his. "I ask your forgiveness." He dropped to his knees. "You have given Potnia Athene your whole life. She will not turn away because of one crime I alone forced upon you."

She made no reply. Her breathing was shallow and rapid.

He stood and led her to the edge of the pit. "We will pray. I will make sacrifices. I will do whatever is necessary to pacify the Lady."

Themiste stared at him. Dark circles and signs of weeping made the skin around her eyes look bruised and swollen.

"Forgive me, Minos," he said, struck by her misery.

"How do you know that title? Did some careless child tell you?"

"It was Aridela's father," he returned, not wanting to betray Alexiare. "Damasen. Remember? From my death dream."

Her expression turned awed and frightened.

"Come." He lit the censers. Sweet smelling smoke drifted as he knelt and pulled her down beside him.

He closed his eyes, yet could think of no prayer to soothe the outrage of the Goddess he had betrayed.

Themiste's scent brought back the memory of their union in vivid detail. He stole a sideways glance at her profile. Though she'd been inexperienced, she had pleasured him lustfully, without shyness or inhibition, three times.

Her lips moved. She struck her throat then her breast. Fresh tears sparkled on her downcast lashes. Even thin and disheveled, she was beyond compare.

Chrysaleon caught her hand, not knowing what he wanted, other than to touch her.

She opened her eyes, revealing fear. Pulling her hand free, she leaped to her feet and backed away, wadding the front of her tunic in her fists.

Consuming, greedy desire erupted. A lifetime's acquiescence to his appetites took over from good sense. Jumping up, he stalked towards her. She turned to run but he caught her before she'd managed two steps. He yanked her around to face him, grasped her hair in his hands to immobilize her, and crushed her mouth beneath his.

A sob escaped from her throat. She pulled him closer, digging her fingernails painfully into his flesh. He didn't mind. It added zest.

He pushed her backward until the wall stopped them. Seizing the neck of her robe, he rent it in half and flung it aside. He lifted her, pinioning her against the wall. Her thighs crept around his hips; her arms slipped around his neck. She lifted her face, closed her eyes, and released a primal sigh.

The tips of her breasts were sweet as honey in his mouth. He no longer cared about Goddess Athene's anger.

Themiste held his head close. Her thighs did the same, as though she wanted to merge their bodies into one.

Almost as soon as he entered her, unbearable spasms convulsed his body. Through blinding culmination he remembered the same thing happening the night of the Destruction, with Aridela. The memory roused a shiver of dread, as it would be forever linked in his mind with what came after. What consequence might descend this time?

He looked up at her face. A shaft of light from somewhere behind him struck her forehead, illuminating her tattoo, the mark of her sanctity.

She slumped against him and wept.

They slid to the floor. He felt her heart pummeling. Helpless, almost paralyzed, he lay, both awed and horrified, glimpsing the fulfillment of something bigger than he could understand.

"Poseidon Earth Shaker," he whispered. "You did this."

He fancied he heard soft laughter echo in his head.

9

Moon of Fertile Willows

ARIDELA WATCHED HER CONSORT WHITTLE A HORSE OUT OF A CHUNK OF soft pine. Resin-scented shavings floated over his lap and onto the grass as the horse, with arched neck and open mouth, took shape.

Sunlight and the soft buzzing of bees made demands that couldn't be ignored, much as she might want to. She gave in and lay back, closing her eyes against the welcome glare, reveling in the cushion of ripened grass and the seductive sense of nature renewing itself. This glorious warmth made it easier to dismiss the frost of just three days ago. Though they had entered the Moon of Fertile Willows and the time was long past when any freeze had ever struck their temperate island, this year, frosts continued to inflict sudden, swift damage, making today's mildness a thing to treasure.

She and Chrysaleon had fulfilled the morning's requirements then slipped away to the nearby apple grove. They had lazed in the grass beneath luscious white blooms ever since, listening to breezes ripple among the blossoms and laughing over how many at the palace must be searching for them.

Most of these delicate trees were dead. It had taken laborers many days to chop down the withered skeletons and drag them away to be burned. But there was a pocket of survivors, exactly seven—a holy number—which had somehow, inexplicably, emerged triumphant from the stagger of the earth, poison gases, suffocating clouds of ash and black frosts even though all around, their companions expired. These seven trees were granted almost sacred reverence. People made pilgrimage to marvel and admire, to pray and leave offerings. There was much concern when they didn't bloom as expected, but they were not dead. A full two months later than normal, they put forth blossoms, causing widespread celebration. It was considered a wondrous sign.

Here in this peaceful green glade, Aridela could briefly forget everything that had happened. She could put aside the duties and burdens that had, of late, been relentless. She and the Zagreus had begun falling into bed so exhausted they shared no more than a kiss or two, reminiscent of older couples who cherished rest more than lovemaking.

Finding that she couldn't fall asleep after all, she shaded her eyes from the sun and admired Chrysaleon's loose, bright hair. How she would love to weave little plaits through it as she and Neoma had enjoyed doing to each other, back when life held seemingly endless pleasure and complacency. Knowing he would never stand for such a thing, she instead caught his little finger and pulled his hand to her stomach. "Soon we will feel our daughter move," she said.

He dropped the knife and carving to stretch out beside her. "I want sons as well. I want many children with you."

"An exquisite dream." She sighed. "Daughters and sons." She paused, fearful of saying it, then allowed the confession in a small voice. "I want that too." *If only it were possible.*

The breeze loosened a blossom above them. It floated down, landing on Chrysaleon's head like a large snowflake. Aridela giggled. Troubles and anxiety fled, leaving them in a cocoon of intimacy. Not even their attendants, sitting at a discreet distance with their backs turned, could detract from the hushed, perfect harmony.

"We should return to the palace," Chrysaleon said at last. Yet he sighed and plucked a stem of wild grass, chewing one end and pillowing his head on one arm as though settling in for the remainder of the day.

"How I wish we could have more than these pilfered reprieves."

"Aridela...." Chrysaleon stroked her cheek with the tuft at the end of the grass stem.

"Is something wrong? You sound so serious." The grass tickled and she pushed it away.

"Remember how your father came to me in vision when I was Harpalycus's prisoner? He spoke to me at length, of many things."

"Yes." She smiled, proud and gratified that Damasen was taking an interest in her consort's welfare.

"He spoke of the king-sacrifices."

Her smile dissipated as the intensity of his gaze warned her. She sat up.

Chrysaleon sat up too. "He said they must end."

Rubbing her arms, Aridela rose and stepped away, out of the charismatic circle that surrounded him and prevented her from thinking clearly. "If only it could be."

He came up behind her, pulling her to his chest, lifting her hair and placing a kiss beneath her ear. "I care nothing for myself," he said. "Your father claimed the king-sacrifice was never what Athene intended. Men and women were created as a complement, like stars circling the moon, like fish and water. We should sacrifice slaves instead—they are easily replaced. Hundreds, if that's what it takes to make the Lady happy."

She faced him and laced her fingers through his. "The sacrifice of the king is a complement. Woman bears man. Man fructifies the crops. It has been so from the beginning. As Velchanos languishes in the killing heat and rises again with the winter rains, so must our consort. It is his duty to follow in the steps of the god. Athene gave her beloved son. Can we do any less?"

"Man is only man. He cannot rise again."

"But he does. He returns as serpent or crow, to tell the oracles. He might return as the north wind, to make women and beasts fertile. He comes back as a child, when a woman takes in his spirit with her food. His blood renews the land. Never have we needed this sacred gift more. If we betray the way, we also betray her, ourselves, and our children."

"Your people and mine share a word—moera. It is man's share, his portion of fate. The destiny he must serve. Mine is not to die in your labyrinth. I am Mycenaean."

"You accepted that destiny. You fought for it. You gave up Mycenae and became one of us, our Zagreus." Shock and anger flooded, then agony at what duty forced her to say. Would he try, now, to escape his fate, when he'd had so many chances to abandon it before? "We have a word too. *Khalada*. Eternal. It is used only for our bull-kings—nothing else. Ever."

"You will make no protest when Menoetius kills me?" He, too, looked angry.

His words stabbed her like knife blades, making it hard to breathe. "Why do you hold him here? Why did you choose him as your cabal? Why did he agree? I do not understand."

"You cannot understand why I would want my brother, he who has been by my side my whole life? You think it would be better for a stranger to cleave me with your axe?"

She drew in a shaking breath. "If you will not honor your vow, the Lady's wrath will descend again—worse, possibly, than before. Perhaps this time we will vanish into the ocean like Callisti. Our achievements will be obliterated. Only you can save us, Chrysaleon."

He pulled his hands free. "I have done everything you wanted. I gave up asking you to leave this place and follow me to Mycenae. My brother Gelanor sits on the throne there. I put your Lady above the Father of Horses, though my life was dedicated to him when I was a boy. I coupled with you in the presence of every humble peasant, every child on this island. No other man would have done as much."

"Every bull-king gives up his name and home. Every bull-king couples with the queen before the people, and considers himself venerated beyond measure. You came to us. We did not beg at Mycenae's gate for a consort. We refused you because of our differences—it was you who insisted, again and again."

He had never looked at her like this. Pierced by such rage, she faltered and stepped back.

"Have you forgotten the day at the bullring?" He spoke almost gently, though there was underlying ice. "I have not. 'Carry the day and become my sister's consort.' And I did—because you asked it of me."

At last she knew, beyond any doubt. He would not have entered the Games but for her. The wounds he suffered in that terrible struggle were her doing. Now she would put him to death and, because every queen before her had done so, she would take Menoetius to her bed for a year. Then Menoetius would die.

And on…and on…and on for as long as she lived.

She stared into his eyes and he stared back. She opened her mouth to defend herself. *I never said you would not have to fulfill the bull-king's obligation.*

But she couldn't say it. All she wanted to do was beg his forgiveness, give her promise that she would find a way to save him. Whatever she had to do, she would, though she herself might be put to death for it.

Submerged in self-recrimination, trapped by her consort's hard, accusing gaze, she didn't hear when someone spoke her name. She only turned because Chrysaleon did.

Menoetius and Selene stood beneath the branches of one of the trees, shadowed by low-hanging apple blossoms. Aridela's womb clenched fitfully, as though in premonition of labor.

"What do you want?" Chrysaleon spoke curtly.

"To speak to Aridela," Selene said. "Would you leave us, Zagreus?"

"How did you get past the guards?"

"Aridela," Menoetius said. "Will you go with us?"

"Has something happened?" Aridela asked.

"Yes," Selene replied.

"Very well." Aridela shrugged. "Will it take long? Chrysaleon and I came here to be alone."

As she started toward them, Chrysaleon seized her wrist. "She will not go with you. Say what you came here to say."

Menoetius's voice was halting and graveled, but he seemed unsurprised at his brother's belligerence. "I have told Selene the truth."

Aridela sensed Chrysaleon stiffen. She glanced at him, but discerned nothing beyond impatience at this ill-timed interruption.

"And now I will tell Aridela," Menoetius added.

"What is it? What has happened this time?" She wanted to rub her eyes and make the day start over. But such was a child's wish, and she had gone past all that long ago.

"Listen, Aridela," Selene said. "Menoetius knows what lives in Chrysaleon's heart."

"Consider what you do, brother." Chrysaleon's voice held threat.

"You think I have not?" Menoetius released a sharp breath.

The two men stared at each other as Aridela looked on, puzzled. What now? She knew already of Mycenae's plot to find Kaphtor's weaknesses. Chrysaleon confessed it before the Destruction, and Menoetius confirmed it, albeit reluctantly, when they were hiding in the mountains. It was nothing new. Both had abandoned those ideas. Could there be something more, something worse?

"Go on." Selene touched Menoetius's forearm.

"Yes, what is your truth?" Sarcasm weighed Aridela's words. Her legs felt tired, almost as if they might give out. "Please, if it is so important, tell me and go."

Menoetius shifted his gaze to Aridela. "Chrysaleon will overthrow your traditions and rule as king beyond his year. For his whole life, in fact. He has not given up his plots. He means to make Kaphtor a vassal of Mycenae—if you allow it."

In the instant before they were interrupted, she had been ready to give Chrysaleon her promise to somehow stop the sacrifice. She felt her head turn, numbly, warily, towards her consort, as the question rose in her mind. *Which one is lying?*

"Will your jealousy never end?" Chrysaleon said. "Finally, the real beast comes forth. He has concealed himself for years, but here is his true nature. A coward, a liar. A traitor."

Aridela's womb cramped again, suddenly and sharply. She placed soothing hands over her abdomen. The healer had ordered her to avoid strenuous activity and strong emotions. *From the beginning,* Rhené had said, *your woman's parts have resisted everything they are supposed to do. Sometimes I have thought your body never wanted to grow up.*

"No man can defy the fate set by Immortals," she said to Menoetius, but her voice sounded weak, unconvincing.

Surely Kaphtor had never suffered as ill-omened a queen as she. What did it matter which brother was lying? Her selfish need was the root of all this misery. Now she could add splitting Menoetius and Chrysaleon apart to her list of wrongs.

"Chrysaleon will, if you do not stop him," Menoetius said.

Selene left Menoetius's side and approached Aridela. "Tell her all of it, Menoetius," she said, then went on to do so herself. "Chrysaleon plots to thwart the midsummer sacrifice."

"I have never seen you so angry," Aridela whispered.

Selene's lips tightened. "Chrysaleon wants to fool all of Kaphtor— and you. We don't know how, only that he will, if no one stops him. If we do not stop it, the Lady will wreak such vengeance as we cannot imagine." Her sea-colored eyes met Aridela's without guile or guilt, only cold ardency. "Daughter of Velchanos. Athene's blood runs in you, and the blood of her son. Your duty is to her. Look at Menoetius. You can see for yourself the mark of the Goddess upon his face." Taking one step closer, she caught at Aridela's hand. "Chrysaleon is not what he seems. Your blind loyalty risks everything."

Aridela stared at Selene, then Menoetius, and finally at a thunderous Chrysaleon, whose hand hovered above his dagger.

Selene touched Aridela's cheek, drawing her attention. "Have I ever lied to you?"

Aridela shook her head.

"I am not lying to you now."

Chrysaleon shouldered between them roughly and grabbed Aridela's upper arm. "Malice and envy drives my brother. And you are right—this woman hates me. Nothing else could explain these lies, this betrayal. Listen to them—they accuse me of plotting against you. How? They have no proof, no evidence, not even a story to tell. They only want to oust me. Why?"

His gaze returned to Menoetius, who remained apart under the overhanging blossoms of the apple tree.

Selene backed away. She wiped tears from her cheeks and looked at Menoetius.

Aridela, too, studied Menoetius. She felt the air grow still and hot. Rage burned away her contrition. All she had wanted was one day of peace.

Because she was staring at him, she read his intent before he spoke. She knew what he meant to say.

"Have you told him of us?"

Chrysaleon looked from one to the other. His hand gripped the hilt of his knife. "Told me what?"

Menoetius looked at the knife then met his brother's gaze. "Do you believe your crimes will vanish if you kill me?"

"You have lost all reason." The muscles in Chrysaleon's jaw clenched visibly. "You are neither bull-king nor Cretan. You are nothing to these people."

Aridela wanted to turn and run, but it felt as though the Earth Bull's horns had erupted from the ground and coiled around her feet, anchoring her.

Chrysaleon's eyes widened then, as he and Menoetius stared at each other. "You...and Aridela." Incredulity passed across his face, then disgust. "*You*. Of all men."

Menoetius flushed. "We thought you dead."

Chrysaleon turned to Aridela, his lips twisted and white.

"The child I carried was yours or Harpalycus's," she said. "I swear it. Menoetius and I never...we never...." The way he looked at her ripped her voice away, leaving her mute.

In my land, women are put to death for lying with men other than their husbands, even if they are forced. Duplicity poisons every woman's heart. As Aridela stared at Chrysaleon, the terrible words spoken by the Butcher Harpalycus crept through her mind.

But Chrysaleon did come back to me. He never blamed me for what Harpa-

lycus did. Harpalycus lied. Still, a shiver raced down her spine at his expression, which had darkened from the tenderness of earlier into cold, unforgiving blame.

He didn't believe her. Perhaps he didn't even hear her. His head twitched to one side as though he was trying to escape unbearable thoughts. His hands clenched and unclenched, only to clench again. Abruptly, he turned back to his brother, sneering.

Menoetius's face remained resolved.

Panic swelled. Seeing them stare at each other, their hatred palpable, Aridela knew beyond denying that she loved them both. She had never made a true choice, and they knew it, or sensed it.

Who could predict where this might end? Neither could die here today. Not because of her.

Selene remained silent, watching each of them, her face unreadable. Selene, the one she had always trusted beyond any other. Yet now her old friend seemed willing, eager even, to spoil Aridela's hard-won happiness.

"Go with your life, Menoetius," Aridela said, facing him. "Leave us for your mother's country, as you said you wanted to do. Give up the idea of being Chrysaleon's cabal. Go, before more anger is provoked, before too much is said that cannot be unsaid."

"That time has come and gone," Chrysaleon said.

She looked at Menoetius, pleading with every shred of will she possessed. "Do not let him believe what is not true."

"How is it not true? You and I were joined in every way but one."

Her protest disintegrated before she could speak it.

"If he does kill me, maybe then you will accept what I have told you. Chrysaleon does not love you. He wants you, but that is not love. It is glory and power he loves. You are his means to achieve it."

"You act like children!" She stamped her foot against the ground. In the same instant, thunder rumbled from one end of the sky to the other. Somehow, without her noticing, ominous greenish black clouds had formed. The air now resonated with tension and silence, as though all of nature held its breath. The hair on her arms lifted in a shiver.

"So be it." Chrysaleon stepped away from her.

She grasped for his hand but he deflected the gesture, catching her instead. He pinned her arms to her sides.

"Now I know my sacrifice would be wasted," he said, staring into her face almost without recognition. "First Harpalycus, now my own brother. Why would any man give his life for a deceitful whore?"

He thrust her away.

Selene caught her, kept her from falling. "Look how swiftly his love for you dissolves. Look how ready he is to believe you faithless. Almost as though he expected it. You have always given him your trust. Your loyalty. Yet he will not do the same for you."

Aridela straightened and pulled free. "You will not rest until you have destroyed me," she said. When Selene started to speak, Aridela cut her off. "Say nothing more. I will hear nothing more from any of you." She turned her back on Selene and stepped closer to the men, who had drawn their knives and were circling each other. "Can you not see?" She lifted her arms in supplication. "You are opposites, yet you are nothing without the other. Menoetius, you are the skin that covers the heart of the apple, the heart that is your brother. You are the spear of lightning after his roar of thunder. You are the ocean battering his cliffs." She shivered yet felt hot, as though fire had ignited in her blood. The Goddess burned within, speaking through her.

Menoetius glanced at her. Chrysaleon did not.

Thunder growled again, followed by lightning that branched across the heavens. "Light and dark," she whispered. "Joined yet separated— for what purpose? None but Athene knows."

Menoetius's strike was blurringly swift. A chunk of Chrysaleon's hair floated to the ground and lay like a pool of spilled golden twine.

On the rocky mainland, a king's power resided in his hair. Aridela stared at it, remembering her tutor's bored voice. *When coming of age, boys dedicate their first beards to Poseidon and pray for courage in battle. The warriors of the mainland believe their strength, their potency, their very invincibility, has its source in their hair. Only common soldiers shear their hair, so it won't interfere with their eyesight or give their enemies something to grab.*

This was the worst of omens.

Still they circled. Chrysaleon's face remained cold and concentrated. A gust of wind plucked at the fallen strands of hair, separating them, casting them into oblivion.

Perspiration beaded Menoetius's forehead. He leaped again. The two grappled, striving for the upper hand.

"Goddess, my Mother," Aridela cried, turning her face to the sky.

End over end the men tumbled, each grasping the dagger-wrist of the other.

Her cry gained the attention of her retinue. They ran forward. The men drew their weapons, but Selene stopped them with an outstretched hand.

"You use her to get what you want," Menoetius shouted.

Chrysaleon kept his eyes on the blade arcing above his chest. He grimaced and strained. "And you are a traitor. To me, our father, and your country."

Their strength was well matched, but Aridela feared the maddened objective she saw on Menoetius's face. She pictured the blade sinking into Chrysaleon's heart, a last breath seeping from dying lungs. His final look filled with accusation, with hatred.

This could not happen. Not now, when they were finally together. And if Menoetius succeeded, his own death would be unspeakable— no one could kill the sacred king out of his time. Such a criminal would beg for death long before it was granted.

Mistress. She turned her face toward the dark, rumbling clouds. *This cannot be what you want. I beg you, Mother Athene, spare them.*

Dazzling bolts of lightning discharged from one greenish-purple fold and shot down to the ground in the west, somewhere in the mountains of Ida.

She shuddered and ran toward the attendants, stumbling on an uneven patch of ground. "Help me! Quickly."

The willow-waisted men, with their lovelocks and kohl-painted eyes, stared askance at the brutish Mycenaeans who were twice their size. They glanced at each other then, together, leaped into the fray, forcibly separating the combatants. It took four men to overpower Menoetius and drag him, cursing, away to the palace.

Rain spattered, dislodging a flurry of white apple blossom. Quiet fell upon the orchard as the remaining attendants stepped away to give their queen privacy.

"Leave us," Aridela said to Selene. "Unless you want to join your lover in his prison."

Selene's pause was infinitesimal before she turned and followed in the wake of Menoetius and his captors.

Aridela took a deep breath and faced Chrysaleon.

10

Moon of Fertile Willows

Alexiare stepped onto Chrysaleon's balcony and bowed. "It is done, my lord. As you ordered, Menoetius is confined in the labyrinth."

Chrysaleon gave his slave a frigid glance before returning his contemplation to the landscape before him. Hearing the bastard's name was enough to send his simmering rage into renewed, full-blown fire.

"May I stay with you?" the old man asked.

He could manage no more than a noncommittal grunt, but it was apparently enough. Alexiare sat on a stool and for some time, wisely said nothing while Chrysaleon stared over the terraces and walls, over the tips of the cypress trees and olive groves to the haze of the city, grinding his teeth and lashing himself with the day's revelations.

In the apple orchard, Aridela attempted to defend her sojourn in the cave with Menoetius. She told him how they wept when Menoetius learned of his half brother's death. How could they have known Harpalycus was lying? The oppressor held up the mangled, bloody head of a blond-haired warrior and declared it was Crete's consort. All had believed Chrysaleon dead.

Nothing she said could penetrate his anger. Not her awkward attempts at describing her loneliness, her despair and desperation, or her adamant claim that she and Menoetius never mated. He knew these for what they were—the weak justifications of someone caught in a lie.

He had ridiculed her flimsy excuses until her cheeks reddened—with guilt, no doubt. *You condemn me for things that did not happen*, she shouted. *What of you and your Mycenaean wife? Did you see her, did you lie with her when you were at Mycenae?*

Ah, here was the truth at last. She was jealous and possessive, like Theanô and all women, everywhere. *Iros is dead*, he replied coldly.

She seemed startled, and asked, *How?*

Murdered. He watched for her reaction, certain she would reveal a woman's true nature and be pleased by the demise of a rival. But instead, her face betrayed shock, then sadness. She had placed her hands over her stomach and even managed to put a few tears in those black eyes of hers. *The baby too?*

Her reaction infuriated him. He refused to answer and again called her a whore—a word he knew had no meaning on Crete before the invasion of Harpalycus. Now, thanks to the Butcher, she understood it all too well, and the deliberate scorn in his tone. She had run off finally, her attendants forming an impenetrable barricade behind her.

When Themiste first told him that Menoetius and Aridela were hidden somewhere in the remote western mountains of Araden, he'd thought the plan a good one. Never once had he suspected betrayal. Aridela was too pampered, too spoiled by luxury and beauty, Menoetius too ugly and bitter, too immersed in ideals of honor and loyalty. Not once in all the days he'd spent journeying there had he considered such a possibility.

Today's revelations left him wondering if all his beliefs were false. Had she fooled him completely? Had she given herself to Harpalycus as well as his bastard brother? How many other men had she favored by spreading her legs? Lycus, perhaps?

Alexiare finally broke the silence. "My lord, did Menoetius succeed in his attempt to turn the queen against you?"

Reluctantly, Chrysaleon fought to push useless jealousy out of his mind. He'd almost forgotten what should have been more important—the accusations Menoetius spoke against him. Accusations that could destroy their plans. "I don't know. There was an instant. She looked at me. I saw her wondering. The bastard could not have chosen a better time—right after I tried to persuade her to stop the sacrifice. I'd almost succeeded, too. If I'd had just a little longer—but it does not matter. Anything that happens now to thwart the sacrifice will be suspect."

"Things will be harder, but we will find a way. My mind works on it constantly."

Twisting the gold ring off his finger, Chrysaleon placed it on his palm and held it out. "Have you seen this seal?"

"Yes, of course. You use it to stamp the storage jars and regional decrees."

"An image of Goddess Athene, giving the bull-king three golden apples." Chrysaleon balled his fist around the ring. "The apples promise glory and eternal life in the orchards of Hesperia. It has always been the consort's ring. Aridela gave it to me after the ceremonies—after someone removed it from the finger of the king I killed."

Alexiare nodded warily.

Chrysaleon couldn't stop gritting his teeth. His rage was almost too much to contain, making him feel his head might split open like a fig. "Who wore it before him? Aridela would know. No doubt she knows the name of every male who has come to the throne in her lifetime. It would be wrong to forget, since they are such great heroes." He looked at the polished balustrade, where dolphins leaped between crescent moons, and doves carried sprays of poppy in their beaks. He longed to splinter the wood with his fists, but it was oak, and he would probably break every bone in his hands.

"I suspect she has committed their names to memory."

"She could recite them?"

Alexiare paused. "Here, as on Argolis, speaking a dead man's name is tricky. Displays of grief might summon his angry spirit and cause mischief. Only after the required offerings are made, if there is no sign of trouble, only then is it considered safe to speak of a fallen king—and it must always be done with caution."

Chrysaleon bandied the ring from one hand to the other for a few more breaths. His jaw clenched and released, again and again. He hissed a curse and threw it. It sailed over the balustrade, flashing before it vanished among the cypresses.

"My lord," Alexiare said, his voice grating, "your suspicion is clear. You are strangely eager to believe Queen Aridela betrayed you."

"Menoetius's face had an air of truth about it. You think he lies?"

"I think he is consumed by the fires of passion and guilt. He burns alive and seeks relief, as any man would in such pain. Can you blame him? She is young, beautiful, a queen, a born leader. She possesses qualities of courage and dedication that set her apart from ordinary women. Every man covets her. This is something you must accept."

"Eloquent words, old man. And this passion. Was it born in the cave, when they believed me dead?"

"Do you want the truth? I believe it was born when she was a child, before he was mauled. Before she knew you."

It was the last thing he wanted to hear. Jealousy vivisected his gut. "What of Harpalycus? Did she welcome his attentions too? A Mycenaean can kill a wife or daughter who has done what she has done. I've tried to ignore it, though I feel the Kindred laughing at me. I wonder if she lied about him forcing her—"

Alexiare seized Chrysaleon's arm, prompting an affronted stare of surprise. "I cannot believe you would say such a thing. No one hated Harpalycus more than Queen Aridela—or had more reason to."

Pointedly and none too gently removing his slave's hand, Chrysaleon said, "In truth, I long to put this aside and go to her. My time is short. If our plans fail and the rise of Iakchos brings my death, who will take my place? With Menoetius condemned and me dead, it will be as if we never came here. We will be absorbed into Crete's soil and forgotten. Mycenae will fall. My line will end. No doubt their goddess finds it all vastly amusing."

"Sir." Impatience, of a level Chrysaleon had never heard before, tinged Alexiare's voice. "You must not die." He stood, clenching his fists. "If you are truly convinced Queen Aridela betrayed you, your course is clear. Bring your armies. Invade and set up Mycenaean rule."

"My course is no clearer than it ever was. She has committed no crime. These women do as they please—as you well know, old Cretan. They lie with whomever they fancy and care not which one of their lovers plants the seed. They know who the mother is. That is all that matters."

"It is the way of the Lady," Alexiare said. "But don't forget—the queen ended the life of the first child in her womb."

"She didn't do that for me. It was for herself and her country."

"The queen has sought in every way she can to recognize and honor your beliefs, though they are foreign to her and her people."

"Then why give herself to Menoetius?" Chrysaleon slammed his fists against the wood. "Is that her way of mourning, to find a new lover as swiftly as possible?"

"What if she told you the truth?" Alexiare spoke as strongly as his throat allowed. "I believe her. I don't think you realize the depth of esteem and respect she has given you. She didn't have to. Moreover, I doubt Menoetius would have killed you today. All his life he has watched over you, defended you, though you may have blinded your-self to it. Remember when Idómeneus announced your betrothal to Princess Iros? You were so angry. Menoetius drew everyone's atten-tion, giving you a chance to calm yourself. Otherwise, there might have been bloodshed. What about the times he has allowed you to win at wrestling? Or the times he has watched over you in battle? It has always been thus. Don't pretend you didn't know. Not with *me*, my lord."

"You are wrong," Chrysaleon said. "All the loyalty of which you speak is gone. Burned away. You were not there. I looked into his eyes. He meant to kill me or see me condemned. He wants Aridela, and he believes if it weren't for me, she would want him, too. That is why he risked everything, even his life. You tell me, old man. Why would he believe that if there were no reason?"

With a lift of his bony shoulders, Alexiare conceded. "I was not there, as you say. He was alone with the queen a long time. Perhaps it is simply my foolish wish to believe the best of a young woman I admire." He paused, pulling at his lower lip and staring meditatively. "Menoetius will be put to death for what he has done. There is no more serious crime on Kaphtor than harming the sacred king out of his time. We will have to find a new cabal. We should look for a native, one smaller than you, perhaps, and less skilled in warfare, though I am not sure how we can manipulate the choice now."

Chrysaleon turned a furious squint on Alexiare. "I am going to tell you something I have never told anyone. If it comes back to me, I will know who to blame."

Alexiare inclined his head.

Chrysaleon peered into his bedchamber to make sure they were alone. "That day Menoetius and I hunted lion. Remember?"

"Your brother's face is a constant reminder, my lord."

"He didn't want to go. I pestered him until he agreed. This was when my father and he were at odds over his dedication to the Lady."

"I recall it well."

"I liked it when they fought. I kept hoping Father would banish Menoetius or have him killed."

Alexiare said nothing, but looked wary again.

"I have always hated the bastard my father forced me to live with."

"Yes, my lord."

"I belittled his devotion that day. I thought if I could goad him, maybe get him to leave a bruise or two on me, it would be an easy matter to turn Father against him. But as usual, I failed. We came upon the lioness and her cubs. She was hiding them in a cave; we had her cornered. I yelled, I shot arrows, but she stayed out of sight. I told Menoetius to flush her out. He refused, and I called him a coward. He said I was spoiled, and that Mycenae would fall to ruin when I was king. He turned his back on me."

Alexiare sat very still, expressionless but for blinking three times in quick succession.

"I pushed him and he fell, close to the mouth of the cave. The lioness charged. You know what happened next."

"Why has Menoetius never accused you of this, my lord?"

Chrysaleon laughed. "Surely you have heard the gods protect those they admire. Menoetius has never remembered what caused the attack. All these years he has believed I saved his life, selflessly, with my little dagger."

"Why did you?"

"Because just as I thought my troubles with him were over, two of my father's slaves ran up the path, shouting. They had been sent out to find us. I should have killed them too, but I hesitated. Then it was too late. When I look back on it now, I curse myself for letting the chance go by. I could have killed all three of them and blamed it on that lioness."

Alexiare frowned and glanced away, toward the trees.

"Do you understand?" Chrysaleon leaned forward and grasped the neck of Alexiare's tunic in his fist. "More than anything else, more than winning Crete, more than being High King, I want my brother dead. I want him to go to his death under the star Iakchos, knowing I sent him there. I want to breathe in the unraveled threads of his moera. When I take Aridela into my bed, I want to know that's where he longed to be, fought to be, and I cheated him of it."

Alexiare opened his mouth then closed it again, saying nothing.

"What is it, old man?" Chrysaleon asked. "Are you ashamed?"

"No, my lord. Never. I was thinking this must be why Menoetius was born. It is his purpose to die for you here on Kaphtor. Because of that day he was mauled, Menoetius will always believe he owes you his life. He will never let you go to your death, not without giving everything to prevent it—of this I am certain, no matter what you say. His sense of loyalty will allow nothing less. Because he attacked you, the people see you as enemies now. They will be far less likely to believe in some trickery or plot when things don't go as they should. If you can keep the council from slaughtering him, I will take care of the rest. We will turn Menoetius into the Lady's Earth Bull, and Daphoenissa's prophecy will be fulfilled. Oh, yes. I am ever amazed, my lord, at how destiny falls into place, one way or another."

ALEXIARE OFTEN VISITED THE MARKETPLACES OF KNOSSOS. HE USED THE time away from the palace to ponder Chrysaleon's situation and how best to help. He liked measuring the mood of the people, and he loved listening to gossip.

When he first heard the rumors, he was intrigued. His mind began to chew on it. Ideas sparked, one after another, like dry branches ignited by lightning.

It seemed the queen's attendants, those who wrestled Menoetius to the ground and dragged him from the apple grove, had become very popular in the city. They were asked, over and over, to describe the events of that fateful day. Could anyone blame these men for embellishing the truth? One of the more colorful stories making the rounds was that the Zagreus's brother had lost control of his wits. He roared like a bull, they said, and attacked with his hands and teeth, using strength beyond anything they had ever seen. They claimed he overpowered the guards and ran off into the labyrinth's black depths. Even now, the attendants whispered, he was rampaging down there, slaughtering hapless victims from rats to humans. Warriors were posted at every entrance to prevent his escape.

Such tales recalled Chrysaleon's long habit of referring to his half brother as a beast, in contemptuous reference to his scars and disfigurements.

It was a perfect foundation on which to build. Alexiare couldn't suppress a delighted guffaw.

Seeking out a spot on a crumbled rock wall, he sat and began his observation of the myriads of people, high and lowborn, as they congregated.

His gaze followed two middle-aged females loitering beside the spring-fed well. They gossiped and laughed with other women, showing no sign of haste or, for that matter, shyness.

They would fill his needs nicely.

He wandered over, bowed, and asked if they might provide him with a drink of water. One of them shrugged and gestured to her amphora. Both were sadly indifferent, returning their attention almost immediately to others in the marketplace. He thought back to the days when his appearance drew the lustful regard of females and males alike. Old age was a disheartening thing, when one still felt young inside.

He cleared his throat. "I have escaped the palace," he said, leaning on his stick. "The king is angry, and when my lord is angry, he becomes spiteful." He gestured toward his throat. If they thought Chrysaleon had harmed him in a fit of ill humor, he didn't mind. "It's nice to come here and not have to worry about doing something that may call down his ire."

They leveled skeptical stares upon him. Then the heavyset one, hampered by a large, sagging bosom that made his stomach curdle, perked up. "I remember you. Before the trouble with his brother. The consort and queen came through the city on their way to the harbor. You were with him in his litter." She appeared quite proud of her recollection skills.

He smiled. "Yes, my lady. I have been with the king since he was born."

She inclined her head and made a jerky bow, seemingly flustered, as though he had suddenly gained importance merely by close association with royalty. Her companion, after a pause, also offered a slight bow. It was a pleasant feeling. His smile widened. The woman who had recognized him shook out her skirts and set her jug on the edge of the well. "How is the Zagreus?" she asked, dipping her ladle in the water and holding it out to him. "Broken, no doubt, by his brother's cruel betrayal."

"The Zagreus is far too strong a man to be broken by anything, my dear," he said, nodding thanks as he cooled his throat. "But yes, the betrayal wounded him deeply. In truth, I worry more about his brother. For many years, the beast within has been kept at bay, suppressed with special elixirs, provided by no less than Goddess Hecate, who took pity on him. But when he ran away from the guards and into the labyrinth, these could no longer be administered, and they must be given every day to be effective."

"Beast?" Her eyes veritably gleamed and she leaned closer, causing her coarse tunic to gap. Enough cleavage was displayed to make his gorge rise. He had to swallow sharply and avert his gaze. "What do you mean, 'beast?'"

"Yes, what are you saying?" the other woman asked.

"Oh, I shouldn't," he demurred, but peered around cautiously, bent in closer, and spoke softly. "You must not repeat a word of this. It would draw the king's wrath upon you if you do, and upon me for having a loose tongue."

The first woman ran her tongue over her upper lip. "Of course, I understand." The other nodded, a little uncertainly.

"Beneath Menoetius's unremarkable exterior there lives a vicious beast." Alexiare peered around again before continuing. Almost whispering, he said, "His mother was not mortal. She was a magnificent black cow that drew King Idómeneus's fancy. In his day, the High King quickened legions of wombs. His seed was so potent it could cause even beasts to bear offspring. Most of these unholy creatures died before birth, but not poor Menoetius. When the antidote is not given, he transforms into a half bull, half man. He becomes so ferocious no one is safe. In his beast-state, he has killed many unwary men, women, and children, and, I hate to say, has feasted upon their flesh."

Their eyes widened. They exchanged glances and clasped each other's hands. "A beast in truth," the first woman said.

"Loose within the tunnels." The other shivered. "Lady protect us!" Making the sign against evil, she asked, "What can be done?"

"You should keep your children close." Alexiare patted the nearest woman's hand. "Innocents often don't recognize danger, and their curiosity will sometimes bring them to a tragic end. I suppose the queen will have to send a contingent of warriors down there to find and restrain him—perhaps even kill him." Alexiare scooped another drink of water to soothe his inflamed throat, then glanced at the looming walls of the palace. He didn't want to go too far, just far enough to whet their imaginations. With a courteous bow, he said regretfully, "I ought to return before I am missed. I don't wish to be beaten. Please, my ladies, give me your solemn oath you will repeat none of what I have told you. I do feel badly for my lord, and his poor, stricken brother."

"We won't," the first woman breathed.

The second nodded. "Our Zagreus has endured so much."

As hard as they tried to hide it, he recognized the impatient itch of desire that affected true gossipmongers. By tomorrow's sunrise, half—maybe all—of Knossos would have heard the story of the Beast in the labyrinth.

11

Moon of Fertile Willows

ARIDELA'S EYES FELT DRY AND GRITTY, HER BODY WEARY AND SLUGGISH. Sleep eluded her but for short interludes wherein she suffered disjointed, oppressive nightmares. Her womb continued to clench, though Rhené covered her in dittany wraps, designed to quiet an unborn baby, and ordered her to remain in bed.

Days of forced inactivity sent her mind circling in endless ruminations. Anger, humiliation, and disillusionment toward Chrysaleon warred with guilt and bewilderment over Menoetius.

The announcement of Iros's death—or murder, as Chrysaleon so indifferently put it, weighed upon her as well. She lay in bed watching morning fade into night, remembering for some reason the tiny snail she'd befriended while Harpalycus's captive, a creature so small and fragile she had never been able to find it after the eunuch hit her and knocked it away. She thought of how Iros had been foisted upon Chrysaleon while pregnant with her brother's child. Had she found Chrysaleon handsome? Had he ever whispered words of sweetness and ardency to her? The few instances Chrysaleon and Harpalycus had spoken of her left Aridela sensing the girl had been used in some political ploy, given no say or choice in the matter. Chrysaleon had dismissively offered to send her back to her father if Aridela would join him at Mycenae. Poor, fragile Iros. Aridela had no doubt the babe was dead as well, though Chrysaleon hadn't said so. What had Iros's short life been like? Who had murdered her, and why?

She couldn't help remembering Chrysaleon's rage at Lycomedes, Tiryns king, for foisting a pregnant daughter off on him. *Please, Mother, bring Iros joy in the shadowlands*, she prayed, to block out the nagging suspicion that the girl's murderer may well have been her husband.

On the third day of her confinement, Aridela's handmaid confided that something had happened. Repeatedly making the sign against evil, the maid described what she'd heard—that the Zagreus's attacker was no longer mortal. That Menoetius had become, through some horrifying divine curse, both man and bull. She claimed to have heard his terrifying bellows herself, when she took her mother some barley cakes. They had echoed through a weed-choked grate, one of the airways into the labyrinth, and were so terrible they almost stopped her heart. The pitiful girl actually shed tears as she shared even more gossip. Her lover, a guard posted at one of the entrances, had glimpsed this creature. He called it an abomination—a gigantic man with a bull's head and enormous hooves where his hands should be. The Beast's eyes were huge and bloodshot. His mouth dribbled foam and blood as he slavered and raged in incomprehensible delirium.

She also revealed the name that had come to be attached to him. *Asterion*. In Kaphtor's tongue, Asterion meant "Starry." It was an ancient tradition among the people to give respectful names to that which was most feared. The Erinyes had long been known as "The Solemn Ones," out of awe and veneration. The fact that Menoetius had now joined the ranks of beings frightening enough to warrant such a name caused Aridela's flesh to shiver.

She careened between guilt, terror, and disbelief. She blamed Selene. She blamed Goddess Athene. But mostly, she blamed herself.

Could it be true? Could the Lady, in her unquenchable rage, have leveled such a dreadful curse upon Menoetius?

In the privacy of her bed, Aridela made the sign against evil and whispered prayers for mercy. She reminded Athene that she would be dead but for Menoetius's quick thinking when she was a child, and later, when she was Harpalycus's slave. She emphasized Menoetius's devotion. She spoke of his eyes, which reflected those of his Mistress, and his singular crescent scar. Had the Lady not marked him in such a way to signify their bond?

Rhené brought a poppy drink, which eventually plunged her into a nightmare where she and the child-bride Iros wandered together endlessly and blindly through the labyrinth's black passageways, their timid steps accompanied by the distant awful grunting and raging of the Beast who, by his very existence, made Kaphtor's doom all too clear.

"My lady, I hate to disturb you." Aridela's handmaid approached the bed timidly, bowing. "It is Selene. She is here again."

"Bring her in." Aridela sat up, despair making every movement a heavy effort. She had refused to see Selene since the confrontation in the orchard, but the passage of seven days had cooled her anger, and Selene had come every day. It seemed petulant and childish to go on resisting.

Selene paused in the doorway before rushing forward. She knelt and seized Aridela's hands, kissing them. "How have we come to this?"

Dark, sunken circles marred the skin beneath her slanted turquoise eyes. They were swollen and red. Such misery sparked Aridela's compassion.

"Lie here with me." Aridela moved over so Selene could join her.

Together they wept, and for the first time, Aridela felt some portion of her misery dissipate.

"You have to save Menoetius," Selene said at last.

"I want that more than anything. Was he drunk? Is there a way to excuse what he did?"

Selene sat up, wiping her eyes. "Aridela, I love you. But you refuse any truth that casts a shadow on Chrysaleon."

Aridela straightened too. "If you have come to accuse him again of treason, leave now, and you might as well return to your country, because I will never welcome you into my presence from this day onward."

Selene frowned and looked away. "I will say no more."

"Has Menoetius ever confessed the truth to you, as Chrysaleon did to me?" Aridela stroked Selene's forearm, hoping to lessen the sting of her words. "Before the Destruction, he told me why they came here. He confessed his father sent them to find our weaknesses so they could overthrow us. He did not have to tell me, but he did. He swore he abandoned the scheme out of love for me. I believe him. All the time Menoetius and I were stuck in that cave he never once admitted any of this. So I ask you—which man is to be trusted?"

"Menoetius did tell me," Selene said after a frowning hesitation.

"But not until recently. One day, he came to me, angry and upset about something, I know not what, and he confessed his father's plot. Many things were revealed that day. It doesn't mean Menoetius cannot be trusted. It means he respects his father and so would not betray his secrets. That is all."

Sighing, Aridela tried again. "Chrysaleon comes from a foreign land, very different from ours. Yet my mother believed in him, and Helice was not easily fooled. His time is short. As Goddess-of-Life-in-Death, my duty is to make each of his days more delightful than the last. Look at how badly I've managed so far. I must make amends…for the time he has left."

Even as she defended him, his words returned. *I am Mycenaean. It is not my destiny to die in your labyrinth.*

No one could ever know. It was her turn to protect him, as he had protected her the night of the Destruction.

She would shield him, but it was useless to pretend she wasn't still angry. Because of it, she deliberately recalled Selene's words as well. *Look how ready he is to believe you faithless. Almost like he expected it.*

Selene slid off the bed. "Menoetius wants to speak to you."

"More lies. More blame. I won't listen."

"No, Aridela. He regrets the trouble he caused you."

"The council has ordered that no one can see him, though you obviously have. Besides, I have heard—terrible things. That he has… become dangerous."

"Absurd lies," Selene said with a snort. "Who rules this land? You or the council?"

"I am queen. But the council has a say in such matters."

"Aridela, do you realize Menoetius may soon die? If you refuse to see him now, you may never see him again. And I will tell you something else. If you let the council kill him, I will die as well."

"What?"

Selene took Aridela's hands and held them to her chest. "I understand how you feel, Aridela, and it grieves me to cause you this pain. I never knew such love for a man could steal into my heart without my consent and burn it forever to his."

Aridela couldn't hide her shock. Selene had always been disinterested, even slightly repulsed by males. "Then you do know," she said at last. "Even into this, you accompany me."

"Further than you guess. I carry his child."

Wonder and joy blotted out the unhappy situation. Selene had never allowed a man to quicken her womb. "What happy tidings!" Aridela rose to her knees. She slipped her hands from Selene's and placed them over the gentle roundness she hadn't noticed before, due to the many layers of clothing worn by all in the lingering chill. The baby fluttered, causing her to smile. "It seems well-established," she said. "When?"

"The Moon of the Olive Harvest, just before we freed you from Harpalycus. The last night, I think, that Menoetius and I were together before he took you into the mountains."

For one cloudy, somber instant, Aridela knew envy. "Menoetius's baby," she whispered, and quickly blinked away a prickle of tears.

Turning her mind from thoughts she had no right to think, Aridela counted in her head. "Then yours will only be about three months older than mine." She got up from the bed and they embraced. "Does he know?"

"Yes—we both gave up the secrets we'd been keeping. Aridela, Menoetius's allegiance is a matter of honor to him, as it is to you. He thought Chrysaleon might return from Mycenae ready to obey the obligation of the sacrifice. He refused to make any accusations until he knew. He gave his brother a chance. Only when he was certain nothing had changed did he agree to come to you. Do you understand how hard this was for him? Menoetius is one of us now. No longer a Mycenaean. He chose us over Mycenae, over Chrysaleon. He is wholly loyal to you, and to Kaphtor."

Aridela embraced her friend again, this time to hide from Selene's perceptive gaze.

It is not my destiny to die in your labyrinth.

"Will both fathers be dead when their children are born?"

The pointed question sent a cold shiver through Aridela's body. *I won't let you die. I will save you somehow.* She had almost blurted out that impulsive promise, but Menoetius and Selene had interrupted them before she could. Looking back now, she was glad. Yes, she wanted Chrysaleon to live. But part of her, the part he had injured so profoundly with his fierce, cruel condemnation—his swift belief that she had betrayed him, knew he was not, and never would be, a true bull-king.

"Come," she said faintly. "I will see Menoetius, since you wish it. But Chrysaleon cannot know. He would never forgive me."

Selene nodded. "It will be our secret."

"I've been told no one can find him down there."

"I can find him," Selene said.

GUARDS STOOD ON EITHER SIDE OF THE HEAVILY BARRED ENTRANCE leading into the labyrinth—Menoetius's suffocating prison. Aridela waved them aside and took Selene's arm.

"My lady," said one. "You cannot go down there. The Zagreus gave orders."

"He did?" Aridela kept her voice mild. "So you dictate to me where I can and cannot go?"

He flushed and immediately bowed his head. "Allow me to accompany you," he said. "It is not safe."

"I will go too." The other stepped forward.

"Very well." Aridela nodded. "But do you understand you serve your queen, not the Zagreus? You will never speak a word of this if you want to keep my trust."

Each again bowed. "Never, my lady," the first one said.

"I am yours and always have been, my lady," said the other.

Aridela turned to Selene. "Lead the way."

Following Selene into the dank, chilly abyss beneath the palace, Aridela found herself remembering the night she and Selene sneaked out with Iphiboë to seek their fortunes in the Cave of Velchanos. This was where Menoetius now lived. Here, in this dusty, crumbling, eerie place, where water dripped, the slightest sound echoed, and the danger of collapsing timbers was ever constant.

Menoetius, what have we done to you? Tears burned her eyes, blurring the dim, dreary corridor.

Selene walked on without pause. They wound farther into caverns of silence, through passageways hewn in long lost centuries.

At last they came to a heavy door with a corroded bronze latch. Together, the guards struggled to open it.

Aridela peered into a chamber not unlike the cave in the western mountains. Several lamps provided cheery light. No doubt Selene had brought them. His tiger skin cloak was tossed carelessly over a stool in the corner. Selene had probably brought that, too.

"Menoetius," Selene called.

Aridela couldn't quite suppress an uneasy tremor when she heard rustling and footsteps in an adjoining corridor. She remembered her handmaid's frightened whispers. *The Beast is an abomination, his eyes huge and bloodshot, his mouth dribbling foam and blood.*

The guards stared too and readied their swords.

But the figure who emerged from the dark was only a man, one who looked as tired and desolate as Aridela felt. Not dangerous. Not mad. Just pale and resigned.

"You came," he said, his piercing gaze heightening the odd, internal tremor. "I did not think you would." He knelt before her, looked up into her face, and took her hand. "Here I am, again your prisoner."

She was struck fresh with the impression that he and Chrysaleon were joined by some invisible, unbreakable means. She heard echoes of voices as she did sometimes. It lifted the hair on her scalp and sent another shiver through her limbs. Yes—one gold, one dark, opposites yet interconnected, like the sky was connected to the earth, dawn with twilight. She feared the rash willingness of each to harm the other side of himself. Why, when it was so clear to her, could neither one see that doing so would drive a spear through his own heart?

Her womb cramped, nearly forcing a gasp from her. Rhené would be angry if she knew her patient had risen from bed and gone traipsing off into the bowels of the labyrinth to see the maddened criminal, Asterion the Beast, condemned of treason and violence against the sacred king.

She must not stay. But before she left, there was something she needed to understand. "Chrysaleon made you his cabal. If you had fulfilled the duty set before you, the people of Kaphtor would have proclaimed you their hero. They would have carried you to me on their shoulders. You would have been esteemed and adored, and Chrysaleon would be dead. Why, Menoetius? Why did you choose instead to destroy yourself?"

He rose, scowling. "Chrysaleon has no intention of dying, under the star Iakchos or anywhere else. He wouldn't tell me his plan, but I saw it in his confidence, his arrogance. I know him in ways you never can."

Frustration and impatience made her speak bitterly. "Chrysaleon cannot thwart his destiny, but now another man will fulfill it, because you, too, will be dead. The council demands your life in punishment for what you tried to do. That is the only thing you achieved by attacking him." She had to swallow before she could add, in a whisper, "And it will be horrible."

Selene stepped nearer and put her hand on Aridela's shoulder. "If you allow that, you will have to torture and kill me as well. Menoetius and I together made the choice to confront Chrysaleon, and I do not abandon those I love."

Aridela's shock at this challenge and what it would mean to Selene drowned out her anger at the insinuation. She turned back to Menoetius. "How I wish you had left Kaphtor, as you intended. I should not have asked you to stay. None of this would be happening if you had gone."

"I didn't know about Selene when I said that." He glanced at Selene and clasped her hand. They gazed at each other, not speaking, but Aridela sensed all they were communicating.

"Yes," she said. "You are going to be a father, Menoetius." Another tiny spark of envy erupted in her chest.

He returned his gaze to her, smiling faintly.

"But if you are staying for Selene and the child, why do what you've done? If you hadn't confronted Chrysaleon, you would be free. And why agree to be his cabal? You could live your whole life, for however long its threads may be woven. Instead, you chose death. None of it makes any sense."

"We thought you would believe me. I didn't see myself down here, condemned to die. I thought it would be Chrysaleon. Then there would be no need for me to serve as his cabal." He gave a wry smile. "I suppose I should have known better."

Selene nodded. "I, too, have asked him why he agreed to be Chrysaleon's cabal—his scapegoat! I have begged him to withdraw. He refuses, but will not tell me why. And as for you," she said, clicking her tongue to show her irritation, "of course I thought you would believe us. I never doubted it. You and I have been sisters, and more, for so many years. I never thought you would choose the foreigner over those who have proven their loyalty."

Aridela looked from one to the other. Painful, rending guilt sprang up, but on its heels flowed anger.

"It is true you have been with Chrysaleon your whole life and you know him well, in many ways better than I," she said to Menoetius. "But you don't know everything. You said you've changed since coming here. So has he. I don't doubt you told me what you believed, and even the truth as it may have once been. He did come here initially with other ideas. He confessed it. But he is different. He doesn't want to die, but he will, for the sake of Kaphtor. I know he will."

Menoetius started to speak then swallowed. "No," he whispered. Agony turned his eyes dark as slate. "He won't. I cannot stand by and do nothing, even if I have to die for trying." Turning to Selene, he said, "Would you let me speak to her alone?"

Selene nodded. "Be aware, she is as stubborn as you." Motioning to the guards, she herded them out with her, leaving the door slightly ajar.

"What is it?" Aridela asked.

"Do you remember the day you took Chrysaleon as your consort?"

Her smile was tinged with suspicion. "Is there some doubt?"

"Do you remember when you turned away from him to look at me? Your mother and the oracle were speaking over the two of you."

"Yes," she said. "I remember it well." Themiste had been praying over the couple but Aridela hardly heard. She was distracted by her lover's brother, who stood some distance away. That was when the Goddess entered her mind and spoke prophecy. She had seen Menoetius as he used to be, handsome, youthful, heroic, carrying the gored little princess out of the shrine so she could live her life instead of dying in a pool of her own blood.

"Something happened." Menoetius broke into her memories. "A voice spoke." He touched the side of his head and shrugged. "I have never told anyone this, and you will think me witless, but I swear it to you, Aridela. It happened. The Goddess told me what was to come."

"You are not witless," Aridela said with a quiet laugh, "any more than you are the Beast of the labyrinth—the loathsome Asterion that has all of Kaphtor shivering in their beds."

"The bull-man." His mouth slid into a cynical smile. "Well, at least no one searches for me. I have all the solitude I've ever craved."

"Tell me what the Goddess said."

"She told me I will live through centuries, that I will have many faces and names. She even told me what they would be. *Cailean. Nuren. Ambrosio. Daniel. Curran.* The last was *William.*" Bewilderment forged creases across his forehead. "Strange names. They made me think of my mother's country. I sensed I was being drawn there—that it was a place where such ways of speaking might be common."

Aridela could only nod. She didn't want to break his concentration though inside she reeled as she matched the names the Goddess told her that day with his. She almost asked why he was telling her this now, when they had been together all that time in the mountains and he'd never hinted at it. But she knew, and couldn't make him say it. Because he thought this was his last chance.

He scrubbed his hands over his face and through his hair before sighing. "She told me the only way to gain her forgiveness was to return her." His eyes, when he opened them, were profoundly stricken. "I don't know what she wants me to do. Do you, Aridela? I have done nothing right so far."

Voiceless torment and wave after wave of love swelled through her. She reached out and placed two fingers over his mouth.

Without blinking or taking his gaze from hers, he kissed her fingertips then the pulse in her wrist, lingering on the burn mark.

Aridela swayed closer and he brought her in, circling her waist. She nestled her face against his throat and curled her arms around his neck, drawing him closer yet.

He put his hand under her chin and drew her face to his. He kissed her feverishly, holding her as though he feared she would vanish. She returned his kisses, asked for more, and wept against his flesh.

"Carmanor," she whispered, tracing the rim of his ear. "The first I ever loved. My barbarian, so mysterious and fascinating. Menoetius, the angry defender who offered his life for my sake. Asterion, who carries me to the heavens and turns me into a star."

He picked her up off the floor, pressing his face against the junction of shoulder to throat.

"You are my heart," she said. She didn't say *I cannot live without you*. But every fiber of her being vibrated with it. She shivered, and he tightened his hold even as he, too, trembled.

After some lost length of time, he placed her back upon her feet. "The Goddess said something else to me that day. She said, 'the sea claims final possession.'" The crease between his brows returned. "Do you know what it means?"

"That is an old saying among my people." Aridela smoothed his hair and brought his face down for another kiss. "It means that once something descends into the sea, it is gone forever."

"Does Athene want me to disappear?"

She could tell he was contemplating. "No, no, Menoetius."

He looked away from her. Aridela gripped his hair, forcing him to meet her gaze. "I will overturn this. You won't die. I won't let them do it. I admit I was confused before—I didn't know what I was meant to do, how to satisfy everyone, but now, I—"

He was shaking his head. "If you try to stop it, you could be condemned."

"I am their queen."

"Chrysaleon would be very angry."

"It doesn't matter. He does not control us."

Something was different. He was no longer joined to her. He was removing himself, bit by bit, though he hadn't let go of her waist.

"Sometimes I let the lamps go out and I live in darkness," he said, almost meditatively. "There is no sound but the drip of water and the squeak of rats. I have seen…things, in the dark."

"What things, my love?"

"The Lady comes to me, her face as bright as the moon. She tells me, 'What seems the end is only the beginning.' It gives me strength."

"Goddess Athene speaks to you? She shows herself? What else does she say?"

"I can't tell you everything. I don't understand it all yet." He shook his head as though dislodging something from his mind. "This is what I wanted to tell you, without Selene knowing. I was wrong to try to turn you against Chrysaleon."

"You believe he is innocent? This is wonderful. I will go to him and tell him—and the council. Everything will be as it was. But you cannot be his cabal. I will not bear it—"

"No."

Aridela read what was on his face. All hope died. She felt as though a knife blade was searing through her soul.

"I cannot explain," he said. "But you must do nothing."

"If I do nothing, you will die," she whispered.

"Perhaps that is what your Goddess wants. Perhaps she wants Chrysaleon to triumph. If so, you should prepare yourself."

"I told you before. No man can defy his destiny." The words came from far away, as though called from Mount Ida's snowy summit. Chills burrowed into her skin, then a wave of heat and nausea.

Menoetius's eyes were all she could see. They adored. They gave a love as endless as the land of dreams. But the Lady's eyes were there too, full of warning.

Numbness crept from her toes to her ears, drowning out everything but the rhythmic sound of her heart, and the quieter, rapid beat of her baby's. She didn't hear Selene come back into the room, but there she was, frowning into her face, her voice echoing as she said, "I promised to respect your wishes. But there is more at stake than love or loyalty." Softly, she added, "You carry a traitor's child."

Aridela's abdomen knotted. She heard herself gasp. Menoetius caught her as stabbing pain doubled her over and her legs collapsed. He picked her up as he had that long-gone day in the shrine, and again the night he carried her to freedom from Harpalycus. He cradled her against his chest.

"Carmanor," she whispered, before ripping cramps cut off her ability to speak, and forced a miserable groan. Hot, sticky moisture flooded between her legs. "Something is wrong." Perhaps Selene had leveled a curse upon her—upon her child.

"She is bleeding," Selene cried, and called to the guards.

Menoetius held her close, bringing back the sense of comfort and safety only he seemed able to give. She felt his heartbeat now, mingled with her own and the baby's.

Selene's promise came from a distance. "Don't worry, Aridela. We will take care of you."

PART II

Amarantos

———

1

Moon of Fertile Willows

———

ARIDELA ROLLED FROM SIDE TO SIDE, SEEKING ESCAPE FROM PAIN. HANDS held her down.

"Chrysaleon?"

"I am here. Where else would I be?"

The healer held a cup to her lips, ordering her to drink. A cool wet cloth was placed on her forehead.

She drifted into uneasy sleep.

THE GUARDS HAD STRUGGLED TO OPEN THE HEAVY OAK DOOR, BUT FOR HER it moved at the touch of a finger. No longer squeaky, it swept outward in soundless invitation.

"Asterion," she whispered. The chamber was not so well lit as last time. There was but one lamp now, giving off a faint glow that only intensified the weight of darkness.

Again, she heard rustling. This time, instead of fear, she felt a thrill of anticipation.

The Beast loped into the circle of light. Incredibly huge, he smelled pungent, musky, like the wild aurochs they captured for the ring. He nuzzled the palm of her hand. She stroked his face, clasped his heavy horns, and kissed his forehead, where a gold rosette glowed.

He prodded her with his snout until he had her trapped against the

109

wall of the chamber. There he kept her, between his implacable enormous head and the immovable wall, snuffling at her stomach as though he could smell the baby. He backed up, snorting angrily, swinging his head from side to side. His eyes were white-rimmed; she sensed the danger and covered her abdomen, but then divine Athene transformed him, and he who pressed against her was a man.

Anything could happen in the place of dreams, where no boundaries existed.

He was Menoetius, but somewhere inside him lived the bull, Asterion, a most virile and potent lover.

He was irresistible.

Chrysaleon was slumped on the floor beside her bed, asleep, his head and one arm resting on the quilt, his fingers meshed loosely with hers.

Still half-asleep herself, Aridela stroked his hair with her free hand. The people of Mycenae claimed their god Poseidon ruled the waves and weather and caused thunderclouds to boil when angered. In this state between sleep and waking, she imagined Chrysaleon as Poseidon, the Tamer of Horses, he who sent raging sea-storms to sink ships. *The mainland's warlike god has risen from his palace beneath the waves to mate with me, Kaphtor's queen, Goddess-of-Life-in-Death, daughter of Velchanos.*

Far better to weave fantasies than face the sense of fallow emptiness she felt where her baby should be.

Chrysaleon's eyes opened, creating yet another dreamy vision, of sun-struck seawater.

"Forgive me," she whispered.

His smile was weary. "Whatever you have done, or not done, I forgive. And you. Will you forgive me, though we both know you should not?"

"Yes," she said, and her resentment sluiced away.

He met her gaze steadily. There was nothing but guilt and sorrow there, no secrets, none of these schemes Menoetius claimed he was constructing. Menoetius was wrong.

"What happened to me?" she asked.

He caught her other hand and held on tightly. "The healing-woman could not keep the babe inside you."

"She has died?"

"The next will live. Crete has the finest of everything, does it not? So it must have our child."

He climbed onto the bed and held her as she wept. Selene's warnings and Menoetius's claims shrieked through her mind. Had Athene killed her child as punishment for her consort's crimes?

She saw her grief reflected in his face. No, it could not be. Chrysaleon was noble. He would never plot against her. Menoetius was blinded by jealousy. She would not justify his allegations by asking Chrysaleon about them.

From the Oracle Logs
Themiste

Two new moons have passed. I have not bled.

I search for answers, in vision, in the entrails, in the logs, but I receive only silence. Should I admit my crime? If I do, everyone will know how I cast aside my sacred vows, and for what? To lie with a man, like some goatherd's daughter.

I am afraid. Yes, my Mother, afraid to die, but more than that I fear my confession will send Kaphtor into another uproar, more confusion, renewed chaos. Our land is weakened. Any admission I make can only bring more harm.

I cannot tell if I make these statements out of concern or a childish wish to escape the punishment I deserve.

After the defeat of Harpalycus the Butcher, Aridela confided that she will take no man to her bed but Chrysaleon until he dies. She puts his customs above ours. How can I admit what I have done in the face of such artless devotion? One look in my eyes would tell her how I would defy everything, even her trust, to lie with him again. Would she not feel deceived by both of us? He has made it clear to her that he will never forgive her intimacies with any other man, yet he lay with me twice.

Such is the barbarian way.

At last I understand the powers of lust that drive men and women. I feel those drives deep in the center of my being. "Run to him," my body cries. "Beg him to touch you." These are the thoughts controlling my nights, my days, my very breathing.

I investigated what herbs to take. I acquired them and mixed the potion that would kill this child. I held it to my lips.

I could not drink.

Its presence threatens my position—even my life. Every day it lives, my moera slips further away. Yet something presses against my mouth like an invisible hand. A dark inner voice tells me, "No. Do not." I fear it is my own longing to hold his child in my arms.

The council has condemned Menoetius. Chrysaleon's brother abandoned everything, his loyalty, his homeland, his honor and his life, for love of our queen. I have heard he is no longer a man, but a howling, desperate thing. The Beast of the labyrinth.

I understand his pain as I never could before. I pity him. I pity all those resigned to hopeless love.

Though it will tear apart everything I have ever tried to be, I will keep this secret. Not only for Aridela's sake, but my own and Kaphtor's.

Aridela was alone when she woke, but her handmaid soon arrived to wait upon her. The girl helped her sit up and shared all the gossip she had missed while trapped in the haze of poppy.

The council wanted Menoetius put to death immediately. At first this news sent a bolt of fear through Aridela. Had the guards revealed her clandestine visit to the labyrinth? But as the handmaid chattered on, she realized their reason was the same as before. They wanted vengeance upon him for attacking the consort in the apple grove. Surprisingly, Chrysaleon was protesting this, but not out of care for his brother. For some reason Aridela didn't understand, he was adamant that Menoetius serve as his cabal. Following that plan would erase the crime Menoetius committed. He would become bull-king, consort, and Aridela's lover. How could Chrysaleon want that when the idea of them lying with each other in the cave sent him into blindly jealous, raging fury?

What would happen if Chrysaleon found out his wife had been with his brother when she lost her baby? It made her shudder to imagine, and not only for herself. She could easily picture his rage exploding outward to engulf Selene, Menoetius, even the two guards.

She sent the maid away to fetch bread and honey, and something to help her poppy headache. While she was alone, she took a comb to her hair and pondered. She thought about the village of Natho, and the day Chrysaleon became her consort. She thought of the strange way his face had melded with his brother's. She remembered her conviction that they were more than they seemed, separated parts of a whole.

In her mind, the Goddess had voiced a bleak and somber prophecy.

I have lived many lives since the beginning, and so shalt thou. I have been given many names and many faces. So shalt thou, and thou wilt follow me from reverence and worship into obscurity. In an unbroken line wilt thou return, my daughter. Thou shalt be called Eamhair of the sea, who brings them closer, and Shashi, sacrificed to deify man. Thy names are Caparina, Lilith, and the sorrowful Morrigan, who drives them far apart. Thou wilt step upon the earth seven times, far into the veiled future. Seven labyrinths shalt thou wander, lost, and thou too wilt forget me. Suffering and despair shall be thy nourishment. Misery shall poison thy blood. Thou wilt breathe the air of slavery, for as long as thou art blinded. For thou art the earth, blessed and eternal, yet thou shalt be pierced, defiled, broken, and wounded, even as I have been. Thou wilt generate inexhaustible adoration and contempt. Until these opposites are united, all will strangle within the void.

Even after so long—seven months—and so many catastrophes, she recalled every nuance, including the odd names, and knew that was part of its design. It had burned itself into her memory the same way the scars left by the Destruction had permanently burned her skin.

The more she thought about it, the stronger grew her resolve. She would forge forgiveness between the two brothers. Determination blazed so fiercely she suspected it was instruction planted by the Goddess herself. Besides, if she lay in bed doing nothing, grief might defeat her.

Themiste's appearance offered a welcome distraction. The oracle came in at Aridela's invitation and sat by the bed.

"I longed for this child, Minos," Aridela said.

"All Kaphtor mourns with you." Themiste's earrings trembled, as did her voice. "I wish I could heal your sorrow. If I could, with some divine power, place Chrysaleon's child inside you, I would. But you have only lived seventeen years. Your *kaliara* has barely flowed a year. Remember how long it took to begin? I think you will have a healthy child, according to Athene's plan." Her words held confidence and she squeezed Aridela's hand reassuringly, but her smile was shaky. "Does not Velchanos rise after his season of sacrifice? There is never new life without death, no new god without annihilation."

"But it is Chrysaleon's child I want."

"There is still time. If not, perhaps his brother can accomplish the goal when he becomes bull-king."

"Menoetius...." Aridela shied away from the memory of his stricken face as she had begun to bleed. "Have you not been told? He will be put to a traitor's death before Iakchos rises."

Themiste paused. "I do not believe Menoetius would have harmed his brother. I have spoken to the council, and so has the Zagreus."

Aridela's throat constricted so tightly in her effort to stave off weeping that it hurt to speak. "Perhaps you're right. But you didn't see their faces. Such hatred as I hope never again to witness."

"There is long-standing hostility there, but something more, as well. I cannot name it, but I feel it must be as deep and enduring as their rivalry."

The handmaid carried in a platter of bread and honey, and a drink made of bitter feverfew.

"Headache?" Themiste asked.

Aridela nodded as she choked down the brew. "Rhené insists on giving me poppy." She couldn't help making a face at the acrid taste, and took several bites of honey soaked bread to sweeten her tongue. "I have been lying here for days with nothing to do but think. I realized I never told you what happened the day Chrysaleon became my consort and sacred king."

"I remember nothing out of the ordinary," Themiste said. "Until that night."

"No one knew of this—" She started to say *except for Menoetius*, but hesitated, then didn't. "I should have told you long ago."

Themiste leaned closer, nodding her encouragement.

"We were kneeling by the water. You and Mother were performing the rites. You had just begun the prayer to Athene." A shiver, caused not by chill but rather a sensation like hot sparks, leaped across Aridela's skin. She hugged herself, rubbing her arms and shoulders, trying to erase the foreboding that accompanied the memory. "A voice spoke." She touched her temple. "Inside my mind."

Again, the prophecy was there for her. She related it without hesitation.

When she finished, she was flushed and sweating, and Themiste's eyes were wide. "That was not all," she said, fanning her face, and repeated the last part.

I have split one into two. Mortal men have burned my shrines and pulled down my statues. Their arrogance has upended the holy ways. I decree that men will resurrect me or the earth will die.

Silence lay heavy and oppressive. Themiste and the handmaid stared at her.

Finally Themiste drew in a deep breath. Turning to the servant, she gave the order to go, quickly, and fetch her scribe.

"I don't understand. Where did this come from?" Themiste asked as the woman bowed and left. "A dream?"

"No, Minos. The words came to me in the middle of the marriage rite. Neither you, nor my mother, nor Chrysaleon, heard it." Should she relate the part Menoetius had played in the prophecy, the promise he'd been given? No doubt the oracle should know. But something stilled her tongue. For one thing, it was not her secret to reveal, and she was afraid of somehow giving away that she had been with him when she miscarried. Also, there was something odd about Themiste's expression when she'd said, *I have spoken to the council, and so has the Zagreus*—a flush and a faltering of her gaze that spoke of secrets, of something being deliberately withheld.

The priestess and the handmaid returned soon after. Themiste and Aridela went over the passage until Themiste was satisfied that she had it faithfully recorded on several sheaves of papyrus. "This voice," Themiste said. "It spoke at length and in detail, yet you seem to remember it exactly. It has been so long. Are you sure?"

Aridela nodded. "Yes. It is always there. It never fades." Weary and drained, she rested the back of her head against the wall and closed her eyes.

Themiste sent the other women away. When she and Aridela were alone, she said, "It sits ill upon me to do this now, but I am going away. I promise to return before the honey gathering begins."

"Why?" Aridela opened her eyes, frowning. "Where must you go?"

"You know a few of the prophecies were dug up from under the palace. Only tablets. I fear those inscribed on papyrus are forever lost, but I have worked to recreate them as best I can."

Aridela nodded. "Yes, I know."

"In dream and vision, I see myself putting the tablets in a dark, rocky crevice, a well-hidden place. I think if I do this they will be safe, even when the earth shakes. I would like to take Selene with me. She can help me find a likely spot. Do I have your leave?"

"Surely." Aridela's heart plummeted. Still, the honey gathering would begin in a fortnight, so the separation wouldn't be long. She stifled her protests and smiled. "We will miss you."

"I ask you not to tell anyone where we have gone. Whatever I find must be kept secret. I need time as well, Aridela, time to commune with the Lady in silence and solitude."

"I understand." Aridela's reluctance melted. "You have done so much since the Butcher's invasion. Go away, Themiste, and recover. Regain your strength."

Again Themiste's gaze faltered and she flushed, setting off alarms in Aridela's mind. "There is something else. You should know first. Soon enough, everyone will know."

"What is it, Minos? You look so…odd."

"A child grows inside me." Tears shimmered in her eyes, and her hands trembled.

"Themiste?" Aridela's mind dropped into an instant of numb blankness before shock catapulted through her, then envy, and finally, apprehension.

"It is true. Two dark moons have passed with no *kaliara*. I saw three cracked empty birds' eggs, and last night a cat gave birth in the corridor outside my chambers. Remember when Rhené could tell you had quickened by the signs your body gave? I have similar symptoms. It is very early, but I am certain. A child has taken root inside me."

"Did you…break your vows?" She was almost too afraid to ask, but she had to know. Always, Aridela had been the child and Themiste the adult. It felt strange to be the one requiring an explanation instead of giving one.

"No."

Aridela gave a sigh of relief. "Then Athene sends a miracle. You conceived in the old way, the sacred way, from the north wind."

"I love sprouting beans and eat them often." Themiste gave the faintest of smiles. "Perhaps they planted the soul of a dead hero in my womb."

Aridela threw back her covers.

"What are you doing?"

"I want to kneel before you. Without doubt you are the holiest of women."

Themiste knocked over the stool in her haste to rise and back away from the bed. A strangely terrified expression passed over her face. It must be due to the reverence Aridela wanted to show her. Themiste was shy and solitary. Kaphtor's holy oracle wanted no recognition. Yet she would have it—much recognition and acclaim.

"Never kneel to me," Themiste said. "Never."

Stammering something unintelligible, she fled before Aridela could protest.

FOR A FORTNIGHT, WHILE THEMISTE AND SELENE WERE GONE, ARIDELA followed her healer's orders and rested. She spent most of her time, when the weather allowed, on an undamaged terrace that gave a southern view towards Mount Juktas, and was out of the way of the laborers and architects.

A rather surprising, attentive companion was Chrysaleon's slave, Alexiare.

"I hope when you regain your strength, my lady, you will come out of the palace and see your land's splendid recovery." He lifted his face to the sun and swept out one arm. "Do you feel the returning warmth?"

"Yes," she said. "I wish I could go out now. I feel perfectly well, but Rhené is overly zealous." She sipped at a drink made from barley, which had been transported by boat from Aptara especially for her.

He gave her a deferential pat on her forearm. "I doubt that, my lady, given the facts. Putting aside the Destruction, there has been invasion, captivity, brutality, isolation, hunger, and then the battle, in which you took such an active part you were wounded near unto death."

"True. It has not been our easiest year."

His smile was admiring. "Yet none of it defeated you. May I ask how the knife wound fares?"

"It aches and the scar is ugly, but no infection came of it and the flesh has completely healed over." Beyond everything else, it was the loss of Chrysaleon's child that remained unbearable, but she said nothing of that, and neither did he.

He seemed satisfied and puttered about, making sure she drank every drop of her stimulating barley-honey concoction.

"Have you seen the Zagreus?" she asked.

"He went to Amnisos to rule on a dispute between your builders and the Mycenaeans. Would you like me to send a messenger after him?"

"No. You stay and keep me company—if it doesn't bother your voice too much."

He bowed again and lowered himself onto a nearby stool, propping his stick between his legs. "Never, my lady. It's good to be in the place I think of as home. I lived in Tamara for part of my childhood. Your mother's mother's mother was queen."

"But you were with Chrysaleon when he was young?"

"Yes, my lady. I have been with your consort since he and Menoetius were born."

"You would have known their mothers."

"I did, Menoetius's mother more so. Chrysaleon's mother, Clematia, was a reserved woman, but Sorcha—Menoetius's mother—and I spent quite a lot of time together."

"He told me a little. The rumors, that she was a priestess, and had the gift of augury."

"I was rather afraid of her. I believe she saw it all before it happened—that she would be captured and enslaved. She could have changed the course of her life, but chose not to in order to give birth to Menoetius." He brushed hair out of his eyes and added with a quirked eyebrow, "One time I watched her make lightning in the sky. Wherever she pointed, it burned, and she laughed like a child with a toy."

Aridela stifled any expression of disbelief out of courtesy. Surely only an Immortal could do such a thing. Alexiare must be mistaken. "Before all this trouble with Chrysaleon, Menoetius told me he wanted to go to her country and find her."

Alexiare's head angled and his shoulder rose slightly, saying without words, *No chance of that now.*

Aridela thought of the day she and Menoetius sat on the crumbling brink of a cliff and discovered they shared something—a memory from a dream. *For longer than you can imagine, I will be with you, in you, of you. Together we bring forth a new world, and nothing can ever part us.*

Menoetius's death would break that promise. She lowered her face, not wanting the observant Alexiare to see her despair.

Her time in the labyrinth with Kaphtor's Beast remained foggy. When she tried to remember all they had said to each other, a headache would begin pounding like hammer blows, and she could recall no more than glimpses of an angry black bull mixed with Menoetius's anguished face, the Lady's eyes, and someone saying, *The sea claims final possession.*

Rhené came then, wanting Aridela to have her daily massage and herb bath, but two mornings later, Alexiare again joined her on the terrace. This time, Aridela had arranged for a chair to be placed next to her so he wouldn't have to crouch on an uncomfortable stool. They resumed their pleasant dialogue almost as though there had been no interruption.

"Many at the citadel of Mycenae call your consort 'Lion killer,' Alexiare said. "You know, of course, how he saved his brother's life."

"Yes. Menoetius told me."

"Did Menoetius tell you of his nightmare—the one where he fights a lion?"

"Yes."

Alexiare paused; his study of her was suddenly speculative, making his thoughts obvious. *What happened between you on the mountain?* He knew, as did Chrysaleon, that Menoetius never spoke casually of either of these events—the actual attack or the dream that accompanied it.

Hoping to divert his conjectures, she said, "I, too, once experienced a mystical dream."

"Yes, my lady?" He reached out and tucked the coverlet over her shoulder.

"It was last year, before—everything. I had asked the Lady to let me dance with a bull." She contemplated how the dream of entering the bullring had forced its way into her sleep nearly every night, but now it was gone, evaporated, its purpose, to spark Chrysaleon's desire to stay, to win the Games and become her consort, completed. Once that was done, it was no longer needed. How could anyone doubt that Athene took an interest in the affairs of mortals?

"Which you did," Alexiare said as her silence continued.

She brought herself back to the terrace, a little startled. "We were on the holy mountain. That one." She pointed at Mount Juktas. "Preparing Iphiboë for the coming grove rites."

His gaze upon her darkened in sympathy. She hurried on, tears stinging her eyes. "I dreamed the statue of Velchanos came to life. He walked across the clearing to me, a man with long golden hair and green eyes. Because of that dream, I knew Chrysaleon later, when I saw him for the first time."

Alexiare's gaze intensified into a shocked stare. "When was this, my lady? When, exactly?"

"The Moon of Mead-making, last year. A month, almost two, before the Games. Before Chrysaleon and his brother came to Kaphtor."

"Ah." His smile was both mysterious and gratified. "Did this—vision—say or do anything? Or merely appear to you?"

"He vowed he and I would always be together."

But when the god initially transformed from stone, he hadn't resembled Chrysaleon. He was darker. She recognized him. She even named him. It was Carmanor who began the phrase, *For longer than you can imagine*. Then a fracturing noise, like that of a lightning bolt striking a tree, interrupted him. When her sight cleared and the ringing in her ears faded, it was Chrysaleon's face above hers.

Since then, both men, in their own ways, had convinced her they had each heard this promise.

She wanted to tell her new friend these details, to have his insight. He was a man she was growing to trust and value. But he spoke again, disrupting her thoughts.

"This is most intriguing, my lady. Our dreams, I think, are not meaningless, but methods for deities to tell us what we need to know. You would not have been so quickly drawn to your consort if you had not envisioned him this way first."

"True. I have thought many times it molded my heart to his before I ever saw him."

Chrysaleon's slave wore such a delighted expression it nearly caused Aridela to laugh out loud. Maybe it was only that he was pleased for his lord and the queen of Kaphtor, but truly, he seemed to think he had played a part in the enchanted dream that bonded her so swiftly and wholly to his master.

"My mother once claimed she saw my future," he said. "She wouldn't reveal it in detail, but made me promise to always remain with High King Chrysaleon. She said if I did, I would experience the tilting of the world, and I would be part of causing this, and would achieve immortality. So far, nothing of any note has happened, and I begin to wonder if she was mistaken." He shrugged, adding wryly, "I cannot pretend many years are left to me."

Aridela could think of no way to refute this. He was a very old man.

But his mind, still sharp, had already flown to another topic. "May I ask you something, my lady, about Harpalycus the Butcher? Only if you are strong enough. I don't wish to upset you."

"I am not so fragile. What do you want to know?"

"It was you who killed him. You were there as he died."

"Yes."

"Did anything unusual happen? Anything that seemed different, hard to explain?"

"It did seem so...but he'd stabbed me." Aridela absently rubbed the wool tunic over the spot where Harpalycus had sunk his blade. The scar throbbed, perhaps in memory of that instant when the knife penetrated flesh and muscle. "I was close to death myself. I'd forgotten, but yes, there was something."

"Can you describe it? I would be most grateful."

"I slit his throat with the knife he used to stab me. His blood spilled over my face and into my eyes—that's why what I saw cannot be trusted, but I thought smoke came out of the wound. There was a stench, as of something rotting."

Alexiare's knuckles whitened on the arms of his chair. "Yes, my lady?" he said, his voice filled with tremors.

"I seemed to lose myself. I still lived, but in some fashion I became joined to him." She shuddered. Speaking of it brought back his heaviness as he'd straddled her, his breath, the murderous glow in his eyes, all too vividly. She swallowed hard and clenched her jaw, fighting for control. "I felt his thoughts. His hatred. I saw his life. I saw him—"

"My lady?" Alexiare leaned forward. "Something must have happened to separate him from you, for I vow you are Queen Aridela alone. Did something—someone pull you apart?" He'd forgotten his manners, for he gripped her wrist, even shook it a little.

"There was a flare of light, and a woman, with a spear. It was not Selene or anyone else I recognized, but it must have been one of our warriors. She shouted at Harpalycus to release me, and he did."

"What are you doing?"

Neither had heard Chrysaleon's approach. He stood, frowning at Alexiare's hand upon the queen's arm.

Alexiare released her as though she'd burst into flames. "I beg your forgiveness, my lord." He rose and bowed. "Allow me to leave you in peace." He bowed again and hobbled away, leaning upon his cane.

"You frightened him," Aridela said.

He gave her a demanding stare.

She laughed. "Are you jealous?"

After a lengthy pause, during which he regarded her darkly, his mouth slid into a sheepish smile. He dropped into the chair Alexiare had vacated and briefly clasped her hand.

"Clematia was your mother's name, was it not?" she asked.

"Yes. Clematia of Seriphos. Queen of Mycenae."

"Alexiare told me about Menoetius's mother, but he said hardly anything about yours."

Chrysaleon scowled. "The slave who birthed Menoetius claimed to have the power of sight and sorcery. It makes a more exciting tale than one that begins and ends with, 'She was a loyal wife and queen, who spent her days caring for her children and the kingdom.'"

"I don't think he meant such a thing."

"I grew weary long ago of hearing about that bitch. She brought unrest wherever she went. Sorcha made the queen appear as nothing. Throughout my mother's life, until the day she died, she had to endure the humiliation Sorcha brought upon her. For the stories never waned, my lady, though Sorcha herself was gone. To this day there are tales and songs of Sorcha the White Seer, of her reckless power, her cruel heart. She was cruel. Of that I am certain." His lips whitened as they pressed together.

"Forgive me. I asked about your mother because I wanted to know more about *her*."

He flushed, but his hands unclenched.

"Is it true she was a priestess? Themiste told me your sister wants to come here and enter the shrines."

He rose and paced to the edge of the terrace, frightening away a line of preening sparrows.

"Why are you angry?" she asked.

He turned and faced her. "My father is dead. My mother is dead. Mycenae hangs suspended like a gemstone before the greedy eyes of the Kindred. I am bound to die and my sister will vanish into your holy caves as though she was never born. Menoetius lives only at my pleasure, which has run dry. If Mycenae is attacked, Gelanor, too, will likely be slaughtered."

"Chrysaleon—"

He returned and picked her up in his arms, his eyes fierce beneath lowered brows, his cheeks flushed. "Only you can save me from disappearance. Only you, by giving birth to my child." As the fire of anger transformed into the burn of desire, he said, "Don't let me be forgotten. Don't let my line die."

I won't let them kill you! She wanted with all her being to whisper the promise. *I will save you.* But no matter how softly she spoke, Athene would hear.

She pulled his face to hers. "I swear I will not fail you," she said instead.

2

Moon of Mead-Making

Cool twilight breezes filtered into the queen's bedchamber, ruffling the draperies between the pillars and teasing the delicate gossamer around the great bed. The tiny disks and shells woven through the material sparkled and chimed.

Chrysaleon took in the scene as he entered. Aridela was lying on the bed; she parted the curtain and beckoned, greeting him with a smile and a kiss as he joined her, and, more subtly, suggestions of sex. But Glauce, greatest of Kaphtor's living artists, stood nearby, mumbling as she labored over a wet plaster fresco on the north wall. She seemed oblivious of the couple as she crushed various pigments— ground lapis, red ochre, charcoal, and gypsum. When finished, the scene would depict Kaphtor and Mycenae united through marriage.

Rhené had acquiesced to Aridela's stubborn insistence that she was recovered, and gave permission to again conceive. The determined glint in his wife's eyes, the playful nips on his ears, and the way she tickled his chest and shoulders with her fingertips made it clear she intended to waste no more time, though as of yet not a day passed without inconsolable weeping over the loss of the previous child, and even now her eyes were red.

They kissed and caressed as they waited for Glauce to finish her work and leave. The nightingale twittered in its wicker cage. Shadows deepened, fading the color on the walls. A maid came in with pitchers of scarlet anemones, which she arranged on either side of the bed. It was believed their fertile aroma would generate fertility. Wine also enhanced the mood.

"I must tell you a secret," Aridela said. "About Themiste."

Chrysaleon stiffened then forced himself to relax. "Where has she been?" he asked, working to sound indifferent. "Today is the first time I have seen her in a long while." He didn't add that as soon as she'd caught sight of him, she turned sharply and walked the other way.

Aridela didn't meet his gaze as she shrugged. "Seeking a safe place for our stories and history. But now she is back, in time for the festival tomorrow."

"What is this secret?" he asked, though he wasn't sure he wanted to know.

Aridela paused, causing his nerves to whine with tension. When she spoke, her tone carried awe. "She has conceived. She carries a child."

Again, Chrysaleon's muscles stiffened and this time, his breathing shortened as he waited to hear what Aridela would say next. Had she tricked him with her kisses and wiles? Perhaps now she would call the guards and have him dragged away to join Menoetius in the labyrinth.

Then the full revelation washed over him, drowning out his anxiety. Themiste had quickened. He could scarcely believe it. Themiste, the arrogant oracle, too good for any man to touch, heralded as the living moon, had surrendered to the same fate as any peasant woman when she opened her legs and let a cock have its way. He almost grinned. His seed was indeed invincible, if it could stir that haughty womb.

Immersed in his self-congratulations, he nearly missed Aridela's next words.

"Athene sends this child for some holy purpose, perhaps to show us her forgiveness. Tomorrow we begin the fermentation of the mead. Themiste will enter a trance. No doubt all will be revealed at that time." She threaded her fingers through his beard. "I wonder how it was done, and if she enjoyed it? I hope she did."

She kissed him. Light as feathers, her fingertips stroked his chest, then lower. His skin responded in a wash of gooseflesh.

So Themiste hadn't told Aridela the truth. She'd protected him, or more likely, herself. Themiste, the proud visionary, was capable of lying in order to hold onto tattered dignity and power.

Chrysaleon's thoughts careened on without pause, though

Aridela's hands and mouth sent his body into stupefying waves of lust.

It is my child. If you knew that, you wouldn't hope for her pleasure. Or would you? I do not understand the women of Crete.

"Grant me a wish," she said.

"What do you want?" He was rapidly losing his ability to think coherently.

"You have exerted your influence over the council to pardon Menoetius. Now let him go. Send him away. Do not force him to fight you. Kaphtor needs no more ill fortune. Let us choose your cabal in the old way, as it has always been done."

He yanked her hands off his thighs. "Is that why you kiss me, to soften me towards my brother?"

She pressed her palm to his temple and stroked his hair. "Do you believe that?"

Slowly, the blaze of anger subsided. "No."

"As a woman and your lover, I always want more of you. More and more still. As a queen, I must think as I was taught. I fear the consequences of changing the rite. I don't understand why Themiste agreed to it, and it makes me uneasy. It is wrong, Chrysaleon. I think it will bring bad fortune upon us."

He closed his eyes and put his mouth against her throat before answering. "I can refuse you little, Aridela—but Menoetius remains my cabal. On this I will not relent. He and I will meet at the rise of Iakchos, and he will remain in the labyrinth, under guard. I forbid you to worry about him anymore."

"You forbid me?"

He didn't take back his words, though the way her brow lifted and her lips tensed suggested that might be the wisest course.

"You will force him to kill you then share my bed for a year," she said tightly. "And yet this is not my concern? I don't understand. Not when the mere suggestion of him lying with me—or me even thinking of him—sends you into such rage."

He forced a mollifying tone, and stroked her cheek. "I know you have a soft spot for him, but he is my brother, and we have spent our entire lives together. If I am to die for you, I need him to be the one who takes my life. He understands. I cannot explain it to you any better than that."

The mood seemed lost. Another thing to thank the bastard for.

Almost as though she read his mind, Aridela hesitantly returned her hand to his chest and traced one of the burn scars from the night of the Destruction. When he made no protest, she sent her tongue on an exploration of the sensitive spot behind his ear. "Let us not be angry," she whispered. "Instead, we should give each other our love and trust."

"Yes," he said, nodding.

"If I quicken, then the three of us—Themiste, Selene, and I—will bear children very close in age. Their bond will be strong. We shall raise them as sisters, or sisters and brothers." Sighing as he gathered her close and folded her beneath him, she said, "I will take such care. I shall not rise from this bed, if only the Lady will grant me the gift of your child."

He forgot Menoetius, Themiste, and even Glauce, as Aridela twined her legs around his hips.

ALEXIARE NOTED HOW HIS LORD'S REGARD TURNED REPEATEDLY UP TO THE sky. It was no wonder. The evening's lofty turrets of color drew everyone's attention, even, apparently, Chrysaleon's, though Mycenae's king was seldom moved by nature's artistry. The pinkish glow was not uncommon, but there were also greens, blues, oranges, and purples. The hues were vivid and startling, as though the heavens had donned a layered gown woven of rainbows. It had been this way ever since the Destruction. Perhaps the gods wanted to soften what they had done.

Alexiare couldn't help a few errant imaginings of he and Chrysaleon lying together, holding each other, washed in this beautiful light. But such fantasies were dangerous, and he quickly squelched them.

Themiste stood before the people as she did every year on this day, to mark the beginning of the fermentation of the mead. This year she also offered the revelation of her quickening. Holding her head high, she swore without blushing, stammer, or pause that no man had touched her. Though she spoke with impressive confidence, Alexiare noticed her hands, half-hidden by the drape of her robes. They were clenched into white knuckled fists.

Would she keep the secret? Or would she, perhaps in a trance brought on by one of her potions, confess her crime and Chrysaleon's part in it? Alexiare wondered if he or his beloved would ever again draw an easy breath as long as they lived on this singularly cursed island.

The people fell to their knees, gripped in awe and astonishment. Prince Kios and two other counselors guided Themiste through the crowd so everyone could touch her and acquire a small portion of her miraculous sanctity.

She was gifted and ambitious. She had as much, if not more, to lose by confession than Chrysaleon did. Surely Themiste would never betray her mortal weakness and its consequences.

He leaned closer to the king and plucked at his arm. "My lord, you have inherited your father's legendary potency," he said quietly. "He fathered many children besides those your mother bore and delighted in every one."

Chrysaleon didn't reply immediately. Perhaps he was thinking of his imprisoned half brother. It was quite true that Idómeneus had scattered his seed indiscriminately. Chrysaleon himself had fathered several children on the rocky mainland citadel—if their mothers could be believed.

"Yes," Chrysaleon said at last. "Yet the child I most want is Aridela's. I would give a fortune to know the secret of enticing that stubborn womb to produce."

With a sympathetic smile, Alexiare said, "Please the Lady." He added, "Daphoenissa spoke truly. Yon priestess bears the fruit of your sowing. You must take care, my lord, or you will always be surrounded by heavy-bellied shrews clamoring for favors."

"You love to bait me, old man. Watch yourself, or I will send you back to the citadel. You'll have nothing to do but annoy Gelanor and live a life of dullness."

Alexiare blinked in mock surprise. "Have you given up your throne? You intend never to return?"

Chrysaleon snorted. He rose to leave, but paused as Alexiare said, "My lord?"

"What do you want now?"

"I've had an idea." With a cautious glance around them to make sure they hadn't drawn undue attention, Alexiare led Chrysaleon to the periphery of the crowd.

"What is it? The queen will be looking for me."

"Patience." In a low voice, Alexiare asked, "What if the Immortals caused Themiste to quicken with your child because the queen never will?"

"She has started children, and could again," Chrysaleon replied, scowling.

Alexiare had decided not to share the rumors he'd lately been hearing in the marketplaces. It was being whispered that the queen's miscarriage was due to an accidental glimpse of Asterion, the Beast imprisoned in the labyrinth. Menoetius had become so dreadful that people believed the mere sight of him was enough to cause a woman to bleed and lose her baby. Alexiare knew what would happen if Chrysaleon heard these tales. It didn't matter that it couldn't be true. The king would lose all semblance of control and Aridela might well suffer the brunt of his rage. For some reason Alexiare didn't quite understand, he felt very protective of her. He must be getting soft.

"I don't mean to anger you," he said soothingly, "but the signs are not good. The queen ended her first pregnancy and one since has ended itself. Though we may wish and pray for her to achieve this desire, we should not blind ourselves to a more unhappy possibility."

Chrysaleon gestured impatiently. "Yes, yes. What is it you want to say?"

"Lay claim to this babe—no, not by confessing. Lay *mystical* claim to it. If Themiste bears a daughter, you and the queen could announce your intention of bringing up the holy oracle's child as your heir. A female would strengthen your ties to the throne, and who knows what we could accomplish with a boy? Daphoenissa said this child will somehow halt the king-sacrifice. You should align yourself with it in all possible ways."

"Yes...." Chrysaleon turned his head and stared, narrow-eyed, at Themiste. People thronged around her, pulling at her skirts, clasping her hands. "And so one more piece of my moera falls into place."

Alexiare folded his arms and smiled.

"I will propose it to Aridela," Chrysaleon said. "She won't like it. She continues to hope she will conceive."

"Make her agree, my lord. I feel certain this is the course you must take. And there is something else."

"Does your mind never cease plotting?"

"Not when the plot may assist you, my king."

"Tell me."

"I have been perfecting our plans to avert the sacrifice. Come, my lord. Allow me to explain." Almost floating with satisfaction and a renewed sense of achievement, Alexiare led his master farther from listening ears.

CHRYSALEON MADE HIS WAY TO THE ROYAL SEATS.

Aridela patted the space next to her. "You're frowning," she said. "Has Alexiare irritated you again?" She often teased him over their unique relationship, one almost of father and son, she liked to say, or mentor and pupil.

He glowered. "I knew I would regret bringing him back with me from Mycenae."

She leaned against his arm as they watched Themiste move through the crowd. "It seems to me the priestess must have quickened with this child for a reason," he said. "We should not ignore the Lady's blessing. Perhaps she sends it for you, since you seem unable to carry one."

Dismay wiped the pleasure from her face. She straightened, pulling away from him. "Athene placed the child into Themiste's womb. It would never be ours, even if we said it was."

"Why can't the priestesses say words, make a rite of it?" He paused, biting his lip. "My time grows short. I fear I will leave no mark upon Crete or the world. I will be nothing—forgotten when your acolytes pour my blood on the land and you take my brother to your bed."

He watched his words cut into her. Her eyes clouded and her shoulders hunched. He forced himself to speak no words of reassurance, and kept his expression cold.

"Because you ask, I will consider it," she said at last. "But only if Themiste has a daughter, and if I do not quicken. Only as a last resort."

He nodded and kissed her.

Themiste returned to the hillock, the bangles in her skirts and her bare breasts glowing in the strange, shimmering light from the sky.

Aridela and Chrysaleon joined her. Only the briefest glance passed between Chrysaleon and Themiste before she looked away.

The queen presented Themiste with her golden labrys. There was cheering. Pennants flew into the air. The people were exhilarated by this miracle that represented new life and a return to plenty. No one doubted the promise it offered.

The sun descended behind Mount Ida. Torches were lit.

Hobbling their legs and tying wings made of partridge feathers to their arms, men crowded onto the wood and marble dance floor with its sacred maze pattern. They dragged one wing in imitation of the revered birds and circled, calling to prospective mates. Women shouted encouragement and made lecherous conjectures about the elaborate codpieces on display. The men grew bolder, making lewd thrusts towards the women, several of whom stepped onto the maze and joined the dance.

Wine, beer, and mead flowed freely. As the moon ascended, Chrysaleon was urged to begin the mead-making ritual. He found Aridela, who must have had her share of drink, for she giggled and leaned against him, her eyes heavy-lidded. He hoisted her onto his back and carried her, clasping her legs around his middle. Someone handed her a kylix filled with wine, which she offered to him. Laughter erupted as wine spilled through his beard and over his tunic, and the image of a man preparing to take a woman from behind was revealed in the bottom of the bowl. He cantered, mimicking a horse, forcing Aridela to drop the bowl and grab his shoulders to keep from falling. The pervasive air of arousal affected him too; he felt the press of her breasts against his shoulders and choked down a desire to lay her in the grass and satisfy his lust. He wasn't drunk enough to yield to such uninhibited behavior, though he saw other couples slinking away hand in hand to do that very thing.

One of the priests brought forth a goat, its back padded with fur. Themiste adorned Aridela in an embroidered robe covered with crystals that sparkled in the torchlight, and gave her a golden apple and a staff, wrapped in ivy and topped with pinecones, which the Cretans called a thyrsus. The apple was sobering, as Chrysaleon knew by now what it symbolized.

The priest assisted Aridela onto the goat's back. Two priestesses walked on either side, one carrying a live hare and the other a raven in a withy cage. Led by a priest holding the goat's bridle, Aridela, her priestesses, and the effusive crowd circuited the path to the oak grove at the foot of Mount Juktas. Cheese and wine passed from hand to hand. The talk grew louder, more amorous, the closer they came to the grove. Hands slipped beneath Chrysaleon's tunic. Women, young and old, rubbed against him. He couldn't help responding, though his wife rode just ahead. Men pressed close around her. Were they touching her as these women were touching him? Red-hued jealousy tore at him, yet he couldn't reach her. Too many people blocked his way.

The clearing held seven carts, piled high with leather sacks already filled with the proper combination of honey and water, which would gradually ferment into mead over the next forty days. Aridela slipped off the goat and joined Themiste in the center of the clearing. The crystals in her robe reflected light from the tall torches.

Chrysaleon finally reached her side.

"We need not participate," she said. "They only want us to begin the rites. Then we may please ourselves."

Themiste held up the hare by its ears and lifted the withy cage, waiting until she had silence and expectant attention. "See and know what will come," she said.

The people chorused assents.

"As the hound gives chase to the hare, so does Goddess Athene chase the bull-king. With her net she snares him. He returns from death as raven, bird of prophecy."

A pavilion stood at the edge of the clearing. Inside, a cauldron simmered above an ember fire. Themiste handed the hare and raven to one of her attendants and went into the hut.

"She will breathe the fumes and enter a trance," Aridela told Chrysaleon. "I hope Athene speaks through her and explains the holy child's purpose."

He shrugged, hoping she would not.

When the oracle reappeared, she moved slowly, with assistance, back to the queen and consort. "Help me," she said. "I feel strange." The queen supported her on one side and Chrysaleon on the other.

Aridela spoke to the people surrounding them. "Lady Athene offers us her divine forgiveness. She shows it by placing a holy child in the womb of Themiste, her faithful servant. Can this be anything other than a promise of life and new beginnings?"

A wave of nods and agreement met these words. Many made the sign against evil, and some wept.

Sending her voice out over the assemblage, Themiste announced, "The labyrinth is still dangerous, impassable in many places. We cannot think of sending the contestants down there. Instead the sacred contest will be held here, in this clearing."

Chrysaleon barely stifled a sneer of cynicism as he watched the smiles and animated praise for the decision. This would be the first time in all of Kaphtor's history that commoners could view the famous confrontation and slaying. He knew that was the only reason it was accepted so quickly.

Themiste's next announcement didn't go as well. "Kaphtor will hold no Games this year." She lifted her hand in a demand for silence at the immediate shouts of protest. "I have seen this. Our bull-king has been given my permission to choose his cabal, and he has chosen Menoetius, his blood brother. All will be as it was but for these two things. For one year only, the Games are suspended. This we do in mourning and respect for the loss of Queen Helice, and for the many deaths each one of us has suffered."

Moans of *the Beast!* undulated through the crowd. Some seemed fearful, others intrigued. Fascination energized the people.

Gradually, the mood changed. What Themiste asked was not too much after all. The most important aspect—Chrysaleon's death— would remain the same. Excitement overrode everything else. The people would witness brutal bloodshed, and they would see for themselves the ghastly Asterion.

Themiste's knees buckled. She drew in a ragged breath. Aridela seized her waist, struggling to support her. Together she and Chrysaleon lowered her to the ground. Startled cries replaced the cheers. The throng pressed closer.

The oracle's hands clawed the air as if to ward off an attack. Her eyes rolled up in their sockets until only unnerving white remained. Her back arched. She panted and gasped. Then she seemed to stop breathing altogether.

"Goddess," Aridela cried. "Spare us, Athene, my Mother. We need our oracle."

Horrified silence fell. Then, thankfully, Themiste released a soft, drawn out moan. Sweat beaded her forehead.

"Bring Rhené," Aridela ordered one of the maids. "Hurry." The woman kneeling beside her rose and ran off, calling for Kaphtor's royal healer.

Themiste turned her head to Aridela, but her eyes remained unfocused, the irises sliding from side to side. When she spoke, her voice offered no inflection—nothing but cold dispassion.

The youthful sun will marry the ancient moon. He who laughs will lie with she who is beautiful to men. Curse the usurper, the changer of the Way. He shall follow without rest, without joy, without relief, until the final devastation of the heavens. He shall follow begging, but love will run from him, and he will receive only sorrow and regret until the world is old and tired, and razed by war.

Her eyes closed and her breath escaped in a long sigh. Chrysaleon stared, chilled with apprehension. Aridela screamed, "No!"

The oracle's eyelids trembled. Her hands moved restlessly. "You cling to your blindness," she muttered. Again, she turned her head toward Aridela. "You will suffer. The world will suffer. As you are betrayed, so you will in turn betray those who put their faith in you."

The crowd parted for Rhené. She felt Themiste's face and hands, and listened to her breathing.

"Carry her to the palace," she ordered, and several men came forward, lifting the oracle in their arms.

Chrysaleon rose, his muscles stiff and cramped. Consumed with unease, he met Aridela's gaze. She stood still, her eyes black and fathomless.

What had Themiste said? He strained to recall. *He who laughs will lie with she who is beautiful to men.* What omen was this? Who did Themiste curse?

The changer of the Way. The usurper. Everyone would think she spoke of Harpalycus. They would shake their heads and wonder how a dead man could still threaten the people of Kaphtor.

But he couldn't fool himself so easily. Certainty crept through him. Somehow Themiste, or the Goddess who spoke through her, knew what he planned to do.

3

Moon of Mead-Making

ARIDELA REMAINED AT THEMISTE'S SIDE, HOLDING HER HAND, UNTIL Rhené assured her the oracle was in no danger. She needed rest, the healer said, and that meant she needed to be left alone.

Neoma talked Aridela into going with her to Mount Juktas, where they would leave offerings at the temple. As they were leaving they came across Selene. Hardly anyone saw her these days, for she was always in the labyrinth with Menoetius. Struck by her paleness and the grief in her eyes, Aridela convinced her to go along, using the health of the baby as an excuse the Phrygian couldn't ignore.

The temple priestesses came out to greet them, bringing refreshments. Aridela's companions accepted eagerly, as the day was warm and the journey dusty. After Aridela had a drink of water, she decided to walk on to the clearing that held so many memories.

She was pleased at the appearance of the forest. The trees were thick and leafy upon either side of the path, the water in the creek cold, swift, and fresh. Wildflowers peeked from shady soil, waving as if to say *pick me, pick me,* which she did. Perhaps the storm of suffocating ash had missed this area altogether.

In due course the trees gave way to the clearing where she, her mother, and Themiste had brought Iphiboë last year, to prepare her for the grove dedication.

She sat on the ground and began weaving a flower necklace as she reminisced about her sister, and her reckless cousin Isandros, her childhood nurse Halia, and then of the day she had brought Menoetius here, when she was ten and he seventeen. It felt like lifetimes had passed since then. He'd been young, handsome, his smiles easy and quick. Neither had any premonition of what was to come.

"My lady?"

She released a small gasp, startled by a man's voice right next to her, and scrambled to her feet.

Then it struck her. The acrid stink of smoldering ashes.

Her heart began to pound so furiously she thought for an instant she might faint. But this was not the shade of Harpalycus. He was an older man, dressed in a typical loincloth, with armbands that signified he was a soldier. His hair was black but for a few streaks of grey. His eyes, too, were black, not anything like the cruel blue gaze Harpalycus had leveled upon her as he sought to make her lose control and release her hatred so he could then punish her for it.

But that smell. She couldn't get it out of her nose, and stepped away from him even as she chastised herself. Why did this keep happening? Why did she continue to fear a dead man, when she knew he was gone?

"Who are you?" she asked. "Why do you disturb me?"

He bowed, his face and manner respectful. "I apologize, my lady," he said. "I saw you here. I wanted to make certain you needed no assistance."

She relaxed a little. "Thank you," she said. "I am perfectly well."

The man glanced briefly around them then he lifted his gaze to hers.

Terror writhed from her core and raced up her throat, blocking it so she couldn't breathe.

"Have you told your consort the truth yet?"

She hardly heard this strange question, for memories of Harpalycus's attacks were flooding her mind.

He stepped forward, seizing her wrists, pulling her close. "Have you told him how much you liked what I did to you?"

A sound ripped through the air. What was it? A cross between a moan and a scream. It sounded like an animal being tortured.

She tried to yank free, but his grip was immovable. How well she remembered his strength.

"Are you ready to take what I offer? Do you want to be one of the Immortals with me, and rule at my side?"

He leaned in close, suffocating her in his singular, pungent smell, and spoke close to her ear. "I see you haven't lost that succulent hatred that sets my blood on fire. I have not yet tired of you, queen of Crete. My slave." He licked her cheek.

Awareness faded beneath a cold black wave, sliding in at the edges of her mind and blotting out everything it touched. Nothing like it had ever happened to her before. What would he do if she were insensate and unable to fight him?

But she couldn't stop it, no matter how deeply she breathed or how hard she yanked, trying to break his grip. The drowning swell crashed behind her eyes and carried her away into a deep black ocean.

"Aridela, can you hear me? Wake up."

She opened her eyes. Selene's face was just above hers. Gradually, she realized her head was cradled on Selene's lap.

"What...?" Her voice was hoarse and rusty. "Water."

Selene motioned to someone. Neoma's face appeared, holding a bowl. Selene held it to her lips and she drank. The water was refreshing. They must have scooped it from the stream in the forest.

Yes, she was in the clearing—her clearing, a treasured place of dreams, of stars and magic, of Iphiboë and her mother, of Menoetius when he was her beloved Carmanor, and perhaps most importantly, of the Goddess.

Had she fallen asleep? If so, her friends would not be so anxious and afraid. They would be laughing at her.

"My head hurts." She had to whisper, though the water soothed her throat somewhat.

Several of the priestesses from the temple helped her stand. She leaned on them and they supported her all the way to the temple, where she was put into a bed and given soup with leeks and barley.

After a few sips, she fell asleep, only to wake like a flash of lightning at some point, remembering all that had happened. She screamed, bringing Selene, who had been sleeping on a pallet next to her bed, upright and bending over her.

Selene sat on the bed and held her as she sobbed. The priestesses and Neoma came in, startled and fighting off vestiges of sleep.

"What happened, Aridela?"

"It was Harpalycus." Aridela choked on the name. "He is not dead.

He followed me. He was in the clearing." An unnerving thought came over her. What had he done to her after she fainted?

She nudged Selene away and put her hands under the coverlet, under her tunic, feeling, searching for evidence. There was no soreness. No blood. No scent of him. Surely something would remain if he had raped her again.

"Aridela." Neoma's forehead wrinkled with concern. "Harpalycus is dead. My cousin, I swear to you he is dead."

Selene held Aridela to her breast and rocked her. Aridela felt her friend's sigh, felt her exchange a worried glance with her cousin and the priestesses.

They must think her mad.

Maybe it was true.

THERE WAS NO WAY TO KEEP WHAT HAPPENED FROM CHRYSALEON, EVEN IF Aridela wanted to. Their attendants were dismissed so they could be alone.

"Tell me," he said. There was an odd, dark look to his eyes she couldn't quite decipher, but it brought back memories of his furious jealousy in the apple grove. He crossed his arms over his chest.

Aridela tried to make her voice sound reasonable, tried to make the shivering subside. "I went alone to the clearing beyond the temple. I was merely sitting there. I didn't hear the man come up behind me. He was just there, all at once. He—he—" She stopped as she heard her voice rise, felt the panic rise too, with hints of the same black swelling wave.

"Did he look like Harpalycus?"

"No," she said. Then her throat closed and she couldn't speak. She began to weep and shake. He took her to the bed and lay beside her, holding her against his bare chest.

CHRYSALEON FELL ASLEEP. WHEN ARIDELA LIFTED HIS ARM OFF HER, HE rolled onto his back, releasing a snore, but didn't wake.

Every sound, no matter how faint or innocuous, prompted nauseating rushes of fear. She'd bitten her lip so often it was sensitive and swollen. Her eyes stung.

She rose from the bed and padded across the chamber, into the corridor, and down the central staircase to the courtyard.

All was awash in the pitch black of deepest night. Cool breezes eddied around her. As her eyes adjusted to the dark, she made out the vast flat space of the courtyard, and beyond that, the hulking shadow of the palace wall. Here and there a lamp glimmered.

She went down the steps on the west side leading to the shrine, but didn't enter that chamber. She passed it, running her fingertips along the wall to keep her bearings.

Low voices broke the silence. She knew there would be guards, two at least, at the entry into the labyrinth. She slipped past them soundlessly, hidden by shadows.

She had to drop to her knees and crawl forward as she searched for the grate she remembered from childhood. When she found it, she felt around its edges. It was simply an air duct, not much bigger than the width of her body, covered by an ancient, rotted latticework of wood that was easily pulled away.

Not allowing herself to think, she worked herself head first into the shaft, creeping along a downward sloping incline carved into the earth like a wormhole, until her hands encountered nothing but air before her. She grabbed a clump of roots sticking out of the dirt on one side— still there, after so many years—and slid free, using the roots to keep herself from falling on her head. She twisted, turning herself upright. Her bare toes touched the dirt floor and she released the roots, straightening. She was in the labyrinth.

Moving on instinct, she walked. Her body knew where she wanted to go. Her thoughts gave way to her body's will.

Eventually she found herself in the corridor leading to Menoetius's prison. Lamps placed in the walls provided illumination for those who brought him food. Most had expired but a few still gave off feeble light.

She came to the door and stopped. Her mind dropped into what seemed an empty, bottomless crater. She lost awareness, of the chill in the air, the musty smell, and of the dim passage stretching away in either direction.

Perhaps she should have been startled when she felt someone approach from behind. One hand rested on her shoulder briefly then slid across her chest to her other shoulder, followed by a second arm around her waist, effectively trapping her. Menoetius's door was still closed and there had been no sound of warning. Yet she knew it was he, the one she sought. The lord of the labyrinth.

He put his cheek against the side of her neck, as he had often done during their time in the Araden mountains, and, more recently, within this prison. His body infused her with warmth, surrounded her with the faint scent of clouds and fallen leaves. She remembered the first time she had inhaled that essence, when she was ten, and he was carrying her to safety, to life.

Like a deluge breaking through a dam, her mind woke. Fear slid away. She leaned against him, the Beast, her bastion, and closed her dry, burning eyes.

She wished they could somehow return in time to the day she, a silly, spoiled child with a topknot and a heart full of callow infatuation, had taken him to Lady Athene's clearing. If only they could find a way back, and from that point on, do everything differently.

"Do you feel her?" she asked softly. "The Goddess?"

She hadn't really thought he would remember. But he whispered, "Yes," as he had that day, and added, "Don't leave me alone this time."

4

Moon of White Light

THE MOON OF WHITE LIGHT REPLACED THE MOON OF MEAD-MAKING, and the days crept inexorably on towards the rise of Iakchos. In ten nights, then nine, then eight, Crete's foreign king, the king who would forever be associated with the Destruction and the invasion of Harpalycus, would die.

Knossos and the palace grew stiflingly crowded as the citizens of Kaphtor, high and low, peasant and lord, poured in from every corner of the island. Alexiare spent his days in marketplaces and other haunts, listening, watching, gauging the mood.

"Our plans are working better than I hoped," he reported to Chrysaleon. "Much unhappiness is brewing. The people love and admire you, my lord. Ah, how they love you. You are foreign, for one thing. That draws everyone's interest, but they know this worked in their favor, for it was your father's army that helped defeat Harpalycus the Butcher, and would he have involved himself in the troubles of Crete had his son's life not been in danger? No. I've heard many declare they would still be slaves but for you." A lump formed in his throat as he added, more tenderly than was safe, "The women coo and flutter over your beautiful face, your skin that reflects the light like a statue of gold."

Chrysaleon snorted his disgust at this poetry and fondled his dagger hilt. "That won't stop them from screaming in rapture as their axe spills my blood." He speared a date with the point of his blade while making a bloodthirsty grimace. "How many of those women will sing hymns as they tear flesh from my bones?"

"Do not lose hope, my lord. These strong emotions work in our favor. The people of Kaphtor will gladly follow new direction if given the chance. Inside, in here," he struck his chest with his fist, "they want to save you." Peering keenly at his master, he added, "Many spoke of seeing you at the queen's side when she gave the decrees, and how she allowed you to make the offerings in her stead. Helice rarely allowed her consorts such distinction. Though she doesn't realize it, Queen Aridela helps our cause. She, too, truly needs but a nudge, the slightest excuse to embrace our changes."

"What of the vision? Have you turned it to our favor?"

"I described how the dead hero Damasen came to you and called you his brother. I had them all gawping when I told them he swore an eternity of friendship with you. That story has spread, gaining renown, as I knew it would, as did the rumor I started about Menoetius. Everyone believes him a monster, frothing and raging in the labyrinth. No one wants the Beast to be Kaphtor's next bull-king." He laughed and slapped his thighs. "I heard one man claim he eats nothing but human flesh, and every citizen will be required to sacrifice their daughters for his unholy appetite."

Only then did Chrysaleon smile. It was his first in many days. Alexiare's exultation soared. The time was ripe for change. People drank in his suggestions like honeyed milk. They were more than willing to see the king-sacrifice end, as long as it didn't anger Athene or wake the Earth Bull.

Alexiare returned to the Knossos marketplaces, eager to hear how his carefully crafted gossip was affecting people. Many bewailed their hero's upcoming death. He lingered near one of the wells, where he could eavesdrop on the common women who gathered there every day. It was easy to listen. No one ever paid a bent old man any mind.

"What of the cabal?"

"The Beast, you mean?"

"Is it really true? Has he been…changed?"

"The Lady did it—a just curse and punishment for attacking our Zagreus."

"My daughter heard him bellowing one night. She was terrified."

"The council decided to spare his life. He will still perform his sacred duty."

"Asterion won't die?"

"The Zagreus himself requested leniency."

The women shook their heads and clucked.

"Queen Aridela's dearest friend grows heavy with the Beast's spawn and begged her to intercede."

Amid a flurry of fingers making the sign against evil, someone breathed, "She will give birth to a monster!"

"My sister is handmaid to the queen's cousin. She said the consort loves his brother too much to see him put to death, though it is surely what he deserves."

"Do you think the Solemn Ones drove Prince Menoetius to such an act?"

"And now they punish him...."

This was far more frightening than the Goddess's levied discipline. All the women made swift signs against evil and murmured prayers to ward off the attention of the unspeakable Erinyes.

"They don't plague mortals over any transgression," one grey-haired woman said. "Who did Asterion outrage?"

"All the gods," Alexiare volunteered. "He is cursed beyond any mortal."

The women stared at him, doubting yet fearful.

Prince Gelanor arrived at the head of a massive naval convoy. The fleet's sails, adorned with images of open-jawed lions, made a powerful impression as they snapped in the wind and caught the glint of the evening sun.

Alexiare heard unhappy conversations about how Mycenae now exceeded Crete in riches and might, and how High King Chrysaleon could no doubt overthrow Kaphtor if he wished. Yet he held back his warriors and consented to his doom at the Lady's hand.

He turned away, grinning as one woman, then her two daughters, burst into dramatic, heartrending sobs.

Gelanor and the Mycenaean counselors, barons, and retinue traveled in bronze-trimmed chariots to Labyrinthos. Their somber expressions suggested no approval of their king's decision to stand by his death-vow.

At the bull-king's final feast, Chrysaleon was given the queen's throne. Aridela sat in a smaller chair next to him.

Keeping to the shadows behind the throne, Alexiare was able to listen to the conversations of royalty without being noticed. When he saw the queen lean in to Gelanor, he crept closer.

"My lord," she said. "I hardly know what to say to you. I can only imagine how you feel."

Gelanor inclined his head. "My brother should be rewarded for what he, and my people, have done to help you. Chrysaleon himself is the only one keeping us from going to war."

Alexiare nodded, impressed at the strength in young Gelanor's voice and manner, and the bluntness in his speech. Who knew how this might aid Chrysaleon's cause? It certainly seemed to add to the queen's guilt.

"Forgive us." Aridela put her hand over his and kissed his cheek. "I am trapped, as is Chrysaleon. I have tried—" she stopped, shaking her head. Tears spilled from her eyes. "I cannot say it, for fear of what might happen."

"I know you don't want this," Gelanor said. "You are queen of these people. Why can you not do something?"

Chrysaleon broke in. "It is the council who wields the power on Crete, not the queen. And even more, it is the Destruction. No one, from queen to poorest peasant, wants to draw the fires and ash. You do not know what it was like, my brother."

Minos Themiste interrupted this exchange by entering the chamber and making her way to the queen's table. Aridela rose to greet and embrace the oracle, who had slowly recovered from her illness at the mead-making rite. During the ensuing forty days, she had remained cloistered in her mountain shrine, refusing to see anyone. Tonight was the first time she'd left her self-imposed seclusion. Alexiare perused her, but saw no sign of her pregnancy, and could only hope she hadn't ended it somehow.

He remained hidden behind the Zagreus, observing Crete's holy oracle as he considered the words she'd spoken in her smoke-induced trance, her threats of devastation, sorrow, war, and punishment.

Even as prophecies went, the one Themiste spoke was difficult. It sparked in him a niggling unease.

Aridela moved so she could sit next to Themiste at the end of the table, leaving Gelanor and Chrysaleon to talk in relative privacy.

Chrysaleon drank too much. His eyes glittered. He swayed and slurred. Alexiare willed his master to show some control. Did the young fool not realize he had to keep his wits, now more than ever? Yet right after, the slave lost all rational thought as he imagined touching Chrysaleon's cheek and receiving an ardent caress in return, though he well knew such a thing could never happen unless Chrysaleon was drunk beyond reason.

At last the bard finished his long tale of Kaphtor's victory over Harpalycus and the part Chrysaleon played. Banging their cups, the grim-faced Mycenaean nobles cheered…and muttered.

Alexiare moved as close as he could to the queen and Themiste, counting on his status as a slave to keep him invisible.

"My friend." Aridela rested her hand on the oracle's arm. "I must ask something of you, something monumental."

Themiste blinked. She clutched the curled tendril of hair in front of her ear and pulled on it. "Yes?" Her voice was like a faint exhale, quick and breathless.

"Chrysaleon and I want to give your child the veneration she deserves. Such a holy gift from Athene should be properly recognized."

Alexiare's throat closed in sympathy at the startled terror that flashed across Themiste's face. "G-gift…?"

Aridela squeezed the oracle's hand. "I have loved you like a sister. Like a second mother. I would do anything for you."

"I know." Themiste's gaze faltered and fell. Her face turned alternately white and red.

"Though I pray and make offerings, I have not conceived. Chrysaleon and I have tried so hard, yet nothing."

Themiste covered Aridela's hand with her own.

"I beg you not to think me heartless or selfish," Aridela continued. "If you have a daughter as the omens suggest, I want to name her my heir and Chrysaleon her mortal father. This child is a wonder—of course the true father is a god, perhaps Velchanos, or there may be no father at all. We will never attempt to hide that. But we can give her power and glory, and she will inherit the country. Your child will be queen." She paused to close her eyes and rub them tiredly. "I don't know if Chrysaleon's seed won't live, or my womb will not bear. Perhaps something happened to me after I lost this last baby. My most ardent wish is for a child I can call his, and now, unless I have conceived in the last few days, it is too late for us."

Themiste blushed as her gaze left Aridela's and met the consort's. They stared at each other while Alexiare cringed and worried his beloved, drunken prince would give away their secrets.

"Yes," she said at last. "Surely Goddess Athene placed this child inside me to carry for you. When she is born, I will place her into your hands. I pray that with her birth, an era of prosperity will begin, even as our new crops blossom."

Alexiare sensed her grateful relief. She actually smiled. Chrysaleon had upended the woman's life. She had vowed to remain untouched by man and she had guided the citizens of Kaphtor, enjoying unquestioned awe and respect. Now she was forced into reluctant collusion with the barbarian, and had to lie—not just to Aridela but all the people. Twinges of guilt plagued him as the oracle lifted one thin hand and pulled again at her hair, a nervous gesture he'd never noticed before. Perhaps she could convince herself that this was Athene's intent all along, and she had only done what was necessary. He hoped so.

"Our brave year-king gives everything he has," Themiste said. Tears flowed from her eyes and Aridela's too. "But Velchanos always rises, renewed after his season of sacrifice. There is never new life without death. No new god without annihilation. Wise men accept their fate, and in the acceptance earn glory unimaginable." She stumbled over the last part. She and Aridela embraced.

Chrysaleon's fists struck the table so hard the crockery clattered. "We are moved like playthings to the whim of the Immortals. No matter what we want, they have their unfathomable way."

Themiste flushed, but Aridela rose and went to him. She put her arms around his neck, kissing him repeatedly. "That is as it should be," she said. "Be easy, my love. I am with you."

Alexiare slipped from the room, stealing through deserted corridors and down gloomy stairwells, for nothing but a sliver of moon remained in the sky. It would be gone, invisible to mortals on the night Chrysaleon faced his cabal in the killing field.

At length he came to the underground shrine, illuminated by faint lamp glow. Alexiare stifled a shiver as he approached the silent, looming goddess pillar, flanked on either side with six-foot cypress poles topped with double-axes, and over a thousand years of blood at the base. Beyond the pillar was the image of Athene, carved who knew how long ago? The delicate wood had turned black with age and smoke but she was still beautiful, and seemed to stare at him without surprise.

Lingering musky incense hung in the air.

Seven years ago, in this very chamber, the child-princess Aridela would have died if not for Menoetius. Alexiare remembered fearing that the king of Mycenae's son would be put to death and war would come to Crete. Instead the bastard had been lauded and praised for his singular role in saving her life.

Now he was again imprisoned in their labyrinth. "The Beast," he was called. His life-thread was nearly unraveled.

"Forgive me, Mistress." Alexiare picked up the holy labrys from its stand and by the light of a clay lamp, unwound the leather strapping on the handle, exposing pale virgin wood. He set to work making deep narrow cuts with a fine craft saw. When finished, he filled the incisions with softened beeswax and smoothed the edges. He shortened the leather strap and abraded the underside until it was thin and fragile, and would easily snap. Then he carefully rewrapped it, taking his time so his interference would be undetectable.

He replaced the axe in its stand and bowed to Athene's image. "My king will make a fine ruler, Lady. He will give his best to you and his home country. How can he do this, if he is dead?" Stretching out his arms, palms up, he sent his mind into deep contemplation. "If you are angry, send me a sign, and I will undo all I have done."

Nothing happened. The earth didn't shake. There was no whisper of thunder, no warning call from raven or owl. The lamps didn't even flicker.

He gave another respectful bow and left, pondering the ways he could slip a debilitating amount of poppy into Menoetius's wine. For he knew, though he was wise enough to keep it to himself, that Menoetius was the better combatant, and would defeat Chrysaleon unless extraordinary measures were taken.

As he had done a year ago, Chrysaleon entered into seclusion to prepare for his battle, alone but for a trio of handmaids who would wait upon him and see to it he had no food and only the prescribed amount of water. No handmaid could be persuaded to attend Asterion in his labyrinthine prison, so all he had was Selene.

Aridela went into seclusion as well, too grief-stricken to bear the company of anyone. The future could no longer be postponed, denied, or ignored. Next time she saw Chrysaleon, he would die.

She wept until no more tears flowed. Then she lay, staring at the wall. Fed by her despair, the shadows that once sought to engulf her during her month in the mountain cave leaped up with revived energy.

One hand pressed to her stomach kept alive her grief for the baby who might have anchored her and returned some happiness. Now there was nothing. No reason to continue. She didn't possess Helice's strength or wisdom, and could not pretend she did. Not even the knowledge that Menoetius would be pardoned after he fulfilled his deadly obligation could lessen her misery.

Deep in the stillness of her second sleepless night, she thought she smelled ashes, just a whiff then it was gone, but it sent her thoughts back to what happened in the clearing on Mount Juktas. The smell of the man, the threat he exuded, the panic he caused. She felt as though someone was in her chamber, hidden by darkness yet staring at her, and she came up out of bed with a cry that brought her handmaid running. The girl lit lamps and searched every corner but of course she found nothing.

When Aridela remembered the comfort Chrysaleon's slave provided after her miscarriage, she sent for him. It seemed to her Alexiare was the only one who could understand her agony. Perhaps they could suffer together over what was coming. He arrived promptly, coaxed her onto her balcony, and sat beside her like a devoted dog, respecting her need for silence yet somehow lending her solace simply by being there.

It was little surprise that at some point she would confide in him about what happened on Mount Juktas. He had always been gentle, he seemed to truly care about her, and moreover, he was extremely intelligent.

She related the incident as best she could remember it, and was surprised at the intensity of his interest.

"Call Kaphtor's warriors out for inspection," he said. "I will help you. We will search until this man is found. He is dangerous, my lady. I find it hard to believe nothing has been done about this before now."

She shrugged, giving an embarrassed laugh. "No doubt because I claimed he was Harpalycus. Everyone knows that cannot be, so they dismissed it as a bad dream."

"He could be one of Harpalycus's men, though, who managed to hide from us. Did no one think of that?"

This made so much sense that she thought perhaps she wasn't being persecuted by the Erinyes or descending into a frightening sickness of the mind after all.

She gave the order.

Alexiare hobbled along with her as she came out of the palace. Her soldiers stood in precise lines, dressed in polished battle gear.

Each one inclined his head or went down on one knee as she passed, searching for the one face she never saw.

"He isn't here," she said after the last man was perused.

"Not here, perhaps," said Alexiare, "but that does not mean he isn't on Kaphtor. These are only the soldiers and guards of Knossos and the palace. He could be anywhere by now." His aggravation was clear to see.

The general who walked with them asked her who or what she was seeking. She gave him a description, at which point he frowned. "That could be one of my men—a troublemaker called Duripi, but unfortunately he was found dead yesterday, my lady, in one of the back alleys in the city. He had many enemies."

Alexiare insisted on seeing the body.

"I warn you," the general said, "it is badly decayed."

The putrefaction and smell was so severe Aridela had to keep her nose and mouth covered with a swatch of perfumed linen.

A pinkish, stinking, gelatinous substance covered the body and seemed to be rapidly decomposing it into liquid. Even as she gazed upon it, a finger fell off the hand and disintegrated into formless goo.

Hadn't she glimpsed a similar secretion oozing from Harpalycus's sliced throat the day she'd killed him? She couldn't be certain. Her memory of that event had never been easy to recall, no doubt because she'd been only half-conscious, and nearly blinded by his blood.

Alexiare didn't seem repelled by the stench or horrific moldering. He examined the corpse with great interest, even squishing the goo between his fingers. He nodded when Aridela said she thought it was the man who had terrorized her in the mountain clearing.

"There will be no way to find him now," Alexiare said, "unless he wants us to."

"What?" Aridela said, startled out of hypnotized revulsion by this unfathomable statement.

"Forgive me, my lady." He dismissively waved away his comment. "It appears your tormentor is gone, and can no longer bother you."

"Yes, thank you for helping me." She gave him leave to go rest. He did look tired. His eyes were shadowed, and his wrinkles seemed deeper. No doubt he was as grief-stricken as she at the imminent loss of his master. She watched him limp away. *No way to find him now unless he wants us to.*

She held great affection for Chrysaleon's old slave, but he really was odd at times.

Moon of White Light

CHRYSALEON ROSE FROM THE BATH. TWO DOE-EYED PRIESTESSES PATTED him dry, intoning the holy words as they waved branches heavy with oak leaves.

Our brave year-king gives everything he has. Does not Velchanos rise after his season of sacrifice? There is never new life without death, no new god without annihilation. Wise men accept their fate, and in the acceptance earn glory unimaginable.

They painted his eyelids and drew bold scarlet serpents across his back and chest. As they bound his hair, praising it for its uncommon color and softness, they brushed against him, their fingers creeping between his legs to make him erect and powerful.

The third priestess offered him wine and bread. Chrysaleon was monstrously hungry after three days of fasting, but he would never forget how their concoctions had nearly unmanned him at the last great sacrifice, and curtly refused.

They dressed him in a white loincloth and bronze-studded belt. A lion skin was arranged over his shoulders, and a heavy gold circlet carved with holy designs placed on his head.

"Where is my cabal?" he asked.

"Being purified," the youngest priestess replied.

He knew better than to believe Alexiare's naïve claims that

Menoetius would sacrifice himself rather than kill his brother. Alexiare was an old man. He had long ago forgotten how the blood could rage over a woman. Besides, too many unforgotten, unforgiven harms had built up through the years.

Menoetius would kill him if he could. The reluctant debt birthed from the lioness attack had vanished. Aridela had decimated it with her smile, her black eyes and warrior's body, her courage, her willingness to love, her devotion to the people of Kaphtor, her fierce loyalty. Menoetius must have surrendered his heart even as Chrysaleon had, that day they'd hidden in the forest and watched her swim with her companions in the pool on Mount Ida.

It was hard to hate his brother for sharing this particular weakness, yet somehow, at the same time, it fanned his hatred to murderous explosive heat.

The heavy flap over the pavilion's entrance was thrown back and in she walked, the object of his obsession. She waved to the maids. As they bowed their way out, she approached him, her gaze never leaving his. Her black eyes were like onyx.

He stiffened. His jaw clenched. *Your face holds neither guilt nor sorrow, queen of Crete.*

She placed one hand on his chest, spreading her fingers over the coiling serpents painted there.

"Do you dream of your next lover?" He ground his teeth, inwardly cursing. He hadn't meant to say that. But the picture of Aridela mating with Menoetius before the people of Crete flashed through his mind with cruel and bitter clarity.

Her gaze didn't waver. "My role bids me accept whatever male triumphs at the New Year. This man I invite into my bed. I cherish him above all others for the length of his days. Then his cabal comes to me, and after that, another."

Chrysaleon stepped back from her, breathing hard, his fists clenching and the tic beneath his eye throbbing.

"I will never care for any of them," she said. "No man will touch my heart, for you possess it, and will until the day of my death. Long years of loneliness will I endure until the time I can again see you and touch you, Chrysaleon of Mycenae."

Chrysaleon heard the truth in her words—saw it in the set of her lips, in the glistening, haunted obsidian of her eyes. She would remember.

Neither had slept during their last night together. Chrysaleon refused to recognize the desperation behind her kisses, and almost managed to forget his grim future in the seductive opiate of her embraces.

They stared at each other as untold crowds gathered to witness and celebrate his death. More had come than ever before, drawn by the enticement of watching the sacred battle, pulled by the fear and anticipation of seeing the terrible bull-man of the labyrinth. The number of bystanders was augmented as well by loyal Mycenaeans and members of Boreas, the secret council dedicated to overthrowing Crete and all like places.

He trailed his fingers over her brows, her cheeks, chin, and throat, where he felt the rapid beat of her pulse.

"We will share the communion," she said. "Your blood will flow with mine. Your heart will beat with my heart. You and I will be one."

"For as long as you live, if you speak my name in the night, I will come."

She clasped his hands. "Then, Zagreus of Kaphtor, I shall call you every night."

BY THE TIME CHRYSALEON ARRIVED AT THE KILLING FIELD, THE HEAVENS had succumbed to deepest black. Iakchos would soon rise above the mountain summits, the brightest light in the sky, for there was no moon to give challenge.

His priestess companions chanted to the low music of flutes and drums. Chrysaleon heard the intoxicating potions in their voices. They had chewed laurel leaves, and even now must be struggling against the primordial urge to fructify the earth with the supreme talisman of his lifeblood. If he failed to sway the people, his genitals would be placed in a ritual basket and carried to the sea in offering to the waters. The two priestesses who had bathed him might soon wash in his blood. He was glad he had refused their amorous invitations.

Torches placed around the clearing crackled as they spat uneasy light across the ground. A hush fell over the gathering when he stepped from the litter.

With no weapon and garbed in nothing but a loincloth, he felt nakedly defenseless. But perhaps he wasn't. At the king's feast, after returning from his clandestine errand, Alexiare had given him a reassuring nod and the faintest smile. Chrysaleon had dismembered that smile a thousand times over the last three days, hoping he'd read it right.

Prince Kios assisted Aridela from her litter. He continued to hold her elbow, a sign of respect she gave to both him and her dead mother. On her other side walked a richly attired Gelanor; his lanky height made her appear even smaller than she was. Following close behind this threesome were Themiste, Selene, Neoma, the rest of the council and other high-ranking women, and priests and priestesses, heads bowed, hands clasped.

Aridela stopped before Chrysaleon. Her face was a queen's, expressionless and regal, but he neither wanted nor needed tears and hysteria. The words she had spoken in private were enough. He returned her gaze as a king would, knowing his own people were watching, and when she turned away, he exchanged a sober glance and the slightest of nods with his brother.

Themiste offered him a bowl of wine. Again, barely suppressing a sneer, he refused.

A covered structure had been erected at the north edge of the oak clearing, bordered by torches both tall and short that bathed it in light. Seven steps led up to a platform, placing the occupants above the crowd and combatants. A high-backed throne sat in the center, leaving just enough space around it for several people to cluster. Ivy wound around the corner pillars and hung from the roof.

Torchlight revealed images of the labrys and holy knots carved into the surface of a stone column, which rose from the ground directly beneath the throne. The priestesses had explained it to Chrysaleon, so he knew it was an ancient, mysterious symbol, representing the passage between life and death.

Aridela climbed the steps and sat upon her throne, taking on the guise of Goddess-of-Death-in-Life. Gelanor stood to her left, Prince Kios to the right, while Themiste and Selene fell in behind. A drummer boy sat in front of them, his bare legs dangling over the edge of the platform.

In a steady voice, the queen said, "Bring the cabal."

Stillness fell. The crowd seemed to not even breathe in their excitement at glimpsing the Labyrinth Beast. A lone baby started to cry, and was hushed by its mother.

Three priestesses held Menoetius's forearms as they led him into the clearing. He wore a black loincloth with a scarlet tassel, and a boar's skin over his shoulders. In his right hand he carried the ancient king-killer, the labrys-axe. Planting his feet unsteadily one after the other, he swayed, shook his head, and stared at the onlookers with a puzzled frown.

Alexiare had succeeded. Menoetius had been dosed with something—probably poppy. Chrysaleon knew what signs to look for, having suffered similarly during his own struggle for kingship. Hopefully, no one else would notice.

Whispered muttering replaced the silence. Most had never seen Menoetius. Many gasped. Some cried out in ridiculous artificial hysterics about his ghastly face. Women shuddered and drew their children close.

They saw what they wanted to see—a fearsome, inhuman creature. The devotion he had enjoyed as Aridela's twice-over savior was forgotten.

Lifting his face to the night sky, Chrysaleon sent out his prayer. *Poseidon Earth-Shaker, Zeus of Thunderbolts. Gods who stamp great cities to dust. Here I stand, your loyal servant. I am High King of Mycenae! Leader of Boreas! Fill me with your strength. Help me now, and I will destroy the ancient power of woman. I will bend her to our will.*

Far to the west, he saw a flash of lightning followed by the faintest rumble of thunder. He stretched out his arms in homage and brought his fists to his chest.

The drum echoed like a heartbeat. He likened it to Aridela's, slow and even. Many times he had listened to that rhythmic sound as he rested his head between her breasts.

Menoetius raised the axe, his knuckles whitening on the handle. His eyes narrowed; the rise and fall of his chest gave away his shallow breathing.

The crowd had again fallen silent. This was the first king killing any had ever seen; their faces revealed awe and fright. The silence was a heavy thing, broken only by the slight crackle of flames beneath the drumbeat, and the drone of cicadas.

The priestesses backed to the edge of the clearing, leaving Chrysaleon and Menoetius alone in the center.

"Remember the day we hunted lion?" Chrysaleon ripped off the lion pelt and threw it on the ground.

His opponent made no reply but his head twitched slightly.

"Boys," Chrysaleon said. "Vowing brotherhood, wanting to risk our lives together. You bear the scars of the attack."

"You killed her." Menoetius's voice was nearly as raw as Alexiare's. "You threw yourself on her back with nothing but your dagger."

Chrysaleon shrugged. "I would have died to save you." He didn't need to say, *The time has come for you to repay that debt.* The warrior inside Menoetius would understand.

Menoetius swayed, awkwardly shaking his head as though trying to rid himself of the effects of the poppy. "I feel sick." He wiped sweat from his forehead with the back of his hand then clawed at the neck of the boar's skin, tearing at the clasp. The pelt slid to the ground behind him.

"I brought the cubs to the citadel," Chrysaleon said.

"They became our father's pets." Menoetius lowered his arms. The axe dangled loosely from his hand. He squinted at the flickering torchlight then peered at Aridela on her throne. When he turned back, he was grimacing, his fury clear to see. "You have always wanted me dead, son of Idómeneus. But tonight, you will have to fight hard to get your wish."

He leaped, raising the axe, aiming for Chrysaleon's skull.

Chrysaleon bent at the knees, tensing to block the weapon on its descent.

Yet, as the blade curved towards him, Menoetius paused, his arm inexplicably hesitating, giving Chrysaleon the opportunity to seize the ancient handle. Menoetius's hand felt ice cold under his.

Their legs tangled as they fought for control. Chrysaleon dropped, pulling Menoetius down on top of him.

As the axe blade slashed into the earth next to Chrysaleon's ear, the head splintered free of the handle. A loud, hollow crack echoed across the clearing.

Gasps and cries erupted. Chrysaleon felt a wash of relief. Everything, so far, was proceeding as planned.

A confused frown darkened Menoetius's face as he stared at the broken weapon. With a curse, he threw away the useless handle and fell on Chrysaleon, fighting for a stranglehold.

The two had wrestled countless times, but never had Chrysaleon experienced such desperate ferocity at his brother's hands. Alexiare's suggestion that Menoetius deliberately threw their matches to let Chrysaleon win was clearly true. It was also clear he had no intention of doing that now.

Could he overpower his brother, even with the added assistance of mind-numbing poppy? Doubt crept through him.

He grasped Menoetius's wrists and jerked hard. At the same time his knee slammed into his brother's groin.

Menoetius fell away, groaning.

Chrysaleon scrambled on top of him, but, twisting to the side, Menoetius managed to unbalance his rival, just enough to break his hold.

Chrysaleon forgot their audience as the two sprawled, rose, slipped, and lurched. They battered each other's faces until blood soaked the very air between them. Menoetius succeeded in looping his leg around Chrysaleon's and yanking him off his feet. With uncharacteristic savagery, he twisted his brother's arm as he fell. The bone cracked and Chrysaleon's shoulder sprang out of joint.

Knowing his life depended on it, Chrysaleon used all the strength he could muster in his good arm to strike Menoetius on the chin. Menoetius's head flew backward; his arms flailed. Chrysaleon pivoted, bringing his leg around in a powerful swing, and connected with the back of Menoetius's knees, bringing him crashing to the ground, where he lay, eyes closed, gasping.

Chrysaleon released a hoarse groan as he shoved his dislocated shoulder back into its socket. For what seemed an eternity, he was blinded by jagged bolts of unstaunched agony. He bent over, swiping blood from his eyes and panting, fighting to catch his breath as pain and hatred flowed in wave after shuddering wave.

Menoetius dragged himself to his feet. He staggered then collapsed onto one hand and vomited.

Chrysaleon waited just long enough for his brother to again rise. Before he could fully straighten, Chrysaleon took a deep breath, lowered his head like a bull's, and charged, striking Menoetius in the stomach and knocking him flat.

Chrysaleon smashed his bastard brother in the face with his closed fist, once, twice, and a third time. The meticulously constructed plan almost evaporated beneath an irresistible need to shatter every bone beyond recognition, but somehow, from somewhere, he found the will to stop, force himself off, to straighten, as best he could, to stand still and wait.

Menoetius lay unmoving, his arms and legs splayed. Blood spilled from his nose, eyebrow, and lip.

Chrysaleon peered at the crowd. No one spoke. Countless eyes stared at him. The boy with the drum faltered and glanced back at the queen.

Hippos Poseidon, he prayed. *Bring the words. Make them believe.*

Swords drawn, Cretan guards ran into the clearing and prodded him to the base of Aridela's platform.

She leaned forward as if about to stand. The only other signs of tension were her wide eyes, the rapid rise and fall of her chest, and her white-knuckled grip on the arms of the throne.

Gelanor remained calm and quiet, his arms crossed. Alexiare had obviously explained the plan to him.

"Kill him," someone in the crowd shouted, and, in the next breath, a wild brawl erupted. Screams merged into a cacophony. Punches were thrown, hair pulled; smaller figures disappeared and were trampled. The horde undulated like a swarm of bees over the clearing, coming perilously close to Menoetius's body.

A few individual shouts overcame the incoherent roar.

"Potnia will be angry!"

"Our crops will fail!"

"Athene cannot be defied!"

The palace guards jumped into the fray, slashing and hacking. Others clustered around the platform, pointing their blades at the crowd.

Aridela removed her gaze from Chrysaleon. She stood, and moved to the edge. Looking out at the furious riot, she waited for the mob to howl itself into silence. Now that her initial shock was past, she appeared composed, resolute. Or maybe it was resignation he saw. Acceptance.

Gradually, the uproar burned out as people were wounded, beaten, or knocked down by the guards. Chrysaleon glimpsed his Mycenaeans scattered among the crowd, using intimidation to subdue those who were most volatile. Many stared up at Aridela; her stillness and silence seemed to exert an unconscious influence over them.

"Is Menoetius dead?" Aridela asked, when her voice could be heard.

"He lives." Clenching his teeth against the pain, Chrysaleon yanked free of the two warriors who gripped his arms and stepped closer. "The cabal must live, to fulfill his sworn duty and take my place."

He tried to read her expression. Was she remembering the day in the apple grove, when he asked her to stop the sacrifice? He couldn't tell. Her eyes were impenetrable.

The nearest spectators hushed each other in order to hear. He waited until all was quiet, then he approached the mob, lifting his good arm. "I cannot die," he said clearly. "I refuse the sacrifice."

Angry murmuring instantly escalated into shouts. Several in the crowd closed their fists and appeared ready to attack and kill him themselves. He hurried on, motioning for calm. "Many have heard of the vision I was given when Harpalycus of Tiryns invaded your country. While I lay near death, I spoke to one of your bull-kings—Damasen." He swept his arm toward Aridela. "Queen Aridela's father."

Blanketing silence descended as curiosity overcame rage.

"Damasen ordered me to serve as your king for the term of a great year. I didn't understand, being only a man, never initiated into the Mysteries. When I recovered, I asked Themiste what it meant."

He waited again, prolonging the suspense. An owl hooted in the distance. Taking a few steps toward the platform, he gestured to Themiste, who had come forward to stand beside Aridela, her hand on the queen's shoulder. "Tell them what you told me."

She looked to Aridela, who nodded. "The sun and moon come into alignment every one hundred months," she said. "Initiates call this holy phase the thinara, a great year."

Gasps swam through the crowd. Conjecture flurried like an auguring wind.

Chrysaleon raised his voice. "When I traveled to Mycenae to claim my throne, I consulted the holy oracle, as is the custom of the new king. She spoke the same words to me. 'Rule,' she said, 'until the sun and moon shift into perfect alignment.'" He lifted his chin and stated with all the confidence and arrogance he could muster, "I am the great-year-king your legends have prophesied."

Some gazed at him silently. Others grumbled. Chrysaleon crossed the field to Menoetius, trying to ignore the radiating blaze from his shoulder and wiping away blood that kept seeping into one eye. He picked up the handle of the labrys, lifting it so everyone could see the broken, jagged butt. "The Goddess has made her wishes clear in vision, in trance, and here, on your field. Do you doubt it? Look upon this axe. Her sacred tool has worked its bloodletting for longer than anyone can measure, yet it split apart rather than take my life. Surely defiance of what she so clearly wants will call down another rage of fire upon this land."

The crowd gestured and argued. A few again came to blows. Chrysaleon dared a glance toward Aridela. She stood at the edge of the platform, as straight and motionless as the golden staff she gripped. As he watched, she turned her gaze to the inky night sky, causing pangs of guilt and remorse to run through him.

He felt her bewilderment, her ambivalence. She was young, alone, and had endured one catastrophe after another. She must feel crushed by opposing desires—to see him live, to submit to the Lady's demands, and to somehow appease her people.

A shiver ran down his spine.

Help came from the crowd itself. "Goddess Athene brought him from over the sea to save us," an old woman cried. "It is prophecy fulfilled. Surely you have not forgotten when our queen was a child, the words she spoke in trance?"

The collective anger faltered. Chrysaleon watched as faces remembered that old prophecy. Awed wonder replaced fear.

He kept his expression grave, though he wanted to smile. The old woman was probably one of the crones Alexiare had prepared and heaped with bribery gifts.

Many still stared at him with hostility and bloodlust. His goal had not yet been achieved.

"Even then," someone shouted, "the Lady knew he would come— the Gold Lion from over the sea."

"The Zagreus saved us." This raspy pronouncement emanated from deep within the crowd. It sounded like Alexiare himself. "Kaphtor will fall into ruin under the Beast!"

"The consort should not be sacrificed," another female cried. "He should be rewarded with life for what he did. That is what Potnia wants."

"Who else but he can protect us from the mainland threat?" a man shouted.

"The Zagreus is a comely man, beautiful in every way," a matron said as she boldly looked him over, hands on hips. "Who wants a monster as our king? I do not."

How many of these who shouted in support of him were Mycenaeans following Alexiare's instructions? He heard his homeland's accent here and there.

"What of the crops?"

The people fell silent as they turned toward the one who spoke.

Selene approached the edge of the platform, her layered skirts rippling in the breeze. "The consort must die," she said clearly. "It is

Law. The crops must be sanctified, now more than ever. To ignore long established holy rites invites the anger of the Immortals."

Aridela gazed upon the crowd. She frowned.

Fearing what he saw on her face, Chrysaleon swept out his good arm to draw attention back to him. He couldn't allow the momentum he'd achieved to be lost. "She is right," he said. "Blood must fructify the crops. One must die. By doing so, he will earn forgiveness for his crimes, and achieve entry into Paradise."

"No," Selene cried.

"The oracle said it." Chrysaleon's voice carried over hers. "'Slay the Lady's Earth Bull,' she commanded me, 'and rule until the sun and moon shift into perfect alignment.' As of tonight, by rights, the Beast of the Labyrinth is the Lady's Earth Bull."

Chrysaleon returned to his brother, who had begun to stir. He seized Menoetius's wrist and held it up. "The consort must stand at the side of the Goddess-of-Life-in-Death. The sacrifice must continue in obedience to the Goddess-of-Death-in-Life. When the sun rises, the first day of the new year will begin. Menoetius, my brother, will be titled Zagreus and bull-king. He will perform the consort's duties and receive every pleasure and accord. When Iakchos ascends again, my cabal will give the divine offering of his blood and be restored to eternal glory in Hesperia. His death will bring true, complete forgiveness to the people of Kaphtor."

He dropped Menoetius's arm and stepped away from him. "I, the thinara king, will spend the first day of the new year in the tombs, in communion with my true brother, Velchanos." Pausing so this image could sink in, he added, "At dawn on the second day, Velchanos will rise to the call of the offering, bringing abundance and peace in the name of his holy mother."

The hush following his speech was different from the silence of before. He felt the people considering his proposal. Many nodded. They turned to each other, talking among themselves.

Triumph washed over him. Victory. Life. And, given enough time, he would discover a way to halt the king-sacrifice altogether. He would not die now, nor would he die at the end of the great year, no matter what any oracle predicted.

"Mycenae's king toys with us. He would cheat Goddess Athene of her due."

The words spilled from the platform like a flood of icy water.

"Menoetius warned me of Chrysaleon's tricks," Selene said. "He tried to warn the queen, but she would not listen. Here is the proof. Chrysaleon stands before you, mocking our rites to your very faces."

Silence again reigned, thick and heavy, as the people stared from Selene, to Chrysaleon, to Aridela.

"The woman is not one of us," some unseen male shouted. "She carries the monster's seed in her belly. She only speaks to save him."

Aridela took Selene's hand. Chrysaleon's brief sense of achievement crumbled like a seashell smashed against a rock. Death flowed closer, lapping at his feet. She meant to say the words that would send him to a cold and bloody grave.

Gelanor stepped forward, his hand moving to the hilt of his dagger. Chrysaleon sent him an almost imperceptible shake of the head, willing him to wait.

Selene spoke again. "The High King of Mycenae sent his sons here on a quest to overthrow us. Menoetius abandoned the mainland and his father's plots. He has become one with us. Chrysaleon seeks our defeat, even now."

"If our queen is too timid to perform the rite, another should take her place," someone shouted.

Selene put her arm around Aridela's waist. Prince Kios, his face contorted with anger, moved Themiste back and took her place on Aridela's other side. He gestured for one of the guards to hand him a sword, and when it was given, he pointed it at the crowd. "Who dares say such a thing?" he demanded.

Then something happened neither Alexiare nor Chrysaleon had anticipated. A man somewhere shouted, "The queen herself can be sacrificed if she defies our laws."

"It is Chrysaleon, not the queen, who would harm Kaphtor!" Selene returned the shout, her cheeks burning with fury.

"He could not if there was strength on the throne," some hidden male cried. "She will sacrifice us all to save her barbarian lover."

Aridela looked out over her people. "You threaten me?" she asked. "When I have listened to every argument, as any judge should?"

Breathless silence fell. The man who broached the possibility of Aridela's death said nothing more, yet Chrysaleon saw countless faces staring up at their queen, narrow-eyed, hostile. One wrong word would send them forward. They would go through Selene, Kios, and the guards. They would rip Aridela to pieces before his eyes. Then they would turn on him.

He didn't know what to do. If he continued to argue for his life they would kill her. But he wasn't yet ready to give in and accept his own death. His mind sprang and tumbled but provided no solution. This was Alexiare's fault. The old man hadn't planned for every possibility. Now where was he? Somewhere in the crowd, too frightened to speak up.

He dared another glance at Gelanor. His brother had left his spot by the throne. He now stood beside Selene, his dagger drawn and ready. He appeared to be defending the queen, but Chrysaleon knew if he raised his hand, his brother would toss him the weapon.

Barely audible over the crackle of torch flames and sough of a suddenly chilly wind, another voice spoke. "I will make the sacrifice."

Chrysaleon swiveled, the hair on his arms and scalp lifting.

While no one was paying attention, Menoetius had dragged himself to his feet. He stood, swaying, staring at Aridela, one eye swollen shut, his face covered in blood.

Complete silence descended upon the oak grove. No baby cried. Not even a cricket chirped. Then, from the west, a low growl of thunder rumbled. It didn't fade but went on, and on, and on.

"I will give myself to your holy blade," Menoetius said. "I will guide your hand to my throat. When the earth holds my blood, you will come scratching in it to find me."

He wiped blood from his eyes with the back of his hand and limped across the field, passing Chrysaleon but never even glancing at him. He staggered up the seven steps. Aridela and Selene reached down, one on either side, to help him. He knelt before the queen.

She dropped to her knees and took his face in her hands.

Menoetius said something. He leaned forward, resting his face against her throat. She put her arms around him, holding him close.

Selene gave a wordless, miserable cry. Sobbing, she ran down the steps and disappeared into the night.

A flash at the corner of his eye pulled Chrysaleon's attention from what he saw before him—this betraying, incriminating intimacy between his brother and his wife.

Iakchos broke free of the shadowed bulk of Mount Dikti's summit and took its place beneath the grand, courageous Hunter. Unlike last year, there was no haze around it. The star was bright, strong, and clear, a good portent for the coming months.

Menoetius's agreement, coupled with the appearance and clarity of the holy sphere, seemed to transform the mob.

"Chrysaleon," someone shouted.

Another joined in. "Zagreus!"

Others took up the cry. He was called hero and savior. Menoetius was heralded. Aridela was praised for the loyalty she inspired.

The boy on the platform beat his drum wildly. The crowd pounded the earth with their feet and clapped. Laughter and cheering echoed into the heavens.

Chrysaleon hardly heard any of it. He stared at Aridela as she rose. She met his gaze before she spoke.

"The people have chosen," she said.

Bending, she linked her arm through Menoetius's. She helped him to his feet and guided him down the steps. He stumbled a little. Themiste ran after them and put her arm around his waist. Together, the two women led him away into the night.

One strange memory of something Alexiare had said overtook every other, causing Chrysaleon's flesh to shiver as he watched their retreating forms.

He will never let you go to your death, not without giving his life to prevent it.

Everyone, including Alexiare, would think Menoetius had indeed chosen death in order to save his brother. But Chrysaleon knew better. Menoetius's choice had nothing to do with him at all.

6

Moon of White Light

MENOETIUS'S SINGLE DAY OF KINGSHIP FLOWED LIKE A MIGHTY RIVER emptying into the sea. Rhené tended his injuries. Aridela cleansed him in a hot bath of sea salts and soothing oils, though he hardly released her hand long enough for her to wield the sponge. She and another handmaid massaged the soreness from his muscles.

Revived and fortified, though with one eye still swollen closed, he held the reins as he and his queen made the circuit of Knossos in a gilded cart drawn by white oxen. Garlands and wildflowers rained upon them.

The title he was given while imprisoned lost its stigma of fear and horror. He was hailed as Asterion the starry god, lord of the labyrinth. Aridela was his queen and dark mistress. Kaphtor's grateful people sang of his courage, strength, and nobility. Glauce worked rapturously on a fresco that would span an entire wall in the chamber of judgment; standing in a field of lilies, their hero saluted the Goddess and made offering of a winged sphinx.

Washed in dusky twilight, the queen and her surrogate-consort formally mated in the barley as demanded by ancient tradition and more recent fears.

After she presented him with three golden apples and the divinatory knucklebones, when the pageantry, songs, and feasting were done, he carried her away to their chamber, leaving behind a wreckage of giggling, sighing maids, a smiling retinue, and many wistful would-be lovers.

"Kiss me," she whispered as he kicked the chamber door closed behind them. "Again. Kiss me again."

Menoetius kissed her until she could no longer feel her lips, until she could no longer speak or think, and could remember nothing but the feel of his mouth against hers. Taking his time, he moved from her face to kiss every curve, every angle, even her toes, as though he wanted to know her body as well as she did. Such tenderness threw her off balance a little, it conflicted so dramatically with the brutal combat she'd witnessed between the brothers on the killing field.

"You remind me of the lioness," he said. "You protect your people like she protected her cubs. Tell Chrysaleon I remember that day. He gave me back my life so I could be here, with you now."

She didn't want to think about lionesses, or Chrysaleon, or what was to come. "Kiss me, Menoetius."

He poured wine between her breasts and watched it pool over her navel. His tongue tickled her when he licked it off, making her giggle. Yet soon he left her gasping, then weeping. "How can I pretend any of it matters?" she asked, her voice hoarse with grief. "I want you with me every night, every night for as long as I live."

He made no reply, gave no consolation. He offered no desperately formed idea to escape his fate. He kissed her tears, and the line of her jaw, up to her earlobe.

She tried again, longing to understand at least. "Selene and I begged you not to be his cabal. You had a choice. You could have stayed with us. Why did you let him do this to you?"

He lifted his head and met her gaze. "When I looked at Chrysaleon and saw the crowd's anger, it became clear, at last, what the Lady required from me."

"What?"

"My blood." His eyes darkened. She watched him travel within to some place she sensed must be awe-inspiring, and maybe terrible. "I didn't want to tell you what I saw in the blackness of the labyrinth, what I heard. She said it many times, as she has in dreams, for as long as I can remember. *Thou wilt give to her the offering of thy blood.* All my life she has prepared me for this. I couldn't tell you because you might have tried to sway me. Whenever I felt fear over what was to come, she repeated her covenant. Remember? I told you. *What seems the end is only the beginning.* I knew she didn't make that vow lightly. I lost all doubts. I understood that whatever might happen, it would not be the end. I will go into my nightmare. I will fight the lion. If I defeat it, you will be free. If I succeed, maybe she will bring us together again."

Ah, so that was what he'd meant on the platform in the killing field, when he'd knelt before her. *The lion is calling me,* he'd said.

Though she held out little hope, she argued anyway. "I cannot bear this. I will not stand for it."

He brushed her hair from her face and kissed her temples. "A sacrifice has to be made, Aridela. Did you not see the mood of the people? They were turning against you. As soon as I agreed, they calmed. They accepted. If I hadn't, you might have been hurt."

He didn't say anything about Chrysaleon putting her in such danger by refusing the sacrifice. She thought of it, and wondered what Chrysaleon would have done if Menoetius hadn't stepped in to soothe the mob's bloodlust. Would he have let them attack her?

"I will find another way." She stroked his hair, as she'd wanted to do for so long, letting it glide between her fingers. "I am the queen," she whispered. "I must be obeyed."

His lashes descended, hiding his thoughts. For a space of time he was silent, then he admitted, "I don't want to die. I want to stay with you and Selene. I want to hold my child." He took a deep breath then shook his head. "The Lady won't allow it. It's my punishment and reward. Punishment because I left you, years ago, reward and redemption now. I can only consent. Maybe it will help Kaphtor. My hope, my plea, is that she will reunite us, somehow, somewhere, if I do what she wants. That is what I think she meant with the vow she made. Whatever happens, wherever she sends me, I will wait for you." As if to further strengthen his word, he removed his gold seal ring and slid it onto her middle finger.

His promise, and the way he kissed the palm of her hand, forced her to blink away tears. But a niggling question remained. "So this is not to save Chrysaleon?"

"My debt to him is great. But no. Not for him."

Menoetius kissed the crescent scars below her ribs, then her knuckles, then the bend of her elbows. She had nearly succeeded in forgetting what was to come at the end of their night when he said, very quietly, "I ask your forgiveness."

Her eyelids felt almost too heavy to open, but she managed. "For what, my love? What could you think you have done?"

"I should have kept him from lying with you in the Cave of Velchanos. I should never have allowed him to enter Kaphtor's Games. Even after, I had a chance to stop him from becoming bull-king and consort, but I did nothing. I was too afraid."

"You, Menoetius, afraid?"

She laughed gently, but he remained grave. "I knew it was you in the cave. I wanted to be with you more than I have ever wanted anything. But I let Chrysaleon best me. I, who could have stopped him, instead turned away and allowed him to drag us all here, to this. The Destruction, the suffering and deaths of your people, are they, too, the result of my fear? I have failed you, again and again, because I could not bear your revulsion."

"You're wrong about Chrysaleon."

Menoetius turned away from her a little, so his scarred cheek was almost hidden. "But he found a way to escape his fate, as I told you he would."

She knew her sidestep into excusing Chrysaleon, almost a habit by now, a defense she wasn't sure she believed any longer, hurt him. She held out her arms, looking down at the marks left by burns. Truth spilled with a storm of tears she could no longer contain. "It's true. In the beginning, your scars disturbed me. If I saw you coming I slipped away. I couldn't accept the loss of my Carmanor, how he had changed. I was spoiled, never tested. But on the mountain, when we were alone, I learned how little they matter. I loved you when I was ten years old. I love you now. I will love you…Menoetius…until only dust remains of my bones."

He didn't reply. He offered no smile, nor did he weep or laugh. Instead, he kissed the bull's-head mark on her wrist, and she watched the shadows leave his eyes.

She held vigil while he slept.

Aridela thought about the oath she'd given Chrysaleon—that no bull-king would ever touch her heart. Less than a day and her words were proven a lie, but she felt no guilt. Her declaration was given too easily, too quickly, without understanding what was to come.

Her lover's hair lay across his face and shoulders, shadowed oak and obsidian, yet it seemed to reflect light like a dark mirror. Her fingertips discerned the faint twitch of a muscle in his shoulder. Perhaps, in a dream, he ran with one of his lions.

There was little chance of him waking. She had ordered his wine steeped with enough poppy to bring him to the edge of death. He must have known, but he obediently drank when she offered him the bowl.

His hand crept across the bed until it touched her stomach, but he didn't wake, only gave an almost imperceptible sigh, as though reassured.

Misery battered her like a storm surge as she thought of Selene and the child. She clenched her hands to keep from shaking him. She wanted the comfort of his arms around her; she wanted him to proclaim that all would be as it was, but this induced repose was for the best. Selene had asked her to make him oblivious, and Aridela, remembering the faces of other bull-kings, had quickly and thankfully agreed.

Selene would suffer as much as she at the close of this night. Together, they would have to find some way to endure, to survive. Could they do it? She wasn't sure.

Her mind veered away from the present and future, back into the opiate of their earlier lovemaking. She watched him, stifling any sound of weeping, and traced the outline of his face carefully, fearful of disturbing his slumber.

One other thing had he told her before he surrendered to the poppy. He'd held her face in his hands to make certain she was listening, so he could see that she understood.

I have never raped a woman.

She hadn't set out to lie to Chrysaleon, but there was one other she would take to her heart.

This one. This one who died so she, and his brother, could live.

The lines in his face were smoothed, his lips serene. Aridela traced the scar curving from brow to mouth. With his eyes closed and his face relaxed, it seemed beautiful. "Athene's mark," she whispered, and kissed his eyelids. "Carmanor."

All her life she had glorified the legendary queen of Kaphtor who had adjusted the twice-yearly sacrifice to give herself more time with a beloved consort. Aridela had always hoped she could leave her own mark upon the history of her people. She'd prayed that somewhere within her lived the same boldness, the same courage.

Lying beside Menoetius, observing him as he slept, she realized she had achieved that hope. She would always be remembered as the queen who dramatically transformed Kaphtor's most sacred tradition. Yet she didn't feel bold or courageous. The change had been thrust upon her, much like the monstrous tide of water after the Destruction. It had swept her along in its wake. She was no more than a shred of flotsam.

Her handmaid entered. "They are waiting, my lady."

She rose. Taking a knife, she bent and sheared off a lock of his hair. She twisted it with one of her own and slipped the talisman into an ivory coffer. After one last, lingering kiss, a final instant against his skin, she accompanied her maid from the bedchamber, so stricken by the weight of what was to come that her legs began to shake and she had to accept the woman's support. While she and the priestesses prepared, Menoetius would be carried back to the field of barley. If he did wake, he would be given more poppy-laced wine. Her instructions had been clear.

Themiste and the priestesses waited in the shrine. Only Selene was missing, Selene, who was somewhere lost and alone, maybe in the labyrinth chamber where the father of her child had spent his last days.

Neoma handed her a bowl.

Aridela chewed the leaves, hating their bitter taste, hating more the devastation they would wreak.

With an ancient sickle of bone, more ancient even than the king's death-labrys, Themiste sacrificed a white calf and poured the blood around the base of the pillar. When it was done, she spoke holy words, made the sign against evil, and handed the sickle to Aridela. "*Khalada,*" she whispered. Tears coursed over her cheeks.

The shrine seemed to darken, as though Goddess Dictynna had covered the torches with charmed fishing nets. Tremors crept through Aridela's muscles. It felt difficult, unwieldy, to breathe.

One of the priestesses sobbed. She craned her head backward and scratched viciously at her face, drawing blood.

They left the shrine, emerging into a night lit only by the glow of Iakchos and the thinnest sliver of a new waxing moon. Aridela led the procession, the blackened sickle resting across her palms.

Themiste, the priests, and Aridela's serving women knelt, bowing their heads, as the sickle passed. Twenty priestesses followed Aridela in a single line through the courtyard and palace precincts, chanting, the sound no more than a hum.

The people of Knossos lined the path to Menoetius. He lay on his side upon a bed of flattened barley, knees drawn up to his chest.

A dreaming god, cast in ivory.

The priestesses circled him, chanting, lighting him with their torches. Breezes rustled the ripened pasture around them, adding to the paradoxical sound of hushed tranquility.

Stepping into the light, Chrysaleon seemed a natural part of the god's dream.

He held out his hand.

"Anathema," Aridela whispered, giving him the sickle. She knelt by Menoetius's head, stroked his hair, and kissed his cheek.

Could those be tears glimmering in Chrysaleon's eyes, or did the laurel leaves create a fancy she needed to see? He gazed upon Menoetius's unmoving form for an endless, breathless passage of time. With his foot, he turned his brother onto his back and brought the sickle down with a hiss, ripping flesh from throat to stomach.

The world erupted in horror and blood.

A hand clutched Aridela's wrist. Menoetius's eyes were glazing, yet he held her with desperate strength. "Selene," he said, his voice hoarse and ragged. "My child...."

The thunder in Aridela's head faded. The chanting that had hypnotized her mind evaporated, leaving cold, sober sense, burning clarity. She paid no more attention to Chrysaleon, who dropped the sickle and backed away. She cradled Menoetius's head on her lap and stroked his face. "I will take care of them," she promised.

"Swans," Themiste cried. "The Lady sends swans! They will carry his soul to Hesperia on their wings." She prostrated herself and so did her priestesses as the flock, oddly silent, landed in the clearing and encircled the tableau.

"Not even this will part us," Aridela whispered. "What seems the end—" Her throat closed. She couldn't speak. Couldn't finish.

Menoetius's grip faltered. His hand fell. "Aridela..." he sighed. "Aridela."

Then he died.

CHRYSALEON'S OX-DRAWN CART WAS DRAPED WITH GARLANDS, OLIVE leaves, and purple grapes. A priestess handed him a carved, heavily adorned thyrsus. He gladly abandoned the tombs, following a path created by torches and the citizens of Kaphtor.

At the south palace entrance he left the cart and approached a waiting litter. He opened the draperies and offered his hand.

First Aridela then Themiste stepped out. Both wore stiff ceremonial garments. Firelight glowed against their diadems, armbands, and earrings.

The three surrounded a freshly dug pit in the center of the road. Priestesses brought a bundle wrapped in white linen. As Chrysaleon accepted it, the wrapping loosened and a bloody lock of his brother's hair slipped from the folds. He knelt and placed the bundle in the hole, swallowing his disgust.

Poseidon, look what I have done for you. Protect me from vengeance.

A soldier shoveled dirt into the hole and replaced the paving stone, covering over the last he would ever see of his nemesis. He'd believed this would be his great triumph, but he felt strangely empty.

"Menoetius, great warrior, son of High King Idómeneus of Mycenae." Chrysaleon lifted his face so his voice would carry. "Protect this land. Allow no invasion, drought, or pestilence to harm the faithful."

There were no cheers. Those who watched remained silent and somber.

He escorted the women to the queen's hall. "I missed you," he said softly, close to Aridela's ear.

Her gaze remained opaque. "The first king of Kaphtor to thwart his death."

"In truth, I did not want to leave you."

One of her brows lifted and her eyes narrowed, just for the space of a breath, but before she could speak, her retinue of women closed in around them and swept her away.

"Are the people satisfied?" he asked Themiste. "I cannot tell."

Her hypnotizing eyes stared straight into his without blinking.

"What is it?" He gripped her arm. "I have heard nothing but the voices of long dead queens."

"Did they question your resolve?"

He released her arm and backed away. "What resolve?"

"To betray the will of the Immortals."

He glanced around, skin prickling, half-expecting the palace guards to march forward and drag him to their underground prisons.

"Happiness fills the people," she said. "You are the hero who saved them from Harpalycus the Butcher, who brought the queen back from the mountains when all despaired of ever seeing her again. You restored her to the throne. You are fulfillment of old prophecy—the Gold Lion from over the sea. What the people have forgotten are the last lines. *Isle of cloud, Moon's stronghold, see your death come in spears of gold.*"

Chrysaleon fought to remain calm and expressionless, but those eyes of burned umber penetrated like dagger blades. Against his will, his breath shortened.

"Yesterday, while you were at the tombs, the council asked me to become your second wife. They want to strengthen the ties between you and Aridela's chosen heir, the babe that grows within me. They believe marriage is the way."

"Do you want this?"

She frowned. "It is only symbolic. Do not think it anything else."

"I would not." But he had, and knew his face betrayed it.

"So many changes in such a short time. It is puzzling. Have you spared your brother any thought?"

The rage he dared not show made his teeth grind. "I didn't want to ask."

"His last words were of Selene and *their* child."

A shudder washed over him. He grabbed Themiste's arm again, this time brutally, knowing he would leave bruises. "Menoetius was a traitor. Selene put Aridela into his care, yet he tried to steal her, from me and from her country. Then he sought to murder me. He had to die. Even so, I should never have applied the sickle of death against my brother. No cleansing can free me of what I have done."

"And yet you chose him. Not only chose him but insisted, and fought to keep him alive so he could meet you as your cabal in the killing field. Did he truly agree to it, or did he simply give you his obedience?" Her gaze turned speculative. "You considered our traditions so carefully. You found a way to alter every phase of the rites to suit your wishes and still appease the people. Lying with me was no more than a piece of that plan, though I have not yet seen how it benefits you. Was it meant to seize my power? In that you succeeded. I bow to your cunning. I only wonder where your ambition will take you, and how far we who have become your pawns will be dragged in your wake."

Yanking her arm free, she turned and walked away.

Look upon what you have accomplished, my brother.

Blood flowed from Menoetius's torso. It ran down his legs and pooled on the floor, yet his voice held no heat or resentment.

Chrysaleon recoiled from the spilling entrails and congealing blood. *I did not want this.*

You have wanted this from the day your life began. I've always known. And I know what you did that day with the lioness. You cannot hide your lies from me now.

There was no excuse Chrysaleon could make, so he said nothing.

Listen to me, brother. Lady Athene has offered me retribution. Do not think this is the end. I mean to return.

I will return.

Chrysaleon jerked upright. Sweat stung his eyes. His heart drummed against his ribcage. He got up and crossed to the table, light-headed, queasy, trembling like an old man. With every step, he felt the cold gaze of the Erinyes upon him. He poured wine, his hand shaking so hard liquid splattered from the bowl.

I will return.

The pitcher fell from his numbed fingers. The sound of shattered clay reverberated through his head like a bolt of lightning splitting a tree.

Wine, red as blood, spread across the rich blue tiles.

7

Moon of Winemaking

Selene opened her cypress coffer and brought out a bundle swaddled in wool.

Unwrapping and smoothing the fabric, she examined the ruined king-labrys, from the faint old stains of blood on the stone blades to the place where the handle had snapped in two.

The fracture revealed symmetrical ridges, like those a saw would make. These extended halfway into the wood. Only the break at the very core was jagged and rough. Remnants of dark wax still clung to these ridges, wax that would make the saw marks difficult to spot, and would help the wood remain bonded if no pressure was applied. Next she studied the leather strap. It was thin, fragile. She broke it with a slight tug. It could be rotted, but the holy king-killer had been carefully tended for well over a thousand years. Selene was sure it had been replaced or tampered with.

Instinctively she felt that someone had weakened the handle and disguised the interference with wax and worn strapping. But who?

"Themiste should have let you die in your prison cell," she said. "Menoetius would be alive but for you, and all Kaphtor would be better off."

She leaned over the cradle where Xanthe lay sleeping, her thumb in her mouth. Just two months old, the baby's breathing was sweet and deep. She was born nine days after Menoetius died, almost a month earlier than she should have been, and it had taken all of

Rhené's skills to keep the infant from dying—her mother too, who contracted a fever during labor. For many days delirium trapped Selene in a place between death and life where she saw her lover again, and lived in joy. She didn't even know she had given birth until the fever finally broke.

"Menoetius," Selene said. "I wish you could see her."

She gathered the child in her arms and lay on the bed.

"Aridela won't listen." She pressed one finger against Xanthe's palm, smiling at the way the baby, even while asleep, latched on and gripped. "She is deaf and blind to everything beyond the lion's growling lies. But I will avenge your father. You won't grow up the child of a traitor."

Though Chrysaleon had pardoned him and Menoetius had been given every bounty due a royal consort, there would be those who would remember how he concealed Aridela in the mountains even from Selene. Rumors would linger about how he attacked the bull-king out of his time. For generations, maybe longer, people would believe the gossip that he'd become a savage beast, slaughtering and consuming innocents, and had to be confined in the labyrinth.

"When you're older you will learn of your queen. You will be taught how Themiste chose her name from holy vision. It means 'Utterly Clear,' and has never before been given to any princess. But Themiste's vision was false. Aridela isn't utterly clear. If she were, Chrysaleon could not fool her as he does. Aridela is utterly blind."

Selene wept quietly, not wanting to wake or frighten her daughter.

He means to halt the king-sacrifice, Menoetius had told her. *Your people will be his slaves.*

Chrysaleon had fulfilled Menoetius's prediction. They were not yet slaves, but, given time and Aridela's continued loyalty, Chrysaleon might make that happen as well.

The lamp sputtered out and they lay in shadow and soft moonlight. It seemed the weight of another body slipped into her bed. She started, but moonlight reassured her.

Menoetius's wounds and scars were gone. He was as beautiful as the first time she'd seen him. He held the baby, smiling, then lay her down and put his arms around them both. Selene felt his breath in her ear.

Children deserve to be loved, no matter what their fathers do or don't do, whether they are good or evil.

He kissed the beating pulse in her throat.

Do not be angry with Aridela. She follows the Lady's design. The Goddess knows what has been and what is to come. It is too much for us to understand.

She made a weak sound of protest and pressed her cheek to his.

Be strong, he said. *Search and you will find your proof. It lies within the palace. Cut the lion's mane, and send him to his reckoning.*

IN THE MOON OF WINEMAKING, ONE YEAR AND TWO MONTHS AFTER THE cataclysm that left Kaphtor's great society doddering like a sick old man, Aridela and her retinue journeyed south to Arhanes, a village on the lower slope of Mount Juktas, for it was here that an abundance of healthy, ripe grapes could be found, more so than anyplace else. The pickers enjoyed their usual competitions as they cut fruit from the vine and dumped it into wooden vats. Girls kilted up their skirts and jumped in, stamping the grapes to the rhythm of drums.

Aridela climbed upon a boulder covered in ram's fleece and blew the painted conch shell in each of the four directions. The gathered people shouted *Alou!* and young girls performed the wild wine-dance to the beat of tambours, flutes, drums, pipes, and cymbals. Intoxicating music, shouts of encouragement, and an ever-quickening beat dissolved inhibitions. Gowns were lifted above knees stained a rich purple. Men sent streams of wine from goat-belly flasks into the mouths of friends and lovers. Everyone sang the bawdy grape-crushing songs.

Selene held Xanthe up to watch. The baby took it all in, seeming to laugh with her entire body.

"Do you see them?" A nearby woman, who had managed to retain a double chin and layers of fat through these bad times, gestured toward a group of Mycenaeans. "They are everywhere these days."

The men swaggered like conquerors, elbowing through the press of locals. Bearded and tall, they stood out among the small-framed, elegant natives. Selene frowned as she studied Chrysaleon's brash countrymen. A royal upbringing may have smoothed his edges, but underneath he was like these men, arrogant and barbaric, itching to fight, to steal, to overpower. To take what he didn't deserve by whatever means necessary.

"My sister is priestess at the palace shrine," the woman said. "She told me she caught three of them sacrificing to Poseidon in there—right at the foot of the Lady's statue. And they were drunk."

One glance told Selene the woman was serious. Xanthe whined in protest at her angry mother's tightened grip. "In the public shrine?" she asked.

"Oh yes. They wouldn't know how to find the other one. She said she surprised them, and one of them pulled a knife on her. She got out of there in a hurry and hid in the maze. They stumbled around looking for her then gave up and returned to the courtyard."

"Themiste should be told."

"One of them wooed my niece awhile back," the woman said with a sneer. "She wanted to imitate the queen, I suppose. He carried her off to the mainland. Now she sends word that he is seldom home, rarely comes to her bed, and when he's drunk, beats her. Why must the young be so foolish?" She added a disgusted "bah," and stalked away.

Newly arrived clerks from Mycenae swarmed over Labyrinthos with their tablets, noting everything, making endless lists. After the harvest, these would be used to set up a first-ever tax collection. Chrysaleon had convinced the council it was necessary to help Kaphtor recover the greatness it enjoyed before the earthshaking, drowning ash, the Butcher, the loss of olive and grain stores and the theft of treasure. In the old days, farmers gave freely in support of their neighbors and country. Trade thrived; everyone benefited. Now their crops would be summarily taken, leaving them with little on which to survive.

Mild weather continued, bringing new growth and hope. Wildflowers bloomed. Saffron was picked. Heat wavered on the horizon. Next month would herald the start of winter and the olive harvest, but for now, Kaphtor enjoyed a welcome respite from the persistent frosts that had afflicted the island all summer. Many gave the dead hero, now almost exclusively known as Asterion, credit for this budding prosperity. To glorify him, a luminous blue-tinged beacon beneath the North Star was given his name.

For several days after the grapes were crushed, it seemed to Selene that she saw Mycenaeans everywhere. Wherever she walked, she heard Poseidon invoked, or this newer thunder-god the Mycenaeans called "Zeus." Some named him a spirit of the crops and claimed Kaphtor was his birthplace. Others said mainland warriors introduced him from the far north. Once she heard an absurd tale that claimed Velchanos and Zeus were one and the same. From what she could tell, worship of him was confined to a few villages at the foot of Mount

Juktas. The Mycenaean farmers who had settled there must have brought the notion of him.

This was more evidence of the polluting influence of the barbarians, as even the smallest children knew that Mount Juktas had from the beginning times been dedicated to Athene's lithe and beautiful son, Velchanos, who shared his name with no foreign god, and never would.

Strolling along the rocky cliffs near Amnisos, Selene was startled and angry to see Poseidon's trident carved into a boulder outside Eleuthia's cave.

The hair on the back of her neck stood on end as she ran her fingers over the scratching. Grabbing a handful of sand, she tried to scrub it away.

She stood, scowling at the boulder. The trident had been carved too deeply, and wouldn't be erased. She turned her face to the heavens.

Lady of the labyrinth, of the moon, the mountains, the seas, and wild beasts. Lady who gave us the olive and the secret of weaving. Chrysaleon steals Kaphtor from you. With guile and trickery, he overthrows us, exactly like Harpalycus, but for Chrysaleon, we make no protest.

Kaphtor was slowly disappearing into the maw of Argolis.

Suddenly cold, Selene rubbed at a shiver of goose bumps on her arms.

How well she remembered her pride in Helice's youngest child. Aridela was called *Shariheid,* Daughter of the Calesienda—a divine gift given by Athene to mortals. Yet Aridela had sacrificed her closeness with Lady Potnia to appease her foreign lover from Mycenae. *I am in my Mother's hand,* she used to say. Selene seldom heard Aridela refer to Goddess Athene anymore—usually only during formal ritual and ceremony.

He corrupted her. She no longer sees anything but what he places before her and wants her to see.

Buffeting winds from the north drew her gaze outward toward the isle of Callisti, lost to destruction so violent it had nearly obliterated Kaphtor as well.

She looked back at Knossos and the shining palace on the hill. Deep within Labyrinthos, the artist, Glauce, was busy covering the ancient paintings in the throne room with new artwork. The queen herself had ordered the change in celebration of her consort. When finished, strange, crouching gryphons would replace the awe-inspiring scenes of bulls. Chrysaleon had made the request, claiming he'd ridden on the back of one in his now-famed death-dream.

Even as she shivered, resolve flowed through her blood like a river of fire.

I hear you, Mistress. I will see Chrysaleon dead and his gods routed. To make the promise stronger, she slit her forearm and smeared the crude trident with her blood. *I will not rest until all is as it was.*

SLIPPING INTO THE CONSORT'S CHAMBER WHILE HE AND ALEXIARE WERE AT supper with the queen, Selene opened cabinets, baskets, and coffers—even lifted the covers and peered under the bed. What did she hope to find? He was too sly to leave evidence of his crimes about.

She drew up straight.

Alexiare. He would do anything for his barbarian king.

Though it grew late and she risked being discovered, she entered the small chamber next to Chrysaleon's.

It was austere almost to barrenness. She would find nothing here. Hope fading, she opened the single olivewood chest and rummaged underneath the folded clothing.

Feeling the hard edges of a bronze coffer, she drew it out and opened the lid, inhaling the faintest scent of apples.

At the bottom of the box, beneath a jar of perfume, an ivory ring, and an old, frail cluster of pressed apple blossom, lay a craftsman's saw, the kind a mason or joiner would use for fine, finishing detail.

Holding it up to the light revealed bits of wood stuck to the sharp grooves. A picture formed in her mind of the king-killer axe and the narrow cuts in the handle. A saw such as this would have completed that task perfectly.

"My lady...?"

The saw fell, clattering onto the tiles between them as she whirled. He'd managed to come in without making a sound, no doubt alerted and wary when he saw his open door, or heard her make some sound.

Alexiare looked from it to her. "Curiosity as well as beauty," he said in his ruined voice.

She knew by the way he arranged his face into studied blankness that he was guilty. But Alexiare would never betray Chrysaleon, and a saw with bits of wood dust in the teeth proved nothing. She would have to force his hand.

"The father of my child should have lived as consort for his year," she said coldly. "That is the Way. You stole it from him, from me, from Aridela, and from Athene. You and the coward, Chrysaleon. I will show Aridela what you have hidden. I will tell her what you did. You and your king will be declared traitors and finally, you will be put to death."

"Forgive me, my lady. I don't understand. What have I done?" He lifted his shoulders and pursed his lips in a fair imitation of puzzled innocence.

The more time she gave him, the less likely he was to give himself away. His mind was quite sharp.

"Aridela will see the evidence and decide," she said. "I will show her the king-killer. I will show her how it was manipulated."

He made a move towards the saw so she bent and picked it up. As she pushed past him, he seized her arm and from some fold or pocket in his tunic produced a dagger. Slaves were not allowed to possess weapons on Kaphtor. Apparently, this was another law Alexiare thought himself above.

"I cannot let you do that, my lady," he said, almost gently.

Selene was taller, and looked down into his eyes with bitter contempt. "Then you must kill me too," she said.

"How could you expect him to embrace such a death? He is a great king and must lead his people as his father did. He loves your queen and wanted to see his children born. Does that make him evil, or merely a man, like any other?" He shrugged. "Lady Athene accepts what we did. There was no punishment."

She smiled.

His eyes widened then narrowed. Tightening his grip on the dagger, he raised it. She dropped the saw. With a shout, she threw herself against him, grabbing his wrist.

Each fought to gain control of the blade. Selene stumbled over a tripod, knocking both it and its bronze statue of Poseidon over. The statue in turn struck the lamp stand. It teetered and fell, sending oil-fed flames splashing across the floor. As she tried to recover her balance, Alexiare shoved her, and she hit her head against the corner of the chest.

It was a hard blow, sending her spinning into near unconsciousness. She fought to recover, blinking and taking deep breaths. The hand she put to her head came away wet with blood. She was oddly breathless and dizzy. Her muscles tingled as if she'd drunk too much wine. Even so, she had no doubt she would overpower him. He was an old man, constricted by a bad leg. He had no strength to speak of. She would try not to hurt him too much. That would be for the executioners.

Menoetius would be vindicated.

Alexiare threw himself on top of her, seeking to pin her arms, but she freed one and punched him in the mouth. His grip on the knife loosened and she took it from him.

She hesitated, reluctant to stab him. Taking advantage of her pause, he struck her breasts with both fists, bit her, and bashed her forehead with his own. As she reeled, unprepared for such a vicious attack, he hefted the statue of Poseidon from the floor and leveled it against her temple.

There was an instant of searing pain then she seemed to drift in and out of the room. She looked down from the ceiling, watching him straddle her. He was gasping, sweating, shaking, clearly at the end of his endurance.

"We have come too far to go back." His broken, rusty voice returned her to her body.

The quick flash of the dagger blinded her. Numbness spread through her limbs. She wanted to throw her enemy off, but her strength had leached away. With the last of her will, she lifted one hand and placed it on the side of his face. "I curse you," she whispered.

Heavy nets tumbled from the painted spirals on the ceiling. Behind Alexiare's grizzled features she saw something. The pale outline of a woman's serene face. With it came a vision of the future. Everything became clear—the reason Menoetius had to die. Aridela's blindness. Chrysaleon's plots. They were all part of a magnificent, complicated tapestry the Fates would weave over the next millennium—or longer.

Calm acceptance washed over and she felt strong enough to speak one last time. "You and your master will wander," she said. "Glimpses of joy will be ripped from you. You will beg for death but death will refuse you. You will follow…and follow…without end."

Alexiare's face disappeared behind a thick inky cloud.

"Lady," she asked. "Are you taking me?"

"I have come for you, Selene of Phrygia," a melodious voice replied. The Goddess held out her ivory arms. "Your tasks are finished for now."

Selene's head dropped limply backward as Alexiare drew her to him. Burying his face against her throat, he wept and shuddered until burning oil threatened to set them both on fire.

He had to crawl his way up, holding onto a stool then using the wall to support his weakened body. Every bone made seething protest. He stared at Selene, astounded that he still lived while she lay dead. It was happenstance—mere unlucky fortune—that she'd struck her head so hard. If not for that, surely he would be the one soaked in blood, and she would be searching out Aridela to tell her the truth.

Things did not happen as they should have.

Panting, trembling from pain and exhaustion, he tamped out the fire with the wool cover from his bed. The palace remained quiet, wrapped in sleep. Chrysaleon must have joined the queen in her chamber.

Alexiare rolled Selene into the singed bedcover. But what to do next? He sat down heavily on the floor, weary beyond belief, defeated. Gradually his mind took over and formulated a plan, as it usually seemed to do. He heaved himself up and left the chamber, slipping through dark corridors to a set of storerooms, where he found what he wanted—ropes and an assortment of leather sacks, commonly used to make mead.

Selene was tall. He took the biggest sack in the storeroom, but still couldn't stuff her completely into it. Using sturdy rope, he tied the bag around her neck, leaving her head exposed, and fashioned the rest into a crude yoke. He staggered through the deserted corridors, dragging the sack to the north entrance. There he waited in the shadows a long while for the sentry to leave his post.

He struggled through the warm, scented night. Many times he stopped to catch his breath. His heart pounded like a smithy hammer then skipped erratically as though struggling to find its proper rhythm. He felt dizzy, nauseated, and wondered more than once if villagers would find their bodies, side by side, at sunrise. The rope scoured his bony shoulders until they were raw and bleeding.

At last he and his burden reached a steep, isolated spot on the northern cliffs. There was no moon, not even a sliver. Alexiare listened to the sea wash against the shore below. He sat next to Selene, giving his heart time to slow, his breathing a chance to calm. When he felt strong enough, he collected stones, packed them in the bag around her body, and retied the sack at her neck with the rope.

He lifted her heavy flaxen hair in his hands. He buried his face in it, smelling its fragrance, feeling its softness. His mind brought forth images of the baby who now had no mother or father.

As the eastern horizon lightened to a rich cobalt blue, he rose again. "I salute you," he said. "You are a great lady and the queen's true friend. I am sorry to have orphaned your child. We will miss you, Selene of Phrygia."

He rolled her over the edge.

He waited at the precipice until the rising sun offered enough light to search the shoreline. There was no sign of the sack. "I will never tell Chrysaleon of this," he said aloud, and turned away.

8

Moon of Flying Swans

THEMISTE'S PAINS BEGAN LATE, AFTER A LONG SUPPER MADE LONGER BY AN eager traveling bard.

Aridela woke at a word from her maid and came to the oracle's side in a sleeping tunic, her hair hastily pulled back.

"Darling Minos," she said, clasping Themiste's hands. "Soon our child will be with us. And it is nearly the full moon—a good omen."

"I've assisted women in labor, but I never realized how...." Themiste grimaced. "Sharp the pain can be."

Aridela cooled her friend's forehead with a wet cloth. "It's hot in here." She glanced at the other women who waited nearby, ready to help when needed. A brisk fire burned in the hearth, plus several stands held flaming lamps. Outside, it was a typical winter's night, cold and raining, but any hint of chill, along with fresh air, had been chased out of Themiste's birth chamber.

Neoma entered, yawning, also in her sleeping gown. She held Selene's five-month-old daughter.

"Here is Xanthe, wanting to greet her new sister." Aridela held out her arms to cuddle the baby. The child gurgled, kicked, and grasped Aridela's nose.

It was easy to see Selene in the baby's face, and hard to look at her without thinking of her mother.

Aridela had never voiced her secret fear in the months since Selene vanished. Had she abandoned Kaphtor because of Menoetius's death?

Had she gone because Aridela refused to believe their accusations against Chrysaleon? Would Selene leave this child, her lover's only offspring? Aridela couldn't believe it, yet those who searched for over a month never discovered any substantial clues to explain the sudden disappearance of the Phrygian warrior.

Chrysaleon had reminded Aridela of Selene's singular hatred toward him. He was convinced she had returned to her homeland to join the moon cult that allowed no men.

Aridela remained unsure. She and Selene were closer than sisters, as close, truly, as lovers. If Selene meant to leave Kaphtor, she would tell her best friend goodbye, and she would take Xanthe. Selene had never run from anything. But months passed, Aridela continued to wonder, and Selene's confession played through her mind.

I never knew such love for a man could steal into my heart without my consent, and burn it forever to his.

Themiste broke into Aridela's thoughts by asking for a sip of water.

"Only a little while longer." Aridela handed Xanthe to a nurse. "My mother used to say that when a babe is born, all memory of pain vanishes into joy as radiant as the sun."

Neoma settled on a stool next to Aridela's.

Aridela held both her friends' hands. "Let us make certain these children are always together. If I conceive, we could have three daughters, lifelong comrades. That is my vision, my dream. I only wish Selene could share it."

"Yes," Themiste said.

"Xanthe has a look that reminds me of her father." Neoma gave a conciliatory sign against evil. "It's these long lashes over blue eyes. I remember his eyes from before he was mauled. His child offers memories of better days."

"And she has Selene's beautiful white skin." Themiste squeezed Aridela's hand.

"Her mother and father live on in her," Aridela said.

Themiste gasped as another pain struck. The labor quickened and there was no more time for idle talk. Moving the friends aside, Rhené and her midwives spoke words of power as the baby's head crowned. A frowning, angry red face appeared between Themiste's legs.

Pulling the newborn free, Rhené cut the umbilical cord with a sickle-shaped knife and sang the blessing. Themiste fell back, gasping and scarlet. Perspiration glistened on her forehead, darkening the tattoo and dampening the fine auburn hair at her temples.

"A girl," Neoma cried, laughing.

Aridela cleaned the infant with cloths soaked in warm scented water.

Two priestesses carried torches, lit at shrine fires, twice around the crying child to shield her from evil spirits.

"Look." Aridela brought her to her mother. "See how lovely she is!"

Themiste's smile was weak.

"We will call her Pasithea."

"Beautiful," Themiste whispered. She nodded her approval. "'Beautiful to all.' It is a good name."

ALEXIARE ENTERED HIS MASTER'S BEDCHAMBER TO FIND CHRYSALEON sitting at a table, hunched over an empty cup. A dagger lay beside his motionless hand. The slave cleared his throat, fighting off fond exasperation.

"Themiste has borne you a daughter, my lord."

The Zagreus's face revealed no pleasure, no dismay, nothing.

"The mother recovers and your child is healthy. Comely, from what I hear. The queen named her Pasithea."

Chrysaleon wearily turned his face away and gazed at the hearth fire. "Themiste never speaks to me unless she is forced."

"The queen believes in you, my lord, and no one dares refute her. Other than Minos Themiste, perhaps, the whole island believes in you, adores you in fact."

Chrysaleon made his opinion clear with a snort. "Are you so certain about what Aridela believes?" He stood, carelessly scraping his chair over the swallows and cuttlefish so painstakingly inlaid in the floor tiles. "Though we never say his name, my brother lies between us every night. She spoke of him only once—to give me his message."

"Message, my lord? You told me of no message."

"He wanted me to know he remembered the lioness, and his debt to me." A strange, almost desperate expression passed across his face, at odds with his laugh. "Before he died, he believed he owed me. Since then, I have had dreams that tell me otherwise."

"Sir, you did the only thing you could. Menoetius knew your fate was to live, to be a great king." Alexiare came closer. "It is every vassal's duty to die for his liege."

"It was not me he died for, you fool. It was her. You saw how the mob was acting. And why didn't he tell Aridela this baby was mine? He hated me—he wanted me declared a traitor. All he had to do was reveal that secret. Both Themiste and I would have been condemned."

Giving one of his customary shrugs, Alexiare said, "What makes you think so? The queen did not believe him when he and Selene told her you meant to thwart the sacrifice. It would have been his word against Themiste's, and she has quite obviously chosen to keep your secret."

Chrysaleon frowned at his slave. "Was it worth it? Before she disappeared, Selene longed to see me slaughtered. Themiste has been forever changed. My blood brother lies dead at my hand." His voice lowered. "I can no longer tell what Aridela thinks. She shares nothing; her eyes give as much away as a moonless night. I am left with the memory of the way she embraced Menoetius the night of the battle, like a lover. Bastard of Idómeneus—he feels more alive to me than ever." Smashing his fist against the surface of the table, his voice turned hoarse. "I want to go back to Mycenae and leave this god-cursed country behind."

After many days of chilly rain and gloomy skies, the sun finally emerged. Though it was humid, the unseasonable warmth was intoxicating. Themiste suggested she and Aridela take the baby and sail to the little isle of Dia just off the northern coast of Kaphtor.

They beached near the ruin of the stone harbor and walked inland, leaving the sailors with the boat. Aridela served as handmaid, carrying a basket of bread, honey, cheese, and a jar of wine, while Themiste held Pasithea.

Themiste protested that she felt strong and was tired of her confinement, so they climbed to the highest point overlooking the bay. From there Kaphtor's coastline was clear and they could even make out the hazy snow-capped mountains of Ida. They settled on the ground and Aridela fed Themiste cheese as the new mother nursed her child.

"I have not told you where Selene and I put the tablets last summer," Themiste said.

"I thought you wanted to keep it a secret." Aridela poured a little wine into a clay cup.

"Not from you." Themiste accepted the offered cup. "We talked about several places—Mount Juktas, Mount Ida, Mount Dikti—even Velchanos's cave. But we went farther, to the Araden mountains."

At this, Aridela almost dropped the second cup she was filling. Her gaze shot to the oracle's.

Themiste gave a brief nod. "Yes, it is far, but I sensed it was where Selene wanted to go. You have already guessed. We went to your cave, yours and Menoetius's."

"Oh," Aridela said faintly. *Yours and Menoetius's.*

Themiste set down her cup and clasped Aridela's hand. "I've wanted to tell you, but you never seem to be alone. That's why I asked you to come here today."

The cozy fire pit, the comfortable pallet, the sense of security, and the discerning gaze of her scarred guardian ran through Aridela's mind. Loss speared so acutely it was nearly unbearable, and she heard herself draw in a sharp breath.

You'll tether me like a goat? That is your image of victory?

I will have victory, Aridela.

Themiste was watching her much like Menoetius used to, with eyes that seemed to see every secret. "We put the tablets in the back, where it is dark and narrow. We had to crawl. Even if someone finds the cave, I think the tablets will be safe."

Aridela worked to maintain a stoic expression.

"Everything was still there," Themiste said. "The pallet where you slept, the pit that kept you warm. Bowls. Cloth. Even that log he brought in. I confess I laughed as I imagined him binding you, and how you have told me you responded."

Tears burned despite Aridela's efforts to stop them. She blinked, but knew the perceptive oracle had seen.

Themiste squeezed her hand. "The air had a wild, clean taste. It renewed and strengthened me. I have not felt so well in a long time."

"Really?" Aridela said.

Themiste nodded. "I sensed I was following the Lady's wishes. Truthfully, I believed I was putting the tablets in a holy place. Selene had the same sensation. We spoke of you, and of Menoetius. She said there was something divine between you."

Trying to recover a semblance of calm, Aridela gave all her concentration to pulling apart a hunk of cheese.

"You loved Asterion, our Beast of the labyrinth."

"Star of the labyrinth," Aridela whispered.

Out in the bay, three dolphins leaped from the water as though trying to reach the sun. Light glittered against the spray and their wet bodies.

"I believe he watches over you," Themiste said.

For longer than you can imagine, I will be with you, in you, of you. Together we bring forth a new world, and nothing can ever part us.

Aridela's throat worked as she fought the urge to crush her face against her knees and yield to grief-stricken howls.

"He had substance," was all she said.

Aridela fell into the habit of summoning Themiste and Neoma on the days her queenly duties didn't demand attention. The three spent endless time playing with the children of their hearts, the one who might someday be queen and her sister in spirit, Xanthe, who gave sweet memories of her mother and father. When Aridela made faces to spark their laughter, she felt joy, reminiscent of the time before Harpalycus.

Several days after they sailed to the isle of Dia, Themiste brought her daughter to Aridela's chamber for a visit. Pasithea had fallen asleep, one tiny fist clenched against her mother's smooth bare skin.

Aridela was preparing for a bath. "Sit with me," she said. "We'll talk of the old days."

They passed Chrysaleon on the way to the bath chamber. Aridela noticed how Themiste glanced at the consort then quickly away. Neither spoke to the other.

When Aridela was soaking in perfumed water, she said, "I understand why Selene hated Chrysaleon. Yet I feel within you an ill will too. Why do you never speak to the Zagreus? He is your mate as well as mine. You could invite him to your bed, unless of course you wish to remain untouched for custom's sake."

"I have no desire to lie with him." Themiste's tone was suppressed yet oddly forceful. "And he should remain as constant to you as you have been to him."

The tension and distaste in the reply left Aridela briefly speechless. She managed to nod and agree. "Yes, he should." She frowned, and sought to explain. "My bond with Chrysaleon is more than physical. It was created by the Goddess, and transcends mortal concerns and jealousies."

Themiste seemed to understand. "You think of the night on Mount

Juktas, when Velchanos wore Chrysaleon's face." She rested her cheek against the fine black curls on her daughter's head and was quiet for some time. "Lately I feel a great worry and anxiety," she finally offered. "I sense something is coming, something that will change us all profoundly. I have seen things, in vision, that I have not shared, with you or anyone, but I woke today convinced you should know of them."

Aridela waited as her maid massaged her scalp.

Themiste's face darkened. When she did speak, her voice trembled faintly. "I have seen men with beards—Achaeans—holding sway over us with lists and taxes. Kaphtor's people starve as the best of what they have grown is taken to enrich mainland storehouses. I have seen our sacred word, *cabal*, lose its meaning and become something differ-ent, something unholy and dangerous. But this is the least. In vision, I see men pulling down the statue of Velchanos and throwing it into the sea—" Her voice hitched. She had to stop, swallow, and compose herself. "Our mountain shrines demolished, the sacred bulls stolen by the mainland god, Poseidon." She lifted her gaze, her anguish unhid-den. A single tear trailed down her cheek. "I have seen sacrifices…of children. That is how desperate the people become."

Aridela sat up straight in the steaming water. She forced herself to keep silent, though she wanted to cry out denials, shout promises that she would never allow such things to happen.

"Labyrinthos lies in ruins," Themiste said, "buried in drifting sand until even the memory of it is lost." She drew in a harsh breath. "In one of my visions, my title was stolen and given to a male. They laughed and kept it, and called themselves *Minos* for all time. Whenever I look upon your consort, these visions manifest, and I am fearful."

Themiste appeared so distraught Aridela didn't know what to do. Finally, she reached out a wet hand. The oracle hesitated then clasped it.

"In this I have joined you," Aridela said. "Not with vision, but dreams. More and more of late they come to me. I wake sickened with misgivings. I, too, have seen our ancient rites discarded, the Goddess forgotten. More than forgotten—betrayed. Just last night, Minos, I dreamed the mainlanders' sky-god, this *Zeus*, gathered an unholy strength right here on Kaphtor. Our honey made him invincible. He murdered or subjugated all the other gods. Once I dreamed he ate Velchanos, and Velchanos was no more. I have dreamed that our people forget Kaphtor's history, that they come to believe Zeus gave birth to Goddess Athene." She laughed. It held no humor, but still she attempted to lighten the heavy subject, and wondered if she really sought to vanquish her own fears. "Does that not prove how foolish dreams can be? Even babies know Athene's name meaning. 'I have come from myself.' No matter how many warriors sprout upon the rocks of Argolis, no matter how they try to change the truth, truth can never be changed."

Themiste's stare was fixed. "Your dreams are not foolish. Goddess sends them as warning. She wants us to prevent this from happening. But how?"

Aridela had no answer, and could only shake her head.

Her handmaid added a mixture of grapeseed, scented with Aridela's favorite musk oil, to the bathwater. Seductive scent infused the room. Themiste entertained Pasithea by swinging her gently and dipping her plump feet into the water. The baby laughed, giving voice to simple delight. Even the oracle smiled, though she still seemed disturbed and sad.

Aridela considered what Themiste described. It was defeat she saw in the oracle's shadowed eyes and slumped shoulders, more so than sadness. The weight of vision and fears for what might come was a heavy burden for anyone to carry. Themiste hadn't escaped that burden. In fact, she suffered more than most, and it was beginning to show. For the first time Aridela noticed the threads of grey in her hair, the fine lines around her eyes and mouth and across her forehead.

Themiste had changed since the miracle that formed a child in her womb. She seldom smiled or laughed. She was often distracted, away in some secret place she shared with no one.

Aridela knew that she, too, bore no resemblance to the spoiled girl she had been before the Mycenaean brothers came to Kaphtor. Any shred of innocence left to her after Harpalycus's brutality had died with Menoetius in the barley field. Not even the gradual reemergence of sunlight or disappearance of the hateful ash could return that carefree child. Only two could make Aridela forget, for short spaces of time, how everything had altered from light to dark. Her two treasured children, black-haired Pasithea and lovely Xanthe, although the pleasure Xanthe gave was bittersweet, thanks to a blue, straightforward gaze that was uncommonly like her father's, and fragile, blue-veined skin so reminiscent of her mother's.

Aridela asked her handmaid to fetch wine, and when she'd gone, said quietly, "Menoetius shared something with me before he died. You should hear it. It might give you ease and hope."

Themiste waited, her luminous eyes still haunted.

"He, too, had visions and dreams. For years, he had a dream where he was confronted by a lion. He knew he must fight the lion in order to protect me from some awful thing—he was not sure what. There were words that accompanied this dream. *What seems the end is only the beginning.* He was puzzled by it, until he was confined in the labyrinth."

She paused for so long that Themiste gently prompted her. "What happened to him there?"

"He heard and saw the Lady as though she stood before him. He said she glowed like a star. She showed him many things—much of which he didn't tell me—and she repeated that promise. There, in the silence and solitude of the labyrinth, his long-abandoned devotion to her returned. He was transformed, ready to submit, no matter what it might cost him. He understood that no matter how it seemed, whatever happened, it was not the end. He told me about this, I think because he believed we would be reunited. It has given me comfort since the night he offered his life to Kaphtor. I believe it too. Somehow…I know I will see him again. Somewhere."

The handmaid returned with a pitcher of wine and two bowls.

Themiste wiped away her tears. "Thank you for telling me, Aridela." She looked down at her baby, who laughed and grasped her finger. "Perhaps we have not given our Mistress enough trust. It could be that we simply cannot see as far as she does."

In the other room, Chrysaleon called to one of his men in a rough, impatient voice. Themiste startled. Her head turned sharply and she stiffened. She only relaxed when it again grew quiet and it was clear Chrysaleon had gone away.

Aridela tried to dismiss a creeping conviction that Chrysaleon had something to do with the changes in Themiste. The oracle had said the very sight of him caused her fear, but Aridela dismissed that, as she did anything that seemed critical of her consort. Besides, the way Themiste said it suggested all Achaeans frightened her, not just Chrysaleon.

There was no denying Kaphtor's recovery was due overwhelmingly to the Zagreus. Ships again entered Kaphtor's harbors, perhaps not as many as in days of old, but such things took time—time Kaphtor would not have been granted without the impenetrable shield provided by Chrysaleon's presence. As High King over the mainland citadels, Chrysaleon cowed those bloodthirsty warriors and kept them from invading. How could Themiste fear the man who contributed so much to their recovery? It was unfair and cruel.

Though she would never betray Chrysaleon by speaking of it to anyone, Aridela knew how tortured he was over what he had done to his brother. She doubted if even the favored slave, Alexiare, knew. Six months had passed, yet he still woke nearly every night, crying out, sweating. She held him and soothed him and he clung to her almost desperately. In his sleep he whispered his dead brother's name, sometimes cursing, sometimes asking forgiveness.

Themiste appeared to be lost in thought. Aridela's own mind wandered backward as it often did, to the mead-making festival and the oracle's frightening prediction. *You will suffer*, she had said. *As you are betrayed, so you will in turn betray those who put their faith in you.*

Had her consort plotted to avert his death and lengthen his reign? With months to consider, she knew he had. But it was his motive that remained a question. Had he used Kaphtor's best interests as an excuse, mouthing words with no intent but to save himself? Selene and Menoetius swore it was so. Now Menoetius was dead and Selene, her beloved friend, vanished. Every time Aridela held their orphaned child, loss and grief reopened old wounds in her heart.

She still didn't fully understand why he had insisted on Menoetius as his cabal, and when awake, Chrysaleon placed a wall so high and thick around any mention of his brother that she despaired of ever receiving an answer. The only thing that made any sense was that he somehow knew, though their bond was frayed and damaged, that Menoetius would do what no other man would: fall in line and offer himself in his brother's stead.

The memory of Menoetius carrying her from the underground shrine when she was ten remained amazingly clear and vivid. She remembered peering into his face, struck by his vivid indigo eyes. He raced in dreamlike slowness up the steps, shouting for help. Even then she had believed him no mere mortal. She often caught herself conjuring the days in the mountain cave where the stalactites glittered. He'd done so much more than protect her from Harpalycus. He returned to her the desire to live, then gave his own life for her sake. It was unendurable that she had broken her promise to take care of Selene and the baby. He'd asked so little of her. When Chrysaleon happened upon her at such times, she was forced to disguise floods of anger and put on a false smile. Sometimes she couldn't manage it, and simply had to walk away from him, which always caused an argument.

All those months leading up to the king-sacrifice, she had wept, prayed, and imagined how to avert it. Had she acquiesced too easily, too quickly, when Chrysaleon offered a way? This pervasive sense of guilt suggested she had much to answer for.

As she sipped wine, the maid smoothed her tangles with an ivory comb.

It is glory and power Chrysaleon loves, Menoetius whispered. *You are his means to achieve it.*

You carry a traitor's child. Selene now, her voice mingling with her dead lover's.

Too many questions. Too much doubt. Aridela was weary of forcing herself to defend what could very well be a lie. In the privacy of her mind, she admitted that since the rise of Iakchos, her single-minded loyalty to Chrysaleon had gradually shifted. Now it seemed to consist of obligation, tinged with suspicion, and the uncomfortable sensation that she'd been deceived. *You see only what you want to see*, her wise mother had once said. By allowing herself to be blinded, Aridela had played a part in the death of Menoetius, in the desolation of Themiste, in the disappearance of Selene, and in the duping of the people of Kaphtor. Her mother had said something else that day. *Damasen's most loving gift to me was his refusal to allow me to change things. It showed his love more than any other act could.* She'd added, somberly, *When Iakchos rises, that is when Chrysaleon's truth will emerge.*

Since the initiation of taxes, Aridela had noticed a change in the people's manner. Once so adoring of Chrysaleon, they no longer bombarded him with flowers and praise. Now they observed him in silence when he left the palace, which he did less and less, and he had replaced all his Cretan serving men with Mycenaeans.

She pushed away nagging guilt and uneasiness. This recovery was hard. But so had been the Destruction. Chrysaleon promised the taxes were temporary and would be discarded as soon as the coffers were replenished. It made sense, and the council had given him their enthusiastic approval.

Menoetius's eyes held an expression of profound sadness. *Even now, when my blood calls you, still you blind yourself.*

Aridela rose from the bath abruptly, turning her face so Themiste wouldn't see her anguish. The maid wrapped her up and briskly toweled the water from her hair.

Hoping to offer some comfort, she said, "From the beginning, kings have spilled their life-giving blood for the good of the people. Nothing can stop the great sacrifice. Think of the bounty Chrysaleon will release upon Kaphtor when he at last descends into the labyrinth—many times more, I think, than any king who lived but a year. His gift will be eight times stronger, for he absorbs the strength and purity of each bull-king who dies in his place."

"Perhaps." Themiste's voice lacked inflection. "I cannot tell. The Lady no longer speaks to me. I see nothing in the entrails. All I am given are these visions of warning, these offerings of curses, death, and endings."

Alarmed, Aridela tried again. "She showed you the highest possible favor by placing a holy child into your womb. Surely Goddess Athene loves you more than any other mortal. You are Minos—Moon-Being. Her holy oracle."

Themiste's face blanched, as it did every time Athene's singular favor was mentioned. "No, Aridela. You speak from ignorance." Pasithea began to cry. Themiste looked down, frowning, as though puzzled by the sight of this infant on her lap. "I am giving Pasithea my title," she said. "I no longer want it. Let it go to the next generation, with prayers that they will take better care of what they have been given than I have done."

Aridela started to protest, but stopped when she noticed how interested the maidservant was in their conversation. "Leave us," she said impatiently. "I will comb my own hair." The maid bowed and backed, a bit reluctantly, from the room.

She knelt by Themiste's stool. "You told me you are afraid of Chrysaleon. I am too, at times."

Themiste couldn't hide her surprise.

"It's true." Aridela took Themiste's hand. It was so cold. She rubbed it—even blew gently on the oracle's fingers in an attempt to warm them. "Don't be afraid. Chrysaleon will live for eight years as my consort, but the labyrinth will claim him. I swear it. There is no escape from Goddess Athene, not for any of us."

When Iakchos rises, that is when Chrysaleon's truth will emerge. Aridela's skin rose into goose bumps. Helice had made true prophecy that day.

As she and Themiste gazed into each other's eyes, she allowed herself to feel what she had denied and suppressed every day and night since that interlude in the apple grove, when Chrysaleon called her *whore*, the insult he knew would hurt her the most, and suggested she had willingly given herself to Harpalycus.

Relief.

PART III

The Reckoning

1

Moon of Mead-Making

IN THE MOON OF MEAD-MAKING, AFTER THE WILD PEAR TREES BLOOMED, Chrysaleon brought his daughter home from Mycenae.

Aridela, Themiste, and Xanthe, alerted by the lookouts, were waiting for them on the pier. Xanthe clutched a new black kitten. Gusty sea-winds played with their skirts, and Aridela had to repeatedly pull her hair out of her eyes.

Rising on her toes, Xanthe waved at her best friend. The kitten gave an anxious meow.

Pasithea, standing beside Chrysaleon on the ship, leaned out and returned the wave. Her unbound hair flew wildly about her head. It would be a chore to untangle. Aridela wondered, as she had numerous times, why she had allowed Chrysaleon to talk her into abandoning Kaphtor's custom of shaving children's heads until they were twelve.

Two long months had passed since she had last seen father and daughter. The returning child looked taller, older than her six and a half years.

Aridela noticed a dark-headed man on Pasithea's other side. From this distance he bore an uncanny resemblance to Menoetius. She drew in a sharp breath and glanced at Themiste, fearful of her thoughts betraying her, but the oracle was talking to Xanthe and hadn't noticed anything.

Tears stung her eyes as she was swept back in memory to Menoetius's silence and frowns, which for months she had assumed were signs of censure. She remembered how he would lower his face and raise his shoulder in an unconscious attempt to hide his disfigurement.

Yes, she wept with joy at the return of Chrysaleon and Pasithea. And a few of her tears were birthed in sorrow for the other, for Asterion. The man who, to this day, was praised in song and art.

No wonder Queen Helice grew so weary that murder at the hands of Harpalycus became a welcome escape.

"She looks older," Themiste said. "And lovely, Aridela. I have missed her so."

Aridela could only nod as emotion flooded.

Pasithea jumped from the tender and ran to them on her short strong legs, crying, "I am going to marry Gelanor!"

Aridela met Chrysaleon's sheepish grin as Pasithea threw her arms around her mother's waist, nearly pitching her over.

"What is this?" Aridela asked, laughing. "You know you must wed the strongest male who wins the Games for you. You're no peasant, to choose a husband."

"I will be Gelanor's wife." The child's lower lip pursed into a familiar pout. "I shall never marry anyone if I cannot marry Gelanor. You changed the customs to suit you, Mother. I will too."

"Where did she get such an idea?" Aridela leveled an accusing stare at Chrysaleon.

He shrugged. "Blame Gelanor. He did nothing but spoil her with trinkets, food, pets—anything she wanted. They were never apart but for sleeping."

"I love Gelanor," Pasithea said.

The queen peered into her daughter's eyes. They were greener than usual just now, due to a fierce gleam, strongly reminiscent of Chrysaleon's when he felt thwarted. The two were uncannily alike. In truth, Velchanos must have made it so, to encourage Aridela to take the child for her own and name the Mycenaean king her father.

"I will consider it," she said at last, not wanting to argue so soon after being reunited.

"I love you." With another hug, Pasithea struggled free of Aridela's embrace. She hugged Themiste with the same exuberance, saying, "Are you well, Themiste-mother? I want to show you the gifts Gelanor gave me." Then she seized Xanthe's hand. Together they ran chattering up to the litters, tugging Themiste along with them. The kitten escaped and all three leaped after it, laughing.

"Chrysaleon," Aridela murmured. A two-month separation made her notice things she paid no attention to in their day-to-day lives. The lines burned into his face by the sun were deeper than she remembered, and his abdomen not as flat as when they'd begun their tempestuous affair in the Cave of Velchanos, eight years past. Sunlight reflected off strands of silver at his temples, and his mane of tawny hair had lost some of its brightness. He still retained his strength, however; he picked her up in his arms without any obvious effort and swung her in a circle.

"I've missed you," he said.

"And I you. Oh, put me down...." Aridela staggered and pressed a hand to her forehead as the hills and beach spun crazily.

"What is wrong, my love?"

"Nothing is wrong. I have been keeping a secret. Chrysaleon—I have conceived at last."

Startled pleasure flamed across his face. He scooped her into his arms again and carried her to the waiting litter. "It's been so long," he said. "I confess I'd given up." Then he added bluntly, "I want a son."

"I have my daughter." She kissed his mouth and cheeks. "I shall make offerings and ask for a son."

"Chrysaleon...." The voice came from behind them. He turned.

"Gelanor," he said. "I've just discovered my queen is carrying a child."

Aridela hadn't seen Gelanor in seven years. He was taller than Chrysaleon now. He had the same green eyes, but hair as black, thick, and curly as Pasithea's.

As she stared at him, Aridela couldn't help thinking this man and her daughter could have sprung from the same womb, they looked so much alike.

"This is happy news." He stepped forward, grinning, and kissed her on both cheeks. His voice was deeper too. When he smiled, his teeth flashed like ivory in a face of bronze, and faint lines crinkled around his eyes. She recalled Chrysaleon telling her that he was her age, which would make him twenty-four, a man now in every way and an assured, imposing ruler. All hint of naivety was gone.

Pasithea ran back to them and threw herself into Gelanor's arms so forcefully he took several hasty steps backward to avoid falling.

He laughed and perched her on his hip as naturally as if he was accustomed to her spending all her time there.

"Gelanor, you truly are 'Laughter' in mortal form," Aridela said.

"Chrysaleon, do you remember telling me his name meaning? Isn't there a goddess of mirth on the mainland? She must have blessed you when you were born. You make all around you want to smile. Chrysaleon—please. You're hurting me."

He set her carefully on her feet with an apology.

"You look strange," she said. "Is it sea-sickness?"

"No." He frowned. "Why is Alexiare not here?"

"He has fallen ill."

"You sent no word."

"I didn't want to worry you, and neither did he. His eyes are worse. I'm sorry to tell you he's blind. And some disease makes it painful to breathe. He cannot hold food and wastes away."

"I want to see him."

"Of course, my love." Aridela turned, clapping for the litter-bearers.

CHRYSALEON HURRIED TO HIS SLAVE.

When he entered the chamber, the smell struck him, instantly bringing back the night Idómeneus died. He paused to compose his features.

"Old man," he said, approaching the bed. "You neglect your chores."

Alexiare turned his head slowly to face his master. The strange cloudy film that had accumulated over his eyes during the last few years had thickened during Chrysaleon's absence. Chrysaleon could tell by the way his slave didn't look directly into his eyes that Aridela hadn't been wrong. He was indeed blind.

"Alexiare." Chrysaleon knelt beside the bed.

"Do not fret, my lord, I beg you. I have had a long life. Too long, some might say, and I would agree." His voice, always gravelly, had degenerated further, into barely comprehensible wheezing.

"What do you need?"

"Water, if you wouldn't mind."

Chrysaleon held the cup to his lips.

"I've been waiting for you to return," Alexiare whispered. "There are things I need to tell you—before it is too late."

"What things?"

"I have seen the Goddess. All these years I thought she didn't exist."

"You've been dreaming."

"No, my lord. I have angered her, brought her wrath not only on myself, but you."

"You have not done anything that cannot be remedied by a few prayers and the sacrifice of a goat."

Kaphtor's royal healer, chosen by Rhené just before she died, entered from one of the side doors, accompanied by a maidservant with a bowl of clean water. She pressed a cloth to Alexiare's lips as he coughed, long, painful expulsions that brought up blood. Exhausted, he fell back.

"He should rest," the woman said, inclining her head. Chrysaleon could never remember her name.

"I'll return later," Chrysaleon said to his slave, "and I expect you to be on your feet."

Alexiare's pet warbler sang as Chrysaleon left. Its voice was sweet yet lonely, sparking a strange sense of foreboding.

He pondered as he strode through the corridors and across the courtyard to the feasting hall. When Aridela mentioned Gelanor's name meaning at the pier, something had coalesced. Never before had he connected Themiste's prophecy to his brother. Yet now it seemed obvious.

The youthful sun will marry the ancient moon. He who laughs will lie with she who is beautiful to men.

He wanted to hear what Alexiare thought, but the old man was too weak, too feverish. It sounded as though he'd become anxious as well, by what awaited him on the other side of life. He must have forgotten how much they had accomplished, and without any sign of anger from Potnia Athene.

A year after Menoetius gave his blood to the crops, the council met to decide the future of the sacrifice. Surprising everyone, Chrysaleon most of all, they followed the precedent he set. Chrysaleon could only wonder how much Aridela had influenced their decision, for she never revealed what was said in those secretive council meetings.

The augurers and star readers drew up their charts and examined the portents, searching out the next perfect configuration of the sun and moon. They concluded that in order for Chrysaleon to achieve the prophesied great year, his reign would have to start over. His first year as king, the year of the Destruction, was discarded, and the counting began anew with the death of Menoetius.

A young Cretan won the Games that year, on the holy day lying out of time between the old year and the new. Nineteen years old, with long black hair and a lean, graceful dancer's build, he ruled at Aridela's side for one day, the first day of the new year, just as Menoetius had done. He was feasted and praised, and he coupled with her that night. Under the burning glow of Iakchos, Chrysaleon emerged from the tombs to slay him with the ancient sickle of bone. The youth's body was torn by the priestesses, his blood sprinkled through the groves and barley, his manhood fed to the ocean, and Chrysaleon began his second year as bull-king.

Every year since, Chrysaleon spent one day and most of a night in the Cretan tombs, listening to the sighs of the dead while envisioning Aridela and her winning consort lying together. Every year he wondered if she would grow heavy with another man's spawn. But it never happened…as far as he knew.

He'd slain six youths so far, men who suffered violent death so he could remain alive and absorb their sanctity.

Time slipped past so quickly. In less than a month the seventh cabal would die, and Chrysaleon would begin his last year as Zagreus and bull-king. In one brief year, he would again face his own death when the sun and moon came into rare coincidence.

Rule until the sun and moon shift into perfect alignment, the oracle Daphoenissa had decreed. *Then you will die, Lion of Mycenae.*

She herself was dead—killed by a Spartan warrior who didn't appreciate one of her auguries.

Chrysaleon entered the feasting hall and returned Aridela's smile even as he squinted in an effort to hide his tumultuous thoughts.

He would blast Daphoenissa's prediction into splinters. Nothing could stop him. Chrysaleon would fly upon the wings of his moera as he had upon the death-gryphon's back, and triumph over all those who plotted to destroy him.

AT THE WELCOMING FEAST, AS PASITHEA ENTERTAINED THEM WITH HER adventures at Mycenae, she played with Gelanor's fingers in a familiar, possessive fashion. It was hard to believe this outgoing, sophisticated child had not yet seen the rise of Iakchos seven times.

After the bard finished his tale, she leaned toward Gelanor, saying, "I want to give you a gift." With great ceremony and flourish, she climbed up onto her chair, sending her bright gaze and winning smile around the hall. Lifting her arms to gain everyone's attention, she made her announcement. "Prince Gelanor," she said, "when you become my husband, you will have my title. You will be Minos of Kaphtor."

She grabbed his hand and pulled him up beside her. He grinned, though he sent a bewildered glance toward the queen.

Shocked silence descended like wet fishing nets. Then someone laughed. Gradually, more people joined in, and soon, nearly everyone was buzzing and thumping their cups on the tables—especially the Mycenaeans. All who saw her loved Pasithea—impetuous in spirit, guileless, incomprehensibly lovely. Spoiled, true, but was that a bad thing? No one else could have secured such a mild reaction to something so shamefully improper.

Giving the onlookers a rueful smile and helpless shrug, Aridela rose and assisted her child back into her seat. "You have been taught better than this," she whispered. "Your title is between you and Mistress Athene. Not for the ears of the uninitiated. You have just broken a tradition that has been in place since Kaphtor's beginnings. Without asking me."

Pasithea shook her head, causing her curly hair to fluff in a cloud. "Is the title not mine? I had a dream that Gelanor shall be known as King Minos."

Aridela sighed. "You have winning ways, Prince Gelanor."

"I don't know this title, my lady," he said. His ever-present smile faded into concern. "Has she done something bad?"

Before she could make any reply, Chrysaleon intervened. "Perhaps we should consider this union. Crete would benefit from a stronger bond with Mycenae—especially when I am gone."

Not so long ago, none among the Kindred Kings would have dared make such a statement. Aridela tamped down a wave of annoyance. Things had changed since the fire clouds and suffocating ash from the sky. It had happened slowly, subtly; only now, hearing Chrysaleon's tone of arrogant confidence, did she realize the full reversal of their positions. This last war on the mainland had been a success. The

Kindred Kings must have clearly displayed awe and respect for their overlord's glorious achievements.

A bowing servant interrupted her thoughts. "My lord," he said to Chrysaleon. "Your slave is asking for you. The healer can do nothing more and the end is near."

"Shall I come?" Aridela asked.

"No." Chrysaleon rose. "It would make him ill-at-ease."

She touched his hand. "Give him my love."

Sad, how the man who had been with Chrysaleon for so long was dying. She thought of how patiently he'd entertained her when she had suffered the loss of her baby, and how he hadn't laughed at her after her scare on Mount Juktas, when she believed Harpalycus had returned from the dead. Alexiare had devoted his entire life to the royal sons of Idómeneus. In many ways he had fulfilled a father's role. At least his existence had not been snuffed out too early, as had the lives of so many others.

Thinking of those lost loved ones made her morose, so she turned her attention to her daughter.

Pasithea was flirting. Seemingly mesmerized by her in return, Prince Gelanor curled strands of her black hair around his fingers. Then he made her giggle by marching two little clay dolls across the table. These were becoming more and more popular. Crafted to resemble Aridela, they were a symbol of the power of Kaphtor's queen to inspire Goddess Athene's mercy. Many believed that when hung in the fruit trees around the time of the Games, these dolls gave off a blessing or alchemy that fructified the crops on their own, without the blood sacrifice of the king. Their effectiveness could hardly be dismissed: every year they'd been used, the crops had burgeoned, and women everywhere were pregnant—even Aridela's cantankerous womb had become fertile.

Aridela traced the designs on her wine bowl.

No more children. No more love. Not until they all lie dead. Then we will begin again.

The remnant of memory from some lost period in her life intruded into her wandering thoughts. A woman had shouted the warning from a hilltop. It had left her as uneasy then as it did now.

Themiste experienced a frightening dream once, shortly after Pasithea's birth. Aridela tried to recall the oracle's words. Something about the sacred bulls being preempted by the mainland god, Poseidon, the destruction of Velchanos's statue, and even the sacrifice of children. *Every time I look upon your consort,* she had said, *I am fearful.*

Change comes to all things, Harpalycus had announced from the head of his invading army.

Could mortal men destroy Labyrinthos? Even after the damage Harpalycus wrought, it was still hard to imagine any but Athene's Earth Bull having that much power. But Aridela had to admit that the bulls, which, in her youth, were sacred only to the Lady, were now considered holy to Poseidon as well. He was routinely called the "bull-god." Rites and sacrifices revering him had become commonplace, even within the palace. Priests and priestesses devoted to his worship resided in chambers next to those devoted to Athene.

Pasithea stopped giggling long enough to interrupt Aridela's conjectures. "Mother," she said, "Why were you upset by what I did? Father said I should give Gelanor my title. He called it a fitting gesture."

"What?" Aridela was so shocked she forgot to control her expression, and stared at her child, enraged. "How did he know the title? Did you tell him?"

Pasithea shook her head forcefully. "I thought you did."

It took all of Aridela's will to grit her teeth and make her face appear calm, though she didn't seem to fool Pasithea, who looked alarmed.

"It's all right," she said, patting the child's hand.

Somehow, though Gelanor seemed appropriately startled, Aridela suspected he'd known about this all along, and was merely putting on an act of surprise, perhaps at Chrysaleon's instruction.

But now was not the time to lose her temper. It was Pasithea's first night home in two months. She would talk to Chrysaleon later. She would watch his face and get to the bottom of this.

As she took a deep breath and sipped her wine, the last bit of Themiste's gloomy prediction ran through her mind as though of its own insistent will. This part had frightened the oracle more than the rest.

My title was stolen from me and given to a male. They laughed and kept it, and called themselves Minos *for all time.*

Aridela glanced at her daughter as a chill enveloped her. The title, so carelessly bestowed by the child, would remain with the Mycenaean prince. It would become for all time the way Cretan kings were addressed.

Aridela only realized she'd risen from her chair when Pasithea, Gelanor, and several others stopped what they were doing and peered up at her.

Almost desperately, she searched for one face at the end of her table.

Themiste returned her gaze. The oracle had already worked this out, Aridela saw. Her eyes were haunted, glistening with tears. She looked old and tired.

Minos, Aridela mouthed.

Themiste lifted her shoulders and covered her face with her hands.

So did things change. Not with the Earth Bull's terrifying explosion or the brutal invasion of armies, but softly, whispering into darkness on the wings of a child's laughter.

2

Moon of Mead-Making

My love....

Aridela woke instantly at the sound of Menoetius's voice, but realized almost as quickly that she'd been dreaming.

Only one lamp flickered, leaving most of the room netted in shadow. She felt for Chrysaleon.

He wasn't there. He must still be with Alexiare.

The draperies between the pillars at her balcony fluttered, stimulated by night breezes. Propping herself on her elbows, she looked around the room. She'd been dreaming, as she often did, of that long-ago night when she and her mother took Iphiboë to Mount Juktas. The stars in the dream glittered more brightly than they ever did in real life, and the air tasted of honey. Velchanos stood over her, his marble face melting into the features of Menoetius, then Chrysaleon. *Save me, Aridela. Open your heart.*

Aridela....

Her head snapped toward the whisper as her heartbeat trammeled. She stared into the darkest corner of her bedchamber. Something moved on the dressing table—an eruption of silver, green, lavender, and crimson phosphorescence.

More intrigued than afraid, she left the bed and crossed to the table. Ribbons of glowing color fountained, lost momentum, and fell again into a pool. She reached out to this silent, wondrous spray, delighted as a child.

Her fingers passed through the rainbow, carving a hole in the center. There lay the source—a gold seal ring.

She picked it up, rolling it one way then the other on her palm, causing the rainbows to scatter in every direction. They grew and expanded, surrounding her. Her hair drifted as if she were underwater. Her feet lifted off the floor. She floated, yet in this extraordinary fluid color, she could breathe, and she could taste the colors—the rich royal flavor of purple, verdant, earthy green, wet, salty blue, and the hot cinder burn of red. Her senses filled with song, awe, and soaring acceptance.

Aridela.

Menoetius stepped into the waterfall with her, his face and body unmarred, his eyes the shade of twilight. He was as he had been at seventeen, the beautiful youth from Mycenae. Her Carmanor.

He took her cheeks in his hands and kissed her, long and yearning, and held her close, cocooned against his body, but in the next instant he dissolved into flickering lamp-lit darkness, leaving behind the mere hint of words.

Be wary tonight, my love.

The waterfall vanished. She stood again upon cool tiles. An exhale of wind from the open balcony nearly extinguished the lamp.

Her heart beat with fearful thudding strength as she pressed her hands to her chest, forgetting she held the ring. It dropped to the floor, flat face turned down. She bent and retrieved it.

It was his. Menoetius had given it to her the night he died.

She woke then, gasping, and jerked upright, staring at the ceiling. She lay in bed, her cheeks wet with tears.

Moonlight flooded from the balcony, pooling across her. Everyone knew that sleeping in the moon's light brought prophetic dreams. Once, it had brought her a god.

As she realized the vivid rainbow fountain and Menoetius's presence hadn't happened, she slumped, pressing her face against her knees. Theirs had been an affair of opposites, of attraction and disgust, respect and resentment. Yet that enigmatic lover taught her things she could never learn from anyone else.

The balcony draperies billowed inward then stilled.

Rising wearily, Aridela went into her bath chamber, rubbing at the ache in her temples and pushing back her sweat-dampened hair. She scooped handfuls of water from the bowl and refreshed her face.

A lamp illuminated the festive rosettes, spirals, and tessellations ornamenting the edge of the ceiling, but they brought no sense of pleasure or peace. She couldn't rout the blaze of color streaming from Menoetius's ring, or the dream-image of his face. Tender. Grieving.

She left the bath and went straight to her dressing table. Shoving combs, mirrors, and paint-pots aside, she seized upon a small ivory coffer.

The ring lay next to the twined locks of their hair. She picked it up, but it was nothing more than a well-fashioned piece of jewelry, cool to the touch, smooth on the inside from years spent on his finger. The engraving was of a man brandishing a dagger as he held off an attacking lion.

Hopeless longing swept through her. If she could, somehow, she would say all she'd neglected to say when she'd had the chance. She would hold him fast and refuse to let him go. Collapsing to the floor, she stared at the ring a long time, kissing it, bathing it in tears.

Somewhere in this misery, the voice from her wedding day returned, offering gentle reassurance.

Thou shalt be called Eamhair of the sea, who brings them closer, and Shashi, sacrificed to deify man. Thy names are Caparina, Lilith, and the sorrowful Morrigan, who drives them far apart.

It gave her mysterious comfort to hold his ring and think of the night in the labyrinth, when he shared the promise he had received at the same time. It was hard to remember, but she worked at it until she recalled every name he'd told her. *Cailean, Nuren, Ambrosio, Daniel, Curran,* and finally, *William.*

She dried her cheeks and rose. Kissing the ring one last time, she put it back into the ivory coffer.

Sleep would be impossible now.

She wanted to ask Chrysaleon why he had told Pasithea to give Gelanor her sacred, secret title. How had he even known of it? But that could wait until tomorrow. Right now she needed him to distract her. His laugh and his kisses would dissolve her fears, and the unhappy sensation that she had betrayed everyone who ever trusted her.

He'd probably dozed off in Alexiare's chamber. He wouldn't mind being awakened. It would give her a chance to tell the slave goodbye, as well.

Only with Chrysaleon could she release her obligations, her masks, and be simply, finally, a woman.

$$3$$

Moon of Mead-Making

"THE IDEA CAME TO ME ON THE VOYAGE TO MYCENAE," CHRYSALEON said, "as the sun rose in the east and I watched dolphins leap about the ship. The dead god, Damasen, first suggested it in my death dream from long ago."

"Tell me again, my lord," Alexiare said. "My memory fails me these days."

"He said that Potnia Athene's true origins would be forgotten, and she would be known as a hater of women. He suggested a day would come when Athene would be thought of as the child of Zeus."

"Did the queen's father want to help you defeat the sacrifice?"

"No," Chrysaleon said, thinking back. "He was devoted to the Lady. He wanted me to protect Aridela. He thought I would be long dead by now." He gave a defiant shake of his head to rid his mind of the king's face. "At Mycenae I called together the members of my Boreas council and put forth this idea. Together we perfected it. Before I left, our bards were setting the new stories to song—even a new meaning for Athene's name. 'I have come from myself' has changed to 'She who has never known man.' That tidbit came from Damasen as well."

"You and I understand how a well-told story can root in the hearts of the people." Alexiare smiled tremulously, though tears dribbled across his temples.

"All the years we spent trying to destroy her," Chrysaleon said. "Changing her—we never considered that." He laughed. "You would be proud of all I have accomplished in the last two months. Perhaps I don't need you so much after all, eh, old man? At Mycenae, Pasithea told me she'd been given Themiste's secret title. She didn't tell me what it was, but she didn't need to, thanks to you. I convinced her that if she gave the title to Gelanor, it would bind him to her. There's nothing she wants more than that. She adores my brother. She made the announcement tonight. Neither Aridela nor the oracle could do anything to stop it. It is done. Themiste's holy title belongs to Mycenae now."

"Gelanor did not resist, my lord?"

Chrysaleon laughter was now cynical. "Not at all. He lost his infatuation with Aridela when he saw she meant to go through with dispatching me in the sacrifice. I told him how sacred the title is, how much power it wields. He made a decent pose of bewildered, humble surprise to keep her from suspecting."

"Yes, my lord," Alexiare said. "I truly am proud of you, and of Gelanor. He has become a surprisingly valuable ally. You know, I have been lying here, thinking back over everything we have done. It seems to me your true success began the day Menoetius was mauled. On that day, you discarded fear and impotence. You embraced your moera when you caused the beast to attack your brother. At that instant, you became a true heir to your noble ancestors. You chose your destiny, and accepted what you would have to do to achieve it. Every year since, you have grown more formidable, more determined."

Chrysaleon nodded, though Alexiare couldn't see. Before he could say anything, Alexiare began coughing. Chrysaleon gave him water, which helped a little.

"I only wish I could expunge the evil I have created," the old man wheezed, his voice as grating as an avalanche. "I am so afraid."

"You have done no evil."

Alexiare coughed again, hacking until he spat out curds of black blood. He fell back, his battle to breathe obvious. "Oh no, my lord," he gasped. "You are wrong. I've caused much evil, and dragged you into retribution with me."

Chrysaleon bit back impatience. More blithering about some silly crime. "Whatever you have done, old man, it can be nothing too reprehensible."

Alexiare blinked as if he could somehow rid himself of the obscuring cloud over his pupils. "Are we alone, my lord?"

"There is no one here but you and I. Tell me what causes such shame and whimpering."

"She cursed us before she died." Alexiare's voice was so soft it forced Chrysaleon to lean closer. "I fear what comes to me. Yet I asked the Goddess to give me a sign if she was angry. Nothing happened. I told myself she didn't care, perhaps even approved, but now I know how wrong I was. She does care. She cares very much."

"Who cursed us? Have you forgotten how adored I am?" He paused, caught in uneasiness by his own words. The people no longer adored him, thanks to the taxes he'd begun and never stopped. But peasants the world over did as they were told if they knew what was good for them. "The bards compose songs about my glorious deeds every few days," he added with bravado.

"Selene."

Chrysaleon stared into his slave's wasted, yellow face. "You know what happened to her?"

"I killed her, my lord."

"You—*what?*"

"The child, Xanthe—you stole her father from her, and I stole her mother."

Shock numbed Chrysaleon's ability to think. Then, slowly, he began to wonder if it could be true. His mind hummed. Alexiare had been a weak old man for many years, Selene a practiced fighter. Still, Alexiare seemed to have his wits, and believe what he was saying.

"Selene found the saw I used to weaken the king-killer axe." Alexiare managed to speak almost normally. "I meant to get rid of it, but I forgot. It was just a saw. Many men have saws. I confess I desired a memento of what you and I brought about—changing Kaphtor's ancient tradition. But she tricked me. She said she would take it to Aridela and she acted as if she knew everything. I couldn't allow her to plant suspicions in the queen's mind." His voice broke and grew steadily fainter. "I didn't want you to know, but now I go to the shadowlands, and you must be on guard against her curse."

"What is this curse?" Chrysaleon remembered the morning no one could find her. Alexiare kept to his bed, seemingly ill. There had been a fire in the old man's chamber the night before. When asked, Alexiare said he stumbled and knocked over a lamp. Chrysaleon had laughed at him, ridiculed him for being so clumsy. Now that he thought about it, his slave's lip had been cut and swollen. Maybe he was telling the truth.

Alexiare stretched out his arm, grabbing at Chrysaleon. His fingers were nearly transparent, the nails thick and yellow, curled like talons.

"Seize your happiness, my lord," he gasped. "Do whatever you must to make a full life with Queen Aridela."

Chrysaleon gripped the old man's cold, dry hand. "Curses mean nothing to me. You know that. Have you forgotten my grandfather's motto? *Fortune favors the bold*. I have done nothing but construct my fortune in the same manner as my ancestors. Tell me now of this curse of yours. I will defeat it as I have everything else that's tried to stand in my way."

"You must understand—I saw the hand of the Lady on Selene's face. It was she who spoke. Here, my lord, here it is, as she said it. It has had years to burn itself into my bones, but so I could never forget, I had it carved into my flesh." He lifted his thin, papyrus-skinned arm. Chrysaleon had to seize it and hold it still, for it was so shaky he couldn't decipher what was there. Once he had it steady, he saw a series of faded tattoos spelling out a phrase.

Glimpses of joy will be ripped from you. You will beg for death but death will refuse you. You will follow and follow, without end.

Chrysaleon spoke it haltingly, for the symbols were faint and hard to read. When he finished, Alexiare nodded. "This is what the warrior Selene said to me as she died." His voice degenerated. He coughed again, but was too weak to clear his lungs. His breathing rasped and hissed.

Even as Chrysaleon formed words of derision, his throat closed. This curse, so frightening to Alexiare, revived a memory of Themiste at that long-ago mead-making festival, when she had fallen into a death-like trance and spoke prophecy about Gelanor.

The youthful sun will marry the ancient moon. He who laughs will lie with she who is beautiful to men. Curse the usurper, the changer of the Way. He shall follow without rest, without joy, without relief, until the final devastation of the heavens. He shall follow begging, but love will run from him, and he will receive only sorrow and regret until the world is old and tired and razed by war.

His skin erupted in waves of gooseflesh. Gelanor's name meaning was "laughter," and Pasithea, "she who is beautiful to all." Themiste had predicted the alliance that Chrysaleon, Gelanor, and Pasithea herself now wanted. The oracle's words cursed the *usurper, the changer of the Way*. It was easy to attribute such a statement to Harpalycus. But in the end, Harpalycus hadn't really changed much about Kaphtor. Chrysaleon had changed everything. The smallest children knew how much.

Selene, in the throes of death, spoke words so similar they could not be discounted or shrugged off. This had to be a true omen. Not even he could bluster it away.

"No...."

The word floated in a horrified whisper from the door. Chrysaleon swiveled and rose, tensing. His fingers embraced the hilt of his dagger.

Aridela approached, each step slow, unsteady, as though she was ill or injured.

"Alexiare is close to death," Chrysaleon said. "Delirious. He knows not what he is saying."

"My lord." Alexiare's hand clutched at the air until it found and latched onto Chrysaleon's forearm. "You said we were alone...."

"Quiet, old man."

"He speaks the truth, and I will hear no more." Aridela turned her gaze from Alexiare's ravaged face to Chrysaleon's. "You did trick us. All of us. All but Selene. Because you were too selfish—or too cowardly—to die. Look how many have died in your place."

Her hands rose to her lips, tremulous as the wings of a dragonfly. "Themiste said my blindness would cause untold suffering. She was talking about you. I see it now. She told me I would betray everyone who believed in me. And I have."

"Aridela—"

"How I loved you, Chrysaleon. But what...what was it I loved? A shade. A dream—a vision I thought Athene sent me. I loved you like a child loves a hero in a legend. I forgot that bards exaggerate their stories to make them more interesting." Her eyelids fluttered. Color rose then fled through her cheeks. "When you professed such desire for me that you were willing to relinquish your country and die in our rites, I believed you. When the time came and you refused, I told myself it was because you were cheated of so much of your promised year. I allowed you to change our ways, to set yourself above us.

Selene tried to tell me. So did Menoetius, but I would not listen." Her voice dropped to a whisper. "Now Selene is dead. Menoetius is dead." She drew in a breath. "And I cannot bring them back. I cannot repair what I have done."

As he sought desperately for the words to soothe her, she continued, almost to herself. "I have always been told I was meant to fulfill a great purpose. How stupid and arrogant I have been. I didn't make use of my mother's wisdom. I didn't heed the warning in the prophecy or even my nightmares. I blinded myself to everything but you. What will become of the people now? What new horrors have I brought upon them?"

Tears swam in her eyes. She swayed as though she might faint.

"You didn't want me to die," Chrysaleon said, worry fading beneath an explosion of anger. "You were happy for me to trick you, as long as you didn't get blamed." He shook off Alexiare's clinging hand and stepped closer to his wife. There was something in her face he had never seen before. Horror. Self-condemnation. He must control this situation. If she would let him hold her, he could kiss her into submission. He was certain of it.

"It is true. Kaphtor was my covenant, not yours. It is my treason alone. Potnia Athene will never forgive me. She saw my thoughts, how I wanted you to live. Only my fear of reprisal kept me from ordering it." She ground her knuckles into her cheeks, hard enough to leave bright red marks. "Yet if I had given the order, there would have been no reason to kill Selene or Menoetius."

"What's done is done, my love." He took another step and held out his hand. "We did it together. Nothing need change."

She glanced at Alexiare then turned her unblinking obsidian gaze upon Chrysaleon, reminding him uncomfortably of the Spartan seer. "You deliberately caused that lioness to attack your brother. Why? What did he do to make you hate him so much?"

She had been standing there that long? She'd heard everything then, every incriminating detail. "No—I didn't. Alexiare slips in and out of delirium. His memory is faulty. He's confused. Everyone knows the story of how I saved Menoetius's life."

Those eyes penetrated his brain like knife blades. "He died believing it."

Screaming silence crowded close, thick, and suffocating. Then she blinked, and her gaze turned even darker, more intent, as her brows lowered. "I would like to know if you murdered your Mycenaean wife, Iros, and the baby she carried."

"What? No." He shook his head. "No I did not, and punished the ones who did."

She stared at him, visibly shaking. He could see she was reluctant to let herself believe anything he said. "In the craze of battle," she added, so softly he could hardly hear her, "have you done to others what Harpalycus did to me?"

The question took him by surprise. He started to deny it, but he knew any protest he might make wouldn't sound convincing, and that gaze missed nothing. In an attempt to deflect her, he tried resentment and anger. "Why am I being interrogated like a slave?"

Her expression didn't change. Softly, she said, "I have been such a fool."

She stared at him and he stared back, not knowing what to say or do. At last she turned away. "Themiste shall know, and the people. They will decide our fate." She staggered toward the door, pressing her hands to her stomach, hunched as though in pain.

"You cannot tell them. They will kill us. Everything I have done will be for nothing."

He caught her from behind, pinning her arms to her sides, covering her mouth to prevent her from shouting.

She struggled mightily, and managed to free one hand. Lifting it, she seized a fistful of his hair and ripped it from his head.

He released some wordless animal sound. Pain obliterated everything. He didn't mean to, but it happened so quickly. His fighting instincts overpowered his wits.

It was an effortless twist, one he'd performed many times, both in battle and practice. He only realized what he'd done as she convulsed then sagged against him, and the sound of her snapping neck echoed through the room.

WAS THAT A SCREAM? THE SOUND WAS FAINT, FAR AWAY, BUT CHRYSALEON heard and straightened.

"Hippos Poseidon," he whispered. "What have I done? Why did you not stop me?"

The strength drained from his legs. He slumped to the floor, still holding her. "Wake up, Aridela," he shouted, shaking her. "Wake up. You can't be—"

He stopped as the tiles under his feet rippled and cracked in an undulating wave. The bowl of broth next to Alexiare's bed fell and shattered, followed by the lamp stand. The room plunged into murky shadow.

The earth shakes.

His instinct was to run, to hide. But he couldn't let go of Aridela's body, couldn't just leave her lying here. Someone would soon come to make sure they hadn't been injured. He moaned, pulling her lifeless head against his throat, pretending for one glorious instant that it had been a dream, that she was still here. Then he forced himself to rise.

As the chamber sighed and shuddered, he carried her to the bed and pushed her underneath it. Crete's Earth Bull, believed to live deep inside the mountains, accompanied his labor with eerie, echoing growls that made the hair rise on the back of his neck and prompted him to glance over his shoulder, again and again.

"What happens?" Alexiare struggled to lift himself. His breathing came in shallow wet gasps.

"Quiet. For once in your life be silent, old man."

"The earth is shaking." Alexiare frowned into the gloom. "Queen Aridela! My lady, are you there?"

"She cannot answer. Because of you, cursed slave, and your loose tongue, she is dead." He choked as he said it, and clenched his hands. Rage flared, leaving him trembling.

Alexiare's hand groped for Chrysaleon's. "Your ambition takes you too far. It is my fault. I led you to this. Oh, that I could have died before now."

"Stop talking before I kill you as well."

"I see the face of a king. I see all Crete's kings. They will force us to repay this debt."

"Quiet!"

Alexiare fell back, sobbing like a child.

The earth's quiver subsided. Everything grew as still as the death around him. A maid soon arrived to ask after Chrysaleon and his slave. Working to keep his voice measured, he sent her away.

The warbler rustled in its cage and made a sad, plaintive call, which sounded like an accusation.

Chrysaleon glanced into the shadows as uneasy prickling ricocheted over his skin. His bare toes touched Aridela's arm. Clerks and servants began their days early. More would have been awakened by the earthshaking. There was no time to waste. What should he do? How to dispose of the body so none would suspect the truth?

Alexiare continued to sob. The sound grated against Chrysaleon's skull. He clenched his teeth to keep from ordering the old man to die and leave him in peace.

Glimpses of joy…ripped from you. Follow begging until the world is old and tired and razed by war.

It began softly. Chrysaleon hardly noticed the cool breeze skimming past his face. A sheet of papyrus on the table across the room blew into the air then drifted to the floor.

He looked up.

Stabbed by spears of dread, he rose, fumbling at the hilt of his dagger and pulling it free of the baldric.

A man stood on the opposite side of Alexiare's bed, motionless as a statue. His long black hair blew wildly in this strange wind that had somehow found a way into the chamber. Bluish-lavender light circled his body like a halo.

"Who are you?" Chrysaleon cursed the unsteadiness of his voice. The man's face struck him as familiar. He flailed, trying to place him.

Alexiare's weeping faltered. "Who is here?" he asked in a whisper. "I feel so cold."

Chrysaleon ignored him.

The breeze strengthened. The man's expression darkened. As his fists clenched, a hard gust hit Chrysaleon. The papyrus flew up again like a disturbed leaf.

The man's lips pulled back in a wolfish manner, baring teeth.

Something fell and broke. Chrysaleon couldn't tear his gaze away from the specter before him to see what it was.

Outside, thunder rumbled.

"What is it?" Alexiare's gnarled hands gripped the edges of his bed. "A storm?"

Chrysaleon braced himself, suddenly remembering. This was Damasen, Aridela's dead father, but there was no hint of the kindness or serenity he remembered from his death-dream.

The wind died. The temperature in the room dropped. Chrysaleon's breath steamed and he shuddered uncontrollably.

Intensely aware of Aridela's body beneath the bed, he fought the urge to kneel and beg forgiveness. Instead he squared his shoulders and tightened his grip on the knife. In truth, he hadn't felt such raw, lashing terror since the night of the Destruction.

Damasen spoke. "You have betrayed all who trusted you."

Vomit clotted in Chrysaleon's throat. Speckles swirled through his eyesight. He hardly realized when he dropped the dagger. The sound of it clattering was faint, far away.

"You have set this world upon its path, and so you will live it. You will watch it unfold, and you alone will remember everything you have done. Until you honor your vow, you will carry the burden of all your deceptions, and they will grow heavy."

Chrysaleon's blood pounded. His ears thrummed. He staggered and almost fell.

"You will remember and despair," Damasen said.

With those words he erupted—vanished in a flash of silver, leaving nothing but a deathly chill and the echoes of his promise.

The room returned to dim stillness. The sensation of fire licking through Chrysaleon's veins subsided.

Alexiare lay motionless, his mouth open, his blind eyes staring. Chrysaleon thought the old man had died of fright, but then he sucked in a breath and coughed.

"My lord," the old man whispered. "Now do you believe me?"

Chrysaleon gritted his teeth. He wanted to throttle that ugly, wrinkled throat, but instead he dropped onto the stool, willing his heartbeat to calm. For some time he jumped at every sound, but no more shades from the underworld appeared.

Clearing his head with a hard shake, Chrysaleon went to the door and studied the corridor. He saw no one, but he knew that could change in an instant. He must hurry or he would lose his nerve. Aridela's body felt soft and warm still. He slipped from Alexiare's chamber quietly, keeping to the shadows as much as possible. Holding her against him in a lover's caress, he carried her to the nearest set of stairs and balanced her at the top.

"Farewell, my love." He blinked away persistent, blurring tears, and willed the annoying tic beneath his eye to quiet.

Sending a nervous glance one direction then the other, he removed the necklace she always wore, the one with two crescent moons cupping a blue star, and meandering lines representing the holy temple of Labyrinthos. "This I will keep," he said into her ear before he kissed it.

Such a small woman. Light and fragile as a bird. She barely made a sound as she fell, step over step, coming to rest in a sadly disjointed posture at the bottom.

Fortune favors the bold.

Great societies were created in such ways, molded from rough clay, shaped into amaranthine civilizations that would endure until the end of time.

Crete would be his monument. It would tower, invincible, inde-structible, growing greater and stronger throughout eternity.

He stared at the shadowy form. "You and I will find each other again," he whispered. "I vow it. For as long as the pyramids stand in Egypt, you and I will be together."

"Is it done?" Alexiare asked.

"It's done." Chrysaleon dropped wearily onto the stool. "Now be quiet. I need to think."

"Yes, my lord."

No more deep, thick nights shadowed in green. No more murmured words of passion and soft warm limbs nestled against his. No more huge black eyes, windows to trust, although of late, he had seen that trust less and less.

And she had at last conceived the child who might have been his son and heir.

He couldn't bear to look at Alexiare, who sputtered and gasped.

Wiping away tears with the back of his hand, he bit the inside of his cheek hard enough to draw blood, afraid to allow such thoughts, afraid they would fracture him into pieces. Later, after he envisioned a way to mend this disaster, he could mourn her, the only woman he had ever loved. But not now. Not yet.

The sacred king of Crete rose to his feet as the answer formed in his mind.

So simple, neat, and believable. Pasithea, as Aridela's successor, would be crowned. Chrysaleon would find a way to make Gelanor the cabal, and would protect his brother by naming him Zagreus. The couple would be formally betrothed, and would marry when Pasithea came of age. Chrysaleon would return to Mycenae and rule for the rest of his life, putting this tiresome place forever behind him. Together, he and Gelanor would decree the final end of the king-sacrifice. The people were ripe for change, partly because they'd grown used to him continuing to live, and partly due to crushing taxes. More and more had started hanging miniature clay dolls in the trees, and accepted the idea that these "Aridela dolls" pleased the Goddess and fructified the crops on their own.

Glimpses of joy will be ripped from you. You will follow without end.

He shall follow begging, but love will run from him.

You will remember and despair.

Words meant to intimidate and frighten him. But he was no untried boy. Time and time again, he had proven his invincibility. He was the one to be feared. He alone of every bull-king who had ever taken the throne of Kaphtor had changed history and thwarted his death. In true warrior fashion, following in the footsteps of mighty Zeus, he killed his blood brother, achieved power over the Goddess, and accomplished what no other man ever could.

Fortune favors the bold.

He would live to see the day Cretans sacrificed bulls, rams, and goats. Maybe women. Never men, for men would be as gods. A new era was coming. The ancient worship of female to female would be forgotten.

You will harness the force that brings wondrous change to the world, Damasen had promised long ago, in the death dream.

"May it be true." Chrysaleon spoke fervently to the empty room, to Damasen, if he still listened.

He remembered the dead king's other statement. *You have set this world upon its path, and so you will live it. You will watch it unfold, and you alone will remember everything you have done.*

Triumph crept through his limbs. He nearly laughed as he worked it out. Somehow, death was not to be his end. He would return, or never die. Perhaps the gods meant to make him immortal—a god himself.

Until you honor your vow, you will carry the burden of all your deceptions, and they will grow heavy.

The last part of Damasen's speech pricked at his mind, but he pushed it away. Burdens were like guilt—designed for women. He would not be swayed by such things.

He fell so deeply into thoughts and plans he didn't realize night had succumbed to morning until another handmaid entered to check on them.

She inclined her head, saying, "Did you feel the earthshaking in here, my lord?"

Not trusting his voice, he gave a curt nod. The rising sun had brightened the room in a soft pink glow. It was only a matter of time now before she was found.

She babbled on, not noticing or ignoring his tense, unwelcoming expression. "Blessings to the Lady," she said, "it caused little damage. I came to ask if you have seen Queen Aridela, my lord. The earth-shaking caused a landslide on the northern cliffs. A skeleton was uncovered. Some fishermen found it and brought it here. They think it might be murder, for it was stuffed into a leather sack."

"Selene," Alexiare cried. He began moaning and thrashing. "Oh, Lady Athene...."

The maid stared at him, her brow crinkling, before returning her attention to Chrysaleon. "The queen is not in her chamber," she said haltingly. "Has she been here?"

Chrysaleon pressed his fingers against the pulsating tic beneath his eye. "She said she was going for a walk on the plain."

"Did she take no one with her?"

"Sometimes she wishes to be alone, as I do," Chrysaleon replied impatiently, and waved the maid out. She inclined her head and apologized for disturbing him, but he watched her glance back when she reached the door, her expression frowning and wary.

"Is she gone?" Alexiare asked.

"Yes."

"We are alone?"

"Yes, old man. We are alone. What is it you want to say now?"

"I know it was Selene they found. I put her in a leather sack, and filled the sack with stones so she would disappear forever. But the Goddess brought her back. It's judgment. A warning."

"You should have kept your mouth shut about it. That woman will tell everyone she knows what you said."

"My lord, my lord, I am so afraid for you. How can you doubt after this night that the gods are watching, or that you will be punished?"

"Shall I give up, then? Throw myself off the cliffs? I am not ready to admit defeat, even if you are."

Alexiare blubbered a bit longer then he wiped his eyes and said, "Please don't hate me, my king, but there is one more thing.... I was not going to tell you, but after everything that has happened here, I dare not keep this secret."

Chrysaleon didn't want to hear any more revelations. He rubbed his eyes and groaned. "How many plots have you birthed and carried out in that shriveled mind?"

Alexiare swallowed several times. He grimaced as he tried to gain control over his emotion and reached out, but Chrysaleon ignored his searching hand and eventually Alexiare let it drop to his side. "It is about Harpalycus."

"Harpalycus!" Chrysaleon sighed, disgusted. *I am ready for you to expire. Why do you cling to this life?*

"He is not dead."

Snorting, Chrysaleon rose and crossed the room. He picked up the papyrus from the floor and tossed it on the table.

"Harpalycus and my old acolyte, Proitos, discovered how to outwit death," Alexiare said. "I am not sure how…but they did. You must believe me. I know of what I speak, for I myself taught Proitos the rudiments of these cursed abilities before he abandoned us to serve the prince of Tiryns."

Chrysaleon returned to the bed. "What you claim is impossible." He squinted at his dying servant. Yet he remembered the rumors about Alexiare, whispers that Far-Reaching Hecate had shared her knowledge of plants and alchemy with the secretive old man, and that he knew far more about women's mysteries than he should.

There was also that covert mission Menoetius made to Tiryns. When he returned, he reported the people there believed Harpalycus was seeking a way to achieve life without death.

Alexiare shook his head emphatically. "I tell you the truth, my lord. They found a way. When I began delving into these matters, I sensed the rage I was causing, and knew I would be punished if I continued. I abandoned it, but Proitos did not, and Harpalycus joined him in the search. I didn't know, and still do not, how they slip into other living bodies. So I took every precaution when we captured Proitos. I made certain no one came near him or touched him. But Harpalycus did manage to consume someone after the queen slit his throat—I believe it must have been one of Kaphtor's warriors. Do you remember when she returned from Mount Juktas that time, claiming Harpalycus attacked her? She spoke the truth. Later, just before the rise of Iakchos, while you were in seclusion, she and I searched for him among the troops. We were shown the dead body of the man from the mountain. She thought she was free of the soldier who had terrified her, but I know better. Harpalycus found a way to consume another before he died. Unless something has happened to him in the last seven years,

Harpalycus is alive, my lord, and there is no way to expose him. I don't know if he is still on Kaphtor. But I do know he hates you above all else, and will harm you if he gets the chance. I doubt he has left."

"Are you saying he can…place himself into other people's bodies? That would make him a god."

"I am not certain how he does it, my lord. But I've considered it carefully. I don't think he can simply consume a body whenever he wishes. Otherwise he could have taken you over at any time, and become High King of Mycenae. What better vengeance upon you than that? I suspect he has to be on the verge of death. If this is true, there is always a danger for him. What if he's alone? What if something prevents him from passing into another body before he expires? Still, even if I am right, you are vulnerable, for he is utterly disguised. He could be a trusted friend, a servant—perhaps even a woman. And if he were to get you alone, and fatally injure himself, he could steal your body from you."

"He could have easily done so when I was his prisoner."

"I've thought of that." Alexiare's voice was failing, forcing him to grate out a whisper. "But why would he? He thought he was winning, and would soon be king of Mycenae without having to impersonate you. You understand don't you, my lord, that given a choice, Harpalycus will always choose for you to suffer and be humiliated?"

Chrysaleon thought of the day he and Menoetius had gone eagle hunting, and how the bird handler had stared at him, his face so menacing, so filled with hate. His flesh had crawled with warning. If that man were in truth Harpalycus, it would make sense.

"Part of me believes your mind has rotted," he said, but grudgingly added, "Maybe you are right."

Alexiare lay back and gave himself over to weak coughing. He died soon after. Chrysaleon watched as the corner of his mouth drooped into a deformed grimace. He pulled the blanket over the old man's face so he wouldn't have to see it.

All of this was Alexiare's fault. He should be dumped above ground for scavengers to dismember. Why hadn't the god-cursed man carried his secrets into death? Aridela wouldn't have overheard his incriminating talk. She might have announced her presence before any harm was done. She would have walked with Chrysaleon to their chamber, held his arm, expressed her sadness at the impending loss of his long-time slave. In their bed she would have held him in her arms and comforted him with her smooth young body.

His teeth chattered. Shivering threatened to overpower him.

He thought of King Idómeneus's other son, the one elevated beyond his station. He heard Menoetius's voice echo in his mind.

My Mother promised me retribution. I mean to return.

"Come then, bastard!" Chrysaleon clenched his fists and stood, shouting into the gloom. "If you have courage enough! We will see who wins."

4

Moon of Mead-Making

From the Oracle Logs
  Themiste

The Oracle Logs tell the story of Kaphtor from its beginning. They *give advice and comfort. They bring to life the women who write them. It is a method of immortality for those of us who surrender all we have, even our names, to serve the Goddess.*

I have always loved writing in the log. Now I dread it.

What is my legacy to those who have not yet been born?

A change is coming. I sense it getting closer. I cannot rout the fear that no one will remember Kaphtor's holy seers. The prophecies and predictions will be forgotten. None will know the true meaning of "Minos."

Tonight, at the welcoming feast for Chrysaleon and Pasithea, the child gave her secret title to Gelanor, Chrysaleon's brother and a prince of Mycenae. Everyone laughed. It was taken as a child's harmless prank. I looked at Chrysaleon when she did it—I saw his satisfaction. It was he who planned this.

I felt the cold grip of approaching doom. Gelanor will accept the title and become Minos Gelanor. His son will be Minos something else—probably Idómeneus. Mainlanders love to name their sons after their grandfathers.

Our subjugation is almost complete.

Aridela and I are to blame. We have betrayed Kaphtor. I gave my shame and fear more power than truth and honor. Aridela lost herself in stubborn, consuming loyalty and love.

As I looked upon Chrysaleon, I finally understood. All of it was clear—him lying with me, getting me with child, killing Menoetius, using Gelanor to beguile Pasithea…it has all been part of a maze-like design to this end. I suspect Alexiare is the true master of these plots. Chrysaleon is like a wild bull —directed by emotion and instinct. He could not have thought this up without help.

If Gelanor marries Pasithea, the Mycenaean connection will gain dominion over Kaphtor's ancient royal line. Pasithea carries the blood of our high priestesses, yes, but also the blood of Mycenaean kings, and Gelanor is Idómeneus's son. Their union will change the course of our land forever and bind us irrevocably to Mycenae, for Chrysaleon will be sure to reveal at some advantageous point that Pasithea is his child in truth.

Once that happens, I will meet my death, either openly at the hands of the people, or stealthily, on Chrysaleon's orders. Perhaps it is no more than I deserve.

When he has control of our most sacred title and the heir to Kaphtor's throne, Gelanor will possess complete authority. Whatever he decrees will be done.

He will be not only consort, but king,
…and Moon-Being.

I SLIPPED AWAY FROM THE FEAST, KNOWING I MUST CHRONICLE WHAT happened, and after long pondering, fell asleep at my table. An earthshaking woke me. It does not appear to have caused much damage, but it did leave me uneasy. I suppose that is natural, given what we have endured.

The smoke, the venom, the cara, and the prophecies—they have depleted me. I remember thinking once that I knew of no oracle who lived to be old. Daily exposure to the Immortals burns away our strength, our stamina, even our will. I woke from the earthshaking feeling like charred wood, ready to crumble at the slightest touch.

Of late, more days than not, I find I am looking forward to the end. I have already had a longer life than most of my predecessors, and I am tired.

I have to tell Aridela my suspicions. It will help that she, too, realized the significance of what Pasithea did last night. I know I must do this, yet I hesitate. In telling her, my voice will join the voices of Menoetius and Selene, who also tried to warn her about the Zagreus. How will she take it from me? She has always been loyal to him, but I have seen a change over the last few years. I sense she does not trust him as she used to. Perhaps she is ready to listen, at last.

Today, at sunrise, when I speak the monthly oracles, I will publicly announce that Nephele is to be my successor. She is true to me, patient, dedicated, and I believe she can develop the gift of Sight. She reminds me of my beloved Laodámeia, though Nephele would never be as disrespectful. My choice made Chrysaleon angry. He wanted his sister, Bateia, to be named, but I defied him. From the beginning, I have sensed the poor child was forced to come here and be my disciple. Although she is obedient, diligent in her studies, and has never said a word against her brother, it is obvious to me she was not called to be a priestess, much less an oracle. She and Chrysaleon never speak, and I am told she often weeps at night. He uses her as a scapegoat to assist his plots, like Menoetius, Gelanor, Pasithea, and perhaps Aridela as well.

The time has come to set my life in order. Chrysaleon must not get the chance to wreak more havoc upon us than he already has.

It is time to go to the oracle chamber. When that is done, I will say what must be said to Aridela. I pray the Goddess gives me the words to convince her.

FROM THE ORACLE LOGS
Themiste

THE FOLLOWING IS MY FORMAL ACCOUNT OF WHAT HAPPENED TODAY IN THE *presence of the council.*

I went into the oracle chamber. Io wound up my arm as she always does, yet I felt a change in her. She rocked from side to side. Her tongue flicked in an agitated manner. I soothed her with soft stroking and promised her a bowl of milk.

The council was waiting. Nephele took my hand and assisted me into the pit. She leaned close and told me Aridela had not yet come.

I probably would have worried more if the cara hadn't already set in my blood, causing an inability to concentrate on worldly things.

Io and her sisters wrapped around my outstretched arms. Smoke filled the pit and I breathed it in.

Two priestesses sat on either side to make the translations.

All was as it should be, as it always is, but for the absence of Aridela and the odd behavior of my serpent.

In the beginning I heard and understood my words. I said something about burning an olive branch to frighten away evil.

Everything blurred and echoed, as it often does. The cara was taking hold. A youthful, unscarred Menoetius appeared before me, so clearly he could have been standing in the pit with me, alive. His gaze upon me was somber as he took my arm. He led me down a slope and backward in time, into a long ago dream, where I sat next to Athene's handmaid at the edge of the sea, just before the cataclysm struck. "The holy triad is joined," she said. I saw myself asking, "This marked bull. Who is that?" She replied, "If I told you, you would try to change his fate. Remember this, Minos of Kaphtor. What seems the end is only the beginning."

I looked from her to Menoetius, and at last, I saw.

Menoetius, son of Sorcha. Asterion, the lord of the labyrinth. Chrysaleon of Mycenae's blood brother. Menoetius, whose name meaning is, "he who defies his fate."

He was the marked bull. I allowed the sacred bull of Athene to be slaughtered by his own brother.

I should have seen. I should have saved him. What irreparable damage have I done? How will I, and Kaphtor, be punished?

Menoetius clasped my hand and said, "Do not lose hope, priestess. We have another chance."

Before he died, he told Aridela that he believed they would be together again. His conviction gave her comfort, as it does me, now. We have made mistakes, trusted where we should not have trusted, given where we should not have given, seen things that were not real, ignored things that should not have been ignored. Yet Lady Athene wants us to go on striving. She does not want us to give up.

Menoetius's death in the mortal world set him on a divine path, much like Velchanos's sacrifice and rebirth. It is a rite beyond my understanding, something that will make him infinitely stronger—strong enough, I pray, to fulfill the mysterious destiny Athene has designed for him.

I was given more visions, one upon the next. I reeled as I saw the illusion played upon us by Alexiare, Chrysaleon's slave. It was he who changed Aridela's dream on Mount Juktas, who caused the statue of Velchanos to take on the likeness of Chrysaleon. I remember observing Aridela's thoughts through the use of the mind link, the subliquara. I saw the dream unfold. Velchanos stepped off his pedestal and became a living man. At first, he resembled Menoetius—Menoetius, not Chrysaleon. Alexiare, using some powerful ability beyond anything he should know, altered that image into the Gold Lion of Mycenae, and by doing so, changed what should have been. If Aridela had seen only Menoetius, she would have bound herself to him. Our country would have continued in strength, wealth, and success. Perhaps there would have been no Destruction at all. Our ways might have filtered through history, influencing other societies, other countries. The world would have enjoyed peace and prosperity, into the far distant future. I saw glimpses of that lost world in my mind. It was astounding.

But now Kaphtor will decline. Like a lamp run out of oil, our flame will disappear. Other places, other ways, will take ascendance. Other countries will direct what comes, for I saw, too late and too clearly, that Menoetius was the blessed one, Athene's champion. Not Chrysaleon.

Nephele tells me I fell silent and began to weep. The council members at first were agitated by this, but soon they grew impatient.

My mind soared on the spine of the wind. An irresistible force—I don't know what else to name it—entered into me and overthrew my will.

The snakes coiled around my neck and wrists. I stretched both hands to the sky. "Anathema," I cried, the words promising the great offering—and more, words forbidden to write, even here.

Yet it was not I who spoke. Goddess Athene spoke through me.

Thou hast murdered my children and sent me into darkness.
Thy covenant to me is broken. Until you fulfill your obligation, I
will forsake thee.

Athene has always been with us. She taught us everything we needed to thrive. Athene, my generous, beloved Mistress. I know what we have done. I know why you are angry. I despair that we can ever earn your forgiveness.

There was more, though I cannot decipher the meaning of it. I can only hope some forthcoming Minos, possessing better wisdom, will understand and know what to do.

An immortal corps will be formed from those who give loyalty.
They will bond to her but will not know her, nor will she know
them, for she has become the wounded woman, and will walk
alone.
Through the black and barren times, remember. No death is
final unless I make it so. Life is a winter tree that seems dead.
With warmth and sunlight, it regenerates and blooms, granting
beauty and life to all.

Here, the priestesses stopped writing, because a serving maid ran in screaming and interrupted. I did not hear her. The trance pressed too deeply over me. When I recovered, much later, I was told.

Aridela is dead.

After spending the night with his dying slave, Chrysaleon returned to the queen's chamber, but she was not there. He raised the alarm. Searchers found her at the bottom of a staircase. She must have lost her footing during the earthshaking, and the fall broke her neck.

Following our custom in such rare crises, where the queen-to-be is too young to take command, the council gave me the crescent staff. I am charged with returning order to Kaphtor, though all I want to do is lie on my bed and weep, or flee to my mountain shrine and separate myself from everyone.

My mind travels backward to your childhood, how your brow furrowed as you concentrated in the judgment hall. The way your eyes followed the bull dance, and the many times you slipped past your nurses and caused such uproar.

Aridela, my heart has died with you.

5

Moon of Mead-Making

Nephele sent her mistress an apologetic shrug as she escorted the serving woman into Themiste's chamber. "This is Gaiane," she said.

Themiste rubbed the back of her neck. She had finished a long day with Kaphtor's council, and wanted to offer comfort to Pasithea and Xanthe, who were taking the queen's death very hard.

Trying to hide her impatience, she waited for the woman to speak, wondering why a private audience was required.

Gaiane bowed. "Lady," she said, "my husband is one of the fishermen who brought you the skeleton from the northern cliffs."

"Skeleton? What skeleton?" Themiste dropped wearily into the chair at her worktable.

Nephele knelt beside her. "You have been so busy, I hadn't told you yet. A skeleton was discovered off the coast. Those who found it brought it for your judgment, not knowing what else they should do."

"Many skeletons have been unearthed along the coast," Themiste said to Gaiane, thinking perhaps she didn't know. "It is a sad fact. The mountain of water crushed anyone who had the misfortune of being there when it came."

Gaiane edged closer. "Not stuffed inside a leather sack, with stones packed in to make it sink. My husband and his companions believe it a murder. He insisted I come and tell you what the Mycenaean said, our king's slave—he who was called Alexiare."

234

Themiste sat up straight, her attention captured. "What does he have to do with these bones?"

"When my husband and his men brought the skeleton to Labyrinthos, they showed it to me. Later, when I was sent to make sure the king and his slave were unharmed by the earthshaking, I mentioned it to the Zagreus."

There was anxiety in her eyes as she leaned closer, bringing the kitchen scents of smoke, saffron, and garlic. "I told them what my husband said, that part of the cliffs collapsed and uncovered a skeleton. I told them about the leather sack."

She paused. Themiste began to think she'd misunderstood Gaiane's expression. The woman seemed as excited as she was fearful. "Yes, go on."

"Alexiare cried out, 'Selene!' He became agitated, and wept. Perhaps it is nothing, but my husband wanted you to know."

She made the quick, winding sign of the serpent on her breast, the age-old gesture showing obedience and respect to Athene.

Selene. Could it be true? Alexiare had been old. Themiste remembered someone once claiming he was near ninety. At any rate, his mind, so close to death, could well have wandered.

She pictured beautiful Selene, and thought back to her sudden, inexplicable disappearance. The never-solved mystery.

Themiste tamped down a rising hope. It would be impossible to identify a skeleton, and difficult to determine the cause of death. But she should go along and look, and make some sort of statement.

"Did you see the Zagreus?" Themiste asked as Nephele came into her chamber.

"His man would not let me in, my lady, but I caught a glimpse of him. He was sitting by the hearth fire with a cover over his shoulders. He looked pale and ill. I went down to the slave quarters as you asked. Here is what I learned. They are only allowed into the chamber to bring food and remove the chamber pot. They say he hasn't eaten anything they've taken him. Other than those times, the king allows no one near him but the one man, a Mycenaean. The servants told me he won't be parted from the knife the queen used to kill Harpalycus, that he constantly turns it over in his hands. Some of the slaves suspect he is losing hold of his reason."

Themiste sighed. She longed to retreat from her obligations as Chrysaleon seemed determined to do, but the needs of the country took precedence over personal grief. "He has to accompany the procession to Aridela's gravesite, no matter how inconsolable he is. The people expect it."

"Yes, my lady."

"I must prepare Aridela for her journey to Hesperia." Themiste fought back tears. "It cannot be put off even one more day to make concessions to his suffering. The sarcophagus is ready, the grave dug."

Nephele lowered her head and wiped at her eyes.

"Come," Themiste said. "First we will go and look at this skeleton. Even if it is a murder, what can be done? I suppose I must say something about it, for I have no doubt that gossipmonger Gaiane has told everyone in the city. Our people love their scandals."

"Yes, my lady. Could it be Selene?"

Themiste shrugged. "How can we ever know who this person was?" Her initial curiosity had faded. What did it matter, when compared to the inconsolable sorrow of Xanthe and Pasithea, and the Zagreus's worrisome withdrawal? As certain as she was that Chrysaleon had callously fooled them all in the name of power, it was also obvious he loved Aridela, and was grieving.

They descended into the labyrinth and found the chamber where the bones were being stored. Once the lamps were lit, Themiste took in the scene.

Someone had laid out the skeleton on a large table. She examined it, her nose wrinkling. Most of the skull was gone, leaving only a chunk of the lower jaw and a few teeth. The spine was intact, and one side of the torso—the collarbone, ribs, arm, and hand. The other arm, the legs, and the feet were partially crushed, and all the bones were sorely blackened from their time in the mud. This unfortunate must have been submerged for many years, to cause so much breakage and discoloration. Probably since the Destruction.

The leather sack lay on the floor, remarkably preserved, though it smelled quite bad, of seawater and rot. Beside it lay the pile of stones the fishermen claimed were packed inside.

Then she saw what else time and the sea had not destroyed.

Themiste picked up the skeleton's one remaining hand, eliciting a faint moan from her handmaid, who hung back in the shadows. She worked the ring off the second finger and rubbed away the embedded mud as best she could.

Shivers edged along her flesh as she contemplated the ring then the skull. "I remember when the queen gave her ring to Selene," she said. "It was when Harpalycus held Kaphtor and Selene sent her to hide in the mountains with Menoetius. Aridela would not take it back when she returned to Labyrinthos, and Selene never removed it from her finger."

Nephele came closer, curious despite her fear.

Themiste held out her hand, the ring resting on her palm.

It was the queen's ring, depicting the three faces of the Goddess, the maiden, the mother, and the crone.

"Alexiare did know," Nephele said softly. "But how?"

The two women stared at each other, horrified by the obvious answer.

From the Oracle Logs
  Themiste

Who understood Aridela's heart? Who never betrayed her? Who had the courage to brave her wrath by speaking the truth?

Selene. Always Selene.

It is said that the sea claims final possession, and leaves nothing behind.

The sea claimed our beloved Phrygian warrior seven years ago. It took her into its cold, fathomless embrace only to return her, for some inexplicable reason, on the heels of Aridela's death.

Why did Selene rise? Does she seek to reveal what really happened?

Our queen, a woman of such promise, refused to see any wrong in her lover. She allowed him first one transgression, then another and another until he stole our land and made it into a likeness of his own.

I did nothing to stop him. My selfish fears took precedence over Kaphtor, over the queen, over even Goddess Athene. I will be punished, of that I am certain.

I have been wrong about many things. But it occurs to me I did not fully misread the signs at Aridela's birth.

They said she would bring great change to Kaphtor, and she did.

6

Moon of Mead-Making

From the Oracle Logs
  Themiste

Before purifying Aridela's remains, I tried once again to understand her by studying the prophecies. The first I read was her recounting of the voice she heard the day she became wife to Chrysaleon.

I read until it blurred before my eyes, and only a word here and there stood out. The name Eamhair, and the sad promise that she would wander alone, in misery and slavery.

As I stared at the tablet and brooded, my eyes locked on one line.

Seven labyrinths shalt thou wander, lost, and thou too wilt forget me.

A memory revived, a sense of recognition. This was not the first time I had seen this phrase.

I found the papyrus where I recorded the dream I had just before the Destruction, and scanned it until I came to the sentence I wanted.

She must find her way through seven labyrinths to learn what she must learn.

I again pulled forward the prophecy from her day of joining to Chrysaleon, and read:

Thou wilt step upon the earth seven times.

So much was offered to me through the years, yet somehow understanding remained elusive. It hurts my pride to admit I have been as blind as the queen.

Because I failed to see what I should have seen long ago, and took no steps to change it, we have been thrust onto a narrow path, one leading to an unfathomable future. I sense that up until Aridela's death, we had a choice, but now our future is set.

It seems to me that the prophecies use seven labyrinths to mean seven lives. Six more names will Aridela bear, although the vision from her day of union to Chrysaleon only gave us five.

Her death here is not her end.

As I realized this, I was filled with euphoria, a thrilling tremor of perfect consummation. I knew I had finally woven the missing strands together, and pleased the Lady. I was able to go to Aridela, to wash her body and say good-bye, knowing this farewell would not be final.

An immortal corps will be formed from those who give loyalty.

Will I be part of this corps? I have committed many crimes. I owe Aridela, and our Lady, recompense. I will beg her to let me make amends, to become Aridela's acolyte in lives still to come.

I believe Lady Athene saw all of this long ago, perhaps before any of us were born. I think she knew we would fail, and she set in motion some plan only she understands. Aridela is truly her child, as I have always claimed. She is the fulcrum. It is from Aridela that all will evolve. Those who seek her, seek also the Goddess, and a future of hope.

DID OUR BELOVED QUEEN LOSE HER BALANCE AND FALL DOWN THE STAIRS AS everyone believes?

I purified her body.

I pried open her stiffened hand.

I found what she gripped at the instant of her death.

Long ago, in vision, a god transformed from the serpent Io into a man—Aridela's father. Damasen said many things to me, things that have puzzled and worried me ever since. He told me that she would betray all who love her, and all she loved. When I protested, he said this:

Betrayal cannot birth from nothing. It weaves backward and forward, into and out of the thread of life and death, of faith and love, of envy and desire. This future will only come to pass if the child is first deceived by those to whom she gives her trust.

Seeing what was in her hand, I understood at last.

Damasen told me that at the end of oblivion lies hope, and only Aridela can find it. Was she killed before she could fulfill her destiny, or is it still to come?

I know what I believe.

"I SEE THREE STARS, AGAIN AND AGAIN. A TRIAD OF STARS," WROTE *Melpomene in one of her logs. If I am right in my suspicions, only one star is left. He murdered Menoetius and Aridela. Either he or his slave killed Selene.*

Themiste stopped writing. She frowned at the papyrus and chewed on the end of her stylus. Then she added a few more lines, glancing every now and then at the clump of hair she'd placed on the table—long, golden hair, with dried blood and bits of skin still attached.

"Nephele," she called.

"Yes, my lady?" Her maidservant entered from the adjoining chamber.

"Bring me a man," Themiste said. "One who will do what I ask without question, no matter what it is."

Nephele inclined her head and went off on her errand. She returned sooner than Themiste expected, a man in tow.

"This is Rusa, my lady," Nephele said.

Themiste studied him as she rose from her chair. He was a rough-looking fellow of indeterminate age, his body solid, powerfully muscled, his nose badly set from an old break, leaving it crooked and oddly flat. "I have a problem and need help solving it," she said. "Are you willing to assist me? You will have to subdue someone of importance. You might have to kill him."

Rusa bowed. "I have killed before," he said, "and will do so again, as long as you make it worth my while."

"Then come with me," Themiste said.

As they left, Themiste was struck by his pungent odor—the bitter, rather stifling scent of smoldering wood or ashes. It was somehow familiar.

No matter. The man looked strong and cruel. She could only hope he didn't turn into a coward when faced with the identity of his prey.

Themiste led Rusa down to the royal family's private shrine, where she retrieved the bone knife that had killed Menoetius. Strangely, as she held it, instead of dwelling on what she meant to do, her mind took her back to Harpalycus's occupation, how he had overthrown the village of Natho and imprisoned her, Aridela, and Helice in the villa's underground storerooms. The memory caused a cold fluttering to race across her skin. Harpalycus had threatened her, yet in the end, he didn't attack her the way he had Aridela. Too fearful, no doubt, of the wrath and vengeance of the Goddess.

Motioning to her silent companion to follow, she left the shrine. "We will enter his chamber through a secret corridor," she said as they crossed the courtyard, the stillness of deep night surrounding them. "When the task is finished, you will leave Kaphtor. It is the only way to keep you safe. You will be taken wherever you wish to go, and given everything you need to thrive."

He inclined his head. "Who am I killing?"

She hesitated then took a chance. "The Zagreus," she said, watching him.

His eyes narrowed and his mouth curved into the faintest of smiles, one that renewed the shiver across her flesh. She was suddenly afraid to go with him, alone, into the passage leading to Aridela's bedchamber. Again something about him pricked her memory with sharp warning, but before she could examine the feeling, they came to the staircase and climbed swiftly to the top story. It was too late to go back. She would see this through to the end.

Nephele went into her mistress's room. She folded a blanket and blew out two lamps, leaving one flickering on the table to greet Themiste when she returned.

On her way out, she picked up the papyrus Themiste had been working on, intending to stack it with the others.

The name of the Zagreus caught her attention—that and the uncharacteristic sloppiness of the writing. Had the Minos written this while trapped in a vision?

She read on, shock and disbelief turning to panic.

What is Chrysaleon's obligation? To die. If he will not walk willingly to his death, I will drag him there.
This will be my last entry in the Oracle Logs.
I must rectify my sins. I must silence the call of my queen's blood, and earn my place at her side in lives still to come.

I will not fail again.

THE END

Historical Notes

Robert Graves said Aridela's name was actually a title, and meant "The Very Manifest One," while Carl Kerényi defined it as, "The Utterly Clear." Both men believed Aridela was actually a goddess, and that her story was deliberately changed later, turning her into the rather pathetic, abandoned mortal, Ariadne. Kerényi felt she was a powerful goddess of the moon, worshipped throughout the Mediterranean, but also more: he describes her as a deity who provides to each one of us that invisible spark that makes us unique.

GRAVES, ROBERT. *The Greek Myths*, 1955
KERÉNYI, CARL. *Dionysos: Archetypal image of indestructible life*, 1976

What really happened to Crete after the terrible eruption of the super volcano on the island of Santorini in the Bronze Age? Archaeologists still aren't sure, though they know more than ever before. They have found evidence of many things: of child sacrifice, of slow recovery, of changing religion, and of a devastating fire. They used to think Crete was overthrown during its time of weakness, but later changed their minds. Now they theorize that Crete recovered, at least somewhat, but that later, the island lost power and became subject to the mainland. What happened to the people of Knossos?

This is my story as it might have unfolded.

To the Reader

Thanks for reading *In the Moon of Asterion!* I hope you enjoyed it.

Connect with me and read lots of extras at my website, where I have:
    Bibliographies
    Maps
    Purchase links
    Histories
    Character details

rebeccalochlann.com

About the Author

While growing up, Rebecca Lochlann began envisioning an epic story, a new kind of myth, one built upon the foundation of the Greek classics and continuing through the centuries right up into the present and future.

This has become her life's work, though she didn't exactly intend it to be that way when she started.

The Child of the Erinyes series is mythic fantasy, inspired by the Greek tale of Ariadne, Theseus, and the Minotaur. As one reader put it, "Loads of testosterone, slaughter, and crazy magic," with a love story, of course.

Though the story is fiction-fantasy, it still took about fifteen years to research the Bronze Age segments of the series, and encompassed rare historical documents, mythology, archaeology, ancient religions, and volcanology.

The Year-god's Daughter is her debut novel: Book One of *The Child of the Erinyes* series. It has been utilized as a study guide in an American university, named a B.R.A.G. Medallion honoree, and was a finalist in the Chaucer Historical Fiction awards. Book Two, *The Thinara King*, a First Place winner in the Ancient History category of the Chaucer Historical Fiction awards and a Next Generation Indie Book Awards finalist, continues the saga. Book Three, *In the Moon of Asterion*, wraps up the Bronze Age segment of the series and leads into the middle trilogy, set in Scotland. These are: Book Four, *The Moon Casts a Spell*, Book Five, *The Sixth Labyrinth*, and Book Six, *Falcon Blue*, which jumps backward in time to the Early Medieval Era.

The denouement comes in the final three books: *When the Moon Whispers, First and Second Chronicles*, and *Swimming in the Rainbow*.

Rebecca has always believed that certain rare individuals, either blessed or tortured, voluntarily or involuntarily, are woven by fate or the Immortals into the labyrinth of time, and that deities sometimes speak to us through dreams and visions, gently prompting us to tell their lost stories. Who knows? It could make a difference.

Connect with Rebecca at her website, BookBub, Facebook, or in a review at your point of purchase.

Erinyes Press and Rebecca would like to thank you for continuing this journey.

Attributions

My author website has maps, bibliographies, and more: rebeccalochlann.com

Front and back cover design: Rebecca Lochlann, Erinyes Press
    Colorization of necklace: Rebecca Lochlann, Erinyes Press
    In the Moon of Asterion cover image: Giovanni Dall'Orto, November 11 2009: File Source: Creative Commons, Attribution License/cropped & colored. Ancient Roman bust of Antinous. Hadrian age ((AD 117-138),National Archaeological Museum in Athens, Room 32. http://commons.wikimedia.org/wiki/File:1642_-_Archaeological_Museum,_Athens_-_Antinous_-_Photo_by_Giovanni_Dall%27Orto,_Nov_11_2009.jpg
    https://creativecommons.org/licenses/by-sa/1.0/deed.en
    Colorized, brightened, cropped, background replaced
    Blue Labyrinth image: exogenesis0, Depositphotos
    Stars: dvargg, Depositphotos
    Ancient Greek goddess: Chris Geszvain, Shutterstock
    Design Elements: A-R-T-U-R, Depositphotos
    Crescent moon, necklace image & Erinyes Press logo by Lance Ganey: freelanceganey.com
    Labrys Axe graphic © "Labrys-symbol" Licensed under Public domain via Wikimedia Commons http://commons.wikimedia.org/wiki/File:Labrys-symbol.svg#mediaviewer/File:Labrys-symbol.svg
    The Moon Casts a Spell cover image: Eve Ventrue, eve-ventrue.com
    Labyrinth (paperback): EcOasis, Shutterstock
    Moon & night sky (Paperback): Jonson, Depositphotos

Titles in The Child of the Erinyes series

Book One: *The Year-god's Daughter*
Book Two: *The Thinara King*
Book Three: *In the Moon of Asterion*
Book Four: *The Moon Casts a Spell* (a novella)
Book Five: *The Sixth Labyrinth*
Book Six: *Falcon Blue*
Book Seven: *When the Moon Whispers, First Chronicle*
Book Eight: *When the Moon Whispers, Second Chronicle*
Book Nine: *Swimming in the Rainbow*

ancient triad together again on the windswept isle of Barra, in Scotland's Outer Hebrides.

The Chief of Clan MacNeil is forced to sell his ancestral island to John Gordon of Cluny, a mainlander. No one knows what to expect. Will life get better or worse? Will John Gordon take care of his tenants or evict them, like so many other landowners are doing?

Lilith Kelso is derided as Barra's irreverent, peculiar changeling. She doesn't care. She has no use for anyone but the orphan, Daniel Carson. Everyone expects them to marry someday.

Then John Gordon buys the island. He sends his steward to collect rents and squeeze out profits.

The steward doesn't come alone. He brings his son, and nothing will ever be the same.

Chapter One: The Punishment

NOVEMBER, 1853

LET IT BE DONE.

A wave washed over him, shoved him down where there was no air. He was too tired to fight, and swallowed yet more water. Another swell surged underneath and lifted him to the surface. The waves were like raging dragons, the cold as sharp as knife blades, the water bitter and abrasive against his throat. Sleet pelted his face.

I'm coming, Lilith. We'll be together again. She won't win.

How many more times would he try to convince himself of that, when she had always won, and made every punishment worse than the last?

Claire. Evie. My girls. Forgive me for letting this happen to you.

How could he have so misjudged the hatred?

It doesn't matter anymore.

His mind grew as numb as his body. He couldn't be sure, but he didn't think he was even shivering. He had died four times already, so he wasn't as fearful as someone else might be. Still, the cold was miserable, and it was agonizing to draw salty water into his lungs instead of air. He should open his mouth and drink. Perhaps it would hurry things along.

When his heart stopped, he would drift, one with the waves, and gradually sink. Fish would feast on what was left.

The rising sun broke up the storm clouds. From one horizon to the other, flames covered the heavens. *Red sky at morning, sailors take warning.* His last dawn.

Wait. There was no need for this melodrama. He would see more dawns. He didn't know where or when, but it would start over, the crazed circle of searching, finding, and fighting.

His mind sparked back to life one last time. He saw the murder of his wife and children. He felt the boot soles holding him down, forcing him to watch. He couldn't block out the screams.

We tolerate no witches here!

Just die, he told himself wearily. *Die and be done with it.*

FAINT SHOUTING. COARSE ROPE PASSED AROUND HIS TORSO, UNDER his arms. More shouts. Dangling in the air. Thudding hard against unforgiving wood.

Pain and shock brought him back briefly, but he soon drifted away again.

CHOKING, SPUTTERING. A RUSH OF WATER BURNING HIS THROAT, gushing from his mouth. Hands shoving hard against his chest.

He retched helplessly.

Some man shouted in his face. "Are you alive?"

"Look at this." Another voice, also male. "Is that a knife wound?"

"It's needing stitches."

"Don't waste the needle and thread. This man won't live another hour."

He floated away.

THE STENCH MADE HIM WISH HE DIDN'T HAVE TO BREATHE. BABIES wailed without ceasing. He heard moaning, creaking, faraway shouts. Swaying movement rocked him, sometimes gently, sometimes rudely.

His chest radiated blistering pain. He lifted a hand and touched the area, feeling a lumpy wad of cloth.

"You're awake." A face swam into view. Young, bearded, shaggy brown hair. A dirty bandage, edged with dried blood, on the man's cheek.

"Can you tell me your name?"

He blinked. Such noise. It hurt his ears.

"How do you feel?"

He turned away and closed his eyes, but the man didn't leave. Instead he leaned over and adjusted the cloth.

"Just tell me what to call you, and I'll let you sleep. Or I can bring gruel if you're hungry. It's the worst thing you'll ever taste, I warn you."

Leave me be.

"Och. I'll come back later. Rest. I suppose that's what you need most."

He thrashed. He heard children screaming and shrank from the glint of a knife blade. He dug at his eyes, seeking to gouge them out, and with them, all memory.

Someone had shoved a wet hemp bag, stinking of piss, over his head. He was pushed, kicked, dragged, and thrown into a boat. Much later, several hands hoisted him. Just before he was thrust overboard, he felt something being wrapped around his arm. The sharp tip of a blade slid up his ribs, one by one, then sank into his chest and ripped downward. "Just in case," he heard through his own agonized groans.

The bag was removed and his wrists untied. A soft voice spoke next to his ear. *My father could not save you this time, could he?*

A kick in the spine sent him sprawling into icy water. He fought his way to the surface, choking, hearing the sound of drunken laughter fade as his murderers left him.

He was so cold. He could no longer remember how he came to be in the water, or why.

Da, look at this shell I found. Isn't it pretty? Luminous green eyes full of mystery and magic. A child's arms around his neck. Who was she?

A woman, loosening her glossy dark hair. Sitting on the edge of a bed, crooking her finger. *Show me how Prince Chrysaleon of Mycenae makes love.*

"Wake up, man!" It was that same brown-haired fellow who kept pestering him.

A piercing jolt of pain shot through his head. His throat felt raw. *You killed Daniel. You think you can hide behind your slave?*

"Mother of God! Did you have a bad dream? You're safe. You're safe, I tell you. If you don't stop screaming, you'll bring the captain down on us."

He stopped struggling. Every part of his body ached. The shooting pangs in his head retreated, leaving a dull, repeating throb. "Wh-where am I?"

"You're on the *Bristol*, headed to Nova Scotia. D'you mind what happened? I plucked you out of the ocean."

"O-ocean?"

"Aye, you were half-drowned, but I think you'll survive. There were some wagers on it, I admit."

He could only stare and try to understand what the man was saying. His mind was sluggish, his throat thick and aching. His ears rang and the man's voice echoed.

"Can you at last tell me your name?"

Name?

"What do folk call you, man?"

"I—I don't know." He didn't care, suddenly, where he was, where he was going, if he was alive or dead. He suspected this man had saved his life.

He doubted he would ever forgive that.

Chapter Two: The Boy from the Sea

Lilith was feeding lettuce to the kit when a change in the **air** caught her attention. She rose from a squat. There, that unnatural movement of shadow. She squinted into the sunlight, trying to see what it was. Not one figure but two, one shorter than the other, both silhouettes with the sun behind them. The light was blinding, stinging her eyes.

Was that Mam? Something about the outline made her think so. But who was the other?

Inexplicably frightened, she grabbed the kit, holding it tight against her chest, stroking its soft long ears and whispering nonsense.

She watched her father get up from his perch near the front of the cottage, puffing on his pipe. A pungent whiff of smoke drifted her way.

As the approaching figures stepped out of the sunlight and into the shadow thrown by the bulk of the cottage, she blinked, and when her sight adjusted, she saw that it was indeed, her mother, and an unfamiliar boy. Her mother held the boy's hand.

Her mother and father spoke. The boy said nothing, just kept his face pointed at the ground. She couldn't hear what they said, but her father's tone was irritated.

Her mother led the boy over to Lilith. "This is Daniel," she said. "He'll be living with us."

Lilith clutched the kit more tightly. It responded with a protesting squeak and a strong kick of its back legs.

"Can you say something?"

No. Lilith wouldn't even shake her head. She wanted to know why this strange boy was going to live with them. She didn't think she liked it.

The boy squinted at her, revealing brilliant blue eyes and an angry sickle-shaped wound that cut through his left eyebrow, curved around his eye, and ended halfway down his cheek. But before she could properly take in everything about him, he sighed and turned his face down, back to the ground. His shoulders lifted.

He smelled of the sea.

When she'd found the kit, its leg had been bloody and broken, probably from a failed eagle attack.

That boy's glance told her everything. He was wounded, like the kit. Pain rolled off him, an awful sadness that swelled like a cold wave right through her stomach and heart, and lodged in her throat.

She shifted the kit into the crook of her left arm and held out her right hand. Her mother released the boy. Lilith clasped his hand in her own.

He looked up again, his eyes glistening with unshed tears.

Ever since she could remember, she had sung to the sea, and the sea listened. She asked it for a gift, to prove it loved her. This boy was the answer. Her mother must have caught him in a net and was giving him to her to bring back to health.

The sea was there in his eyes—not the cold grey sea that lived in the Outer Hebrides, but a clear blue sea, like a polished stone; the sea as she dreamed it when she stared into the fire at night.

Lilith gave him the kit. He took it carefully. It cuddled against him, lifting its nose to his neck, and he smiled, very faintly.

He would be well and whole again. She would see to it.

———————————————

Chapter Three

———————————————

STUART WATCHED HIS WIFE TRUDGE BACK TO HIM. HIS TEETH clamped on
the stem of his pipe and he sucked in a mouthful of smoke, cursing as
he blew it out.

"There's no help for it," Faith said. "You know that."

"I can barely feed those I've already got."

"Claire was my friend. She asked this of me as she died. I could
hardly refuse. There's no one else will take him. He's alone in the
world now."

"I know that, woman. The others would let him starve, and who's
to say that wouldn't be best?"

"I say."

"I wonder if anyone but me realizes what a tender heart you're
hiding under all that acid."

"There's a vast difference, I think, between tender-heartedness and
common decency."

Giggling drew their attention. Lilith had taken the kit from the boy
and put it on the ground. Now both of them were following the creature as it hopped about. Under Lilith's care, the rabbit was growing
spoiled and fat. It trailed along after his daughter like a puppy. Stuart
knew he'd be feeding that rabbit for as long as it lived, though he'd
prefer it in the stew pot feeding him.

Another giggle. Lilith had no patience for anyone or anything but
beasts, and she did have a way about her that soothed the wildest,

most frightened creature. Stuart watched, astounded, as his daughter put her hand on the boy's forearm. Together they dropped to the ground and took turns holding the kit on their laps. He would have been far less surprised if Lilith ignored the Carson lad, or ran away from him.

Stuart puffed. "She's not right in the head."

"She's fine."

"She says nothing to anybody, but will talk without ceasing to beasts—not a word of which I understand. And the moon—I've caught her talking to the moon. Singing to it even. She's fey. Queer. Maybe a changeling."

"She's not a changeling. She'll come out of it."

"She has no' a single friend. And she should have at least a few words by now."

"She's only five. A bit slow, maybe. You'll see. In another year, she'll be like any other child."

Stuart shivered. He quickly dismissed it as a chill breeze, but he couldn't dismiss his inner conviction so easily.

No, she won't. She'll never be like other children.

THE MOON CASTS A SPELL
BOOK FOUR
Available everywhere in digital and paperback

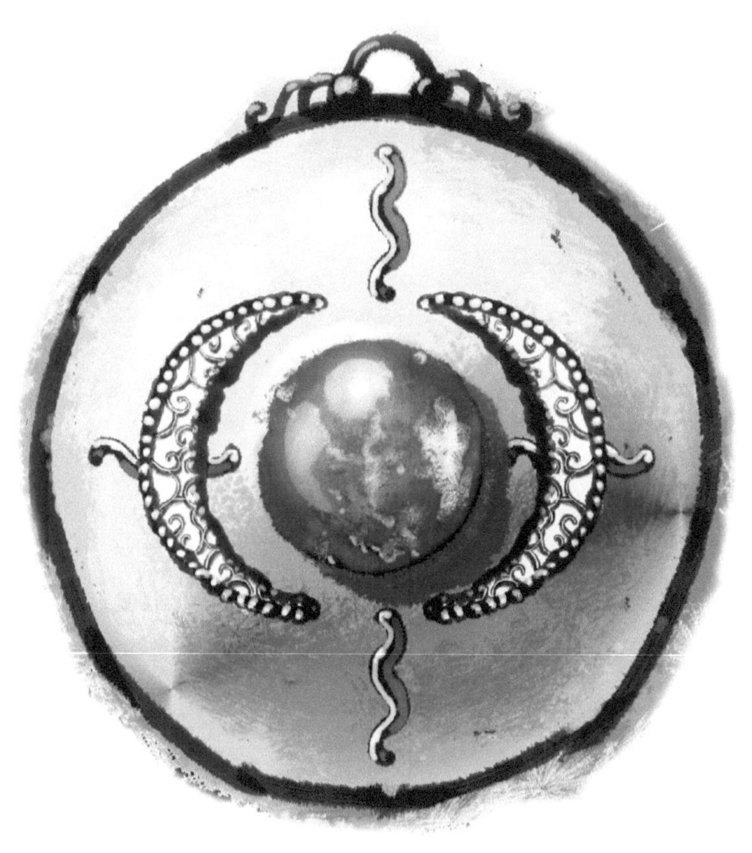